W9-APS-249

THE AMAZON LEGION

BAEN BOOKS by TOM KRATMAN

A State of Disobedience

A Desert Called Peace
Carnifex
The Lotus Eaters
The Amazon Legion

Caliphate

Countdown: The Liberators
Countdown: M Day (forthcoming)

WITH JOHN RINGO
Watch on the Rhine
Yellow Eyes
The Tuloriad

THE AMAZON LEGION

TOM KRATMAN

THE AMAZON LEGION

A Baen Books Original

Baen Publishing Enterprises
P.O. Box 1403
Riverdale, NY 10471
www.baen.com

ISBN: 978-1-4391-3426-9

Cover art by Kurt Miller

First printing, April 2011

Distributed by Simon & Schuster
1230 Avenue of the Americas
New York, NY 10020

Library of Congress Cataloging-in-Publication Data

Kratman, Tom.
  The Amazon Legion / Thomas P. Kratman.
      p. cm.
  "A Baen Books original"—T.p. verso.
  ISBN 978-1-4391-3426-9 (alk. paper)
 1. Space warfare—Fiction. I. Title.
  PS3611.R375A65 2011
  813'.6—dc22
                                                2010052403

10 9 8 7 6 5 4 3 2 1

Pages by Joy Freeman (www.pagesbyjoy.com)
Printed in the United States of America

Dedicated to
Kat and Kelly and Sergeant Hester...
and all the other *Amazonas*,
past and potential

WHAT HAS GONE BEFORE

5,000,000 BC through Anno Condita (AC) 472

Long ago, long before the appearance of man, came to Earth the aliens known to us only as the "Noahs." About them, as a species, nothing is known. Their very existence can only be surmised by the project they left behind. Somewhat like the biblical Noah, these aliens transported from Earth to another planet samples of virtually every species existing in the time period approximately five hundred thousand to five million years ago. There is considerable controversy about these dates as species are found that are believed to have appeared on Old Earth less than half a million years ago, as well as some believed to have gone extinct more than five million years ago. The common explanation for these anomalies is that the species believed to have been extinct were, in fact, not, while other species evolved from those brought by the Noahs.

Whatever the case, having transported these species, and having left behind various other, typically genengineered, species, some of them apparently to inhibit the development of intelligent life on the new world, the Noahs disappeared, leaving no other trace beyond a few incomprehensible and inert artifacts, and possibly the rift through which they moved between Earth and the new world.

In the Old Earth year 2037 AD a robotic interstellar probe, the *Cristobal Colon,* driven by lightsail, disappeared en route to Alpha Centauri. Three years later it returned, under automated guidance, through the same rift in space into which it had disappeared. The *Colon* brought with it wonderful news of another Earthlike planet, orbiting another star. (Note, here, that not only is the other star *not* Alpha Centauri, it's not so far been proved that it is even in the same galaxy, or universe for that matter, as ours.) Moreover, implicit in its disappearance and return was the news that here, finally, was a relatively cheap means to colonize another planet.

The first colonization effort was an utter disaster, with the ship, the *Cheng Ho,* breaking down into ethnic and religious strife that annihilated almost every crewman and colonist aboard her. Thereafter, rather than risk further bloodshed by mixing colonies, the colonization effort would be run by regional supranationals such as NAFTA, the European Union, the Organization of African Unity, MERCOSUR, the Russian Empire and the Chinese Hegemony. Each of these groups were given colonization rights to specific areas on the new world, which was named—with a stunning lack of originality—"Terra Nova," or something in another tongue that meant the same thing. Most groups elected to establish national colonies within their respective mandates, some of them under United Nations' "guidance."

With the removal from Earth of substantial numbers of the most difficult and intransigent portions of the populations of Earth's various nations, the power and influence of trans- and supranational organizations such as the UN and EU increased dramatically. With the increase of transnational power, often enough expressed in corruption, even more of Earth's more difficult, ethnocentric, and traditionalist population volunteered to leave. Still others were deported forcibly. Within not much more than a century and a quarter, and much less in many cases, nations had ceased to have much meaning or importance on Earth. On the other hand, and over about the same time scale, nations had become preeminent on Terra Nova. Moreover, because of the way the surface of the new world had been divided, these nations tended to reflect—if only generally—the nations of Old Earth.

Warfare was endemic, beginning with the wars of liberation by many of the weaker colonies to throw off the yoke of Earth's United Nations and continuing, most recently, with a terrorist and counterterrorist war between the Salafi *Ikhwan,* an Islamic terrorist group, various states that supported them, and—surreptitiously— the United Earth Peace Fleet, on the one hand, and a coalition led by the Federated States of Columbia, on the other.

This eleven year bloodletting began in earnest with the destruction of several buildings in the Federated States of Columbia and ended in fire with the nuclear destruction of the city of Hajar in the unofficially terrorist-sponsoring state of Yithrab.

Prominent in that war, and single-handedly responsible for the destruction of Hajar, was Patrick Hennessey, more commonly known as Patricio Carrera, and the rather large and effective force of Spanish-speaking mercenaries he personally raised, the

Legion del Cid, based in and recruiting largely from *la Republica de Balboa,* a small nation straddling the isthmus between Southern Columbia and Colombia del Norte.

Balboa's geographic position, well-suited not only to dominate trade north and south but also, because of the Balboa Transitway, an above-sea-level canal linking Terra Nova's Shimmering Sea and *Mar Furioso,* key to commerce across the globe, was in many ways ideal. It *should* have been a happy state, peaceful and prosperous.

It was also, unfortunately, ideal as a conduit for Terra Nova's international drug trade. Worse, its political history, barring only a short stint as a truly representative republic following the war of liberation against United Earth some centuries prior, was one of unmixed oligarchy, said oligarchy being venal, lawless, and competent only in corruption. Perhaps still worse, during the war against the terrorists, the security needs of the country had been filled by the introduction of troops from the Tauran Union to secure the Transitway and its immediate surrounds.

Carrera had learned well from the Salafi *Ikhwan,* however. The drug trade through Balboa was ended by war and terroristic reprisal to a degree that left the surviving drug lords quaking in their beds at night. The oligarchy was beaten through the electoral process and the final nails driven into its coffin—and into the heels of the oligarchs—when it attempted to stage a comeback in the form of a coup against the elected government and Carrera, its firm supporter. Carrera's second wife, Lourdes—Balboan as had been his first, Linda, murdered with her children by the Salafi *Ikhwan*—figured prominently in the suppression of the coup.

The problem of the Tauran Union's control of the Transitway remains, as does the problem of the nuclear armed United Earth Peace Fleet, orbiting above the planet. The Taurans will not leave, and the Balboans—a proud people, with much recent success in war—will not tolerate that they should remain.

And yet, with one hundred times the population and three or four hundred times the wealth, the Tauran Union outclasses little Balboa in almost every way, even without the support of Old Earth. Sadly, they have that support. Everything, every*one,* will have to be used to finish the job of freeing the country and, if possible, the planet. The children must fight. The old must serve, too. And the women?

This is their story, the story of Balboa's *Tercio Amazona,* the Amazon Regiment.

CHAPTER ONE

...a failure, but not a waste.
—LTC (Ret.) John Baynes, *Morale*

A phone was ringing somewhere. People—women and children mostly—screamed. Others, men and women both, shouted. Their voices were distant, as if they came from the mouth of a tunnel. Runaway freight trains, having jumped their tracks and taken off into low ballistic flight, crashed into scrap metal yards, one after another. Over that was the sound of jet engines straining and helicopter rotors beating at the air.

With a barely suppressed shriek of her own, Maria Fuentes sat bolt upright in her trembling bed, her hand going automatically to her mouth to stifle the sound. As her eyes adjusted to the small light streaming in through her bedroom window, she realized that she wasn't asleep any longer.

"It was a..." she began to say. She stopped, mid-sentence, when she realized that she could still hear the trains, the crashes, the screams.

"*Mierda!*" she exclaimed, as she threw off the light covers. "Not a nightmare. Shit. Oh, *shit.*" Maria felt nausea rising, mostly fed by sudden unexpected fear.

The phone, which had stopped ringing, began again as Maria raced for her baby's—Alma's—room. She stopped and picked it up.

"Sergeant Fuentes."

"Maria? Cristina." Centurion Cristina Zamora was Maria's reserve platoon leader. "Alert posture Henrique. No drill." Zamora's voice was strained, nervous. Maria couldn't remember ever having heard Cristina's voice as anything but perfectly calm before. Not ever.

She felt a fluttering in the pit of her stomach. *Zamora's upset? We're so fucked.*

"*Not* a drill?" she asked, pointlessly.

"No, Maria, not a drill. Alert posture Henrique."

"Henrique? Okay, I understand." "*Henrique.*" *Call up all the reservists, but only those militia who can be quickly and conveniently assembled.* "I guess time's more important than numbers, huh?"

"They don't tell me these things, Maria. Later."

The phone's tone changed, telling Maria that Zamora had hung up.

Maria's phone was already programmed with the necessary numbers to conduct an alert. She scanned through until she found the number for her assistant, Marta Bugatti. She pressed that button, then the button for "speaker." She placed the phone on her bed and, while the phone was ringing, pulled out her legion-issue foot locker. A couple of flicks of the retainers and the top popped open. She was pulling her tiger-striped, pixilated battle dress trousers on when the ringing stopped and a deep voice—deep for a woman, anyway—answered, "Bugatti here, Maria."

"Marta. Alert. 'Henrique.' No shit."

"Oh, *really?* I would never have guessed!"

Unseen by Maria, a mile and a half from Maria's small apartment, Bugatti shook her head in general disgust and then held her own telephone receiver towards the nearest window. On her own end, Maria could easily make out the sound of chattering machine guns.

Marta's voice returned in a moment. "So what fucking else is fucking new? I'll take care of it. I'll—" Marta's phone went dead.

"Marta? *Marta?*" Maria pounded her own phone on the foot locker's plastic edge in frustration mixed with fear. "Shit. Dead." She closed the cell and tossed it on the bed. She thought, *Okay, Marta. You're a bitch . . . sometimes. But you're a lovable bitch and you're* my *bitch besides. I'll trust you.*

Maria pulled on her boots, green nylon and black leather, tucked her trousers into them, and then speed laced them shut. She wound the ends of the laces around her legs and tied them to hold the trousers in place. From her locker she took her battle dress jacket. She was buttoning this as she started again for her daughter's bedroom.

She started, then stopped short at Alma's door. *My God, I am going to have to leave her, then fight; maybe die, too, and leave her forever.*

Suddenly Maria felt even more ill. *How can I leave my baby?* Just as suddenly, she felt even worse. *How can I abandon my friends, my sisters, my troops?*

Bad mother; bad friend. Responsible parent; irresponsible soldier? Hero? Coward? None of those words mean a damn thing. Whatever I do, it's going to be because I'm more afraid of not doing it than of not doing the other. I'm going to be a coward in some way, no matter what.

Had she been a different person, *any* different person, she might just have stood there, indecisive, until it was all over. But Maria wasn't just *anybody*. The powers that be had selected her very carefully, then trained her more carefully still. They had even organized her unit very carefully, paying more than usual attention to the needs of single military mothers. With or without Maria, Alma would be all right. She knew that. But without her, her troops—her friends—might not. She had no choice, really. She'd made the decision years before.

I have to go.

Alma was still sleeping soundly in her little bed when her mother entered. Maria smiled as her sight took in her daughter's few dozen pounds and few little feet of soft lines, dark lashes and curly hair. Maria marveled that not only was Alma hers, but that the baby wasn't awake and screaming.

I could never hope to sleep with artillery flying anywhere nearby, not even in training. What makes it so easy for a kid?

Maria looked out the window from Alma's bedroom. She couldn't see much but the street they lived on, and not all of that. Streetlights illuminated the scene. So far as she could see none of Terra Nova's moons had any noticeable part in that. Then the streetlights began to flicker out, leaving nothing but the moons' light.

Below the apartment, people were running in the streets, most of them tugging on uniforms. Just about everybody was carrying a rifle, machine gun, or rocket launcher. A number of those who weren't armed seemed to be trying to hold back someone who was. Somebody's mother, wife, or maybe girlfriend was crying for him to come back. Maria couldn't see where anyone did turn back though.

Returning to her own room, Maria continued pulling gear from the locker. Out came load-bearing equipment, her helmet, her silk and liquid-metal *lorica,* the legion's standard body armor. Her centurion's baton she picked up for a moment, then replaced it in the locker. Last came her modified F-26 "Zion" rifle.

She held the rifle in her hands for a moment, drawing some small comfort from its heft and weight. Then she slapped a drum magazine in, turned the key on the back to put pressure on the spring, and jacked a round home.

I hope Alma stays asleep. She hates to see me in helmet and body armor.

Fully clothed and armed, Maria slung her rifle across her back, walked back to the baby's bedroom, then picked her up in her arms.

Alma almost woke up then, sucking air in with three gasping "uh...uh...uhs." The mother waited a minute or two, holding her, stroking her hair and saying, "Don't worry, baby. Everything will be all right, baby. Don't worry, love. Mama's here." The child snuggled her soft hair into an armored shoulder and fell back, sound asleep.

Once Alma had fallen asleep again, it was out the door and down three flights of stairs. Maria didn't bother with locking the door behind her; crime hadn't been much of a problem in this part of the city for some time; current invasion excepted, of course.

Lance Corporal Lydia Porras, of the *Tercio Amazona's* Dependant Care Maniple, affectionately called "the Fairy Godmothers," careened her van through the streets, barely missing men as they hurried to their duties in the dark. The Fairy Godmothers were not actually part of the *Tercio Amazona,* but seconded to it from a regiment of elderly and late enlistees.

Though Porras was in uniform, her vehicle was plainly civilian, both in color and design. Otherwise, it would certainly have been fired on by any one of the dozens of helicopters that swooped in from time to time to shoot at the soldiers in the streets.

Porras made a sharp left-hand turn onto Maria's fast-emptying street. She jerked the wheel left again to pull up to the apartment building, then slammed on the brakes to bring the van to a screeching halt. Porras killed the lights and listened for a moment for the sounds of one of the fearsome attack helicopters the Taurans had in such abundance. There was nothing or, at least, nothing she could hear over the rattle and *crump* of artillery.

Porras prayed, "*Santa Maria, Madre de Dios,* take pity on an old woman who has borne children. Take pity on children too young to die. Most importantly, Our Lady of Victory, grant it to us."

Porras crossed herself and stepped out of the van. As she did so, Maria and Alma appeared in the doorway. Porras took Alma from her mother's arms—well, pulled, actually; the mother didn't want to let go—and placed the girl gently, sitting up, in one of the seats of the van, taking the extra moment to buckle the child in. There were a couple of other children there, too. One of the others, an older girl, turned sideways in her sleep to throw an arm around Alma. Porras smiled for the first time that night. *Kids can be so sweet.*

When one is young and alone and the call comes to fight, it really helps to know someone is going to take care of the kids. That was Porras's job. She was a nice old biddy. Gray haired, wrinkled; but her eyes shone bright and her posture was immaculate. She had not volunteered for service until she had turned sixty-two years old, with grown children and grandchildren of her own. She'd gone to geriatric basic training then, and then volunteered for assignment to the unit.

Old, Porras might have been. Steady, calm and reliable she was too. She was also a surprisingly good shot. Even so, Porras couldn't hope to do what Maria and the others did; she was simply too old. Still, she certainly made it easier for them to do their jobs.

Alma loved her. So did Maria.

Filled with inexpressible feelings of pity, love, and fear, the old woman looked at Maria carefully, as if for the last time. *Pretty girl,* she thought, eyes glancing over Maria's five feet two inches of height, healthy figure, straight nose and large, well-spaced eyes. She placed a hand gently along the younger woman's sculpted chin, saying, "Go with God, child. And be careful. I'll guard your daughter with my life."

Then, eyes clouding with tears, Lydia Porras jumped back into the van, slammed the door, and pulled away amidst screeching, smoking tires.

For Maria it was *so* hard to watch that van pull away.

Maria Fuentes's hands trembled. She was frightened, damned frightened, and she had reason to be. Her country's enemy had one hundred times Balboa's own population; three or four times that ratio in disparity of wealth. Between their regular and reserve forces they had more people under arms than the entire population of her country. Weapons? Except for small arms and a couple of tricks there was no comparison. Technology? Sister, Balboa wasn't even in the race.

But it's not hopeless, she told herself, forcing her hands to steady down. *We have some things going for us, too. Our weapons are generally decent and reliable. We have a better doctrine for battle and a much better one for training. We have damned good leaders.*

And this is our *country. We have no place else to go.*

Tougher to measure were some *softer* factors: Heart, soul, a pretty good knowledge of their own country, and the fact that the enemy was arrogant—and might, with luck, sometime show all the stupidity arrogance entails.

Besides, the Taurans *did* have some place else they called home. And if they didn't mind much making others bleed, they didn't much like bleeding themselves.

Maria thought, *If we're going to make them bleed, we'll have to bleed some ourselves.*

She looked up at the sky and, with the streetlights gone, saw the thin crescents of two moons, Bellona and Hecate. *Yeah, they've got more night vision capability than we do; they'd hit us at a time with minimal illumination.*

She turned away from the direction in which Porras had taken Alma and, her mind on bleeding, faced in the direction she would have to go. She took the rifle from across her back and, weapon in hand, began jogging.

Left, right, left, right.

From the apartment building it was about a mile to the assembly point, the "hide." This was a small restaurant in Balboa City owned by one of the other squad leaders in Maria's maniple.

Left, right, left, right.

It is not, repeat *not,* fun to run, or even jog, in a tropical environment, when you've got forty-five pounds of combat equipment and ammunition dragging you down. It wasn't fun for a man. For women it was worse. Maria knew it would become even worse than that after she picked up the rest of the ammunition hidden at the restaurant.

Left, right, left, right.

Maria heard the steady *whop-whop-whop* of a helicopter coming closer. Her army had more than a few helicopters, but none of them sounded like this one. She began to look around at her surroundings, desperately seeking someplace she could hide.

"Hey, Johanson, look left. Single grunt. Take 'im?"
"Yeah, sure, why the hell not?"
The helicopter tilted left as its tail swung around to the right, bringing its weapons to bear. The target ducked and disappeared from view.
"Fire a couple of bursts. See if you can spook him out."
"Roger."

In the recessed doorway in which she'd taken shelter, Maria pressed herself against a wall to try to blend in with the shadow. Her heart was thumping so loud in her chest that she was sure even the helicopter's crew would be able to hear it.

Suddenly the shadow disappeared as the street was lit by the strobe of several dozen heavy machine-gun rounds being fired. Against her will, Maria screamed. Again the helicopter fired and she pressed her hand to her mouth and bit down.

More than the sound, it was those solid streams of tracers lighting up the landscape that terrified her. She just tried to make herself smaller, even as she bit down on two fingers again so as not to hear herself scream out loud.

"Fuck it, Jo. If he's still around, he'll be wanting to change his pants before reporting to his unit. Call it a 'Mission accomplished.' We got shit to do. Let's go look for easier meat."
"Roger. Don't like hanging around one place too long, either."
The chopper tilted right as Johanson flew it up and away from where Maria's trembling form crouched unseen.

In combat, fatigue and fear are "mutually reinforcing and essentially interchangeable." So Maria had been told in training. Her training cadre had even done their best to show her, and her sisters, how that worked. *Nothing* could have fully prepared her for the reality. She felt so weak from the terror of that helicopter that it took an effort of will just to start moving again. Once she did, though, it got better. She was even able to start thinking and stop just reacting.

Left, right, left, right.

Maria thought, *The Taurans may be stupid, but they're not that stupid. They know we have to assemble to defend ourselves. I wonder what they. . .*

The Tauran sniper should have had a spotter, and preferably a man for security. Under the circumstances, the desperate need to destroy the Balboans' leadership before they could fully mobilize their not inconsiderable force of reservists and militia, spotters and guards had been dispensed with. His spotter, indeed, was also alone, someplace a mile or so to the west.

Alone, on flat roof overlooking one of the enemy capital's major thoroughfares, the sniper carefully rotated the focus ring on his rifle's scope as he tracked his target down the street. He'd begun to squeeze the trigger once, when the target was in an open space. But the target had disappeared behind a small truck before the rifle had fired. The sniper relaxed the pressure on the trigger, waiting patiently.

Ah. There he was again. The sniper gently slid the rifle over to bring it to bear on the target. He began to squeeze the trigger once again. "Keep your damned head still, asshole. Stop swinging like some *bitch*," the sniper whispered. The trigger depressed. . . .

KAZINGG!

The bullet passed by Maria's head so closely she felt the wind of its passage. *Sniper!*

Even as her mind put a name to the threat, her body was diving behind the nearest auto. In falling, Maria scraped her right elbow on the concrete hard enough to rip her uniform and tear the skin beneath. She ignored it, except to think, in some distant part of her mind, *My God, Centurion Garcia would kick my ass if he ever saw me do a dive like that.*

Her body armor, tougher stuff, protected her breasts, as aramid fiber knee cups protected her knees. Her heart, which hadn't ceased pounding since her brush with the helicopter, began to race: *thumpthumpthumpthumpthumpthumpthump.*

"Shit! Shit! *Shit!*" Maria cursed, even as she crawled to put the engine block and the right front tire of the car between her and where she thought the bullet had come from. It was better than nothing.

Unless, of course, the bullet didn't come from where I thought. In that case, I'm probably toast.

She rolled over to her back, then slithered her posterior around. Trying to make the smallest target possible, Maria sidled her back to get her head flat behind one of the car's tires.

Another bullet sent a cloud of broken safety glass raining down on her. Another and she heard a bullet ring off of the engine block then pass through the sheet metal of the body just over her head. Maria began to pray quietly.

Her back hunched against the tire, Maria looked to her left. The next nearest car was better than twenty-five meters away. She didn't think there was any way she could make it before the sniper put a bullet in her. She knew, too, that he wouldn't be picky, this time, going for a headshot. *He'll put one through my guts then shoot me in the head as I lie there on the asphalt. The lorica's good for shrapnel and light rounds, not heavy, full caliber bullets. I'm pinned, but good. Worse, if all else fails he'll probably eventually go for the gas tank. Then it's going to be fricasseed Fuentes.*

She began to pray a bit more fervently, whispering, "Our Father, who art in Heaven, hallowed be Thy name. Thy Kingdom come..."

Next to the main door to Maria's maniple's headquarters there was a hand-painted sign. She'd seen it a thousand times. The sign showed a duck trying to eat a frog, the frog's legs sticking out of the duck's mouth. The duck couldn't eat the frog, though, because the frog's front feet were wrapped around the duck's throat, choking it, blocking its windpipe and gullet.

The caption on the sign said, "Never give up!"

She stopped praying to think, *Okay. Never give up.*

Maria took the drum magazine from her F-26 rifle, then tapped it against her thigh to make sure all the cartridges were well seated. She then replaced it in the magazine well. The magazine made a click as it seated, soft enough but seeming loud to her. Her finger flicked on the rifle's integral night sight. Maria took one deep breath, crossed herself and prepared to get up and shoot back. She was NOT going to burn without a fight.

Even as her body tensed, she thought, *If they could think of putting snipers on the roofs to block our mobilization, why couldn't we have put people on the roofs to block the snipers? Or, at least, to keep the bastards busy?*

✧   ✧   ✧

"Quietly, Pablo," the old man whispered with authority. "Don't let the ammunition drag on the steps, boy."

"*Si, Abuelo*." The grandson looked overhead, past where a lightly built shed protected the stairwell that ran through the building from the frequent rain. He could see only one moon, and that a thin and weak one. Perhaps another was up; from where he was, Pablo couldn't tell. In any case, he couldn't imagine even the remotest possibility that anyone would or could hear anything over the ceaseless drumming of the artillery, the screaming of the jets, and the *whoosh* of light air defense missiles trying—usually in vain—to bring down an aircraft. Still, orders from his grandfather, more importantly orders from Legion Corporal (Med. Ret.) Vladimiro Serrasin, were not to be ignored. The old man was a veteran not only of the terrorist war, but even of the invasion by the Federated States, many years before. He was the boy's hero.

The boy, himself a junior cadet with a slot waiting at one of the military schools, clutched the bandoleer tight to his chest.

"There, Pablo. See him?" The old man pointed to a soldier, enemy presumably, lying down on the sloping roof with his rifle aimed through a large open chink in the wall surrounding the roof.

"This one is good," *Abuelo* gave as his professional judgment. He had a tone of approval in his voice the boy found incongruous at best. "Good fieldcraft. From the ground only his target would have a chance to spot him. If he is as good a shot, that wouldn't be a problem for him."

Abuelo got on one arthritic knee, the rough gravel of the roof digging into it. Instead of showing a wince, a mild sneer crossed the old man's face. The light machine gun he bore in his arms— an older and more primitive arm than the fancy F- and M-26s the legion carried nowadays—went to his shoulder in a motion so smooth it was obviously long-practiced. The old man leaned into the shed that shielded the stairwell to the roof from rain. He took aim on the indistinct shape on the opposite roof. The old man inhaled, let the breath out, and began to squeeze....

Maria crossed herself quickly, then twisted up to one knee to bring her rifle to bear on the building from which she thought the fire had come. Even as she did so, a long, long burst of machine gun fire came from her left rear. She hadn't been expecting it.

The surprise ruined her aim. Her bullets hit the building opposite, but that was all.

She did *not* wet herself.

From the other side of the street came a scream that might have been heartbreaking if it hadn't also been so satisfying. The machine gun fired again and the screaming stopped.

Mildly faint and more than a little nauseated, she slid down to rest her back once again against the tire.

As Maria sighed her relief, she heard a laugh from overhead. Then an old man's voice called out to her, "I once was young and brave and strong."

Maria answered, loudly as she could, her voice still breaking with terror, "And I'm so now...Come on...and try."

Then a young boy—he sounded all of thirteen or fourteen—shouted to the world, "But I'll be strongest, by and by."

"Go on, girl," said the old man. "We can see for about three blocks. It's clear that far, anyway."

Maria shouted out, "Thanks," then got unsteadily to her feet. Thankful to be alive and substantially unhurt, she resumed her jog again for the restaurant.

The restaurant wasn't in, though it sat very near, the seediest part of the city, just south of Old Balboa. Though the septic-mouthed, genengineered *antaniae* had been eradicated from most of the capital, here their nightly cries—*mnnbt, mnnbt, mnnbt*—could be heard in the distance.

From the restaurant's door came the challenge, "Delta, Oscar?"

Maria gasped out, "Lima Lima." The challenge and password for the week spelled, "doll." Had the sentry asked "Oscar, Lima," Maria would instead have answered with, "Delta, Lima."

"Go on inside, Sergeant Fuentes. The platoon centurion will be glad to see you. It's a freakin' nightmare, I'm tellin' ya."

Nodding, too out of breath for words, Maria brushed past the sentry and eased through the restaurant's door. Sweat dripped from her chin to splash on the floor below.

Inside was a scene of boundless confusion and disarray. Tables and chairs had been pushed against the walls and windows for whatever cover they might provide. Women soldiers crouched low and indistinct amidst the tangle, their eyes searching out the windows for a threat. A six-foot section of flooring had been torn away. From the hole flew metal and wooden boxes of what was plainly ammunition. Women soldiers ran to and fro, moving the boxes to where other armed women were breaking them open and passing the ammunition out.

To one side Maria's platoon's optio, what some armies would have called a "platoon sergeant," spoke frantically into a radio. "What a nightmare! Half of us aren't here yet! Dead, wounded, held up by traffic; I don't know. Everyone is doing someone else's job... No, I haven't seen a trace of Zamora... Yeah, yeah. I know. 'Never to expect a plan to really work. After all, the goddamned enemy gets a vote, too.'... Roger, I'll keep you posted. Out."

The optio dropped the microphone to rest beside the radio. She took one look at Maria and said, "Sergeant Fuentes. Good to see you. Your people aren't here yet. Go help Gupta drag the rest of the ammunition out of the hide."

Obviously, there wasn't time for questions. Maria did as she was told.

The "hide" was that hole in the floor, normally kept hidden under a table, which held roughly three quarters of a ton of ammunition. The women all kept their personal loads at home, of course, but that was mostly rifle and machine gun ammunition. The hide had enough for a real battle: mortar shells, antitank rockets, mines, demolitions, grenades. The hide had never been designed for highly complex and degradable ammunition, like the light, shoulder-fired, antiaircraft missiles. Those would have to come later, from elsewhere, if they did.

As she eased herself down, Maria wondered how many people had eaten at that table never knowing they sat above enough explosives to blow them halfway to La Plata.

"Ouch! Watch where you put your feet, Sergeant Fuentes. That was my shoulder."

"Right. Sorry, Gupta. Move a little so I can get down there with you."

Whatever the origins of her name, Gupta was white and approximately blond. Once she'd stepped out of the way, Maria eased herself into the concrete-lined hole, then planted her feet on the floor of the hide and began to help. Some of the boxes took the two of them just to lift. She was struggling alone with a heavy crate when Marta stuck her face into the hole.

"We're all here, Maria. I also picked up two militia types—Sanchez and Arias—on the way." With that, Marta brushed off an hour's stark terror.

Marta turned her head away and ordered, "Sanchez! Relieve the sergeant down in the hole." Marta reached down a hand to help Maria climb out to make room for Sanchez.

Once back on her feet, Maria reached up to give Marta a quick hug. This was awkward as Bugatti was not only a head taller, but huge breasted to boot. Maria had to really reach.

"Good girl, Marta. Line 'em up."

Bugatti turned away and in that La Plata-accented Spanish that might as well have been Tuscan began to bellow to the troops.

After Marta had put the squad into a line Maria started her inspection. This was no time for parade ground bullshit. Sure, naturally she checked their ammunition, weapons, equipment, food and water. Mostly, though, she checked *them*.

"Your kids get picked up all right, Cat?" She asked of her machine gunner, Catarina Gonzalez.

For answer Cat just nodded her plain face on her stocky neck.

Scared, Maria thought. *Don't blame her. If I had three kids I'd be three times more frightened than I am.* She patted Cat's cheek for reassurance's sake and continued down the line.

Cat's ammunition bearer, Arias—a tall, slender, blond girl— was next. Arias was so new that Maria couldn't for the life of her remember the girl's first name. While hands jiggled Arias's canteens to check the weight of the water, Maria asked about her ammunition to cover the memory lapse.

"Fifteen hundred and ninety rounds, 6.5mm, four ball to one tracer," Arias answered. "One thousand and sixty in my pack; five hundred and thirty ready." Arias tapped the two large magazine pouches at her waist for emphasis.

Arias sounded frightened. Maria couldn't let herself.

Then she remembered the name. Maria squeezed Arias's shoulder and said, confidently, "Vielka, don't sweat it. You're in good company. The best."

Vielka smiled and relaxed just that trifle that said, *Okay, Sergeant. I won't be scared if you're not.*

"Good girl."

While Maria checked her troops, the rest of the platoon showed up, a few at a time. The platoon leader, Centurion Zamora, arrived last of all.

Zamora pulled off her helmet to run fingers through sweat-drenched, long, coppery hair as the other Amazons gathered around. The centurion looked around at the platoon she loved and then fiercely pushed away the thought of what lay in store for them over the next several hours or days.

"Troops," Zamora announced once they'd all been pulled together, barring only a few at the windows and one at the door, "troops, the country is under attack."

Maria rolled her eyes Heavenward, thinking, *What is it about higher leaders in the military anyway, that makes them need to restate the obvious? Ah, well, Zamora has other virtues.*

"Our mission," Zamora continued, "is to assemble, move toward the enemy *Comandancia* on *Cerro Mina,* attach ourselves to Second Legion...and fight as directed."

"Those Tauran Union women who got raped and killed?" Marta asked.

Zamora shrugged, answering, "So far as headquarters knows, it never happened. But did they manufacture an excuse? That's what I figure. Though who can understand a Tauran, anyway?"

Going to one knee, she pulled a map from a pocket, spreading it out on the floor where the troops could see. "Here's our route." A pencil traced a series of streets on a map. "Order of march is Second Squad, Headquarters, Weapons, First, and Third. The platoon optio will take up the rear. Move out in five."

Maria was skeptical. Not all the ammunition was broken down yet. Pulling at a lock of hair, she said, "Damn, that's not much time, Cristina."

"It's as much time as we have, Sergeant Fuentes. So it's as much as we need." Zamora shook her head, though her hair was far too sweat-soaked to move with it, while she thought, *I hate using that tone of voice with people I care for.*

Maria's face went blank as she answered, "Yes, Centurion."

The order of march put Maria's squad first. She told Marta to take up the rear of the squad.

Bugatti twisted her face into a mild scowl and answered, "And just where the fucking hell else would I be, Sergeant, sometime Centurion, Maria?"

Maria chucked her on the chin and led the way out. One by one, the rest of the squad followed, some of the women taking a last chance to stuff a pocket with an extra grenade or meal or drum of ammunition. As they assembled at the door, a light truck, in civilian paint but driven by a uniformed elderly man, showed at the door.

"Anyone here need a couple of antiaircraft missiles?" the old man shouted out.

Maria passed the word back that the air-defense weapons were here. To the old man she said, "Just stand by. The crew will pick them up as they pass."

"Wilco," said the ancient.

Stomach flip-flopping as she slipped out the door, Maria began to move forward, hugging the sides of the street. There was the sound of firing ahead, the muffled patter of her soldiers' booted feet behind. She often heard the distinctive sound of a missile being fired at some helicopter. Sometimes, when she passed through an open intersection and could look south or east, she saw tracers flying high in the air. *I guess that's what "a thousand points of light" look like, after all.*

About halfway to *Cerro Mina*, Zamora answered the radio. After half a minute's conversation, she called a halt. The optio came running up to her.

"Change of orders," Zamora announced. "We hold here until called for."

"Any idea why?" the optio asked.

"Personally, since *Tercio Gorgidas* got the same hold order, I smell politics," Zamora answered.

"*Mierda!*" exclaimed the optio, who then ran back and began directing the troops to find what cover they could in the halls and alleyways off of the street.

Maria took her squad—there were ten of them, all told—and hunkered down between the outside wall of a house and some bushes. Marta flopped down next to her, whispering, "If I were you, Maria, I'd tell Gonzalez to duck into one of those buildings and not come out for several days. I'll carry her gun."

Maria nodded her head for a moment, then shook it in negation. "I know. I considered that already myself. Gonzalez's three kids. I don't want them losing their last parent to be on my conscience. Still . . . no. We'll need everybody soon, especially the machine gunner." *Besides, I like the idea of Alma being orphaned even less than I like the idea of it happening to the Gonzalez children.*

✧   ✧   ✧

The troops began sweating profusely as the sun first rose, and then climbed higher in the sky. Then the spot Maria had picked turned out to have been a good move on her part. The squad was on the wrong side of the street, shade-wise, and would have roasted but for the protection of the bushes. Even so, the building behind them absorbed and then put out a lot of heat as the day grew longer.

Some people, civilians, came out and gave the women cold drinks, snacks, whatever they had to spare. Considering that their country just might lose, and be ruined, it was probably more than they could spare. That made it better in more ways than one.

Curiously, none of those who ministered to the soldiers were healthy young men. Those not with the colors already were perhaps too ashamed to be seen by armed women heading for battle.

It was a long, hot wait until Zamora received new orders. Marta filled the time with idle chitchat, mostly concerning the rumors that flew back and forth.

"Do you think the government's really fallen?" she asked.

"The buildings may be in enemy hands," Maria answered. "The president's way too cagey to get caught himself, though. Not alive. He was a soldier once, too, you know."

One trooper from the air defense team—they had to stay out in the open to use their missiles—stuck her head through the bushes and said, "I heard on the radio that the Taurans were being pushed back into the sea and that the boys of the military schools were on the attack."

Remembering the other half of the machine gun team that had saved her from the sniper, Maria said that she thought it could well be true.

"C'mon, *ladies*," Zamora announced, finally, once the sun was about halfway up the sky. "Enough loafing. We're back on the job."

In a way, the centurion thought, *it's better to go ahead* despite *what's in store than to wait here, helpless.*

It took a few minutes of shouting to get the platoon reassembled in the street. Then the women began to jog again, to move closer to the fighting, as civilians waved to them and cheered. Along their route Zamora's platoon was joined by the others from the maniple, streaming in from the left and right. Maria almost felt sorry for the poor mortar rats struggling under their loads. Then again, they had a couple of mules to help out. She didn't feel all *that* sorry for them. Besides, each of the *Amazonas* except for machine gun and rocket crews also carried a round of ammunition for the mortars. And seven pounds is not something to laugh at when you're already toting over fifty.

They passed some awful things on the way. Bodies, of course, friendly and enemy. Some were uniformed and armed; some looked like civilians who had just gotten in the way. A couple were kids.

Maria thought of Alma for about the five hundredth time that morning. *Please, God? Please help Porras keep my baby safe?*

"Bring me a dozen eggs, child, and the side of bacon," Porras told Alma Fuentes. The pan on the stove was already sizzling. To Cat Gonzalez's eldest, Romeo, she said, "Be careful not to scorch the chorley bread in the toaster."

Chorley was a grain either native to Terra Nova or possibly genengineered by the Noahs. No one was really certain. Growing, it resembled a sunflower that never reached more than a foot or so off the ground. Harvested, processed and baked, it made a yellow bread that was naturally buttery in taste.

"And turn off the television!" Porras shouted at another of the older children. There was no sense in letting them get upset with worry for their mothers.

The safe house for the children was Porras's own. It was on the coast, far enough from the fighting that the children couldn't hear much, if any, of it. Whatever she could hear, Porras still *knew,* at least in general terms, of the battle raging. She forced herself to remain calm, or as calm as she could, and kept the children busy with helping her prepare breakfast. Porras didn't break out the government provided emergency rations. *Time for that later . . . if things get hard.*

"*Abuela* Lydia, where's my mommy?" Alma asked from beneath soulful brown eyes.

"Child, do you remember this morning at all?"

"Not much," the girl answered, shaking her head.

Good.

"Your mommy's with the tercio"—the regiment—"and I'm sure she'll be back by this evening. Tomorrow night at the latest. And you and the other children will be staying here with me. Won't that be fun?"

Alma nodded very deeply and seriously. "Fun," she echoed, even while the child thought, *I'm little; I'm not stupid. My mommy's in trouble, isn't she?*

Before the platoons of Amazons reached the base of *Cerro Mina* they came to an open area filled with smoke, and bodies, and smells both unfamiliar and unpleasant. Marta nearly tripped over two of the bodies locked in what almost seemed an embrace. The knife of one was in the body of the other.

There was also a shot-down helicopter, a Tauran gunship, with two burned charcoal lumps in it, their arms and legs pulled up like a baby's in a womb. Those and their stench made some of the women gag a little.

Maria looked at the helicopter and wondered if it was the same one that had dogged her steps earlier. She hadn't heard or seen a Tauran helicopter since the one that had tried to fire her up and wondered if that absence was because of the eventual and increasing distribution of the antiaircraft missiles.

Marta took one sniff of the helicopter and started to gag herself. She bent over and deposited breakfast onto the asphalt.

The Amazons held up briefly just past that scene of battle, while their maniple commander, Inez Trujillo, went to find someone to report to. While waiting, Maria ordered her squad to take positions next to a couple of wrecked enemy armored vehicles. Yes, there were burned corpses in those, too. And, yes, they stank.

"A bad way to die; poor men," she said.

Wiping her mouth with a hand, Marta answered with a ruthlessness she didn't really feel, "Fuck 'em; better them than us or ours." Still, she shook her head, regretting not the deed, but the necessity.

After several minutes Tribune Trujillo showed up in the open area near Zamora's platoon. With her was some male tribune the women didn't recognize. The man towered over little Inez. Muscular, narrow-waisted, and painfully handsome, he looked as if he could have made a pretty good living as a male model. Maybe he did. He and Inez shook hands good-bye. Then Trujillo began to walk—perhaps a little unsteadily—toward where Maria's squad lay. Halfway there, Inez stopped and forced herself back to reasonable calm. Thereafter, she walked upright and with apparent confidence.

The other two officers and the eight centurions and optios in the maniple gathered around her while Trujillo spoke and gestured to the map and the buildings surrounding them.

Trujillo was nearly finished with her orders. "Our attack to seize the Taurans' headquarters on *Cerro Mina* is to be 'quick and irrespective of losses'; that's how important it is."

"Supporting forces on the right?" Zamora asked. She already knew that one understrength maniple of the *Tercio Gorgidas* was going to be on the left. And that there might be—or might not; things went wrong in war—an artillery barrage to soften the hill up.

Trujillo shook her head. "I'd have mentioned it if there were going to be."

Zamora sighed at those words. "Irrespective of losses," she quoted. "Oh, well. At least our left will be secure. Maybe the TGs are *mariposas*. We've *all* got reason to know they are some *tough mariposas*."

"Other questions?" Trujillo asked. There was some lip chewing, some head shaking. Of further questions there were none.

"Dismissed."

The officers and centurions saluted Trujillo and returned to their places. The Weapons Platoon centurion called her women and their mules over and began setting up the section for firing. As soon as the others saw the mortars begin to set up, they began filtering over by twos and threes to drop off their single rounds of ammunition.

Too soon Maria was crawling on all fours behind her platoon centurion, her squad following her. They passed through tight little alleyways and buildings; their inhabitants staring at them with wide, terrified eyes. A little girl came to stand near where they had to pass, making the sign of the cross at them. Maria flashed the girl her best smile; almost as if she wasn't scared to death.

I guess she means well. And it's nice to know someone cares.

The women crossed open streets with hearts pounding. The whole time they moved they heard artillery—their own, they'd been told—pounding the steep enemy held hill to their front. The blasts made their internal organs ripple in a way that was both fascinating and extremely unpleasant, the more so as they got closer. The sensation wasn't entirely new to any of them as they'd all been shelled, deliberately, in basic training.

Eventually they stopped in a courtyard that abutted onto *Avenida de la Santa Maria,* also known as *Avenida de la Victoria,* the road that marked the partition between the part of the country under Balboan control and the part held for the last decade by the Taurans. Some of the machine gunners, the ones with the heavier .34 caliber belt-fed guns, were ordered into the buildings to support the attack. Cat and her drum-fed M-26 stayed with her squad.

Maria was scared to death. She didn't want to kill anybody; she didn't want to be killed either. The more she thought about it, the more frightened she became. It got so bad that she lay right down on the asphalt, pretending to nap and hoping that its steadiness would help her conceal from her troops how very afraid she was.

Marta wasn't fooled. She sat down, cross-legged, and said, "Don't worry, Maria. It'll be fine."

Foul-mouthed and occasionally insubordinate as Marta was, Maria was awfully glad of her company. She patted her leg and half agreed with her, "Fine. Yeah. Sure."

In a way, having Marta there did help. Maria wasn't *quite* so scared, anyway. She didn't feel so alone. That had really been the worst part of getting to the hide, being all on her own.

Now she was with her tribe. Life was not so bad.

"What do you mean there's no damned smoke available?" Trujillo cursed into the radio. "I can't order my girls into *that* without smoke!...Yes, sir...Yes, sir...I understand, sir. Yes, sir, I'll try."

Inez handed the microphone back to her fire support sergeant, her forward observer. The FO just shrugged and said, "Can't store the white phosphorus with the high explosive. We'll have to wait for the WP to reach the guns."

"We can't wait. It's got to be done now. Suarez promised to paste the hill good with high explosive before we go in. But we're going in."

"Oh, Christ," the FO said. Smiling nervously, she added, "Funny, how you call on the only man who can help you, isn't it?"

Trujillo looked at her watch nervously. "Yeah...funny."

The FO looked up at the sky and said a little, hopeless, prayer; something to the effect of, "Lord, please make them run away." No such luck, of course. The Taurans had their jobs, too.

Trujillo looked around at her command, nearly two hundred women of the *Tercio Amazona*. Her eyes sought out especially those who had gone through training with her back when the regiment was just a dream. They were her best friends; no difference in rank could ever change that.

Her eyes settled on Maria briefly. She smiled with warmth and a little sadness. As she turned her gaze slightly, the smile grew both warmer and sadder. Cat Gonzalez smiled back, encouragingly.

The tempo of artillery fire landing on the hill ahead picked up noticeably. Maria opened her eyes and stood up. Lying on the asphalt hadn't really helped all that much, anyway. She put her arms out parallel to her body to bring her squad on line. Marta fell in behind the squad. It was her job to make sure nobody fell behind her.

"Fix...bayonets!" Trujillo commanded. Word was passed from soldier to soldier. "Fix bayonets...fix bayonets!"

Maria's hands shook as she reached toward her belt. She pulled the bayonet out and fixed it on the end of her rifle. A steady click-click-clicking said the rest of the maniple was doing the same, putting a knife on the end of a modern rifle to turn it into something a caveman would recognize as a spear.

It was not silly, however many thoughtless amateurs thought it was. True, bayonets almost never killed anybody who could still fight. They were not supposed to. What they were supposed to do, instead, was to terrify the enemy into running away or giving up. They did that well enough, often enough, to justify keeping them in the inventory. Of course, part of the terror was in the way they really *were* used; to hack the enemy's wounded into spareribs after winning.

Even though it is against the law of war to refuse to take prisoners, prisoners are almost never taken in a hotly contested assault. Then, too, speeding is against the traffic code.

Arias got down on both knees, right there on the hard pavement, crossed herself, and began to pray. She included the Taurans in her prayers. Another girl, from a different squad, was crying softly. No one but she knew exactly for what or for whom she was crying for.

Then it was time.

✧   ✧   ✧

Trujillo handed the microphone back to her radio-telephone operator. The RTO held it to her own ear, listening. Then Trujillo looked at the F-26 in her hand, shook her head, gave a little "to hell with it" shrug and slung the piece across her back. The tribune took the eagle from its bearer and crossed herself.

There's only one way to do this, to make sure they go up that hill... together. We've got a broad open street to cross. The way the trees are, they cover the enemy from sight of most of our supporting weapons but give them a perfect view of most of the street. On the plus side they couldn't see us where we assembled on our side of the street, what with the trees, the walled courtyards, and the covered vestibules. The Taurans might only kill my girls a few at a time if we try to cross in ones and twos, but there will be a lot more time to do it in; a lot more rifles and machine guns for every second there's a target—my women!—exposed. And there just isn't any more time to wait. A chance at the headquarters for this whole sector? It has to be done, if it can be done, right away, right now. If we fail...

"What the hell? Captain! Captain Bernoulli. You need to see this, sir."

Bernoulli—a stubby Ligurini, a Tuscan mountain trooper—leapt from hole to hole, sheltering from the now desultory incoming artillery. Reaching his machine gunner's side, he hunched his short and stocky frame down next to the man who had summoned him. "What is it, Basso?"

Basso pointed at the street below. "Sir, it's one of the locals. I think it's a she and I think she's giving a speech... right in my line of fire. Sir, do I have to shoot her?"

Bernoulli shook his head at the waste of it all. "Let's wait a sec'. Maybe she telling them all to go home... no, I guess not. Shoot if he... or she comes any closer, Basso."

"Yessir," the mountain trooper answered, though he clearly didn't like it.

On the far side of the street below, Inez Trujillo shouted, "On your feet, *Amazonas!*" Then she waited for the girls to rise, such as hadn't already.

"Now... For your old parents and grandparents back in the City; for the children you have or hope to have; for your country...

for YOURSELVES! The future is at the top of that hill! Follow me, you cunts!"

Holding the eagle high with both her hands, the tribune raced out into the street. She had made it more than halfway across before three things happened: the artillery stopped falling on *Cerro Mina,* the rest of the Amazons realized what she had done, and two enemy machine gunners on the slope simply shot her to pieces.

Perhaps if only one or two bullets had hit Trujillo the rest might not have followed as they did. But Inez was torn *apart.*

The women could see that she was dead, very dead, even before her body hit the ground. She didn't even have time to cry out. Her head was nearly severed, misshapen by a bullet, too. Entrails spilling, her corpse sprawled on the pavement. In an instant she was transformed from a living, breathing woman into an obscenity.

One or two enemy bullets must have hit the eagle's staff, because it fell to the asphalt in two pieces.

The rest of the women—those who could see—just stared for a moment, speechless except for one or two of the girls who screamed. Maria recognized Cat's scream clearly. She looked again at the body, biting her lower lip, tears coming to her eyes.

Maria felt a horrible anger build in her. "They ruined her! They *ruined* her!" She tightened the grip on her rifle and screamed, "*Ataque!*" In the next moment she and her girls were charging across that street screaming like she-wolves and firing from the hip.

The other squads followed right along. Well, men and women *both* are herd animals.

More machine guns—rifles too, of course—joined those that had killed Trujillo. Maria vaguely saw—rather, *felt*—one long sweeping burst cut down the woman—more of a girl really, she was no more than eighteen—beside her. A spattering of angry hornets cracked the air by her head and two or three more Amazons—three, it was three—cried out and flopped to the ground behind her.

Marta's chest hurt terribly where a bullet had struck her breast, penetrating both liquid-metal plate and silk backing to lodge in the soft flesh below. Still she crawled from one body to another trying to do whatever good she could. She stopped briefly by the still-breathing form of Isabel Galindo. Isabel had been an immigrant from Santander. Isabel had been lovely.

She wasn't anymore. From whatever angle the bullet had struck, it had blown away most of her face and both of her eyes. Marta dropped her head onto the shallowly breathing chest and wept, briefly.

"I can't help, Isi. I'm sorry. I'm so sorry. Got to get to the other girls." She bent to give Isabel a kiss from bloody lips before crawling on.

She stopped briefly by Martina Santa Cruz. Martina had just joined the tercio a few months before. She wasn't much past eighteen years old. She would never be nineteen. Marta crawled on.

Marta didn't have to turn the next body over to know whose it was. "Oh, Cat," she moaned, "what about your kids?"

That was one friend too many. Marta collapsed, unconscious.

Maria didn't know, of course, that almost every close friend she had in the world was wounded or dead or dying. She kept running forward, firing short bursts. She kept shouting for the others to follow.

There weren't many others in her squad who could follow. Half of those who began that charge went down before they'd even crossed the broad street. Provided one didn't mind stepping on the wounded, or making the odd short jump, it would have been possible to have crossed it and never set foot on pavement. Even if someone had tried to cross it without stepping on any bodies, they would still have stained their boots red.

The rest of them, the half left standing, reached the wooded slope and, firing from the hip, began to close. It was slow going up that hill. More girls fell with every step.

What few *Amazonas* Maria had left did what she did, dodging from tree to tree, firing ahead without bothering much to aim, mostly just trying to ruin the Taurans' aim.

Then someone ahead of her reached a row of barbed concertina. The Amazon detached her bayonet to use with the scabbard to try to cut a way through. Together bayonet and scabbard made a good set of wire cutters; they were designed that way. Others had the same idea, of course. The Taurans concentrated their fire on those trying to cut through. They were hit, some wounded, some dead. Not one of them got more than thirty feet past the wire alive. The wire itself was draped with bodies hanging grotesquely by the barbs caught on their uniforms and in their flesh. Most were dead, but one woman who had been hung up on the wire kept trying to pick her intestines off of the ground and stuff them back into her torn belly. Her one good arm kept getting re-caught on the wire, forcing her to spill her organs back to the earth. She made a horrible keening sound—hardly human, really—the entire time.

That made Maria very angry, but in a very cold way. When she saw a pair of enemy soldiers come running up, she drew her rifle to her shoulder, leaned into a tree, took careful aim, and fired.

Her first target threw his hands into the air and fell back, dropping his machine gun. The other one stopped, foolishly, for a second or two. Perhaps he was stunned or confused; she didn't know or care. He looked, maybe, eighteen. She shot him in the stomach. With a surprised look on his face, he dropped his rifle, clutched his hands at his midsection and sat straight down. He fell straight back after she shot him, again, this time in the head.

"Sergeant Fuentes," someone gasped. It was Vielka Arias. She had Cat's machine gun in her hands. Maria looked her over and saw that Vielka was hit, too, in the leg. She must have crawled all the way, dragging Cat's gun behind her.

Maria flopped down to her belly beside Arias. Pointing with a finger, she said, "Good girl, Vielka! Now see those two bunkers?"

Vielka nodded deeply.

"Good. Good girl. I want you to use that gun to keep their heads down. I'm going to go for the wire. If I can cut through I'll signal you to join me."

Though Arias winced with pain, she nodded her understanding with great seriousness.

Vielka began firing, first at one bunker than the other, as Maria crawled forward, snakelike. As she crawled, she detached the bayonet from her rifle and the scabbard from her belt. These she linked together.

Once at the barrier, Maria started using her bayonet to gnaw her way through the barbed tangles. Vielka's fire alternated, spitting first to one side of her, then to the other.

"Goddamit," Maria exclaimed as her hand caught on a barb, tearing the skin. She continued her cutting, even so, her work slowed by the ripping barbs. Eventually, she found she had to rise to one knee to keep up her cutting.

Kneeling like that, the work progressed more quickly. Maria

had made it about halfway through when she felt a blow hit her, as if from a great fist. Something tore through her side and out her abdomen. Alma would be the only child she could ever bear with her own body.

Maria cried out in surprise and pain. As her bayonet-wire cutters flew away, she fell down again. Dimly she saw that there was the ragged lip of a shell crater nearby. She started to crawl for it.

After the first shock, her wounds didn't hurt all that much. Then they started to burn like hellfire, especially the larger exit wound. Maria began to cry from the pain. As she lay there, sobbing into the dirt, the bullets continued cracking overhead. That was Vielka, still trying.

Zamora had been trying to make sense of the ruination of her platoon when she saw Maria fall. She didn't think; she just raced for the writhing body of her friend. Bullets split the bark from trees where the enemy gunners sought vainly to bring her down. When Zamora's helmet strap broke and her helmet flew off her head not even her longish, red, woman's hair caused the fire to slow.

Something—luck or God or pulsating prong of perversity—was with her, however. She managed to dive to the ground next to Maria unhurt. She paused only for the briefest moment before taking a firm grasp of Maria's combat harness.

Maria dimly felt the strong grip of Zamora's hand on the back of her harness. She muttered, faintly, "No. No. Leave me here." The muttering quickly turned to one long continuous scream as Maria's body was dragged across the broken ground. The screaming grew to a crescendo, until Zamora dragged her across the rough lip of an artillery crater and down into its muddy, protective shelter. Then Zamora took off, leaping out of the crater like a deer.

A few others, all but one in pretty bad shape, joined Maria in the crater. The Amazons' fire stopped, for all practical purposes, not long after Maria had been hit. One woman—a not so badly wounded one—crawled to the edge of the crater and fired her rifle until an enemy bullet blew her brains out the back of her head. The enemy stopped, too, for a while, then picked up firing again. Maria heard some woman call out to save her, that the Taurans were killing all the wounded. She dug her fingers into the compacted mud of the crater and tried to crawl out to help.

She lacked the strength. Halfway up the slope of the crater Maria passed out.

Somewhere up the jungle-shrouded slope bagpipes were playing "*Boinas Azules Cruzan la Frontera*," Second Tercio code for "No quarter." Down below, medics picked through the one hundred and twenty-odd female bodies littering the street and the hillside. Most, if not by much, were still alive . . . if not by much. Many could be saved.

"Sergeant . . . sergeant we've got a few live ones here!"

The man with three stripes and a Red Cross armband came over and looked down into the blood- and corpse-filled shell crater. He shook his head sadly, muttering, "Stupid women . . . brave women."

Ahead, the sounds of firing told that Second Infantry Tercio was cleaning up the remnants of the Taurans atop the hill. Second had made its attack hours later, but in overwhelming strength—nearly four thousand fresh men, *with* substantial artillery support! When the men of the Second had seen the bloody pulp into which most of the women had been ground, they had gone berserk. There would be few if any enemy survivors on that hill. "No quarter."

"Well, don't just stand around with your goddamned teeth in your mouths!" the sergeant said. "Separate the live ones and get them out of here!"

Interlude

Overhead, at about twenty-five hundred feet, the streamlined shape of an airship wound its laborious way between La Plata, far to the north, and Secordia, way down south. Balboa's Herrera Airport was a routine stop for such. Patricio Carrera stepped out of his armored limo and looked at the ship without much interest. He had more important work to do today to spare a thought for anything but that. *Besides, if it mattered, Fernandez would have told me about it.*

"The Senate is my creation, not my creature," Carrera reminded himself as he walked up the building-wide stone staircase, toward the four dressed granite columns. Compared to a local, Carrera was tall at five feet ten inches or so. He was also considerably lighter than the national norm, with a kind of piercing blue eyes that were essentially unheard of in the Republic of Balboa. Since this was the Senate House, the *Curia,* he wore dress whites, but devoid of nearly all decoration. Despite the light material of the uniform, in the short walk between his staff car and the portico he could already feel sweat building up on his back and sliding down. Balboa had a very hot climate.

The blazing sun shone on columns that held up the thirty foot deep portico. Past the columns stood the dressed but unpolished granite blocks of the front wall of the *Curia,* the Senate House. Centered on that, directly to Carrera's front, were great bronze double doors. In front of those doors stood a liveried servant of the Senate, who was also a retired first centurion of the legion's Fourth Infantry Tercio.

To this man Carrera said, "*Dux Bellorum* Patricio Carrera requests audience with the Senate of the Republic." He then took out and handed over his service pistol. That military officers should never enter the *Curia* while under arms, nor indeed be escorted by armed guards, was a tradition Carrera hoped to establish firmly and beyond question. The best way in his power to do that was to follow it himself.

There was no doubt that the audience would be granted. Otherwise, Carrera would not have come. Still, formalities had to be observed. The retired centurion took Carrera's pistol, said, "Please wait here, *Duque*," and then turned and walked through the doors to announce Carrera's request.

Carrera then waited, patiently enough. It wasn't a very long wait, a matter of mere minutes, until the man returned and said, "The Senate will hear you now, *Duque*."

Raul Parilla, president of the Republic and, pro tem, *Princeps Senatus,* sat a curule chair facing the *Curia's* long, tiled central aisle. The space was flanked by rising levels of marble benches holding a quorum of the roughly one hundred and forty senators. Behind him, to his left, stood a larger than life-sized loricate statue of "*Dama* Balboa," the personification of the nation and the Republic. The statue's model had been Artemisia de McNamara. Carrera had sent far and wide for a sculptor—rather, a team of them—to do Artemisia, and the country, full justice, and just as far for a one by one by three meter chunk of near-molasses-colored marble.

The space behind Parilla to his right was empty, though the Senate had some thoughts on whose statue should fill it. "Victoria should go there," was the consensus, and Lourdes de Carrera's name had come up more than once as the prospective model. Then, too, what the hell, since the sculpting team was just hanging around . . .

Carrera didn't know about any of that, though Parilla and the Senate did. Fernandez, the chief of intelligence knew, too, but he knew nearly everything and told only a fraction of that. Indeed, Fernandez had made only one serious mistake the entire time he'd been chief of intelligence, though that one had been a doozy. All three knew why Carrera was at the *Curia* today, though few if any of the Senate knew.

And they're not going to like any of it when they do know, Patricio, Parilla thought. *Not a bit. We're just not that "enlightened" a country. Pretty unenlightened, as a matter of fact. Barely out of the trees, truth be told. Why . . .*

Parilla's thought was interrupted by the opening words of Carrera, his friend, supporter, sometimes subordinate, and sometimes mentor.

One of these days, Carrera thought, *I really* am *going to begin a speech to the Senate with the words, "Conscript Fathers." And why not? I conscripted the bastards, didn't I? Today's not that day though. Maybe after the next war.*

Instead, he began, "As I'm sure all of you know, I *am* the most progressive, *the* most enlightened, the very *most* multiculturally sensitive human being on the face of this planet."

He kept his own face straight all through that opening but had to wait for the senators to stop laughing before he continued.

"Exactly," he said, and smiled as he said it. "So when I tell you I want to do two things that might strike less astute observers as progressive, enlightened, and sensitive, you gentlemen—and you, too, Mrs. Hurtado—will not be fooled. You, at least, will know beyond a shadow of a doubt that those are the least of my concerns."

He cast his gaze around, seeking eye contact with a few key members of the Senate. When he had caught the eye of one in particular, a dark-skinned veteran named Robles, Carrera asked, "Senator Robles, how old are you?"

"Thirty-nine, *Duque,*" Robles answered.

"How old is your wife?"

"Seventeen," Robles answered defensively. Fernandez had been sure he'd be defensive about his new wife's age. "Why?"

Carrera held up and lightly wagged his right index finger. *Please wait. You'll know in a bit. And Fernandez knows everything.*

"Fifteen days ago," Carrera continued, "I had to witness the execution for mutiny of a senior tribune, aged thirty-seven, and a young corporal, aged nineteen. Both were male. When they joined we didn't ask so they never mentioned that they were homosexual. Note, that there is no law or regulation against being homosexual, but there is a law against two people, conspiring together, to subvert good order and discipline in the legions. That's mutiny.

"The corporal was fairly new, but among the tribune's decorations were three wound badges, the close combat badge, the Cazador tab, of course, and the *Cruz de Coraje en Oro con Espadas.*

"And, despite that, I had to have them both shot.

"No more," Carrera said, shaking his head firmly. "I don't want to have to do that ever again. Ever. Again.

"Because," and Carrera's finger shot out at Senator Robles, "Eros mocks Mars. Love knows no ages, nor sexes, nor conditions. It accepts no bars. And people brave enough to fight and maybe die for the Republic are not going to be dissuaded or deterred by our occasional firing squads. The *most* those do is encourage discretion." He shrugged. "Usually...imperfectly."

Carrera held his hands up, palms facing and parallel, roughly six inches apart, and said, "But, you know, deterrence always seems to fail by about that much."

Senator Hurtado used her hand to hide an embarrassed smile.

"So what do you propose, *Duque*?" Parilla asked, though he knew perfectly well what Carrera intended. And really didn't approve.

Speaking slowly and very deliberately, Carrera answered, "I want to raise a regiment—a small regiment, I think; not many will be suitable for the conditions I have in mind—of married male homosexuals."

Someone—Senator Cardenas, Carrera thought—shouted out from the benches, "This is impossible, *Duque*! You are going to make us a laughingstock among the nations of the world. Raising a regiment of queers; *married* queers? Impossible. And I shudder to think what the church will say."

Bright eyes flashing, Carrera answered, "It *is* possible, Senator. It's been done. It can be done again. And I intend to do it."

"But to what purpose, *Duque*? We don't need them. I don't want them. They make my fucking skin crawl!" Cardenas shuddered.

Carrera hesitated before answering. "No pun intended, but I find them a little, ah, distasteful, myself. But, Senator, as I said, just two weeks ago I watched two good soldiers shot by firing squads for mutiny. Their crime was that they were of different ranks, fell in love and...did something about it. They weren't the first we've had to shoot, either. You know that.

"They died well, those two. I want them to be the last. This is a way, a chance anyway, for them to be the last."

Carrera looked around the *Curia*, gauging support. He didn't think he had it. He said, "Senators...if it doesn't work...what have we lost? Some money for training. A few buildings we could always use for something else. Some uniforms. Let me try this...please?

"Besides, I need them for something else."

"Eh?" Cardenas asked. "What? What else?"

Carrera's eyes lit again as he answered, "I want to raise a regiment of women."

Later, in his own offices beneath the *Curia*'s main floor, Parilla sighed, "They voted against you, Patricio. On both questions. No money for your *Tercio Gorgidas* or *Tercio Amazona*. Even Hurtado voted 'nay.'"

"I'd be proud of them," Carrera admitted, then scowled, "if I wasn't so damned annoyed that they balked me."

"What are you going to do?"

Carrera's mouth twisted before he answered, "When I turned over the bulk of the legion's assets to the Senate, you know I openly kept quite a bit for discretionary funds."

Parilla smiled. "Yeah, I told them you would. I think they were secretly relieved to be able to balk you without frustrating you. I also made you a deal, even against my better judgment."

Carrera's left eyebrow shot up. "What kind of deal?"

"If you can make these regiments worth a damn, on your own ticket, the Senate will recompense your discretionary funds."

"Best you could do, huh?"

"Better than I really wanted to do," Parilla admitted.

CHAPTER TWO

To sleep, perchance to dream.
—William Shakespeare, *Hamlet*

Maria:

I'd had it pretty plush as a little girl. I didn't even suspect just how plush until much later.

My family lived in a big white stucco house, a few miles west of Punta Cantera. We had a maid, a cook, two cars. My mother needed the maid, too, given the sheer size of our house. Maybe by South Colombian standards we weren't quite rich. Certainly we weren't more than distantly connected to the oligarchy that ran Balboa from shortly after Belisario Carrera's revolt against Old Earth until quite recently. Still, we lived better than about ninety-eight percent of the people of our country.

My earliest memory—and I can't really remember how old I was then—was of sitting on my father's lap watching television. Two men, one brown, one black, were fighting. I didn't care about that, of course; sitting on Daddy's lap was better than playing with my dolls, trying on new clothes, or even ice cream or candy. I only paid attention to the fight because it seemed important to my father.

Suddenly the brown man on the TV threw down his hands saying, "*No mas. No mas.*" Daddy went into a towering rage at that, putting me on my feet so he could pace and fume. I remember him using words like "disgrace," "ashamed," and "coward." He used some other words, too, that I'd never heard from him before. Come to think of it, I'd never heard some of those words from *anyone* before. I guess I must have been really young.

There were a lot of things on the television worse than that when I was young. I was maybe seven when I walked into the living room and saw my mother, even paler than she normally was, staring at the screen while biting her finger so hard blood started to drip. Mama was crying.

I asked what was the matter, but she just shook her head while continuing to stare at the screen. Then I looked and I saw the bodies, and the parts of bodies, and the blood.

At first I thought it must be a movie. But Mama never would have cried over a movie, not her. And, when I looked from the screen to her face, I saw tears running.

"Who would do this?" Mama asked of the air, her hands flailing about, helplessly. "Who would do such a thing? Even when we were invaded, twelve years ago, they tried not to kill regular people. This ... monstrous ... *thing*; they intended to butcher innocent folk."

Then she realized I was really there and picked me up and carried me out of the room.

She was too late, of course. I already had an idea of what had happened. And I thought then, as I think now, that the most important lesson I'd learned since starting school was that when someone hits you, you have to hit them back. Hard. As hard as you can.

It was maybe a year and a quarter later before we finally did hit back. I got to watch that on television, too, with Daddy and my brother, Emilio. Mama wouldn't watch. Emilio was enthralled. Daddy was mostly just interested.

I know now why the images on the screen were green and grainy. At the time I didn't. I'm not sure Daddy did either. And there wasn't really that much to see, just bright green flashes on a long steep ridge somewhere they called "Sumer." I didn't know where that was.

The man doing the talking seemed really nervous, and it was hard to make out his words over the other sounds. Sometimes he'd turn his camera around and show what was happening in the other direction, but when he did you could see even less, just the outline of a hill being lit up by flashing lights.

I fell asleep on Daddy's lap before much of anything really happened.

It wasn't so long after that that the country began to really change. Neither Mama nor Daddy were too happy with the changes.

What changes? Oh, I don't recall that I'd ever seen a soldier in my life except on TV or at the movies. But, more and more as time went on you would see them everywhere. Some even came to school sometimes to talk to us. And they had parades in the streets pretty often, too.

In any case, I knew and cared little enough about all of that back then. My world was one of school, friends, beaches, parties and shopping. The latest hit love song was much more important to me than the fact that an army was growing around us.

The first time I ever really *saw* the legion was when the Second Infantry Tercio paraded down *Via Hispanica*. It was on a day when my mother had taken me shopping for clothes at a boutique near the *Iglesia de Nuestra Señora*. We had only just arrived at the door to the store, I having delayed things by successfully talking mother into buying me a new pair of shoes at a different establishment as well as two new music discs at yet another.

Hey, helping Mama spend Daddy's money was my *job*.

The parade itself was very well stage-managed, it seems to me now. Traffic was stopped in both directions for maybe half a mile. That was as far as I could see, anyway. Then smoke appeared as if by magic, a screen of billowing thick gray fog, all across the street. Someone started throwing these little bombs into the smoke. They whistled and then blew up, something like the sounds I'd heard on the TV, coming from Sumer. By that time, I was also able to recognize them from the war movies my little brother Emilio watched whenever he could. I, assuredly, had no interest in war in general or artillery in particular.

Then the pipes started, loud and shrill, and the first rank of the Second Tercio appeared, marching through the smoke and the explosions...as if marching into a fight. I think that was the effect they intended. It was...impressive. It impressed *me,* anyway.

When the boys went into their parade step—a sort of modified goose step, actually—people on either side applauded and the girls nearly swooned. Some of the men and boys marching really were handsome. And there was a *power* in their tread that I'd never experienced before.

I was fairly mesmerized for the moment. My mother just pulled me away into a store, tsk-tsking about what her father would have said had he been there to see it. No one, hardly, in *our* social class would dream of joining the military, back then, and certainly not an infantry tercio. We were all very much above that sort of thing. Mama's whole family explicitly despised the legions. Daddy's was a bit more ambivalent about them.

My father was a businessman, self-made for the most part. He'd started life with very little besides determination, some brains, some guts. I remember him, when I remember him, as being very handsome, very dark. My mother was a *rabiblanca*—a "white ass." She had been something of a debutante, from one minor branch of an old, old family.

My mother's family *never* liked my father. For one thing, he absolutely refused to take anything from them, a position my mother supported him in for the sake of his pride. For another, he just wasn't from one of the old families that usually ran our country. That stain passed on to myself and my brothers and sister. Our grandparents never cared for us as much as they did the other grandchildren. Besides we were too dark from Father's side of the family.

Still, Mother and Father did everything they could to make it up to us. We went on vacations regularly, attended the best schools in the City. Today I shudder to think of how much money they spent on me and my three siblings. We were probably as spoiled as any four kids growing up anywhere. And I? I was the apple of Daddy's eye, certainly through age fifteen. Whatever I wanted, and I recall that once that had even included acting classes, I got.

Age fifteen? Yes, that's when everything changed. The big change? I discovered *boys*. In particular, I discovered *one* boy.

Juan was simply *gorgeous*; tall, muscled and olive. He was curly haired, with green eyes framing a patrician nose. *Yumm.* His family was as old as my mother's. Juan's age? Eighteen. When you're fifteen, eighteen looks very mature and attractive indeed.

I saw him first when I went with some friends to the beach at Santa Clara, east of the *Ciudad*. I was sitting under one of the palm-thatched huts that dot the beach, just chatting with my girlfriends, when Juan came into my view. He looked good in a bathing suit.

So did I, I guess. Juan came over to introduce himself and my girlfriends thoughtfully made themselves scarce. We talked, made some arrangements, met again in the City. Met again. Met again.

He could sweet-talk a girl. I wasn't short, he said; I was "perfection in miniature." I wasn't too dark, no, I was...let me think. Oh, yes, "the shadow of beauty on a moonlit night." Oh, *that* was a good one. He told me I was beautiful, often enough, with enough of what sounded to me like sincerity, that I began to believe that to him I *was* beautiful, not merely pretty. I was his "Heaven and Earth." My eyes, his stars. My body, the paradise he *yearned* to enter.

He said he loved me, too.

I decided Juan was the *one*. The usual thing—err, things, actually—happened. I won't pretend I didn't like it. Even the things I didn't much like for themselves I loved doing with him...for him. I didn't even mind that some of those things hurt.

But then the only slightly less usual thing happened.

"*Madre de Dios!* What is the *matter* with you, Maria?" My mother stood, arms folded, at the door to my bathroom where I knelt, head in the toilet.

I had hidden my pregnancy for a couple of months, too afraid to disappoint my parents. Rising to my feet, I answered, "Nothing, Mother. I just don't feel well."

"Yes...of course...you don't feel well." Uh, oh. Mother wasn't buying.

She looked me over very carefully. Then she slapped me right across the face. "I wonder...do you suppose your bra is getting too tight, little one? Do you think maybe you need a larger size school uniform?" She hit me again, knocking me to the floor, then screamed, "Who was the boy, you cheap little tramp?" When I didn't answer, she pulled me to my feet by my arm. Then she twisted my arm behind my back and bent it. I screamed.

She forced the truth out of me. I wasn't as used to pain then as I later became.

Oh, sister, was there a scene at my house that night. Father screamed at me, slapped my face, too. He'd never done anything like that before, never even raised his voice to me. Mother had always disciplined the girls.

Mother, on the other hand, just cried continuously, moaning about the shame of her daughter being a "cheap *puta*." It wasn't until quite a few years later that I discovered from my sister that Mother had been three or four months pregnant with me when she'd married Father.

Daddy called Juan's parents, demanding that he marry me. They said Juan denied being the father. They said that if Daddy couldn't control his "little whores" it was no concern of theirs or of their son.

Naturally, my father went wild at that, but since Juan's parents hung up and took the phone off the hook there was no one to take it out on but Mother and myself. Finally, I ran to my room in tears.

The next day I took off from school to find Juan, since his parents weren't accepting any calls from me. I was so *sure* he would want to elope right away. There wouldn't be any point in detailing all the places I looked for him. Suffice to say that I *did* find him. I wished I hadn't.

He'd already found a new girl, was with her, in fact. No time waster was our Juan. When I tried to get his attention he turned his back on me. When I insisted, he said—and he said it out loud, so everyone could hear—that the baby could possibly be his, but since I would "go to bed with anybody, the odds were against it." Then he announced that he wanted nothing further to do with me because I was trying to pin this pregnancy on him. I ran out, again in tears.

The son of a bitch *knew* I'd been a virgin.

Well, my parents were no happier that I hadn't gone to school. Still, the big thing was the baby.

"I am taking you to the doctor and you are going to abort that little bastard inside you," Father said. So much for devout Catholicism.

"No, I'm not," I answered. "It's my baby and I'm keeping it."

"Then you'll keep it elsewhere," Father threatened. "I won't have your bastard in this house." Mother said nothing. With Father in charge she was able to just keep crying.

"Then I'll *GO!*" I shouted back as I stormed off to my room.

I went to bed that night brokenhearted. Even then, even with the exhaustion of tears, I couldn't sleep. Juan didn't want me, had used me and thrown me away like old toilet paper. Daddy and

Mother were ashamed of me; so ashamed they wanted to destroy my baby. They'd do it too, I thought. They'd make me do it.

That I just couldn't let happen. I might not have Juan. I might have lost my parents' love. But I had my baby. Already I could see her—I was sure the baby would be a girl—see her smiling face, hear her laugh, watch her clap her hands in innocent joy. No. No one was going to take my baby away—or hurt her. I got up and began to quietly pack a few things: Some clothes, whatever little money I had saved when I wasn't too busy spending it on clothes, music, shoes, or jewelry. I packed a family picture. I took, too, the emerald ring I'd been given on my fifteenth birthday, my *quinseñera*.

I also raided the refrigerator for half a dozen olives, the big gray ones that are about the size of a plum and are said to taste something like real Old Earth olives. Mother kept a couple of trees out back, green-trunked and gray-fronded, but those would have been too bitter. Standing in the kitchen, thinking of her olive trees, I considered for a moment taking some of the tranzitree fruit that grew in her garden as well. Green on the outside, red on the inside, sweet and deadly poisonous; the tranzitree fruit would have been a quick way out.

I couldn't do it. It wasn't just *my* mess of a life at stake.

I crept out of the house, as quiet as a mouse, sometime before dawn. As quiet as I'd been, my little brother, Emilio, met me at the foot of the staircase.

"Are you leaving us, Maria?" he asked, a look of real twelve-year-old's sorrow in his eyes. "Is it because you're going to have a baby?"

I just threw my arms around him, trying very hard not to cry. Emilio had always been my favorite; ever since the day Mother had brought him home from the hospital. I loved my sister and other brother well enough. There had always been something special between Emilio and myself, though.

Emilio asked me to wait a minute while he ran to his room. When he came back he had about twenty-five drachma in his hands... that, and his favorite baseball glove. "Please take these, Maria. I know you don't need the glove... but it may remind you of me. And you *will* need the money."

I started to really cry then. I buried my face in his shoulder to muffle my sobbing. Then he started to cry without any shoulder to deaden the sound. I worried that we'd wake my parents.

I told him, "Emilio, I have to go. But I'm going to miss you most of all."

"But how will I find you?" he asked.

"Don't worry. Once I'm on my feet, I'll find you."

With Emilio's little fortune in my purse, his glove weighing down my satchel, tears in my eyes and a lump in my throat, I left.

I walked for hours through the city, switching my suitcase from hand to hand as I did. I was pretty naive in most of the ways of the world, but I knew I'd need money until I could find a job. So...no taxi. And I didn't know the bus routes; I'd never had to take a regular bus before. Still, by noon I had reached my destination, an even seedier than usual part of the *Rio Abajo Barrio.* There I went looking for a room.

Finally, an apartment manager showed me something in my price range. "For what you can afford to spend, miss, this is about as good as you're going to find."

But, God, it was *awful.* I don't mean merely dreary and dirty, though it was those things, too. The one window was cracked. There were cockroaches scurrying around the floor when the manager of the building turned on the one, bare, light bulb. And it stank, of grease, of dirty bodies...of sex, too. Nasty, you know. And it was the *best* of what I'd seen in my price range.

Well, I did some mental figuring. With the money I had I could afford this place for about six weeks and still eat once a day. I thought six weeks would be enough time to find something to do, some kind of work. Then I could get a better place.

I took the dump.

You can't hold a fifteen-year-old, boy or girl, accountable for being dumb. The money lasted maybe three weeks. And I sure hadn't found work by then.

I'm not going to talk about the next several months. Go ahead and assume the worst you can imagine. It was probably, in most ways, worse than that. But at least it wasn't prostitution.

Eventually, my pregnancy began to show so badly I couldn't get *any* kind of work, even the *Barrio* pimps weren't interested. I lived off charity for a while. You cannot imagine how much that hurt, coming from my family, with my father—to say nothing of my mother.

Then came the big day. My water broke, I went into labor. One of the neighbor women helped me bring the baby into the world, there on my filthy mattress.

It was hard. The baby was big and I was...tiny...inside. Writhing in agony, I cursed Juan. I cursed my father. I cursed every man who'd ever lived. While I was at it, I cursed Eve.

Mr. Rios waited outside while his wife held me and helped me and comforted me. When Mrs. Rios held Alma to my breast, I thought she was the most beautiful thing I had ever seen. I still think so. I can't imagine ever thinking differently.

Alma was fine and healthy. I got sick. If it wasn't for Mrs. Rios and her husband I don't think I would have made it.

After a few months—yes, that's how sick I was—I was able to start looking for work again. Unfortunately, there were no jobs for little ex-rich girls with no skills, a tenth-grade education and a baby to care for. Not unless they were in the new legions, and I was too young to join even if I'd wanted to. Not that the thought ever even crossed my mind.

I'll tell you the truth: I considered going to work in one of the whore bars. I don't suppose that I had any real skill at that sort of thing, Juan or no, but I'd been an eager learner. I might have become a whore, too, if my having been sick so long hadn't made me—temporarily—pretty damned unattractive. I'm just as glad I never had to find out if I could have.

I did find work; as a waitress. It was hard work and the restaurant was hot. And me? I'd never worked a real job a day in my life before I got pregnant. And the odds and ends things I'd done so far didn't require even as much skill as a busboy needed. I was also still weak from being sick so long.

My family had paid for dancing lessons for the girls, fencing for the boys. *I* thought I was pretty graceful. But I seemed to spill more food on the floor than I served the first few days I was there. The manager fired me after an unfortunate incident involving a large bowl of hot soup and someone's trousers.

The next foray into economic independence was as a maid. Now, you understand, I couldn't be a maid for any of my own people. My parents might have found out and died of shame. I still owed them something, I thought. So it had to be for some foreigners. And the Taurans were the most numerous foreigners around.

That first maid job lasted two days. It was for some old man who lived in Balboa and worked on the locks of the Transitway. He was Sachsen-born as I recall. *He* kept insisting I . . . well, it doesn't matter, I wasn't going to do it, not for him. Once he understood, out went Maria on the street again.

After that, I went to work for a Gallic couple, the Mangins. He was an officer, a captain, in their army. She was a housewife. They were really nice to Alma and me. We lived in a little room underneath the house. It was even air conditioned and had its own bath. Life was not bad.

However, all good things come to an end. By the time I went to work for the Mangins they only had about a year left in the country. When they moved away, so did my job. Back to *Rio Abajo* I went. Still, since the job with Mangins had come with room and board, I'd been able to save almost six hundred drachma.

With the money I'd saved I was able to pay for some new clothes and a better room. The new clothes got me another job, this time working in a store on *Avenida Central.* I was on my feet all day, six and a half days a week. The Rios continued to care for my daughter. Whenever I could, I looked for a better job.

"Well, Miss Fuentes, your office skills aren't really what we're looking for. Still, you're young. You can be trained. We'll give you a try." The speaker was *Señor* Arnulfo Piedras, a chubby, jolly-seeming man of about forty. He ran an office in a bank off of *Via Hispanica.*

I gushed, "Oh, thank you, sir. *Thank you.* I promise you won't be sorry."

"I'm sure I won't," he said meditatively. "Please come back tomorrow at eight to begin."

I left feeling some real hope for the first time in many, many months. As I walked past the rows of desks, I never noticed that none of the women working there would meet my eyes.

"Close the door behind you, Maria," Mr. Piedras said gently. I did.

Once the door was shut, his face went from gentle to a mask of utter fury. "Idiot!" he screamed at me. "*Idiota!* Can't you do the simplest little thing right?" He waved a piece of typewritten paper in front of my face.

I stood there by his desk, speechless. I couldn't imagine what I'd done so wrong. I'd only been working for about two weeks.

Piedras continued, "I gave you this job out of the goodness of my heart and *this* is how you repay me? Fool! Blunderer! Moron!" I still had no idea what he was talking about. Hell, I was too much in shock to even begin to understand what he was talking about.

Then he shouted, "You're fired." That hit me. I started to cry. I didn't know what I'd done so wrong. What *could* I have done so wrong? My old job was already filled. I couldn't even go back. I'd taken a better apartment, one I could only afford on my new salary. And he was firing me already. I had a *baby* to support.

At my tears, Piedras seemed to relent. His fat face softened. He put his arms around me as if to comfort me.

I stiffened as I felt him unsnap my bra, one handed. I think now that it must have taken much practice for him to learn to do that so easily. I soon found myself bent over his desk, face down, the sausagelike fingers of his left hand playing with my breast, the other lifting my skirt and tugging at my panties. When he had those out of the way he stuck a hand into his desk drawer.

I didn't start to sob out loud until I felt him rub something, lubricant, I suppose, between my legs. He put a hand over my mouth to shush me. Then he raped me.

Alma looked up at my face from where she'd been resting her head on my chest. She asked, "Whatsamatter, Mama? Why are you crying?"

"No reason, baby," I sniffled. "Everything's fine," I lied. "Just cuddle into Mama and sleep."

It had gotten better at work, actually, over the past several months. Where Piedras had called for me two or three times a week to begin with, now there was another young girl for him to break in. I didn't have to feel the swine inside me more than once every few weeks.

I'd stopped crying once I realized the fat pig enjoyed it. My only protest now was, if he forced me to my knees, to push him so far into the back of my throat that I threw up on him. He didn't enjoy that. After the first couple of times of cleaning my vomit from his trousers, he gave up on it.

He still usually pushed me face down onto his desk. After the first time I threw up on him, he took me...behind...to punish me, I suppose. He still did that from time to time.

Why didn't I complain? Well, the first few times maybe I could have. Just maybe somebody would have listened, too. Then he'd have told his story. You know which story, the one about the little tramp who tried to seduce the boss. They would have believed him. And I'd have been fired. And maybe Alma would have starved.

But what about the law? Same thing; same ending. My country just wasn't set up to protect women who were alone, women who didn't have a husband, son, or father to protect them. Nothing is stronger than custom and that was ours at the time. I had no one. I was alone, nearly without rights. I was helpless.

I took showers all the time, but I never felt clean anymore. I was barely eighteen.

Things began to really fall apart again when the civilian government used the Taurans and our police force to try to get rid of President Parilla and *Duque* Carrera. Everyone knows how they failed to do so, how Lourdes Carrera escaped from captivity, got some help, then fought her way to a TV studio to rally the tercio of Volgans to save her husband. Then came the Revolution, along with a very large number of public executions. Then came the Tauran financial embargo. And with that, my job disappeared. Besides, Piedras had to make room for a new addition to his harem.

I had to find us a smaller place, no choice. Alma was too little still to understand why she had to leave her old playmates behind. I didn't know how to explain it.

It was at about that time that I discovered that we were no longer a democracy, at least what I'd always thought of as a democracy. On the other hand, I was still too young to vote so I really didn't give it much thought.

Also at about this time my sister and my mother found me. Forget the tears and recriminations, forget the money they offered me too. I was my father's daughter, and I had my pride. Still, they would sometimes bring something for Alma that I could never quite bring myself to refuse. The poor baby had so little.

Well, my financial situation just kept deteriorating. The country as a whole was surviving the foreign embargo, but for those of us who were on the margins of society and weren't in the legion, life got grimmer and grimmer. I thought about giving Alma up to my mother but couldn't bear to be apart from her for the rest of my life. And Daddy most emphatically didn't want me back.

I really didn't know what to do. I was rapidly coming to the end of my rope. I had to sell my emerald *quinseñera* ring. I'm pretty sure I was cheated.

During one of the regrettably short stints I did as a waitress I caught a news program on *TeleVision Militar,* the military TV station. It seemed Carrera was officially adding a new organization to the legion. I'd probably have forgotten all about it except that the *Tercio Gorgidas* was eventually, much later, to play an amazingly important role in my life.

There had been a lot of ceremony and drum beating, most of it quite meaningless to me. Parilla led the bulk of the men standing on the parade field through another ceremony that sounded suspiciously like a set of marriage vows, though the emphasis was maybe a little more on mutual support in battle than mutual support in life. Then the camera showed Carrera leaving his wife's side and going to the microphone to speak. He opened a book on the podium.

I heard him say this: "The ancient Old Earth writer, Plutarch, tells us of an extraordinary military unit of ancient times, its life... and death. Listen: 'Gorgidas, according to some, first formed the Sacred Band of three hundred chosen men... it was composed of young men attached to each other by personal affection... For men of the same tribe or family little value one another when dangers press, but a band cemented on friendship grounded upon love is never to be broken, and invincible; since the lovers, ashamed to be base in the sight of their beloved, and the beloved before the lovers, willingly rush into danger for the relief of one another... they have more regard for their absent lovers than for others present, as in the instance of the man who, when his enemy was going to kill him, earnestly requested him to run him through the breast, that his lover might not blush to see him wounded in the back.'

"'It is stated that the Sacred Band was never beaten till the battle at Chaeronea; and when Philip, King of Macedon and father of Alexander the Great, after the fight, took a view of the slain, and came to the place where the three hundred that had fought his phalanx lay dead together, he wondered, and understanding that it was the band of lovers, he shed tears and said, 'Perish any man who suspects that these men either did or suffered anything that was base.'"

On the screen, I saw Carrera turn slightly to send a dirty look to someone to his right rear. I later figured out that this someone was either a senator named Cardenas or a legate named Suarez.

After that, Carrera turned back to his audience and continued, "'Gorgidas distributed this Sacred Band all through the front ranks of the infantry, and thus made their gallantry less conspicuous... But Pelopidas, having sufficiently tried their bravery at Tegyrae, never afterward divided them, but keeping them together, gave them the first duty in the greatest battles... thus he thought brave men, provoking one another to noble actions, would prove most serviceable, and most resolute, when all were united together.'" Carrera closed the book from which he'd been reading.

"Your tercio has a glorious ancestry; quite possibly a glorious future. Don't fuck it up."

TV *Militar* would never dare to censor anything Carrera or Parilla said.

The *Gorgidas* boys did a parade then, in front of the cameras. The people, men mostly, in the restaurant seemed to have mixed feelings. Many of them were in the reserve forces. Some, probably most, were thoroughly pleased at getting whatever *mariposas* had been in their organizations out of same.

One night, sometime later, I heard some heavy weapons firing from not so far away. (Not that I knew the difference at the time; though I know the difference now). This was followed by the sound of a crash and an explosion. I hid with Alma under the bed. The next morning we came out and everything seemed pretty normal, except that the neighborhood was buzzing over some Tauran helicopter that had been shot down the night before. Curious, Alma holding my hand, I walked in the direction of the crash.

Sure enough, just outside the walls there was a helicopter, wrecked and burned. It still smoked slightly.

I saw a man, tall for one of us, though not so tall for the ex-gringo I'd heard he was. Carrera was looking over the wreck as some medical people removed the bodies from it. I saw him lose his temper and strike one of the medics. I don't know what for.

I kept watching. Unfortunately—or perhaps fortunately, as it turned out—Alma drifted away. I didn't worry when I realized she was gone. Say what you want about the people of *Rio Abajo*. They may be poor but, at least since the legion exterminated the criminals, they are basically decent, more decent than the richer folks I'd grown up with, a *lot* more decent than people like Piedras.

Then I saw Alma and I did start to worry . . . though panic might be a better choice of terms. She was running across the street directly toward *Duque* Carrera. I don't know what you remember from that time, but Carrera had a damned terrifying reputation. When one of Carrera's guards began to turn a rifle on my little girl, I nearly screamed.

But Alma just stopped in front of him with her hands behind her back.

Carrera squatted down and talked to her very softly for a little while. She took her hands from behind her back. She had made him a bouquet of flowers. He laughed, took the flowers, and scooped her up in his arms. He spoke to her for a little while then Alma pointed at where I was standing.

Oh, my God, I thought. *He's coming towards me.*

"I take it this is your little girl, Miss . . . ?"

"Fuentes, *Señor*. Maria Fuentes." I guess he'd figured out from the lack of a ring on my hand that I wasn't married.

He consulted his watch. "Well, Miss Fuentes, little Alma here has brightened up my day considerably. Would you do me a big favor and let me take the both of you to lunch?"

One does not refuse an invitation from someone who is not only the second most powerful man in your country, but also has a reputation Attila the Hun would have been proud to own. Still, it was the strangest thing to me, walking through the streets of the City, Carrera carrying my daughter, and all of us surrounded by big men carrying guns.

There was an ice cream shop and delicatessen not far away. When we went in the owner blanched. I suppose of all the people he ever expected to see enter his establishment, Carrera was probably the last.

He bought Alma a sandwich and then an ice cream cone. When I tried to refuse anything he insisted that I at least have a sandwich. He, himself, settled for coffee. Patting his stomach he said to me, "My wife overfeeds me. And I don't get out as much as I used to. If I didn't watch myself, I'd get fat."

The memory of Piedras fresh in my mind, I assumed Carrera just wanted to bend me over a desk, too. I kept my eyes down on the plate while I ate.

I was wrong, by the way.

Carrera asked me a little bit about myself. I told him as little as possible, but I think—no, I'm sure—that he saw right through me. I mean, I really think he saw everything; maybe to include Piedras or someone just like him.

He thanked me for joining him for lunch. He said he almost never had a chance anymore to just sit down with someone and talk. He asked me about my work.

"Well...I'm sort of between jobs right now," I answered.

He asked me about my hopes for the future, but I didn't have any beyond seeing Alma grow up to a better life. Since I rather doubted that would happen, I told him I had no hope for the future.

After a while, I ventured a question of my own. "Sir," I asked, "why did you and *Presidente* Parilla exterminate the opposition government?"

He put his hands behind his head and leaned back in his chair, his eyes staring into space. At length he answered, "Self-defense, I suppose; they were trying to exterminate us."

Seeing I didn't understand, he elaborated, "The old, rump government tried to get rid of us on some trumped up drug charges. Many of my friends were killed; my new family threatened. My wife, Lourdes..." He stopped talking for a moment. I've never seen anybody with that much pure hate in his eyes, not even me in the mirror after a session with Piedras.

He continued, "Anyway...Lourdes saved us. You probably knew that. When our side had won out, Parilla and I determined never to let anything like that happen again. We stamped out the oligarchs to let the country start over fresh.

"Mostly, it's working," he said. Then he looked at my threadbare clothing, looked at Alma's too thin frame. He looked at my face and sighed. I saw then that his eyes really were beautiful, the color of the sky on a cloudless day, and surprisingly full of compassion.

"Unfortunately," he continued, "a lot of decent people have been cut out. We only have so much money to go around, despite some help from some friends who have the same enemies we do. There's only so much we can do. By concentrating only on those with military power, we've left a lot of folks—people like yourself—without any recourse at all. This seems to be especially true of the women of the country. I'm sorry. There's only so much to go around," he repeated.

"God knows," I told him, "I could use some help. One decent break, that's all I need." I *didn't* cry, however much I wanted to.

He looked at me very intently. Then he asked me, if it were possible for Alma to be cared for, if I would be interested in joining up. He said he couldn't do more for me than that, that the benefits of society were for those who benefited society.

When I hesitated, Carrera reached over and pulled Alma onto his lap. She immediately settled in nicely, still intent on her ice cream. He asked me "Don't you think this beautiful little girl deserves every chance you can give her?"

Thinking of everything I'd already given up for Alma—wealth and position for her life, dignity (Piedras!) for what passed for comfort—I wanted for the moment to spit at him. I didn't though. Instead I told him I *might* be interested. He gave me a card with an address and a phone number to call to reach one of his aides. He also wrote a little note on back and signed it, "C."

Before leaving he reached into a pocket and pulled out some money, saying, "Buy her a birthday present from me." He turned his body, too, so no one could see the money.

It was so . . . tactful. He could have said that I looked like I needed the money. I did. He could have made some kind of political capital from it, even. But he just wanted to do a nice thing for a nice baby girl, without embarrassing me.

Then he set Alma back down, paid the bill and left, his entourage of guards following in his wake.

He stopped and waved to Alma from the door.

That was pretty tactful, too, the way he'd let me know where to go. Anyone could see I couldn't afford a phone. But I knew where his office was, if I really wanted to go there. Everyone knew.

Did I? I'd never even considered the possibility. Before Alma, before I was born, my future had been all planned out for me: finish high school, then go to the university; either in Balboa, Santa Josefina, Atzlan, or La Plata. After that, marriage, of course. Then a sedentary life as a housewife *cum* minor socialite. Oh, yes, and produce many grandchildren.

I was living a life a far cry from that. It was a dreary and hopeless life, too.

I thought about it for a few days. I'll confess, I was scared—maybe terrified is a better word—of going into the legion. Then, too, I was sick at the thought of leaving Alma behind, even if I knew she'd be well cared for. Which I didn't *know* at the time, actually.

I asked around the neighborhood. Many of the men were in the legion. They said it was hard, but there were a lot of advantages to going...and that it could be great fun. (I wasn't too sure that my idea of fun and theirs precisely matched.) One of the men was in training to be a civilian machinist with his tercio footing half the bill, lending him the rest at low interest. He could never have paid for that himself. Another had managed to open a small store with a veteran's loan. There were different benefits for different jobs and levels of responsibility. The men didn't know what was available for women.

I thought about what it might be like, to have a fresh start at a decent job, a decent life. Maybe I'd even be able to start my own business. I might not have finished my education but I wasn't stupid or lazy. Okay, maybe a *little* stupid, but I was growing wiser all the time.

Finally, I worked up the nerve to go to Carrera's office, at the *Estado Mayor*. He wasn't in but, as he'd said, one of his aides was.

"Miss Fuentes?" asked the aide, a fairly youngish tribune, not too good looking. At my nod he said, "The *Duque* mentioned that you might be coming by. How can I help you?"

"*Duque* Carrera said something to me about—possibly—joining up."

"Yes, that was my understanding. Do you have any skills now?"

I had to tell him that I really didn't.

He just shrugged his shoulders and said, "Most women who express an interest in the legion do not. Don't feel bad; usually neither do the men. That really doesn't matter. We can teach skills provided that the student is willing to learn and worth teaching." He stopped for a minute, scratched his chin, and then asked, "Tell me, Miss Fuentes, what, if anything, you know about the legion and how women are utilized."

Again I had to admit to having no idea.

"Very good," the tribune said. "Then you should have few misconceptions to clear up. Basically, women are not really necessary. Sorry." He didn't seem to be.

"Oh, yes, they fill certain jobs that would otherwise have to be done by a man, but—if no women were available—we would use very old and very young men in those jobs...boys and pensioners if we had to.

"Essentially, women are cooks, clerks and medical personnel in medical units above the cohort level. Except for a *very* few who have special talents and skills needed by the legion—lawyers, doctors, nurses, a few pilots and such—those have traditionally been the choices open to women.

"However, because we have certain rigid requirements for moving up in rank that are—so far—dependent on qualifications that women have not yet been admitted to, there have been no women officers or centurions accessed in the last thirteen years. The couple of holdovers from before the invasion are kept on merely as a courtesy. They are not *real* officers anyway, but more or less administrative types. They are also frozen in their old ranks. There are a larger number of women warrant officers; those lawyers, nurses, doctors and such I mentioned to you.

"Also, you should know, the major benefits of service—the material benefits I mean, not the benefits of eventual full citizenship—are rank and job driven. Combat arms jobs—infantry, armor, artillery, combat engineers, some military police, and air defense—have greater benefits in terms of civil education and job training. Officers and centurions are entitled to attend higher education at government expense when off duty, sometimes on duty. Women do not, so far, qualify for any of these.

"Women *do* qualify for government protected jobs upon completion of training but...the jobs for which they qualify are less desirable, by and large, than those that men qualify for. This is not because they're women but because they are not eligible, so far, for positions of great hardship or responsibility."

The tribune hesitated, looking me over. I have been appraised by a number of men over the years. None of them ever quite looked at me like that, as if I were a strong and healthy mule they were thinking of buying.

I knew what he was seeing: an olive-skinned female, with good teeth, fair muscle tone, somewhat short. If he thought I was attractive, it didn't show.

At length, the tribune said, "There is one other possibility you might want to think over." He reached into his desk, pulled out a color brochure, and handed it to me. "*Duque* Carrera has directed the raising of a female combat formation; a full tercio if we can find enough women who are both willing and able. If the program is successful, and if you join it, *and* if you finish your training, you would also qualify for all the same benefits as any man who joins."

I really couldn't see myself as a fighter. I told him so.

"You would know about that best, I suppose," he answered. "But take this brochure home with you. Give it some thought. Even if you elect not to join the *Tercio Amazona* you might still want to try some other, female, branch of the service."

"I have a child. *Duque* Carrera mentioned that she could be taken care of for me if I join."

"That's discussed in the brochure."

The brochure was mostly in simple question and answer format.

If I join the Tercio Amazona, *will I be able to be married?*
The Republic takes no interest in whether or not its defenders marry, except that, after accession, marital or romantic relations may not generally be within the same regiment and may in no case be between any members of substantially differing ranks. Enlisted men and women (pay grades 1 through 3) may socialize privately only with other enlisted men and women. NCOs, Centurions, and Officers may associate only with service members of the same corps. Warrant officers are permitted social interaction only with other warrants. This is true whether you are on duty or off. The notable exception to this is the *Tercio Gorgidas* in which de facto marriage to another member, just prior to induction, is the rule. This partial ban on socializing does not affect organizational social activities nor does it cover marriages which existed before enlistment. In the latter case, however, married couples will almost never be permitted to serve in the same regiment.

What about children?
Dependants of members of the legion who have been killed or crippled, in action or in training, qualify for

a number of assistance programs, generally of the self-help variety.

As for already-born children, while other female members of the defense forces do *not* receive much in the way of official direct assistance in caring for their children, mostly due to their being in densities within their tercios too low to make this practical, the *Tercio Amazona* will have a fully staffed dependant care maniple which will provide twenty-four hour care for your children while you are serving.

Both *Amazonas* and other female soldiers may become pregnant and bear children. Non-*Amazonas* are authorized up to two eighteen-month unpaid leaves of absence, which times do not count towards fulfilling their military obligation. Because the Republic does have an interest in strong and brave mothers bearing strong and brave children, *Amazonas'* maternal leave may be taken in the dependant care maniple, if and only if there is an opening. That time *will* count toward completion of service and will be paid, though at a reduced rate. We do not pay soldiers who are not combat effective through their own choice at the same rate as others. The *Tercio Amazona* will have a thirty to sixty percent overstrength authorized to permit both a combat capable unit and adequate opportunity for maternal leave.

It is within the contemplation of the legion, but by no means certain, that members of the *Tercio Amazona* may be given the option of serving four years of active time, then being discharged to the militia or Home Guard to become mothers if they wish. This option is not available to you now, and may never become available.

How difficult will training be?
No harder than necessary.

After training what happens?
The legions are primarily reservists. As an *Amazona* you will attend a fifteen week Basic Combat Training (BCT) Course. For your general information, male BCT is, at this time, twelve weeks. At least some of your class

will then be selected for leadership training. The rest will be offered one or several job or training opportunities, though most will become infantry. You will, if you are given an option, at your own discretion, take one of these. If you are only offered one job, so be it.

Also, after BCT and leadership training, if any, you will have a minimum ten-year obligation as a reservist or in the militia. During your reserve time you will be required to attend weekend training, one long weekend a month from a Thursday or Friday night to the following Sunday or Monday night. In addition, the reservists of your unit will train thirty days a year in one lump period at the *Centro de Entrenamiento,* at Fort Cameron. The militia of the tercio will train together with the reserves for another seventeen days per year. A further eight days of individual training and administration are required and authorized. Additional time may be required of you, based on the needs of the legion.

The tercio dependant care maniple will look after your children, at a legion facility or private home, for all the time you are training. As a special gratuity, your children will be cared for and fed at government expense.

How much will I be paid?

You will receive normal recruit private rates of pay and allowances for every day you spend in your initial training. Thereafter, if in leadership training, you will be paid at the applicable rate for a trained private, or your current rank, whichever is higher.

While in a reserve training status you will earn three months' pay per year for up to three months' training (the typical reservist actually spends seventy-seven days on duty, about half and half, weekends and weekdays). This does not include extra pay for special or additional training. This is only true for the next several classes of *Amazonas.* Once a healthy cadre is formed, most *Amazonas* will be placed in the militia echelon after BCT. They will only be called up for twenty-five days per year, normally, though more time may be required. Militia *Amazonas* will earn a minimum of thirty days pay per year.

As mentioned above, there are also opportunities for extended courses of paid special training for those who qualify.

See the table at the end of this brochure for applicable pay rates.

What if I fail in training?

If the circumstances of your failure are essentially disgraceful, you will be discharged from the legion under other than honorable conditions, or worse. Those so discharged are entitled to *no* benefits.

If the circumstances of your failure are not disgraceful, you will be given an opportunity to train for and finish your term of service in one of the positions reserved for women but not as difficult as the *Amazonas.*

That last part frightened me. But then Alma told me she was hungry. All I had was the money *Duque* Carrera had given me to buy her a present for her birthday. I used it.

The next day I went back to the *Estado Mayor* and signed up for the *Tercio Amazona.*

Interlude

The rain was coming down in sheets, though, given the season, those sheets flew horizontally rather than vertically. One could trace those sheets by the thick pattern of droplets moving in tight lines across the black asphalt.

Professor Rafael Franco, also Junior Centurion Franco, *Tercio Gorgidas,* eased his vehicle into the carport next to the three bedroom house he shared with his partner, Balthazar Garcia. The carport was no shelter from the rain being driven under the roof by the wind. With a sigh and a muttered curse, Franco opened the door. He was pelted then, immediately, and soaked before he'd gotten himself out of the car and the door shut behind him. There wasn't any sense in running at that point; still muttering imprecations he walked to the door leading from the carport into the kitchen of the house. He fought the wind to close the kitchen door behind him. The house was quiet, still, except for the pounding of the rain on the tiled roof.

"Balthazar? Are you home?"

Garcia answered from the living room, "In here, Rafael."

On his way to the living room Franco stopped to draw a beer from the refrigerator. He grabbed a piece of dried chorley bread from a tray. Beer held in one hand, he passed the bread to Garcia's pet trixie, a magnificent gray and green archaeopteryx that his partner had, most unusually, taught to speak. Not that trixies didn't have the capacity to learn, but most were more stubborn than the people who tried to train them. Garcia was an exception in that there were damned few people *or* trixies that could hold a candle to him for sheer mule-headedness.

"Up yours, *cueco,*" the proto-bird answered, as it held the chunk to its beak.

Of all the things, Franco thought, shaking his head, *he could have taught that bird to say... Lord, why did I have to fall in love with someone with such a weird fucking sense of humor?*

He continued on, taking a seat on a chair opposite the one where Garcia sat. Though no one would say that Garcia was much to look at, a hairy fireplug in approximately human form, Franco still felt his heart warm to see him.

"Weather too rough for fishing?" Franco asked.

"You just wouldn't fucking believe it," Garcia answered, with a shake of his head. After taking accession into the *Tercio Gorgidas,* and converting to reservist status from regular, Garcia had gone into the family business, running a forty-foot yawl out in the waters between the capital and the *Isla Real.*

Garcia looked at Franco's soaked form and corrected, "Well... maybe you would. How was class?"

Franco shrugged eloquently, then elaborated, "'One can lead a child to knowledge...'"

"'... But one cannot make him think.' I know," Garcia finished. He went silent for a bit, searching Franco's face. Finally, he asked, "Would you miss teaching so very much if you stopped for a while, maybe took a sabbatical?"

"Probably. Why?"

Garcia sighed. "Tribune de Silva called here today. He wanted to know if you and I might be available for the next eight or ten months to run two or three basic training courses."

"It would be a pay cut from my salary at the university."

Garcia answered, "I know... for me, too. But I think we should consider it."

Franco nodded. "All right. Let's consider it. First, why are you interested? I can see that you are."

"You always could," Garcia chided, with a smile. More seriously, he continued, "I was thinking about obligations, actually. No... not the ones the law or custom lay upon you... more the ones you feel."

Franco sighed. When Garcia spoke of obligations—or worse still, of duty—there was really no reasoning with him. *Mule-headed.* Franco half resigned himself to eight or ten very uncomfortable months in a tent or shack. Still, he tried. "What obligations are you talking about? Something more than the two and a half months a year we already spend in uniform? Why? Who do you think we have to pay back?"

Garcia looked down at the ring on his left hand. Its mate graced Franco's. "I really wasn't thinking about paying anyone back... more of paying forward. Carrera and the legion have given us a lot. You know they have: Marriage, legitimacy, a degree of acceptance we didn't have before."

"He gave us an opportunity not to be put against a wall and shot, you mean," Franco retorted. "I don't see where that makes us particularly obligated to him."

Garcia smiled. "He'd have been right to have shot us, back when you were an adorable young corporal and I was your platoon optio who couldn't keep his mind straight from thinking about you. It was hard, you know?"

Franco laughed. "Yes, I seem to remember that it was."

"Asshole," Garcia said with real affection. "You know perfectly well what I mean. Anyway, Carrera saved us from that, gave us the chance to be together in the *Tercio Gorgidas*. I think we owe him."

Resignedly, Franco looked at the wall upon which hung his and Garcia's helmets, body armor, weapons and centurion's insignia. He asked, "What do you—and he—want?"

Garcia knew he'd won at that point, and more easily than he'd expected. Looking down at the floor, biting his lower lip contemplatively, he answered, "I'll want you to start studying the problem. He needs us to train some women."

CHAPTER THREE

Pity not! The Army gave
Freedom to a timid slave.
In which freedom did [s]he find
Strength of body, will and mind.
  —Kipling, "Epitaphs of the War"

Lydia Porras's van pulled up beside a large sign painted with the number seven and lit by a small spotlight. She showed her pass to one of the sergeants who directed her to a parking space not far away. Already more than two hundred—that was Porras's guess—prospective Amazons milled about in confusion, their voices raising a sound much like a swarm of insects. Lydia saw a few kindly-faced, older noncoms trying to sort the mob into some semblance of order. She, herself, with a few folders tucked under one arm, went to stand very near the number-painted sign. More young women arrived in a steady stream, a very few of them already in uniform. She thought, *Must be some girls who wanted a step up in life. Given the world as it is, I hope they can lift their feet that high.*

A loudspeaker began to blare out names and instructions. Suddenly all talk from the women ceased. The noncoms continued to direct and sort them as best they could, being as gentle as they were.

I know this is all new, Lydia thought, *but I have never seen the legion let any group—even the rawest—sink to the level of a mob like this.*

The loudspeaker blared, "Fuentes, Maria. Fuentes, Maria. Report to Load Ramp Seven. Fuentes, Maria, report to Load Ramp

Seven." Porras checked the photo on one of the files she carried one last time before beginning to look out for the mother of her new charge.

Ah, there they are. Lydia caught sight of a young woman, perhaps eighteen, carrying a baby girl on her left hip and a battered suitcase in her right hand. The girl looked…defeated…already, beaten down. Her face? Porras thought it might have been a very pretty one if it had shown the slightest bit of life—or joy in life.

Lydia walked up and introduced herself. In a warm, grandmotherly voice she said to the baby, "Well, hello, little one. You must be Alma. You and I are going to get along famously, I think. You see, I'm your very own fairy godmother."

Alma opened her mouth into an "O" of wide-eyed surprise and asked, "Really?"

"Yes, indeed. And I bet I know what your first wish is." Porras produced a huge lollipop. Whether that had been Alma's first wish or not, one may well doubt. But it immediately became her first wish.

"Don't worry about her," Porras said to Maria as she took Alma in her arms. "She'll be well cared for. My house has gotten to be too empty since my own children grew up and moved away." She hesitated, and then said, "You know that the legion doesn't allow any communication from the outside during the first half of basic training?"

Before Maria could answer, all other sounds were drowned out by a high-pitched roar. Seven hovercraft approached a long ramp that led up to the land adjacent to the pier. One by one, the hovercraft climbed the ramp from the sea to the land, before settling down at marked spots on the asphalt. As each settled, the sound pouring from it dropped down to a comparatively low whine.

Maria started to choke up. Porras saw tears begin to form.

"Why are you doing this?" Porras asked.

"For *her*," Maria sniffled.

"Then *do* it; for her."

Porras handed Alma back just long enough for Maria to give the baby a last hug. Maria gave the child back, then began to shuffle forward with the other women who—though she did not know it—were to be in the same platoon with her. The suitcase, Alma's meager things, stayed behind.

Maria's tears wet the asphalt where she walked. She wasn't the only one crying.

✧　　✧　　✧

A very short—almost tiny, actually—woman of about Maria's age quietly sobbed onto the shoulder of a young man in uniform. The young man said to her, "Inez, don't be a fool. I'm *in* the legion. I know. It's *no* place for a woman. Certainly no place for a woman I care for. Please don't go. They won't make you, you know. It's purely voluntary."

Unable to speak, the woman, Inez, just shook her head violently "no." Then, with obviously pained reluctance, she turned and followed the rest of the women, drying her eyes as she went.

Across the asphalt and up a ramp, then a scurry to find some piece of the deck to stand on and call her own; Inez grasped the metal railing and tried not to think of home.

A horn sounded three times in warning, then the foot ramp whined its way up to the verticle. The engines of the hovercraft began to whine and strain. Inez gripped the railing tighter—*very* tight, actually—as the big machine lifted and began to turn back towards the ramp and the water of the bay past it.

It was late at night and, while one of the moons, Eris, was up and full, there was nothing to see but water and wave and the lights of the city, receding behind them.

Maria wasn't alone in staring backwards, at those lights, and implicitly at the life and loved ones being left behind. Once or twice she sniffled. A tiny girl next to her sniffled in what seemed to be an echo. Maria looked to see if she were being made fun of but, no, the tiny girl was, in fact, sniffling.

"I'm Inez," the tiny one said, "Inez Trujillo."

"Maria Fuentes."

A tall, white, spectacularly-built woman noticed the sniffling and introduced herself to Maria and Inez, "Marta Bugatti. And, yes, I'm a bloody foreigner. Moreover, I've been in the legion for a while, with the *classis*." The *classis* was the legion's naval organization and it had seen some hard fighting over the years.

Almost uniquely, the woman, Marta, already wore legionary battle dress and had rank and some badges neither Maria nor Inez recognized.

In that La Plata-accented Spanish that might as well have been Tuscan, Marta, having noticed that Maria and Inez had glanced at her stripes, said, "Those come off as soon as we report in.

Except for pay purposes, I'm a private for the duration, just like everyone else." She then asked, "Are you crazy for being here or just foolish?" Marta smiled as she asked the question. She seemed cocky, somehow, and very self-confident.

Before either Maria or Inez could answer, all three of them had their attention diverted by a tall and slender, really stunningly gorgeous blond woman who had already gathered about herself an entourage. The three, Maria, Marta, and Inez, walked over to hear better. It was only later that they found out the woman's name. It was Gloria Santiago.

"Just listen to me," Gloria declaimed, over the hovercraft's whining. "Stop worrying. This is going to be *easy.* Don't fall for the men's lies. We are smarter than they are. We are tougher than they are. Why, if a man had to go through childbirth, he'd cry like a baby. But *we* can and we *do,* all the time." She didn't look like she'd ever had a baby.

Inez muttered, "We're *not* as strong as they are."

Perhaps Gloria had overheard, though given the noise that seemed unlikely. In any case, she said to the crowd, "What difference does it make if men have bigger muscles? They have tinier brains. After all, how much of a brain can you stuff into something about six inches long and usually far, far too thin." That raised a laugh; even Inez found it funny.

"And besides," Gloria continued, "strength is overrated. I've seen it on TV; you all have. These days technology is what wins wars. And if men weren't so stupid, they would realize that, too. Just let us show them."

Gloria went on in that vein for some time. Eventually, Maria, Marta, and Inez lost interest and wandered back to where they'd been standing.

"Amazing," Marta said with disdain. "Imagine how seldom women would be hit by their husbands or boyfriends if they only knew that muscles don't matter."

Ahead loomed the *Isla Real,* its peak rising out of the sea. Lights beaconed from several places near the summit and one set seemed to stand several hundred meters above that.

"It's a solar chimney," Marta explained. "They saved a bundle by running it up the side of the mountain, but it goes straight up even from there. All the power for the island, enough for two hundred thousand people or more, so I've been told, comes from that. They've got it marked so that helicopters and airplanes don't run into it at night or in fog or rain."

"That's right," Inez observed, "you've been out there before, haven't you?"

"A few times, yes," Marta agreed.

"You were navy?" the tiny girl asked. "Why did you switch?"

"Bad memories," Marta answered, then wouldn't say more about it.

Their hovercraft began to veer, causing them all to lean to the side away from the turn. Except for the marking lights, there were no others to be seen. Then, suddenly, a battery of overhead lights, powerfully bright, came on to illuminate a large concrete pad. The hovercraft eased itself over a strip of sand, then came to a gradual stop before descending to land on the pad. The engines gave a last whine of protest at being put to rest.

With a whine of a completely different pitch, the foot ramp went down on one side before settling to the concrete with a jarring clang. Up the ramp trotted a man, close-cropped, uniformed, bemedaled and just flat mean looking. He had a sneer of complete contempt engraved across his face. He carried a small portable loudspeaker in one hand. He pushed aside any women who didn't clear out of his way quickly enough. Gloria went to her rear end with an outraged shriek.

The man stepped up to where Gloria had been sitting, then lifted the loudspeaker to his lips. "All right you stupid twats, get your fucking high heels off." The man waited for all of ten seconds for the women to complete that task. "When I give the order you will have thirty seconds to clear your worthless smelly hides off this hovercraft. When you get off, the men standing below will put you into formation. Then Tribune de Silva, your maniple commander, will speak to you. You will keep your foolish mouths shut. Now *GO!*"

Pushing each other and scrambling, the women crowded the single ramp. Many tripped and fell, to be trodden on by the others. At the concrete base, a number of noncoms, none of them with a kindly face, slapped and pushed and prodded the women into a single block. To the right, other groups were receiving much the same treatment as they debarked from their hovercraft. Being so far from the center, the men herded the women to their right.

At the other end, women were being herded to the left. The end result was a mob of prisoners, surrounded by guards, standing fearfully before a dais that rose about ten feet off of the concrete.

A very handsome man—he introduced himself as Tribune de Silva, and their commanding officer—walked briskly up the steps of the dais. De Silva made a little welcoming speech—sort of a welcoming speech. Had they been asked, most of the women would likely have confessed that they had been made to feel more welcome. De Silva then departed in a legion vehicle, leaving the women to the none-too-tender care of their senior centurions.

Shocked though she was, Maria's eyes widened as a huge bear of a man came to a halt in front of her. The man, she could plainly tell, was less than pleased with his charges.

"I am Senior Centurion Balthazar Garcia. You are shit. Introductions being finished, we will get on with business."

Garcia began to walk slowly from one side of the group to the other, distaste shining in his features. He did not smile. He spoke dispassionately as he walked the line, commenting on each of the women. "Too scrawny... You'll want to see the docs about getting a breast reduction, swabbie; those things are going to get in the way... No arse... Legs too skinny... Nose? Or is that a bus stuck on the end of your face, girl?... Stringy hair... When did you last douche, pigpen?... Bimbos. You! Bitch! Dry your silly fucking eyes. That's right, sniveler. That's right, crybaby..."

It was a ritual that hadn't changed, couldn't have changed, since long before the days when some Roman centurion had first taken charge of a group of new recruits. It made a sort of cruel sense, actually, though none of the women understood it at the time. There was only so much time—which is almost the same thing as only so much money, but harder to come by—any army could afford to spend on basic training. The kind of rule that Garcia was establishing cut down on the silly questions and complaints. That saved money and time. Since the time and money thus saved could be spent training soldiers to fight and live, it also saved lives.

It is often better to be insulted than dead.

Then, too, the best thing about beating your head against a wall is that it feels so good when you stop. A moderately kind word from someone who mostly tells you that you are animate pond scum means more than the same word from someone who routinely says that you are God's gift to the world. It was deflation of the currency of praise.

Garcia went on in that vein for quite some time. He didn't offer to fight any of them, as they did with the men and as the Amazons later would do on the first day of training. There wouldn't have been any point to it, anyway. Not all eighty of Garcia's girls together could have taken him on at that point. That would have taken training and mutual confidence they didn't have even a notion of yet.

Once Garcia had finished engraving their faces on his memory he turned them over to someone else to get them on the buses, stomping away, himself, off into the darkness.

"I am Centurion, Junior Grade, Rafael Franco," that someone else announced. Showing a smile neither friendly nor unfriendly, but ripe with anticipation, he continued, "You are going to be seeing a lot more of me than you are going to like over the next several months. Just to be up front with you, I do not like you. I do not care about you. You are just things. Someday, perhaps, unlikely as it seems right now, you may become more. For now, you are using up oxygen that you don't deserve. Keep your mouths shut and your ears and eyes open and we might—just possibly—learn to get along. Cross me and . . . well, don't."

"Now, you silly little girls, I know you are far, far too stupid to know your right from your left. Take my word on it; that bus over there is on your right. When I give the command 'Right, Face,' I want you to turn those stupid looking things you hang in front of what passes for brains in the direction of the bus. Got it? Right . . . face."

Marta ended up sitting next to Maria on the bus, near the window. She saw their destination first and said, simply, "Oh, shit." They had arrived at Camp Botchkareva.

Maria looked. It took maybe two seconds after arrival for her to decide that *Rio Abajo* wasn't so bad after all. The camp looked more like a prison than a school. It consisted of fourteen large metal huts, some open fields she couldn't guess the purpose of, and about fifty or sixty tents. At the edge of the camp the perimeter was defined by a fence of triple concertina, rolled barbed wire, with two rolls along the ground and one resting above those two. Guard towers and searchlights were at each corner and the solitary gate.

"Off the bus, twats." Franco, with help from a few others, pushed the women into a kindergartenish double line, that being about the limit of their ability at the time. Then he led them through one of the metal huts. There, their clothes and suitcases were taken from them and locked in tiny double-locked compartments. They left the hut bare-ass naked, with only a wallet to call their own.

Predictably, the sight of all that naked female skin had no perceivable effect on Franco or any of the other trainers. The *Tercio Gorgidas* was—mostly—homosexual. The Amazon candidates didn't really exist for them, not as women, not as possible sexual partners, apparently not even as human beings.

There were, on the other hand, a few women in the group who seemed, no, not delighted, but . . . interested.

"Get your fucking eyes off me," Marta told another woman, bunching her fists. That woman made some apologetic sounds and backed off, keeping her eyes carefully away from Marta.

Haircuts came next. As poor as she'd been, Maria had always kept her hair long. But, no, they didn't ask how the women wanted their hair styled, although a few of the men in the *Tercio Gorgidas* did just that for a living when they weren't on active duty. A smiling Franco watched over them as some men detailed to barber duty swiped their scalps clean. "Buzz 'em, Pedro."

When Maria looked in the mirror afterwards, she felt like crying, she thought she looked so ugly. Some women *did* cry. They stopped when they realized no one in a position to help cared in the slightest.

Before they were issued any clothing, the women were marched us into some mass showers, placing their wallets along a shelf on the way in. Most everyone in Balboa took cold showers, at least sometimes. It was no big deal in a place so *hot*. The water for these showers, it turned out later, was specially chilled to be *icy*. Maria screamed when they turned on the water. They all did.

Marta and Gloria complained out loud after the water was turned off. They were just swatted for their efforts and pushed on to the next station.

As the women left the showers, they were asked for their sizes. Each woman was then handed one sports bra, in approximately her size (Marta was a tight fit even in the biggest size they had;

the man passing out the bras made a note of it), two pair of boxer shorts, physical training shorts, two pair of socks—not stockings—and running shoes. It wasn't such a bad outfit, except for the boxers.

Franco gave the women a very few minutes to dress. Then he lined them up again and led them to their barracks. This was a long low arching metal hut with few amenities to speak of; three bare light bulbs and forty pair of bunk beds. On each bed were a thin, useless pillow, a pillow case, two sheets, and a very light and unnecessary blanket.

"Gather 'round, girls," Franco ordered. The women, all of them still in something like shock, clustered in a circle. "Sit down."

He began to pass out red felt-tip markers. When everyone had received one, Franco began to speak.

"Okay. I want you to take your markers and I want you to draw a dotted line just like the one I am drawing on my wrist." Franco drew a six inch long series of red dots lengthwise down his left wrist. "Everyone done with that? Good. Now draw another one on the other wrist... Done? Good. Let me see. *Very* good. Now there's no excuse.

"You see, women threaten suicide and even act it out rather frequently, but you fail so often to carry through that I am forced to question your sincerity and competence as a sex. Therefore..."

Franco turned toward the door. He tossed a package of razor blades to the floor on his way out. "Trujillo!" he called over one shoulder. "Collect up the markers in that box and put them by my office door. Anybody who wants a razor blade, just help yourself. 'Cut along dotted line.'"

Marta and Maria stared at the package of razor blades slack-jawed for a few moments. All the women did. "Cocksuckers," was all Marta said. Maria said nothing.

Since they knew each other's names already, Marta and Maria gravitated to the same set of bunk beds. Marta asked, "Do you care which bunk you get, Maria?"

From Maria's point of view the top bunk looked awfully high. Her doubts showed on her face.

Seeing those doubts, Marta said, "I can boost you up if you want the top. It doesn't make any difference to me."

"I don't care..."

"Let's flip a coin on it." They did, and Maria ended up on top, Marta giving her rump a push to get there. Most of the rest collapsed as soon as they could. None of them bothered to make her bed.

Some of the women, more than a few, cried themselves to sleep.

Maria's last thoughts, as she drifted off, were of Alma. In her imagination, she pictured the life they could hope to have together if this Amazon thing worked out.

Garcia snickered as Franco distastefully told him about the women's reaction to the razor blades.

Franco asked, "Was that really necessary, Balthazar? Poor girls."

The senior centurion nodded, saying, "I think so. See…we're going to be putting them under a lot of pressure, pressure worse than anything they're used to. And we can't watch 'em all the time, not and let 'em grow too. Eventually one of 'em's going to try a play suicide. Problem is, she just might succeed even though she won't be serious about it. This way's a risk, sure. But now, at least, there'll be none of those 'attempts' that might go too far."

Franco just shook his head doubtfully. "You're the boss."

Morning came incredibly early and *impossibly* loudly. One moment the women were peacefully asleep. The next they were sitting bolt upright, eardrums thumping from piped-in music. And—horror of horrors—the music piped in was from *bagpipes*. The next moment and Garcia, Franco, and eight other men were on them like gnats, big hairy gnats with muscles.

"Get up! Get up, you lazy little maggots. Dressed and outside for PT. You! That's right, honey, YOU! Move your lazy, skinny ass!" A couple of quick pushes and Marta and Maria ended in a tangle of arms and legs, a mattress over them.

Half crawling, half running, the women made it outside. More than a few of them did so with stinging buttocks where an instructor's baton had met with a tardy posterior.

Once outside, the two centurions, four sergeants, and four corporals began to push and prod them into some semblance of a formation. There followed a very brief class in "Assuming and Maintaining the Position of Attention." That was possibly the easiest thing any of them learned to do at Camp Botchkareva.

It was so easy, in fact, that the instructors called on some very tiny assistants to help them determine if they were doing it right.

Maria would hate sand fleas to her dying day. The little demons crawled up her legs, into her eyes and ears, inside her nose... more personal places, too. They bit her everywhere except for where her shoes covered her feet, each bite like the point of a tiny hot needle. And she had to just stand there and take it because, while the sand flea bites were painful and present, the instructors were infinitely menacing.

Maria had expected physical training to be worse, somehow, than it was. Not that it wasn't hard, or that the women didn't raise a sweat. It was and they did. And some of the women couldn't do the exercises very well. Failure to exercise properly usually got a snarl, a whack on the fanny, and some direct, hands-on, correction, but no more than that. And the instructors didn't have them try to do anything they really couldn't. It was all "doable," if barely.

After calisthenics Garcia ordered, "Assemble to the Right... Move." The women crowded back to the shallow block formation they'd started in. Then it was, "Right... Face. Forward... March. Double Time!—that means run, you stupid twats!—March! Left... left... left, right, left."

The run was worse than the exercises. It wasn't fast; Garcia knew they were too new for that. But it seemed long to all of them and it was intentionally painful. The women's newness made it more painful still, as none of them really knew how to keep in step, even though Franco called the cadence, "Left. Right. Left." The women still kept tripping each other up.

"I'm sorry; I'm so sorry," the girl behind Marta repeated every time her toes landed on one of Marta's heels. Though Marta was concentrating on trying to keep in step, that woman's toes continued to foul her up.

An instructor named Salazar trotted up. He whacked Marta's thigh with a stick, hard.

"Get in step, dummy... Left, right, left. Your tits can do it. Why can't you?" Then he whacked her again.

And the instructors let no one fall behind. They didn't try to encourage anyone with kind words. They hit and kicked those who stopped trying until they were willing to try some more.

Two women simply stopped and lay down in the road.

"Diaz! Salazar! Take care of 'em," Garcia bellowed.

As the platoon rounded a bend, a brave soul might have looked over her shoulder to see Salazar kicking one of the dropouts while Diaz lifted the other to her feet by her ears. That brave soul might have seen the latter of the two drop right back to the dirt as soon as Diaz's grip relaxed.

Neither of the dropouts was seen on the island again. By the time the rest had returned from the run, those two had already been dishonorably discharged. The remainder heard later, and at the time believed, that the dropouts were paddled pretty badly before being thrown off the island.

Eventually the platoon turned around to head back to camp. All were pretty much nauseated as they passed through the front gate. After they halted and were dismissed, Marta immediately fell to one knee and began to throw up. Maria walked over and put her arm around Marta's shoulders to help her back up.

Marta shrieked, "Get your fucking hands off me!" When she saw how shocked Maria was, she tried to apologize. "I'm sorry, Maria," she said. "It isn't your fault. I just can't stand to be touched by *anyone.*"

Though he was nearby, Garcia either didn't notice, or pretended not to notice, Marta's outburst. He knew some things about Marta that the women didn't.

Marta and Maria were joined by another girl, Inez Trujillo, the tiny one, and her bunkmate, Catarina Gonzalez.

Inez said, "Come on, you two. Let's go hurry and freeze. Garcia's only given us five minutes to shower before breakfast. And I don't know about you two, but I'm starving."

They raced through the icy water as quickly as minimal sanitation needs permitted. Then, dressed again in the same sweaty clothes, they began a slow trot to breakfast.

Breakfast? Gloria, sitting at a nearby table, snorted at it, saying, "This is certainly not what I'm used to."

Truthfully, it wasn't anything special: hardboiled eggs, sausage patties, sliced cheese, bread and butter, fried chorley tortillas, some fresh fruit. There was also a broad, shallow bowl of the gray, plum-sized Terra Novan olives. It was believed they were native to the planet, rather than genengineered like the Noah's tranzitrees, bolshiberries, and progressivines.

To many, the sheer quantity of the food dished out was amazing. Maria, for example, after years of scraping pennies to try to feed Alma and herself, was shocked that the cooks gave them as much as they felt like eating, barring only the sausage, cheese and eggs, which were rationed.

Since no one had bothered to feed the women the night before, most of them fairly pigged out.

Cat, Inez's bunkmate, took over dividing the rations. The way she did it reminded Maria a bit of her own mother, especially in the way she played favorites. Somehow or other, Cat seemed to have adopted Inez as her substitute baby. Maria noticed, anyway, that if there was an odd amount of one of the rationed items, it seemed to end up on Inez's plate.

Maria didn't complain. After all, Inez *was* the smallest and thinnest girl at the table.

There was a can of a thick, rough paste on the table. Gloria, several seats down from Marta, took a slice of chorley and then used her knife to spread some of the paste on it. Marta, who'd been around the legion for a while, started to caution her but then decided, *Screw the arrogant bitch.*

Gloria took a bite, chewed twice, and then her mouth opened, panting, as her eyes widened. "Holyfuckingshit!" she gasped, reaching for a glass of water. "What *is* that?"

Marta smiled and answered, "Well, among other things..."

The morning of that first full day the women drew their equipment; all ninety-five distinct items required for the first five weeks of basic training. With a little help from the four corporals and one of the sergeants they managed to stow everything in their rucksacks. Later in the day, and with a little more help, they managed to put together the fifteen items that went into their load-carrying harness: four empty drum magazine pouches (another magazine was generally to be kept in their rifles, when issued, or in a cargo pocket), two plastic one-liter canteens with covers, first aid pouch with bandage, bayonet and scabbard, "butt-pack," suspenders and belt.

Everything else was stuffed into the rucksacks including, at that point, the helmet, its liner, and its camouflage cover. In all, their Phase One BCT load was about forty-five pounds excluding water, food, and any ammunition they might be carrying.

Sergeant Castro brought out several rolls of thick green tape and, using Marta's set as a model, patiently showed them how to tape all the metal pieces to ensure they stayed together... and didn't dig into their skin.

"Look, girls," Castro said, "no matter what we might call you, or how we might treat you, we're here to help you. Don't let it go to your empty heads, but yes, we're almost always going to be pretty damned patient with the technical and tactical things you need to learn. After all, this is all new to you.

"On the other hand," he intoned, "if you fail in any way that so much as touches on a matter of character or discipline, kiss your little butts goodbye. We really don't assume you are precisely stupid... but you are, literally, ignorant. We are not assuming you are innately bad... but you have been poorly brought up. It's fair to say that so far as your becoming soldiers goes, you haven't been brought up at all. And you *are* weak, soft, and unrealistic. But don't worry; we'll fix all that."

The women spent that first day, when they weren't actively involved in fitting and stowing their gear, learning close order drill: "square bashing," the instructors called it. The sun was hot, but water and rest breaks were fairly frequent. They knocked off just after sundown.

Marta and Maria had dinner together, facing each other over the table. Things had remained a little awkward between them since Marta's outburst of that morning. Still, since they were bunking together, they tended to stay together.

Inez sat down next to Maria. Cat, who was the oldest of them, sat down next to Marta. They were all soon chatting just like old friends. It turned out that Cat was a widow. Her husband had left her with three kids—one just a baby—very little money, and no marketable skills. Only the *Tercio Amazona* offered her a way to have her kids cared for while training and earning a ticket to a better life.

Cat missed her babies terribly, she said. Then she reached over the table to rub Inez's scalp, saying, "But I have a new one to take care of right here."

Inez rolled her eyes and sighed.

Since dinner was better than breakfast, and the mess hall blessedly cool after a hot day in the sun, the women lingered over it, in relaxed conversation.

It came as a considerable surprise, then, when they returned to their barracks and found the doors had all been locked, their packs dumped in a pile outside, and a cross-armed Centurion Garcia standing guard at the landing in front of the main entrance. The other nine trainers, likewise, stood at ground level with their arms folded.

"Girls, girls, *girls*," Garcia chided. "The legion gave you a clean barracks this morning. I looked at it about two hours ago and what do you suppose I found? Dirt! Filth! Disorder!

"Obviously, you people are not fit to live in civilized surroundings. You had time to clean the barracks after breakfast. You had time during the very frequent breaks you were given this afternoon. You had time after dinner. Obviously, you do not know or care enough to take advantage of time. Therefore, tomorrow your breaks will be halved. Tonight you will move into the tents where you will live until further notice. Platoon! Tench... 'Hut! Squad leaders, put your filthy girls into the tents."

And so the women moved, though every morning one of the corporals supervised them in cleaning and re-cleaning the barracks they couldn't live in.

The sun was down but only one small moon had risen. Outside the camp, the nasty *antaniae* called out, *mnnbt, mnnbt, mnnbt*. From somewhere in the surrounding trees a trixie cawed on its nightly quest to kill and eat as many moonbats as possible.

By the faint light of the one risen moon, Maria, Cat, Marta, and Inez sat in the dirt outside the tent they'd been put in. It was dark in the tent; no lights, no beds either.

"It's so damned unfair," Cat said. "Why didn't they tell us to clean the barracks? I don't mind cleaning."

"Because they wanted to put us in these tents," Marta answered. "Men... just bastard men. They're all alike."

Maria had reason to share Marta's opinion on men. To some extent, maybe, she did share it. She was too embarrassed to mention Piedras, though, so she just said, "Well, no matter how bad things look"—and those tents looked dismal indeed—"I guess things could be worse."

Cat asked, "What do you suppose we have to do to get back in the building?"

Gloria must have overheard Cat. From somewhere inside the tent she answered, "Kiss those bastards' asses, I imagine. That's what they want." Gloria had been a little bitter since early that morning when Centurion Garcia had knocked her on her posterior for trying to answer back.

Inez disagreed. "No. My brother—he's a centurion candidate—told me. The legion wants fighters, not ass-kissers. They want people who will do their duty. They want people who, even if they're not sure what their duty is, will at least be thinking about what it *might* be. I think we'll get out of these tents when Garcia decides we can and will do that."

Gloria retorted, "You're giving them too much credit for brains, Trujillo. They're doing this because they think they can. It's just spiteful meanness and envy. I might even call it abuse of power," she finished sullenly.

Inez answered, "I'll admit, it seems like a pretty far leap from tents to training. And maybe I can't quite see the connection either. But these men have been at this sort of thing for a long time. Maybe they really do know what they're doing.

"Then, too, you know, we women tend to be forgiven our little transgressions in polite society. You must admit, this is a pretty good indication that we will not be lightly forgiven by the legion, which is no kind of 'polite' society."

Marta said, "I heard we are going to have to carry everything they gave us on our backs from now on. We don't have any lockers here like we did in the barracks."

"My brother warned me about this," Inez commented. "When they did this to his basic training maniple, he said, 'All the time we lived in the tents we had to lug everything we owned on our backs wherever we went. I got to where I hated my rucksack and everything in it.'"

Beyond harassment, that first week and a half of Basic were pretty much taken up with close order drill, customs and courtesies of the service, military law, uniform and equipment wear and care, and—of course—physical training.

The women had about two and a half hours of physical training every day. In the morning they had an hour and a half of calisthenics and a run that usually left them puking. If at least a few girls didn't throw up then the next day's run would be longer, faster, or both. For evenings there was another hour of combatives. As training progressed they didn't always do the morning sessions. They rarely missed the evening ones.

The men taught them to hit, gouge eyes, crush gonads…bite. They were also trained to a pretty fair standard with a knife. They learned to strangle, smash, break noses, and twist tendons…stab, jab, and slice.

Still, they weren't men. They could never have learned to use the simple male techniques used in bayonet fighting. That took too much weight and strength. Instead, they were taught the older, more intricate, fencing variety of bayonet fighting. That, as with many things for the women, took up a lot more time than was available to the men going through Basic.

"Thrust! Twist! Draw! Thrust! Twist! Draw!"

The swaying bag to Maria's front seemed to mock her. For half an hour or more she had been trying to sink her bayonet solidly into one of the bull's-eyes painted on the side. To her left, Marta was having equal problems. To her right, Inez Trujillo was awkwardly trying to strike from below.

Corporal Salazar literally picked Inez up by her combat harness and shook her. The man had biceps thicker than Inez's legs. "You worthless little midget! Do you think the enemy will all be runts like you? If you can't go in low for the kill, go in high!" He shook her again before dropping her back to her feet.

Salazar then turned and slapped Maria across the face. "Put your heart into it, you stupid cunt. Hate that thing!" She nodded and tried again: Thrust, twist, draw.

Garcia's whistle called a moment's rest. He shook his head, perplexed. *Those old bayonet fencing drills we're using were meant for men. They depend on having a center of gravity a lot higher than a woman's, more height and muscular strength, too. Ah, well, they'll have to figure some of this out on their own. If they don't, I just might let Salazar carry through on his threat to kill one of 'em on the spot.*

Again the whistle blew, signaling, "Break's over."

"Gonzalez, you dumb twat. Picture that sack as a man, coming for your kids. Kill 'im!" Cat lunged…and missed.

Salazar turned back to Maria. "Idiot child! Try again." She missed the bag completely.

Gloria, standing opposite, laughed out loud, right up until Salazar, with a fencing master's grace, took two steps across the sawdust and laid her out with a single punch. He'd pulled his punch, too.

✧   ✧   ✧

After that, Maria had a lot of trouble with Gloria, who seemed determined to make her into the platoon goat. Why this was so, Maria didn't know. That it *was* so was patent.

Maria stood in line outside the mess, right behind Cat and ahead of Marta. The line stood at parade rest, the women coming to attention to take single steps forward as one of those ahead cleared the chow line and went to the tables. For those standing outside, there was no shade and the sun beat down on them. Worse, really, it reflected up from the gravel to ensure they were not just thoroughly but *evenly* roasted. Or perhaps there was another culinary term that would have suited better, given the near one hundred percent humidity.

The mess hall was air conditioned, not for the women but for the benefit of the cooks. Still, whatever the reason for it, it was blessedly cool. Usually, it was as silent as death. Today, the women in line could hear sounds that seemed almost happy. True, they'd done well enough not to be punished much today, but what changed the tone inside the mess Maria couldn't guess.

She discovered why, when she finished passing her tray through the line. The very last thing slapped onto it was a small tub of ice cream.

"I haven't had..." she started to mumble, before Sergeant Castro, standing at the end of the line, ordered, "Seat, woman."

"Yes, Sergeant," she said, then hurried to the dining area to find a place to sit. Unfortunately, the only open seat at the moment was beside Gloria. The latter took one look at Maria, another at the tub of ice cream.

Then Gloria said, "You're fat; you don't need this." She took the ice cream and passed it to someone else, then crossed her arms as if daring Maria to do something about it.

Maria didn't. She just took it.

"Oh...yes, love...yes...oh, please...harder, harder...oh, oh, oh!"

"Goddamned fucking sluts," muttered Marta from the other side of the tent she shared with nineteen other women. "Don't they know people have to fucking sleep? Will you two please SHUT UP!"

The lesbians ignored her. These two apparently had very little sense of shame, though if there were others they were more discreet.

The next morning, one of those two, Sonia, walked up to Marta and suggested that she was just jealous because she wasn't "getting any."

"What is it, Bugatti; do you want to join us? Well, maybe if you're nice. Then again, maybe you already have a little something. Maybe..." Sonia looked at Maria and, then reached out a hand to clasp her breast.

Marta went for her like a berserker. Before anyone could stop it, Sonia was on the ground with Marta sitting on her, pummeling away with clenched fists. Maria felt a little ashamed—*all right, more than a little ashamed*—that she just stood there with her head lowered when the second lesbian, Trudi, jumped Marta from behind. Marta went down under flailing feet and fists.

It was another one of the girls who went to Marta's aid. Cristina Zamora was easily the biggest woman in the platoon. Zamora was pretty enough, in a strong featured way, and with her shining coppery hair. She picked up Trudi and punched her four or five times in the face before dropping her to the dirt. Then she separated Sonia and Marta, slapping both of them senseless with fine impartiality.

"Freeze, bitches!" Garcia's stone face gazed upon them. A few quick questions and he pronounced sentence. Marta, Zamora, Sonia and Trudi were given six hours extra duty each for disorderly conduct.

Then Garcia turned to Maria and asked, "Is this woman your bunk buddy?"

"Yes, Centurion," Maria answered, shamefaced.

"And is it true that you failed to go to her aid when she was attacked and outnumbered?"

Maria's eyes lowered. She hesitantly answered, "Yes, Centurion."

Garcia's voice dripped with contempt as he said, sneering, "For *you*, eighteen hours extra duty, to be accomplished in three-hour increments during and in place of the evening meal. Six days' bread and water for breakfast and lunch. Six days' restriction to your tent when not at meals, extra duty, or training."

"Maria. Maria, wake up."

"What? Who?"

"Shush. Shush. It's Marta. Here, eat this." She handed over a leg of chicken she had stolen from the mess hall.

"Marta?" Maria took the chicken, then stopped. She couldn't eat it, no matter that she was famished.

"I'm sorry, Marta. You know, for..."

"I know. It's my own fault for letting my temper get the better of me. I never think things through first. Now eat!"

Maria did as she was told. She *always* did as she was told. Juan, Piedras, Gloria...

She thanked Marta, over and over. She apologized, over and over, between bites.

"Look, skip it. You can't help being what you are...any more than I can." Marta patted a wet cheek, took the gnawed bone, and crawled back to her own pallet.

"It isn't just Garcia's platoon, sir. We've all had problems to some extent." The speaker, Ernesto del Valle, was a tall, distinguished-looking senior centurion. He rubbed the fingers on one hand across graying temples as he continued. "It's true, the lesbians aren't as naturally promiscuous as, say, we would be. But there are problems. They're human enough. They do develop interests that not only are not requited, but *can't* be requited. Fights, sir, lots of fights."

"Frankly, I can live with lesbians, sir," Garcia said. "What's driving me crazy is the number of women who are just certain, deep down, that they can get to one of *us*. We're having to be twice as shitty to all of 'em as we should have to be to any of 'em just to drive home the futility of the whole thing."

De Silva—Tribune de Silva and a "shoo-in" to be Legate de Silva someday—placed his thumbs in the hollows of his temples and tapped his fingers on his brow.

"Tell me, Garcia...del Valle, are these women human?"

Only Garcia answered, "Extremely human, sir."

"As human as we are?"

Del Valle answered, "Yes, sir."

De Silva raised his gaze to the three other officers, sixteen assembled centurions and sixty-two junior NCOs. "Anybody here ever have a crush on a straight? Hmmm? Raise your hands."

About two thirds of the men present did.

"Right. They're human, just like us. Our gender orientation

doesn't change theirs. And from their point of view we *are* the right gender. The same basic thing holds true for the lesbians. *All* the other women are the right gender from their point of view."

Franco observed, "But, sir, you can't separate them from us. Who would train them?"

"No, I can't," de Silva agreed. "You're just going to have to be shitty to the women. But we can separate out the lesbians from the rest. And we will. Sergeant Major?"

"Sir."

"Put out the call. I need a centurion pair and four NCO pairs for an eighth platoon."

"Sir."

On the tenth day of training the women trudged to the ranges, everything they owned on their backs, nothing to be left behind in the tents. At seven miles, the walk to the range wasn't nearly as far—or done nearly as fast—as some of the later marches. Still, it was no walk in the woods. To their usual forty-five pounds was added another three in food, another nine in water. That was more, in Maria's case, than half her body weight. Some girls had it rougher. Inez Trujillo, all four feet eleven inches of her, had it particularly bad.

By this time, of course, the women had spent a good part of every day with their rucks on their backs. But this was different. Women walked funny. Women sling their hips differently from men when they walk. They're *made* that way. And the rucksacks were made for men, even though the women had small-sized ones. There was no really adequate solution to the problem. Carrying a ruck simply hurt them more.

"Tough luck," as Centurion Garcia said. "Builds character."

Perhaps it did.

When they reached the bivouac area, they were given a chance to strip and clean themselves before pitching the tents. All were ecstatic at being able to remove the rucksacks. The straps had just *killed* their tits.

Marta was leaning against a tree, resting, when she looked at Inez and exclaimed, "Oh, damn!"

Maria followed her gaze and saw Inez, cupping a breast in each hand, rocking back and forth, quietly moaning. Through the spaces between her fingers the others could see two spots, bright red against the dull green of Inez's T-shirt. Cat sat beside her, wringing her hands.

Marta and Maria stood up and went to her. They pulled her hands away and removed her T-shirt, then her bra. Marta said "I haven't seen anything like this since..." Whatever she'd been about to say was lost as she didn't continue.

Inez's nipples were oozing blood where the straps must have rubbed her. They were just *raw.*

"I'm all right," Inez said, through clenched teeth.

"Like hell," Marta answered. "I'm going for a medic."

"No! No, please. I'll *be* all right."

"Sure. Right. Okay. Maria, go clean her bra and shirt. They'll be impossible to wear with dried blood and crud on them. Now... let's see. Cat, help me..."

When Maria came back with Inez's things she saw that Marta and Cat had bandaged the raw nipples and were working on the straps to her rucksack.

"The problem," Marta told them, "is that these packs are made for the width of a man's shoulders. With us... they push the other straps too far inward." She meant the suspenders on the combat harnesses. "So..." And she held up the ruck to show them how she had reversed the straps to point out, rather than in. This would put them on Inez's shoulders, leaving enough room that the suspenders weren't forced across her tits.

Clever girl, Maria thought.

The rifle range was fun, even satisfying. And the women had to develop a whole new set of muscles. There was no reason to believe that men were naturally better shots than women as far as most of the factors in marksmanship go. But the women weren't as strong and even a rifle requires some unusual musculature. The F-26, being heavier than most, required still more.

The girls spent literally hours just holding their rifle and squeezing off dry fires to build up muscle and control of the trigger finger. The technique was simple enough. An instructor would supervise as they took turns in teams of two. One member of the team would place a coin on the end of the rifle of the other, while the other was in firing position. Then the one with the rifle would s-l-o-w-l-y squeeze the trigger until the hammer dropped, or, to be technical, since the F-26 was electrically primed, until the connection was made. If the coin fell off, the woman needed more practice, and got it. They generally also received a large number of pushups, needed or not.

And every day they would march somewhere new. Or back to somewhere old. And they sweated and strained and were generally made miserable. Inez's new strap arrangement caught on with the smaller girls. Soon all of the "little people" had reversed their rucksack straps. It was better, a *little* anyway.

Sweated? Among the ninety-five items in their initial kit were two field uniforms and five sets of underwear—boxers—and five pairs of socks. A few buckets were made available for washing their own clothes but the supply of clean clothing never quite kept up with the demand. They stank.

But the instructors had thought of that. Women can get sick, inside, if they get and stay too filthy. No, not always, but the risks were much greater than for men. About two days after they'd arrived on the ranges a gynecologist showed up. She lectured them on the dangers and on what they could do to keep healthy. Maria's respect for boxer shorts and sleeping naked under her mosquito net went up immeasurably.

After the gynecologist left, Centurion Franco said, "Good. Now you've been told. If you don't listen and rot from the inside out it's your own fault." Most women listened. Some girls didn't at first, lazy or maybe just tired. They paid the price, too.

Not that getting sick got them out of anything. Sick call was held in the field. If a woman was really hurt the odds were better than even that she would be recycled into the next planned class, doing scutwork in the interim. If one of them was just feeling poorly...tough.

Feeling poorly? It was not widely known, but women who live in close quarters seem to tend to get on the same menstrual cycle. Those were bad days; everybody bitching at everybody. Except the instructors, of course. The woman had learned that one never yelled at an instructor unless one had a burning desire to be beaten senseless.

A lot of the women thought it grossly unfair that they were treated so harshly when they had their periods. Actually, almost all of them thought so. On the other hand, though, not one could pinpoint what was so special about a period. If they could be made to march on blistered and bleeding feet, why not with flowing menses? If a bad head cold or the flu didn't keep them out of training why should something more predictable and natural?

That, at least, was the way Centurions Garcia and Franco saw it. And their opinions were considerably more important than any woman's at that point in time.

The women were provided with sanitary napkins, which was something.

"One thousand, two thousand, three thousand . . . down, bitch! Now roll. Rifle to shoulder. Suppress! Number two . . ."

The women were doing short rushes and low crawls interspersed with dry firing. These techniques were used to move forward against the enemy without giving that enemy time or calm to shoot back accurately. Doing the rushes and crawls for a little while isn't so bad. Doing them for hours upon hours, as they had been, was painful.

Maria's tits hurt like the devil from being pounded on sharp rocks. The scabbed sores on her elbows—which she'd gotten from holding up her rifle and herself on the firing range for endless hours—had torn open. Her knees were bleeding, too.

She nearly cried but did blurt out, "Sergeant Castro, why do all of you treat us so *badly*?"

Castro didn't answer immediately. He thought for a few moments then blew his whistle to call a halt. "Gather 'round, girls," he ordered. "And sit down."

When the entire squad had gathered at his feet, he said, "Fuentes here doesn't understand. She probably isn't the only one. So listen: Once upon a time a bird way down south in Secordia procrastinated about flying north for the winter. By the time it got off of its fluffy little ass the weather had already turned. It made it about halfway across the Federated States before its wings froze up. It was also starving because it hadn't been able to find anything to eat. The bird fell to the ground, shivering and expecting to die soon.

"A cow came along and dropped a load right on our little friend's head. Soon it was warm and happy, well fed, too. It stuck its head up and began to sing. A cat heard the singing, raced over, dug the little bird out of the cow flop, and ate it. Do you know the moral of the story, *chica*?"

Maria said she didn't.

"Just this: Not *everyone* who shits on you is your enemy. Not everyone who digs you out of the shit is your friend. And when you're warm and well fed, don't make a ruckus about a little bit of shit.

"Now back to work."

"I wish there were some cheap way to chill that creek."

Franco smiled. "Ice is rationed, Balthazar, as you know very well."

"Mmmm. Yeah. But this is a special circumstance. Why, these women might get to like it out here in the jungle, if they don't have to freeze just to be clean."

Realizing that his partner was, in his own way, merely joking, Franco added his own sally. "They do seem to be having a pretty good time, don't they? Are you sure you weren't being over-generous what with giving them each a whole ounce of shampoo?"

"Maybe...but they did shoot well on the qualification range."

"Well, yes, but a whole one-ounce bottle? Each? Are you sure you're not getting soft?"

Garcia shook his head, as if uncertain. "No...I don't think so. It seems fair enough."

Below the bank on which the centurions stood, their students joked and played and gamboled. Cat, a country girl originally, showed her squad how to wash their clothes on the plentiful rocks.

"When's the chow due?" Garcia asked.

"About an hour, Balthazar."

"Did you arrange for chaplain services?"

"Of course. Even though it isn't even Sunday. By the way...?"

"Don't eat when you're hungry, eat when you can. Don't sleep when you're tired, sleep when you can. Pray always."

Franco couldn't argue with those sentiments.

After washing their clothes, Inez, Cat, Marta and Maria took turns washing each other's stubble. Of course, with so little hair, they really didn't need help. It was a social thing, not a practical one.

Sitting on a stump, Maria spent her meager free time writing a letter for Porras to read to Alma. Even if the baby couldn't contact her, she could at least let her know that Mama hadn't abandoned her. Every few lines Maria would turn her eyes to her open wallet, just to stare at her baby's photo. It was better than nothing.

Marta sat down besides the stump. "Do you miss her?"

"More than anything," Maria answered. "She's the only reason I'm here."

Marta sighed wistfully "She's beautiful. I can't have babies," she added, sadly. "Do you think, maybe, when this is over I could watch her for you? Sometimes? Or maybe take her to the park ... or something?"

Maria thought, *Is this Marta I'm hearing with the fear of rejection in her voice?* "Anytime," she answered. "But why can't you have a baby of your own?"

"I just *can't!*" Marta stood quickly and walked away.

The sun was setting as an outraged shout rang through the camp. Franco trotted over to investigate.

When he returned, he told Garcia, "Someone's stolen another woman's shampoo."

"You know the drill. Do it."

Faster than one can imagine, the women were hustled out from their tents and into formation. Then Franco called the roll to determine they were all present. One by one they went back, with an instructor in attendance, and dumped out their rucks.

One girl, by the name of Rossini, was found with an extra bottle. The rest of the women were sent back to bed. Rossini spent most of the night tied to a tree.

The next morning the formed platoon was called to attention by Centurion Franco, who then reported and turned the formation over to Garcia. Garcia ordered, "Stand at ... Ease.

"A soldier is first and foremost a selfless individual. He, or *she,* cannot be anything but that and still be worth much as a soldier. Recruit Private Rossini has failed to meet even the most minimal standards of selflessness. She is, in fact, a thief who stole something of considerable subjective value from someone who had no more than herself. For this, Rossini has been tried by court-martial, the centurions' council sitting en banc, and found guilty. She is to be dishonorably discharged and her name struck from the rolls of your regiment. There is one little thing to attend to first, however."

Garcia gave a command. The platoon formed in two lines, facing each other. At Garcia's nod two corporals half dragged, half carried Rossini to one end of the double line. She stood, quivering, hands still tied behind her back. Her eyes were an eloquent—but useless—plea. She was clad only in T-shirt and shorts. Most of her skin was exposed.

"Remove your belts," Garcia ordered. "As Rossini attempts to move between your lines you will strike her. I do not care whether you use the tip end or the buckle, but you WILL strike her . . . or join her."

Most of the women held the metal buckle in their hands. A few—whether they were the meaner ones or the ones most offended by theft was not obvious—took the other end, swinging the metal buckles freely. The corporals and sergeants went to stand behind the women to make sure they didn't slack off.

Garcia ordered "Begin." Rossini was pushed—well, kicked, actually—into the gauntlet.

The details would be offensive. Some hit Rossini hard, some held back as much as they could while being watched. Most hit no more or harder than they had to. Still, a few women went out of their way to kick the culprit.

Rossini tried to protect her face, shielding it with her shoulder, but that only made her stumble and left her in the line of blows longer. Welts and cuts appeared on her face, neck, arms and legs. It was only luck that saved her eyes.

A belt tangled in her legs, causing her to fall on her face. She crawled with her knees alone those last ten meters, her face plowing the ground, just like the animal Garcia wanted the others to see her as. Finally, bleeding from multiple cuts, at the end of the line and of her strength, Rossini collapsed.

Garcia ordered the platoon to "Attention," "Left and right . . . Face," then gave the command, "Forward . . . March." A sobbing Rossini, her head sideways on the ground, was left for some of the maniple's headquarters people to kick off the island.

Garcia didn't even order that she be given the rest of her uniform. She'd never wear those particular clothes again.

Four more women, including the one whose shampoo had been stolen, resigned that night.

Maria wanted to resign. She didn't because, while she found the whole thing sickening (and back then she wouldn't even have even hit Rossini were she not being watched herself), Marta and the others made her see the point.

"Look, Mari, Rossini was obviously untrustworthy," Marta said. "*I* certainly don't ever want to have to fight with her or anybody like her at my side. So she's useless. And so the legion booted her out."

"Yes, sure, throw her out," Maria answered. "But beat her? Like an animal? Worse, because we would never beat an animal like that."

Inez added, "The gauntlet? Well, my brother taught me this about the legion. The legal code is damned draconian, in theory. In practice, however, they only use formal corporal punishment on people they're going to dump anyway—a cherry on the ice cream, because that kind of humiliation tends to make someone useless as a soldier even if they weren't already useless. And using a deadbeat like Rossini states a myth that is very important to the military. 'Soldiers and veterans are real people. Everybody else is essentially subhuman. See for yourself how this *thing* was just beaten like a dog, if you don't believe us.' It is difficult to see someone beaten like a dog and still think of that person as a human being.

"Besides, they were actually merciful with Rossini. A man who'd been caught stealing from comrades would have had the same punishment, in theory. But a man would have run between two lines of men; heavier, stronger, quite possibly meaner."

"I doubt that Rossini was offended by the extra mercy," said Cat.

Marta, who had been beaten more than once in her life by various utter bastards who had derived some considerable sexual pleasure from the beating, said, "It wasn't a sexual thing. Our instructors are *gay*. They don't see Rossini as a sexual toy. They barely saw her as a human being. They just wanted *us* to do and see the damage. And see her humiliation."

Inez nodded. "My brother said that after an incident like this, you will never see another incident of theft reported the whole time of basic training."

The sixty-six women remaining in the platoon trained next on special weapons: Machine guns, submachine guns, flamethrowers, grenades, demolitions. Of those weapons, most would, in latter days, remember the grenade range best. This was not because they liked it the best or because the grenades were the hardest things to learn to use. The engineering things, the flamethrowers and demolitions, were much harder physically. Only a very few women, it was found, could even carry and use a flamethrower with any effect. But learning to use the grenades properly made a certain impact on the mind.

It was a blessedly cool, rainy morning when Garcia led the platoon from Camp Botchkareva to the engineering and grenade ranges. The dirt firebreak that paralleled the paved road to the range area and the ground on the ranges stayed muddy, even though the sun had broken out when they were about halfway there. Still, it wasn't all that bad. And, despite the rain, their uniforms were mostly dry by the time they started to train. Smelly, but dry.

The women sat in a semi-circle around a low platform on which stood Centurion Garcia. While he addressed them, they wolfed down their breakfast from sundry cans and pouches. Between the platform and the women was a hole dug into the ground, perhaps two feet by two, three deep, and almost entirely hidden by grass.

"Grenades are made for a man to throw," Garcia said, tossing a grenade up and down, one-handed, as he did. "Oh, we could make them smaller and lighter for a woman but then they'd also be less powerful, so less effective. Besides which, it would be a lot more expensive to make them especially for women as the cost of a piece of military hardware goes up as the number purchased goes down. And, as anyone who has ever been around the military knows, if there *were* two models of grenade serving the same purpose, offensive, defensive, or screening, the supply system would deliver the women's to the men and theirs to the women. That's just how it works."

He flipped a little wire tab off the thing, then nonchalantly pulled a pin. He lifted his thumb and a flat metal thing—a "spoon," it was called—sprang into the air. Equally calmly, Garcia tossed the now fully armed and slightly smoking grenade into the hole a few feet in front of the platform, between it and the girls. He did it so calmly and nonchalantly, in fact, that the resulting explosion took the women completely by surprise, raising a chorus of frightened cries.

Totally unfazed, Garcia picked up another one, began tossing it up and down, too, and continued, "On the other hand, it is also damned rare for a soldier to actually have to throw a grenade all that far. If she's in a hole and the enemy is attacking she can throw it about five feet outside and it won't hurt her much beyond making her ears ring a bit. And if she's the one attacking, 'Get closer.' That's how you will be trained."

Quicker than he had the first one, Garcia thumbed off the safety clip, pulled the pin, released the spoon, and then tossed the apparently live grenade into the midst of the women of his platoon. Screaming, they scattered in all directions. The practice grenade, painted up to look like the real thing, went off with a mild *pop*.

Garcia chuckled. "Gets 'em every time."

The women practiced for hours with blue-painted steel dummies. Then they practiced some more using the same dummies but with low powered fuses inserted that functioned like real grenade fuses. Finally, they were called forward one at a time to any of a half dozen circular sandbagged bunkers to use the real thing.

Garcia wore the nearest thing to a smile any of the women had ever seen on him as Catarina Gonzalez entered the pit. It wasn't a frown, anyway, and that was something.

There were six grenades sitting on a table to one side. Garcia told her to take one. She did, and inspected it as she'd just been trained to do.

"How long is the delay on that grenade?" he asked.

"It will explode four to five seconds after I release the spoon, Centurion."

"Plenty of time, don't you agree, Gonzalez?"

Yes, she thought, *except that quality control at the factory being what it is, the delay might be anywhere from three to seven seconds.* Still, she wasn't going to argue with him.

He continued, conversationally, "You know, Private Gonzalez, any fool can throw a grenade."

"Yes, Centurion."

"We, however, wish you bitches to become very *special* fools. Prepare to pull, Private."

She did, both hands in front of her, one clutching the pull ring, the other on the grenade body.

"Remove the safety clip."

Cat flipped it away with a thumb.

"Pull, Private."

She pulled the ring away, still holding the spoon, the safety handle, down with the fingers of her other hand. She then went into the position to throw, one arm and hand stretched forward, the other—the one holding the bomb—cocked by the side of her head. She was already scared out of her mind by that little hand-held monstrosity. She was, however, rather more frightened of Garcia.

Garcia reached out with a beefy arm, lightning fast, and grabbed the wrist attached to the hand with the grenade. Then he said, "Gonzalez, when I give the command, 'throw,' you are going to release the spoon. That will release the striker to start the fuse burning. You and I will then count together to two . . . slowly. Then I will release your hand to throw the grenade . . . Ready? Throw."

She froze. She would not, could not, release the spoon if she also couldn't immediately get rid of the damned thing.

"Private, that grenade can only kill you. I won't tell you again. Throw."

Cat's bladder let go, liquid running down her legs. But she also let go the spoon and, as soon as Garcia had counted to two and released her wrist, threw the grenade as far as she could. Along with Garcia, she fell to one knee and ducked her head to shelter from the blast. It rattled her, even so.

After the last bits of mud and rock had pattered down, Garcia pretended to notice neither Cat's dripping trousers nor her quivering hands. He just said, "Good," with his customary lack of enthusiasm.

The next two grenades she also "cooked off," though on the last one Garcia did not hold her wrist. (Nor did she wet herself again.) Then the pair went forward and Cat threw two more around the corner of a trench. The little metal fragments made a pattering sound as they hit the wall of the trench opposite her.

"Okay, Gonzalez," Garcia admitted, "You've done well so far. For this next one, the last one, I want you to crawl forward to that little bunker and put it through the firing port. But Private, this time, hold the grenade for a count of three after releasing the spoon. Got it?"

"Yes, Centurion." Grenade in hand, Cat slithered forward, rolling to her back just as she reached the bunker. She flicked away the safety clip, pulled the pin, released the spoon and counted slowly and deliberately, "One thousand . . . two thousand . . ."

On three, no longer shaking, Cat calmly placed the grenade

into the bunker, withdrawing her hand just as the explosion burst out of the narrow firing port.

Wet pants or not, she was damned proud of herself.

That didn't mean she wasn't embarrassed too. When Garcia told her to go back to the rest of the platoon she hesitated, looking down at her trousers. His gaze followed hers.

"Oh...I see," he said. Then, not unkindly, "Gonzalez, do you think you are the first one to ever wet themselves doing something terrifying?" A sigh. "You are probably a little young to be learning this lesson. Let's hope it takes. Anyway, start back to the platoon."

She had just turned and started to reluctantly, shamefully slink away when Garcia bellowed. "You. Gonzalez. Halt, bitch. Drop! That's right, down on your belly like a snake. You stinking reptile, you move like pond scum. You know how pond scum moves? I didn't think so. It doesn't. If you can't walk like a soldier then get down there with the pond scum. Crawl, bitch!"

Garcia directed her into one of the little natural run offs that led from the pit to the waiting area, following her, insulting and cursing her, the entire time. Then he had her do short three-to-five second rushes from one scummy little hole to another. Some of the other girls watched with wide eyes. By the time he let her go, she may have been covered with mud and slime, but no one could tell if she was also covered with urine.

The last thing he said, before letting her go was, "And wipe that goddamned happy smile off your face, you stupid twat."

With some difficulty, she did.

Perhaps Garcia was being kind. Perhaps he was trying to keep her from being needlessly humiliated. On the other hand, maybe he also wanted people to move faster on the range. Certainly nobody else dawdled there, that Cat could see, the rest of the day. Indeed, the women pushed themselves to finish the job as quickly as possible. This may not have been such a good thing.

Marta waited nervously for her turn to throw the grenades. Ahead of her, another woman from a different platoon was shaking pretty badly as she picked up the first grenade. Her instructor went through much the same "very special fools" speech that Gonzalez had heard from Garcia. (The speech went way back to the very beginnings of the legion.) The instructor was very calm, but this did not stop the woman's tremors. Still, she took her grenade, flicked away the safety clip, pulled the pin, and released the spoon. The instructor held her wrist while she counted "One thousand . . . two thousand" with a breaking voice. He released the wrist to let her throw; which she did. Right into the wall of the bunker.

The instructor's eyes followed the grenade as it bounced off the front of the pit, to the back of the pit, and then to the front again before settling on the floor. Perhaps he'd been counting the seconds automatically. Whatever the case, he didn't hesitate a moment. Pushing the woman towards the entrance, he threw himself down atop the bomb. It exploded, sending blood and flesh and bone out of his back to spatter pit and woman, both.

Marta screamed. The blood- and flesh-spattered woman stood, frozen, her face ghastly white where it hadn't been speckled with bits of red.

Within moments another instructor, the dead man's pair bond, entered the pit and fell, weeping, to his knees. He verbally flailed the woman, "You fucking stupid moron. You goddamned fucking incompetent murdering *bitch*. What makes you so goddamned important that my partner had to die for you? What?"

The woman had no answer.

Franco came and led the crushed man away.

Late that night, they marched the women back to their bivouac area (not Camp Botchkareva, with its icy showers). They sang, as they'd been taught to sing on their "slack time." Given the events of the day, they sang mostly downbeat things:

> "Come by the hills to the land where glory remains,
> Where stories of old fill the heart and may yet
>   come again,
> Where the past has been lost
> And the future has still to be won.
> And the cares of tomorrow must wait
> 'Til this day is done."

The women sang much of the time, and nearly all the time they were marching, scores of songs from the legionary song-book, plus a few of their own. In happier moments, they were particularly fond of the children's song, "*Guillermo Hinchese*" ("With the razor's gash he had settled her hash. Oh, never was crime so quick!") and the more adult "Sacred War." At first they were made to sing, but—after a while—they came to love singing together for its own sake. It was fun. Never mind that with every song they were being indoctrinated. Indoctrinating through song was so old a trick it was almost passé.

Marching away from the grenade range, between songs, Gloria fumed at length about all the explicit and implicit insults. She thought they should be considered innocent until proven guilty.

Sick of her bitching, Inez asked her, "Why? If we fail, we might cost them their lives. It strikes me as a lot to ask of someone, to take an extra risk for something that will do *them* no good at all."

"Let them prove there's a risk," Gloria retorted, "before dumping on us."

"They just did," Inez answered.

First aid training came next, almost a whole week of it, and the Amazons were *good* at that; Centurion Garcia even said so. Although when he had them carry the instructors around on stretchers for a couple of hours they found that was *much* harder than carrying each other.

Resting her weary arms afterwards, Inez said, "I'm told that women in tercio medical companies have a lot of trouble with that. Enough trouble, says my brother, that it's an open question whether they'll continue to let women into male tercios as medics. I guess that's one advantage of having a females-only combat unit. We won't waste men's time by having them carry light little burdens like us. Neither will we be overtaxing ourselves, maybe even killing our own wounded, trying to carry men who are just too damned heavy."

At last, after not quite four weeks in the jungle, Phase One was over. The aspirant Amazons marched back to camp. As a reward, Garcia even let the girls use the barracks for a few days. The water in the showers was still icy.

Interlude

"Up yours, *cueco*," the archaeopteryx said from his perch in one corner as it worried with its beak a Terra Novan olive held clasped in one claw.

"Fucking bird," Franco muttered, as he looked out of the tiny shack he shared with Garcia. From the window he saw a squad of women running in a circle, their rifles held over their heads. Their tramping feet raised a cloud of dust that had them all coughing and gagging. Above the suffering girls, in the background, high over the island, the continuous cloud around the mouth of the solar chimney loomed.

"God, I hate this shit," he told his partner and boss.

"I know. Me, too."

"Would you have volunteered us for this horror if you had known what we would have to do to them?"

"I did know. So did you. Deep down, you knew."

"Maybe so," Franco half-admitted. "Christ, why us?"

Garcia didn't answer immediately. When he did, he said, "Because we can. And no one else could. Now stop your bleeding and tell me about third squad."

Franco pulled his gaze from the suffering women. "Mostly, they're coming along. The ones who have me worried are Bugatti, Santiago and Fuentes; our resident sociopath, feminist and wimp, respectively."

Garcia chuckled low. "You know, for a really smart, book learned, university professor, you can be awfully dense sometimes."

Franco looked at Garcia with something between shock and mortal offense.

"Oh, calm down. You're young. You're still learning."

"So *teach* me, O ancient and mighty one," Franco answered sarcastically.

Garcia thought briefly of a terrified young girl, holding a grenade in a trembling hand. "Just trust me, Fuentes is not a wimp. There's steel inside there. Oh, maybe it isn't Atacamas Mountains solid. Maybe it's more like a ... oh, like a rapier, I suppose. In any case, it keeps springing back. I think she'll be all right."

"Maybe you should have a talk with her," Franco suggested.

"Maybe I will at that. As for Bugatti?" Garcia shook his head with disgust. "That poor creature has some tales to tell. Have you seen her file?"

It was Franco's turn to show disgust. "I've read it. But do you really think she can overcome all that?"

Garcia shrugged. "Maybe. Maybe not. She's trying though. And she's doing better all the time. Why, she's even learned to hide the fact that she wants to rip our throats out whenever one of us gives her a whack."

Then it was Garcia's turn to look worried. "You're right about Santiago, though. She's always been out for number one, hiding it behind her concern for 'all women, everywhere.' You would think she'd been a charter member of the National Organization for Upper Middle Class White Women. It's getting worse, too. But I have a trick that might work on her."

"Or might not."

"Or might not," Garcia conceded.

Franco looked back out of the window. "Do you really think this is the best way to get the best out of a group of women?"

"That isn't the point or the mission. We're not trying to get the best out a group of women; we're trying to get the best women out of the group. That's a very different thing. And for that, this way works perfectly. It will be *their* job, later on, to figure out how to get the best from a group of women.

"Now ... what about third squad's children?"

Franco answered, "I spoke to Private Porras last night by phone. The Gonzalez children are doing well enough. The Maceira boy has a head cold, but is recovering nicely. Little Alma Fuentes misses her mommy and cries a lot."

"Should we let Fuentes call home, do you think?" Garcia asked.

Shaking his head, Franco replied, "Leaving aside the fact that it's against the rules ... Yes, yes; I know you can bend the rules for good cause. Leaving that aside; I think it would be a very bad idea to let Fuentes' mind start wandering to her baby. She has trouble enough being apart from her kid. You know; cries a lot when she thinks no one is looking."

"Okay, then. Little Alma can cry a little more." Changing the subject, Garcia asked, "Are you ready to deal with the herstorian we've got coming out to lecture the girls?"

Franco smiled then. "Sylvia Torres? She's mindless," he snorted. "I not only know everything she ever wrote; I just might know everything she's ever read. I knew her at the university, after all."

"Good. Let's make it memorable. Be nice to the woman, but give the girls what they need to recognize silliness when they hear it."

CHAPTER FOUR

The song for the soldier is a war song;
it is *not* "I don't like spiders and snakes."
—Patricio Carrera

Maria:

By the end of Phase One our strength was down by about twenty percent. It would probably have been a lot lower except that our cadre simply would not let us quit easily at this point and punished us if we tried. We were also a lot stronger, though the strongest of us still couldn't have taken on the weakest of our instructors in close combat. Even the three or four strongest probably couldn't have. But it was an improvement. Besides, we could shoot at least as well as an equivalent group of male recruits, and probably better. We could use the weapons that didn't require any unusual physical strength as well as the men, even a little better in the case of tripod mounted .34 caliber machine guns. Garcia had said something about "natural rhythm" when he'd announced that. We had more trouble with firing the machine guns from their integral bipods or from the hip. And carrying them and a full ammunition load was always a pure bitch.

We still could not march as far as the men, as fast, while carrying the same weight. Actually, as a group we couldn't even *pick up* the same weight to start to carry it.

In Phase Two of training they started messing with our heads even more than they had previously messed with our bodies. We can talk about that later.

We also got fresh haircuts. Yes, they buzzed us again. But, then, they issued us two more field uniforms, more underwear, and another pair of the lightweight boots each. Win a few, lose a few.

(We don't do that anymore, in Amazon training, by the way. After the first buzz cut we don't say a word. But we keep the new girls even filthier than the *Gorgidas* did with us. As their hair grows, it gets and stays *rotten*. We leave them the shears, though. When they cut their hair on their own, we know we're training them hard enough. Discipline is always better when it grows from inside.)

One day they marched us into a sort of tree shaded amphitheater surrounded by bleachers they used for a classroom. A pinch-faced, sort of dumpy woman walked to the lectern and introduced herself as Professor Sylvia Torres. She said she was there to teach us about the history of women in the military. She'd obviously never done a day in uniform herself, nor was her degree in history, let alone military history. And the way she wrinkled her nose at our stench didn't precisely endear her to us.

It was obvious that this woman only partly approved of our experiment. She plainly disapproved of our being segregated. Though it was funny that she entirely believed in, and seemed to approve of, the original Amazons, who were entirely segregated except at breeding season.

"There is plenty of history to support the integration of men and women in the military," she announced. "To begin, let us take the example of Lucille Brauer, a Federated States Marine who served aboard the FSS *Charter* during their war of AC 288. She had to keep the fact she was a woman hidden, true. But she did everything the men did, to include fighting in some of the most successful actions in which that ship engaged."

Franco interrupted to ask, "Professor Torres, how did the Brauer woman manage to keep hidden her sex when it was a regulation of the Federated States Marines at that time for the commander to inspect each of his Marines for their health, buck naked, once a week? I'm just curious, you understand."

"Professor Franco," Torres answered, "I'm afraid the record is not specific as to what measures Ms. Brauer had to use."

"*Centurion* Franco," he corrected. "She was successful, though, in hiding her sex, you say. Hmmm. Interesting. Please excuse me for a moment, Professor. Stand up for a moment, Bugatti."

Marta arose with a suspicious look on her face; her chest prominent, as always.

Franco spoke as if he really were interested in finding a solution to a problem that *could* be solved if he could only open his mind enough. Rubbing his face contemplatively, he said, "Maybe if we redesigned the body armor a bit...might be hot...but... yes, we could—possibly—do this. Thank you, Professor. Sit down, Bugatti."

I joined the others in smirking. Trying to make Marta look like a boy was an obvious exercise in futility.

I don't think Torres quite understood what Franco had just done to her, because she continued, unfazed, "As another example, we have the case of a Volgan tank crew in the Great Global War. This tank crew, composed of two men and two women, successfully held up the advance of an entire Sachsen *army* of eleven divisions for three days. This was not the Red Tsar's propaganda, by the way, but came from *Sachsen* records. After the Sachsens finally succeeded in knocking that tank out, they found that the only survivor of the crew was a *woman*." She smiled triumphantly.

Franco raised his hand again. "What were the relationships among those men and women, Professor?"

"They were married, Prof...ah, Centurion Franco." She consulted her notes, briefly, then said, "They were, in fact, the Political Commissar of the unit, his assistant, and their wives."

"Ah, then," Franco said. "So they were married, like us in the *Tercio Gorgidas*. And the political cell of their unit, you say? That's very interesting, too. Were they fanatics, do you suppose, Professor?"

"Well," she answered, "their actions in battle would seem to indicate an unusual degree of commitment."

"So they didn't have any of the typical problems you get when you put men and women together. I see."

Torres did *not* see, it seemed. "Problems?"

"Oh, you know. Problem Number One: 'Won't one of you big strong men help poor little ol' me?' Problem Number Two: 'Private, how *grateful* would you be if you didn't have to pull guard tonight.' Problem Number Three: 'You're what! What will my wife say?' That kind of problem. Tell me, Professor, what kind of tank was it?"

Again she turned to her notes. "It was a very advanced for the time heavy tank, I understand."

"Ah. So women *can* crew a heavy tank. Very good. Do you happen to recall how heavy a tank it was?" She didn't.

"Hmmm. I don't know either," Franco said. "I wonder, though, whether there might not be a problem with putting women on tanks today. Even heavy tanks in those days were much lighter affairs than tanks now. Shells were lighter. Tracks were lighter. Parts and engines were lighter. Today, I don't know that any two women and two men living could adequately fight and maintain a main battle tank which is, at forty to seventy tons, two or three times heavier than its Great Global War counterpart. The tracks are too heavy, the shells are too heavy, *everything* is too heavy."

She asked, "But don't we have tanks that are lighter than that?"

"Well...sort of," Franco admitted. "The legions do have Ocelots. They're pretty light; about nineteen tons. On the other hand, an Ocelot wouldn't stand a chance against a real tank though it does give pretty good service as an infantry support vehicle. I'm sure women—or men and women mixed—could handle those without any *technical* problems whatsoever," Franco concluded enthusiastically.

I guess Torres hadn't ever given any thought to the technical differences between one type of weapon and another. I didn't know myself. She seemed happy with Franco's seeming agreement.

Moving on, Torres said, "Nor is the history of men and women being integrated in combat limited to heavy, high technology, weapons like tanks. Women of Zion, during their wars, gave good service themselves as infantry against the Arabs, mixed in units with men."

Franco inquired, "How did that work? Were there any problems?"

"Well, there were a few," Torres conceded. "It was discovered that men simply would not treat women like they would other men. When the women got into trouble there was an unfortunate tendency for the men to abandon the mission to save the women. I wouldn't blame those boys too much. They couldn't help it, even if it wasn't hard-wired in their genes, there was some strong cultural conditioning. Besides, it isn't like straight young men have any brains." We, even Franco, joined her in a laugh.

"Unfortunately, the women were soon—after about three weeks—removed from units with men and formed into their own, where they continued to do respectably well. This was still patently unfair. It wasn't *their* fault that the men acted like that. Worse, today Zion's women are not even allowed to drive trucks, because trucks go to the front and women are *not* allowed at the front."

"I thought that Zion does still conscript young women," Franco commiserated.

"They do," she said, "but only *if* they haven't gotten married. The drafted women make a pun of the initials for their service; apparently in Hebrew the letters can also stand for 'We should have gotten married!'"

Franco asked, "Do you suppose that the Zionis do it this way at least partly to make sure that old maids of eighteen or nineteen have all the opportunity possible to meet a great many eligible young men so they'll get married soon thereafter...to start working on the next generation of—male—cannon fodder?"

"I'm sure I don't understand the workings of *that* kind of mind, Pro...Centurion Franco."

I saw Franco shrug as if he didn't understand it, either. "Well, it's just a hunch, of course. But, if not, why not conscript young married women who are not pregnant? It surely doesn't seem fair to me either. Do they have any other reasons?"

"Maybe one. It is believed," Torres said, "that there are some cultures—and Arabic culture in particular—in which it would be an unpardonable shame for men to surrender to or run from women."

It occurred to me that my own culture wasn't too far from that.

She admitted, "The Zionis claim that when they put women in combat units, Arab units that otherwise would have given up or run away would stay and fight, driving up everybody's casualties, if they even suspected there were women opposing them. But that's old news. In the Federated States' first war against Sumer, some decades ago, the Sumeri prisoners were glad to be guarded by military policewomen."

Franco commented, "That's vastly different from actually surrendering to women, of course. But there must have been some such surrenders since some of the Sumeris were equally glad to surrender to civilian camera crews. I have heard that some large numbers tried to surrender to passing aircraft. Still, I'm not sure that this proves anything...except maybe that beating an army that's been pounded from the air for six weeks, and was rotten to start with, is not something on which to base a generally applicable theory. Still, it *is* an improvement, Professor, I agree."

Torres continued on with a discussion about the apparently remarkable ability of armed forces to change character. That part of her discussion was in the same general vein, or at least had the same philosophical underpinnings: that the sheer raw power of armed forces was such that all they had to do was order their people to become something and they would become that thing. She said, "Armies do it all the time. This one should be able to do the same with you and men as easily."

The last thing she spoke on at any length was concerning our unmitigated, inalienable right, as women, to get pregnant and have babies any time we wanted, at our sole discretion. She really didn't like the idea of our being administered mandatory implanted contraceptives. Centurion Franco didn't say a word about that.

The next morning, however, we had to do another road march, a fifteen mile hump.

Franco stood in front of the platoon and asked, rather blandly, who among us had agreed with the feminist speaker about our right to get pregnant. At first no one admitted it. He promised us, Scout's Honor, that there would be no retaliation, no personal punishment, against any who might express their honest view.

At that Gloria said, "I agree. You men have no right to tell us when we can, can't, should, shouldn't, or must have a baby."

"Well, we have one honest woman in the group. Have we no more? Surely we must." He coaxed us and cajoled us until he had fifteen women, about a quarter of what we had left by then, who would state that they believed that Torres had been right, that men had no right to tell us when we could and couldn't, or should, or must, have a baby.

Franco agreed with them, said so plainly, even enthusiastically. Then he told them to drop their packs, rifles, load carrying equipment and helmets. He ordered them, very gently, out of the formation. He told them not to worry, they wouldn't be punished, but just to stand by. At that time a couple of the corporals brought out fifteen or twenty long, thick poles.

Then Garcia came out, grinning broadly. You really had to know him at the time to know just how creepy a thing that was.

"Ladies," he said, "it seems I'm going to be a daddy. Who would have believed it? Me?" he rhetorically asked of the women Franco had called out of formation. "For, you see, you are all now, for this day only, officially 'pregnant.' As such, in deference to your delicate condition, and out of concern for the health of your babies, you cannot be expected to—and I, as a mere man, will not ask you to—engage in any strenuous physical labor."

The creepy grin changed to a frown. He tapped a finger against his own cheek, as if he had just realized the existence of an insoluble problem. "Still, we do have a range to go to. My, my. And we don't have any buses or trucks scheduled. Hmmm, pity. So, sorry to say, you will have to walk to the range with the rest of us. But you needn't worry about how your gear will get to training. Your fellow recruits have volunteered to carry it for you."

Then he ordered the rest of us to string their gear on the poles, shoulder the poles, and, "Forward march." We formed in three long columns with the "pregnant" women and the instructors marching in the center, Garcia up front and Franco walking the center and rear.

I cannot even begin to tell you how much that *hurt*. I was—we all were—already carrying as much as we *uncomfortably* could. Between the poles and the other girls' gear we had maybe thirty pounds more than that. It was just too much.

Not that Garcia or Franco seemed to care. Their faces remained impassive as we stumbled along, tears mostly hidden by sweat, for fifteen miles. The poles probably weren't the worst possible way of carrying that extra gear. But they did cut into our shoulders, scrape our necks, throw us off center so that our backs hurt. It was torture. It was intended to be.

The "pregnant" women, all of them—even Gloria, who surprised me by it—begged to be allowed to carry their packs for themselves. Franco, marching next to our squad, was having none of it. When one of the girls tried to help us with the poles he rapped her knuckles with his centurion's stick, hard, for her trouble.

"Sorry, *chica*, you can't have a miscarriage on my watch. Garcia wouldn't like it, caring and sensitive soul that he is."

And even though they carried no loads, the day was still hot. They had to drink from the water the rest of us were carrying for them. They apologized, embarrassingly, sincerely and continuously, until Franco told them to, "Shut up! Stop bitching! You claimed the unlimited right. This is what it means; that someone else has to carry your load. Live with it."

Gloria walked along miserably between Inez and Marta, myself and Cat. Inez and Marta took turns berating her.

"Oh, my," said little Inez, straining more than most under the load. "Poor, poor Gloria. She's so smart, she's so big and strong and tough. She can figure out *anything*. Why, she's even figured out how to have someone else carry her equipment."

"And she didn't have to flutter her eyelashes or look cute," continued Marta. "All she had to do was get herself pregnant. We sure are the superior sex, with Gloria as our leader, showing us the way to the top."

I confess, their verbal abuse of Gloria was becoming annoying. Cat finally got sick enough of it to tell them to shut up and leave her alone. Inez listened, though Marta still grumbled.

That march would normally have taken maybe six hours. It actually took just under ten. And each one of those was several times worse than any hour of marching with a normal load would have been. We tripped; we slipped; we fell. From the awkward walk, the extra weight, most of our feet were bleeding by the end of the day. I never before quite understood how bad Christ's march up Golgotha must have been. (Though that wasn't the worst march we ever did.)

We never even tried the old stand-by of, "Won't one of you big strong men help poor little ol' me?" It never worked with *our* instructors anyway.

When we'd reached the range, Centurion Garcia announced, "From this day forward any member of this platoon who goes on sick call will have her gear carried in this way by the others. To support this, each squad will carry two of these poles to all training sites, and in addition to their other gear."

Three more recruits resigned that night. Two of them were from those whom Garcia had made "pregnant." They were allowed to go to one of the non-combat positions for women in their home town tercios. I don't know if any of them took that option.

We took to calling going on sick call, "getting knocked up." The poles we called, for reasons both obvious and subtle, "pricks."

Not everything they told us or did to us was antifemale, or even antifeminist. I learned a lot about the military history of my sex. Maybe more importantly, I learned to *think* a lot more about the military history of my sex. Centurion Franco did most of that lecturing.

One thing Franco told us, more or less off the record, I'd like to repeat here. Of course, in training now we do tell the recruits that the Amazons might have existed but couldn't be proved. It's better that they not be disillusioned if someone ever really disproves their existence.

But Franco thought it fairly likely they had existed in some form. His reasons were partly technical, partly philosophical. Basically, Franco said, the Amazons, if they had existed, were horse archers at a time when horses could transport men only in clumsy chariots. The early horses were too weak in the back to support a man's weight. Supporting a woman would have been possible centuries before horses were bred that were strong enough for a man but centuries after horses had been domesticated. This also corresponded, roughly, to the invention or introduction of the composite bow, which was—in legend—the Amazons' weapon of choice.

Moreover, said Franco, the people who recorded the legends—the ancient Greeks—were simply not horse oriented, the area being a poor place to raise horses. They would be fairly unlikely to even have thought of putting women on horseback unless there was some crumb of fact or fact-based rumor to support it.

Lastly, he said that the legends were quite accurate in principle about what *would* be required to make female warriors, especially that voluntary giving up of their right breasts, an important part of a woman's appearance and the symbolic reduction of their ability to nurture.

I'm still not sure if I buy it.

Franco told us, too, of some criticisms of military women that, he thought, were patently unfair. It seems there was an instance, thirty or forty years before the *Tercio Amazona* was formed, when women in the Federated States Army stationed in one of the hot spots around the planet had deserted their posts in overwhelming numbers because there was a chance that war might break out soon. Worse, much worse, men took off in droves to see to their wives and girlfriends.

"No wonder they did," said Franco. "They'd never been trained for combat. Why, women at that time, in that army, didn't even fire weapons in basic training. It's perfectly understandable that they ran, though the men should have been shot."

That was, obviously, not going to be a problem for us.

Naturally, at some point in time the question came up of our being raped if captured. Franco had a pretty good one liner for that: "Don't surrender." He didn't let it go at that, though.

"Look," he said, "young men have been having their bodies violated in battle for uncounted millennia. You tell me. In what way is it worse for you to be raped—in a place that's reasonably suited for a somewhat similar purpose—than it is for a young man to have a sword, spear or bayonet driven through his belly? How is it worse for you to be raped than it is to be disemboweled by a shell fragment? How many women prefer death to submission to rape? Your own sex has already voted on the question and their answer has been that rape is preferable."

I thought of lying under Piedras and tried not to weep. It hurt more that it had been true.

Don't get the wrong idea; we didn't have these short lectures in any neat, antiseptic classrooms. There weren't any outside of the camp. Mostly they weren't even formal lectures, but just little bits of food for thought Franco would throw to us from time to time. Usually, they tended to come just before or just after we had to do something really miserable, painful, or dangerous.

Once, for example, near the end of Basic, we did a thirty-mile road march with full combat equipment and supplies in twelve hours. It was part of our graduation exercise. We knew that the equivalent march for the men was forty miles in fifteen hours, longer and a little faster. A lot of our training was like that: something less than the men had to do.

I've thought about that a lot over the years. Did this "gender-norming" (that's what they called it) mean we were inferior to men, that we could never be equal?

That depends, in large part, on what you think the purposes of physical training are in an army. Sure, some of it is building strength, stamina, and endurance. But that isn't its whole purpose, nor even most of it. My sisters who died on *Cerro Mina*, and—later on—in other places, were equal to, better than, most men in every important way, even if they couldn't march as fast. And that isn't just regimental pride speaking.

Think about battle; I have. A terrifying thing, no? But what is terrifying about it? The chance of painful death or mutilation. The fear of failing your friends and yourself.

Think about fear; I have. I have known fear unimaginable when

I was just a girl. I overcame it, as my sisters did. How? Discipline, dedication, determination, morale, courage . . . call it, "character."

And that is what our physical training was mostly about; building those things—character building—through pain. We suffered on marches, we suffered on runs, our hands bled from digging. And all of this we did, essentially, to ourselves because— beyond a certain point, and corporals' boots or centurions' sticks notwithstanding—it just isn't possible to make someone take one more step, dig one more shovel full of dirt, if that person won't do it on his or her own. (I read later that the ancient Greeks and Romans almost never used slaves to row their warships because free citizens could and would do a lot more work on their own than a slave would under the lash.)

You see, it wasn't all that important that we couldn't march as far as men. It was that *they* had to march farther, faster, than we did to suffer as much; to build as much character.

Franco told us, after that march, "Sure we created different standards for you than men have. You're easier to hurt. You don't need as much effort for the same pain."

That was true enough, but it wasn't the whole truth. Moral considerations may be three times more important, but they aren't *all-important.* There are some objective factors that go into the equation, as well. It's a balancing act, I suppose. So far as I know, we are the only army, at least in recent times, that has found something like a proper balance where women are concerned.

I've since had a chance to read about some other armies and how they tried, and generally failed, with making real soldiers of women. Naturally, the tercio newsletter, *Hippolyta,* has articles on just that in almost every issue. You should read some of them.

Although, to be honest, *Hippolyta* can be pretty damned smug when comparing foreign failures with our success. Still, we do have some reason to be a little smug.

Take Secordia, for example. About thirty years before us, they opened up all branches of their military service, and all organizations, to women, including the infantry. A great blow for women's rights? Not exactly. You see, Secordia had previously unified their armed forces. There was no separate navy, air force and army. So a woman supply clerk in what had been the Secordian Navy could easily find herself moved to be a supply clerk in an infantry maniple of the Secordian Highlanders, and some did. No big deal, you think? Try to imagine yourself as a plump, comfortable supply clerk on a plump, comfortable ship. Then put yourself out in a Secordian winter in an unheated leaky tent, or maybe no tent. They had some serious morale problems.

And when they tried to put women right into the infantry? Oh, sister, was that a disaster! The Secordian trainers didn't gender norm anything for those women. One hundred and one women started infantry training. Ninety-eight failed outright. Of the other three—the ones who had to go through the course twice to pass—only one passed and she—maybe because she was the only woman in her unit—left as soon as her enlistment was up. Frankly, I have a sneaking suspicion that the male Secordian soldiers may have eased up on that one woman who made it to ensure that they wouldn't be forced to gender norm anything, while discouraging any more women from volunteering. And no, repeat no, women volunteered to become regular enlisted infantry in Secordia after that fiasco for *years*.

They had a little more apparent success with putting women in artillery and armor. I say "apparent" because the success was more apparent than real. Want to know how many women actually ended up serving guns and tanks in the regular Secordian Armed Forces? Exactly...none. They did fire-direction computing for the artillery—a dead-end job, by the way, in a really modern army, though it still has some future in ours. In the armored corps they drove light armored cars, not real tanks. They did not do the heavy work. And they were mostly despised by the men because of it.

Despised by the men? Maybe not as individuals. But certainly the professionals down south were disgusted enough by having women thrust upon them without any real thought having been put into the very real problems those professionals knew they would have. Complaints were loud and unceasing. So was more than occasional active sabotage of the women in their military.

That wasn't a problem for us. Since our men didn't risk having their worlds turned upside down by women warriors, they could help us rather than try to ruin us. And, in retrospect, I must say that they really did help us...if only to help ourselves.

Other armies had been more pragmatic; and more successful. The Cochinese, during the war there, had made considerable use of women, even as infantry. Not being subservient to the politically and socially dogmatic *and* militarily ignorant, the Cochinese had put the women in their own—all female—companies. They'd done pretty well, too, as long as they lasted. They took casualties, naturally, and women willing to fight are fairly rare, hard to replace. Pregnancy was a big problem, too, one we've solved partly by stringent social pressures and partly by requiring that women serving and not on maternity leave have implanted contraceptives.

Do I seem unsympathetic? Look, I was a woman serving in a combat organization where there were no men to take up the slack left by a pregnant woman. And *I* couldn't.

Garcia was sometimes almost human to us. I don't mean just to an individual; I mean to us as a group.

We had movies, some nights, when we were out on one of the ranges. No, we never got to see a movie we really wanted to see. As a matter of fact, if they showed us one, it was almost a sure thing that it would be something we really, really didn't want to see.

One I remember, in particular, began with a horrifying landing on a hostile beach. They didn't even show us the entire thing; just the first thirty minutes or so. It made me sick; and I wasn't the only one.

Garcia had the projector shut off about the time that someone began to throw up noisily. I didn't blame her; the sight of a man carrying his own ripped off arm in one hand while he tried to continue attacking was just too much.

Garcia stood in front. Of us he asked, "What do you suppose it takes; to do something like those men did?"

Marta stood to attention and answered, "Being dropped on a hostile beach with no way back and no choice, Centurion."

"Bullshit. Sit down, Bugatti." She sat.

"Women are supposed to be more emotional, less logical and rational, than men. Is it true, Trujillo?"

Inez stood and answered, "Centurion, I don't know how we've managed to pull off that little piece of propaganda for so long. It's a bald-faced lie. Oh, sure, we can get away with *showing* our emotions more readily than men do, as readily as we feel like, as a matter of fact, without anyone thinking worse of us for it. Proves nothing. Truth is, we can be, and usually are, damned coldhearted bitches, very logical and *very* rational."

I thought that was kind of funny, coming from Inez. If there was anybody in the platoon you could count on not to be a *coldhearted* bitch, it was generally her . . . or Cat.

"'Very logical, very rational,'" Garcia parroted. "Shouldn't a soldier be rational, Trujillo? Better yet, you . . . Fuentes. Shouldn't you be rational?"

"I . . . I don't know, Centurion."

"Fair enough. A soldier should be rational, some would say. Up to a point, sure. But 'a rational army would run away.'" He paused, meditatively. "Okay, that's not quite right. A rational 'army' might not run away. An army entirely composed of completely rational soldiers, however, surely would. Go back to that movie. Did it make sense for those men to get off those boats under fire, then stay in the line of battle, with death or mutilation staring them in the face every second, when there was a perfectly rational alternative, namely surrendering as fast as they could; hiding, at least? Maybe refusing to even get on the boats?"

"It must have, Centurion, to them, at the time."

Gloria added, "Centurion, a few days ago you told us that an army that runs suffers more loss than an army that stands and fights."

"Yes, Santiago. And it's true. If an army does run its losses will probably be greater than if it had stood fast. But they'll be greater among those who were slower in deciding to run, and slower in running. A really rational soldier, in a really rational army, knowing his or her comrades are also more or less rational, knowing they'll run at some point—and probably sooner rather than later—is left with only one choice, to run first and let the enemy kill the others so he or she will have time to get away."

Inez stood up again. "But they usually don't, Centurion. Why not?"

"*Men* usually don't," he corrected, "because being relatively irrational and knowing their comrades are as well, they can afford to wait a little. Almost any man or woman might make the decision to run. Normal men will wait longer, irrationally long. Often they'll stick it out long enough to win over the soldiers of an army that are just that much more rational than they are."

He sent us to bed then.

How were they going to make us usefully irrational? Garcia and Franco took care of it in three ways. First, they ran out anybody who was notably selfish, or even notably less than selfless. We had twice monthly peer evaluations. The cadre actually took into account *our* views on each other. If enough of us marked another woman down as deficient, she generally didn't have long left in the unit. Getting "knocked up" more than once, and then only with really good reason, usually meant a ticket home . . . out of the tercio, anyway.

The other way was subtle. That it was also fairly vicious goes without saying. It revolved around food.

Sometimes Garcia would issue the food for the next day—maybe one hundred and fifty pounds worth—to four or five of us. He would forbid anyone else to so much as touch the rations, it all belonged to the ones selected. We weren't allowed to break it down or help carry it. So if the rest of us were going to eat, a few girls had to put themselves through hell, lugging our food . . . selflessly.

Garcia gave those girls an exemption from the peer evaluations for a while so they could throw the food away, some of it or all of it, if they weren't willing to carry it.

The other way was meaner still. He would occasionally chop off food for a day or two, then issue double or triple rations to those who had performed well, none to those who had done poorly. He did not make us share. In fact, he told us not to, making the point stick once by withdrawing the rations from a girl he caught sharing.

Well, we shared our food anyway, on the sly, and he smirked behind our backs, I strongly suspect.

The point? When someone who is famished will still, *irrationally,* share food with you or carry it for you, there is a better reason to believe that same someone won't run out on you when the bullets start flying.

It was really rather clever, all things considered. Still, we figured out how to deal with it until Garcia made resort to an even nastier variant on the trick.

We were standing in formation one morning (you might be surprised how much time you can spend just standing around, in the military), all of us ready to head for the horizon. We really weren't looking forward to it, especially as some nasty brand of influenza had been making the rounds of the island and many of us were sick.

Franco called the platoon to attention, then turned around to make the morning report to Garcia. "Centurion, all present or accounted for."

Garcia ordered, "Post!" Franco marched to a place behind the platoon. (My eyes were locked dead ahead. It wasn't until some months later that I discovered where, precisely, it was that a junior marched to when the leader called, "Post.")

Garcia then ordered the platoon to open ranks. Once we had, he sauntered along each rank, never saying a word but looking at each of us intently. Sometimes, as with me, he'd feel a forehead for temperature. After he had finished with the last rank he ordered us to close up again.

"*Ladies,*" he began. He usually called us "twats," or "cunts," or "bitches." I had a feeling that "ladies" was going to turn out a lot worse. "*Ladies,* I have here six cases of rations. This is, as I'm sure you're aware, your entire ration for the next two days." He stopped, somewhat melodramatically. "Privates Nuñez, Galindo, and Miranda, you are to carry two cases each . . . unless some other should volunteer to carry those two cases in your stead. Without any help from anyone else."

He had named the three weakest and sickest among us, the bastard.

"Fall in prepared to march in five minutes. Fall out."

We fell into a sort of gaggle. Isabel Galindo said weakly, "I'll carry my own. Take care of Lara and Edi." Little Trujillo looked Galindo up and down carefully, then nodded and said, "I'll carry Edi's. Who'll take care of Lara's?"

Marta spoke just before Cat did. "I will."

Cat said, "Dear, I'm in better shape than you. Let me."

"Maybe so, Catarina. But I'm still stronger. It's mine."

I think my faith that these were women I could count on in a pinch went up a notch right about then.

We discovered some other interesting things about ourselves, too. There's an old saying: *Women have no friends, only rivals.* It ranks, for truthfulness, right up there with an equivalent man's saying: *Never introduce your girlfriend and your best friend.* Truth, but maybe not the whole and universal truth.

Because there on the island, with no men to compete over, we *did* develop into real friends, some of us.

Have you never noticed how women of merely moderate attractiveness will often gravitate around the leadership of the really beautiful ones? (Maybe that's not true in every country, but it's true enough in mine.) And the beautiful ones will be glad to have the merely pretty ones around, because it makes them look even more beautiful by comparison. You might wonder what's in it for the merely pretty. Simplicity itself: They get a little glamour and if they want they can have the cast-offs. I wonder if men will ever realize that the human race is just one big experiment in selective breeding run, since inception, entirely by *us*.

We didn't work that way, though. Who's beautiful when her head is shaved, she's covered with mud, wearing rags, and stinks? Who's beautiful without men to admire her? Nobody. So who takes charge? Those who have an ability that's based on more than looks.

Not everybody got the message right away. I only did, myself, after getting some help from a friend.

"Centurion. Private Fuentes, Maria; reporting as ordered."

"At ease. Private." Garcia stood in front of me and looked me up and down, carefully, like a surgeon inspecting a diseased organ. Then, without any warning at all he slapped me, right across the face, hard enough to knock me to the floor.

"On your feet. At ease... Why do you suppose I did that, Fuentes?"

Though I'd managed to get to my feet, and automatically back to attention, I was literally speechless. I didn't answer.

"I asked a question, Private."

I started to blubber, "I don't know, Centurion."

"All right... maybe you really are dense. Your file says no but... you could be. I'll help you. What did I just do?"

"You hit me." *For no reason, you bastard. Piedras, at least, had reasons.*

"Did it hurt?"

"Yes."

"Does it still hurt?"

I had to answer, "No, it doesn't... not as much anyway."

"Good... good. Now think back a bit. This morning, Santiago dumped a handful of sand and rocks down your drawers. Almost everybody laughed at you. I saw it. Did that hurt then?"

"A little... Centurion."

"Does it still hurt?"

"Yes... Centurion."

"What hurts more; your face from my slapping you, or your insides from Santiago's being shitty to you?"

I took too long about my answer; he knocked me down again, then picked me up, one handed, and set me on my feet.

"Do you recall when...what was that cunt's name...oh, yes, Ramirez. Do you recall when Ramirez made fun of you for being such a midget?"

I remembered...too well. Again, almost the whole platoon had laughed at me. That *still* hurt.

He let me stand for a bit, then asked, "What hurts you more now?"

He was raising a hand already when I blurted out the answer, "*That* does! Ramirez and Santiago."

"Very good, Fuentes. You can make value judgments."

Then he grew quiet, contemplative for a while. "What I'm trying to show you, Fuentes...to drive into your little recruit pea brain...is that physical pain goes away fairly quickly. It isn't always something to be avoided. But pains of the heart? They last and last. I want you to leave now and think about this: If you cannot stand up for yourself, you do not have what it takes to stand up for your regiment or your country. Dismissed."

I thought, still think, that I was about to be booted. I left there feeling absolutely miserable. It wasn't enough, it seemed, just to follow orders. I wasn't good enough. I was going to be washed out. Too weak. Too accommodating. Too...cowardly. No good. Worthless. A poor woman and a poor mother. A failure... failure...failure.

I can't even find the words to tell you how much that *hurt*.

There are six leadership positions for the recruits in a training platoon, recruit platoon leader, recruit platoon optio, and four squad leaders. The cadre rotated them every few days to a week, or—more typically—until you screwed up badly enough to be relieved.

Gloria was the seventh or eighth one to fill the platoon leader's slot in my platoon. When Centurion Garcia announced her name I would almost swear she had an orgasm. Power does that to some women; some men, too, I understand.

I didn't pay a lot of attention to Gloria, though. I was getting ready to pack my bags, emotionally if not in fact. I was sitting on Marta's bunk, the lower one, contemplating my misery while looking at a picture of the child I was failing.

"Fuentes, go clean the latrine," she said to me one day after we had been allowed to move back to the Quonset huts.

I didn't answer her, just kept staring at my one picture of Alma.

"Fuentes, you nasty little puke, go clean the latrine."

I'd had that duty the day before. Curiously, none of Gloria's favorites had pulled anything nasty since she'd taken over. Without thinking, I said, "Stuff it up your ass, bitch."

Now if Marta had told me, or Inez Trujillo, I'd have done it, even in the mental state I was in. For one thing, neither of them—nor probably any of the other girls—would have spared her special friends.

She walked up to me as if she wanted to paste me. I ignored her. But then she pulled my picture of Alma from my hands, tearing it.

I tell you, I saw red. It must have shown on my face because Gloria started to back up. She never got far enough away. I sprang to my feet and punched her first, right in the solar plexus. Good training tells. She went ass-down to the floor, gasping like a beached fish. But I didn't stop. I kicked her with booted feet five or six more times. As she fell back completely onto the floor and tried to twist away, I kicked her in the kidneys, just as I'd been trained. She didn't have enough air in her lungs to scream, though her face contorted as if she were trying. Another kick rolled her onto her belly. Then I jumped on her back.

Marta and Inez pulled me off of her after about the fifth time I smashed her face onto the concrete floor.

When Garcia came in he took one look, gave Gloria and myself both three days bread and water, then relieved her and appointed me the next platoon leader.

I cannot tell you precisely why, not even now, but I felt good. I mean really, *really* good after that. It felt so great that I laughed for long enough that the others began to look at me strangely.

I lasted as platoon leader for five days, which was about average. I might have done better if I hadn't been so damned hungry.

We marched or ran pretty much everywhere we went. The only time we rode trucks or buses was when there wasn't time to walk. You may think that was hard on us. Sometimes it was.

Other times, though, times when we didn't have to carry anyone else's gear, or had time enough that the pace was more like
a regular walk, it was positively enjoyable. We sang: "...If I can't
get a man then I'll surely get a parrot, and it's oh, dear me, how
would it be, if I died an old maid..." Or maybe "John Henry" or
"*Todo por la Patria.*" Sometimes more warlike songs, too: "...In
the streets of the City, the enemy's falling, and trixies are crying
out, '*arriba Patria*'." We had a bunch of really *dirty* songs, too,
but I won't repeat them.

Another song we were very fond of was an old, old one. I
understand it came here from Old Earth and somehow managed
to survive and stay in currency over the centuries, maybe with
some changes here and there. It was "*Apoyate,*" to the extent
that these songs even have titles. Sometimes, when our tails were
really dragging on a long run, Marta, Cristina or one of the other,
stronger, girls would jump out of the formation and begin to sing,
"Call for the tercio, we'll give you a hand..."

It can really pick you up, when you hear a couple of hundred
other human voices crying out, "*Apoyate,* when you're not stro-
ong, *mi hermanita,* I'll help you carry on..."

It makes you wonder, sometimes, about how much of physical
strength is really mental attitude. Anyway, that was a private song.
We never sang it where men, outside of our instructors, could hear
us. It was only for each girl to strengthen every other...because
we never knew just when anyone of us might need a little help.

Still, for me, my greatest help was the thought of a little girl
back in the city who *needed* me to succeed.

The singing was fun. But if you didn't want to join in, usually
nobody made you. You could be together on a march, but you
could also be alone if you wanted, even in the company of a
couple of hundred sisters. And the cadre generally didn't harass us
on the march, so long as we kept up. I think—no, I know—that
that was so we would learn to *like* to march.

And, once your feet, shoulders and back toughened up, there
was so much to *see* and *hear* on a march.

Once, about halfway through a twenty kilometer hump, I heard
a sort of...buzzing from the ranks in front of me. I didn't know
what it was until I turned a curve and saw it: A waterfall landing in a grove so green I may never see its like again, the water

laughing as it splashed on the rocks at its base. A pair of green, gray, and red trixies—gorgeous things—sat on a rock next to the pool, preening themselves.

You know, it's easier to love your country when your country really *is* beautiful.

One time, I remember too, we marched past a group of young men who were probably about halfway through their own training cycle. Hairless, smelly, and dirty as we were, they still watched us march by with the expressions of a group of starving tigers, looking in a butcher shop window.

Out of pure meanness we sang the sexiest, filthiest, song we knew. It had some really great sound effects, notably that of several hundred women faking an orgasm...in cadence: "Uhh...Uhh... Oh...Ah...Uhh...Uhh...Oh...Ah!"

Interlude

The meeting was in one of the larger conference rooms at headquarters, on the *Isla Real,* near the airfield. The trainers from the *Tercio Gorgidas* had come in two buses, which remained parked outside the white stone building that had once been headquarters for the entire legion. There was also a lot of what had been senior officer housing there, too, in the same general area. Most of that was filled by tribunes and sergeants major, now, what with most of the senior positions having moved to the mainland.

On the parade field the headquarters and housing surrounded, a lone Cricket light airplane waited with the engine running on idle. That was Carrera's.

Carrera said, "So give me the truth; how are the women doing?"

The cadre from the *Tercio Gorgidas* sat quietly at first. They were loath to admit to Carrera, their *Dux Bellorum,* that they had problems.

Seeing their reticence, Carrera changed his inquiry. "Fine. Tell me what's going well."

Centurion del Valle answered first. "They've become good shots."

"How good?"

"About twelve percent better than an equivalent group of men," del Valle said. "But that didn't come free. It took a lot more time and ammunition to get them there...a lot more. Even more than that for the machine guns.

"So? That would be true for men, too, if we'd spent the time and ammo," del Valle finished.

Carrera frowned. "Can they handle the machine guns, Centurion?"

"Sure...on the tripods," del Valle answered. "Firing from the

121

bipods or hip shooting?" He put out a hand and wriggled his fingers. "So, so...at best. And when we load 'em down with a full combat load; guns, tripods, spare barrel and ammunition? It takes three of them to carry what two of us can. And those three have a tougher time of it."

Carrera wrote something in a notebook. "What about if we changed their weapons from 6.5 millimeter to something smaller, say 5.5? We could buy them special weapons that would be lighter, couldn't we?" Carrera didn't wait for an answer. "No... I suppose not. Then they'd be the only ones with those calibers. Make resupply kind of tough. All right; what's the real problem?"

Franco stood to answer. "Sir...sir, we hate this shit! And we don't know what we're doing, not really. So we're *gay*? We don't hate women, any of us. We had mothers, sisters...women we've loved. And we are sick to death of being so damned...rotten to these girls."

Carrera answered, "Tough." Franco shrugged. Garcia reached up a hand to pull him back to his seat, then stood himself.

"Sir, what my partner just said? It's true enough. We'll all be happy when there are enough trained women that we can turn it all over to them. But what's really getting us is that we're failing. What works for men just isn't working right for them. They've formed little cliques and friendships, yes. But they've got no *esprit,* no sense of being part of an important community that's greater than any individual. They're just little groups and pairs of friends. Oh sure, they look from the outside like they're bonding the way soldiers should. They sing well together, for what that's worth. But they don't seem to feel like a maniple of men would towards each other. Or if they do, we can't tell."

"Could they fight?"

"No, sir. Not yet. Maybe never."

"Crank up their training."

CHAPTER FIVE

What does not destroy us, strengthens us.
—Nietzsche

It seemed that Size Did Matter.

No matter how the *Gorgidas* trained them; no matter how hard the women tried; it looked like they were never, never, *never* going to be quite (read: nearly) as strong as even an average group of men. They couldn't march as far, as fast. or carry as heavy a load. All the will in the world didn't make a gnat's ass of difference. Technology didn't help much either; it's a truism that, in total, modern high technology had not succeeded in reducing by so much as half an ounce the load on a foot soldier's back, just the opposite. Caesar's centurions would have mutinied over some of the loads a foot soldier of the late twentieth and early twenty-first centuries had to carry, on Old Earth, and things had not turned out any differently on Terra Nova. Too intent on seeing only what it wanted to see, modern egalitarian feminism simply refused to see *that*.

Still, there were some compensating factors.

When the final scores were tallied it turned out the women actually were *better* shots, on average, than men. That wasn't entirely a natural phenomenon. Their ammunition allocation had been twice that of male recruits. The women spent about twice as much time on the rifle range as the men did. This was true for all classes of training ammunition: the women had twice as many hand grenades to throw, twice as many antitank rocket rounds, twice as many pounds of demolitions.

Carrera had put out the word before the tercio had even been formed: If the women couldn't carry as much they had to make better use of what they could carry. And that meant more training, which meant more ammunition for training.

He had helped them in other ways too. All the men were issued jungle boots; canvas, plastic and leather. Carrera spent a lot of money on lighter weight footwear for the women, more or less high top sneakers, though they looked about the same. Their rucksacks? The same story. The rest of the force made do with standard, heavy packs. After the first few weeks, the women were given better; the latest in carbon fiber frames with hip belts to take some of the load off their shoulders.

Still, there wasn't much that could be done with most of the equipment. Radios were *heavy,* a big surprise for those who'd never carried one for twenty miles. The same was true for night vision devices and the batteries to run them. And Carrera was adamant; the women were *not* going to be assigned men to do the heavy work for them; it was all on themselves, sink or swim.

Machine guns? They had what everybody else had for a light machine gun; the M-26. This was a good gun though it went through ammunition at an incredible rate. The Amazons had to have them, or something just like them. A real machine gun can be made lighter but it *needs* to fire a heavy, high power bullet to do its job. Putting a heavy bullet in a light machine gun makes it damned hard to fire, nearly impossible to keep on target. And if men had trouble controlling the M-26—and they sometimes did—it could only have been worse for women, being not as heavy or strong, to control something that, being lighter, kicked even worse.

The heavier .34 and .41 caliber machine guns were almost impossibly heavy, between themselves, their tripods, and their brass-cased ammunition. Of course, the .41 caliber guns were too heavy for men to tote, also.

Water weighs the same for everyone. And the women needed about as much of it.

The biggest thing Carrera did to help them was, eventually, to make their squads and platoons bigger than the men's. Fourteen or more women per squad compared to eleven for the men, not even counting the overstrength the *Tercio Amazona* would have later on to allow some women to take maternity leave.

Of course, since an infantry unit's firepower is mostly in its heavy weapons, and since the Amazons had just the same number of heavy weapons as a man's unit did, one could say that they weren't such a bargain. The government had to pay an Amazon squad almost thirty percent more than it did a squad of men, for no greater firepower.

But all the things done to try to cut down on the women's load just compensated—and that only partly—for lack of physical strength. If they were going to make it in a traditionally male world—the world of war—they had to be stronger in character than men to make up for being weaker in body. And firepower wasn't everything . . . there's heart, too.

"Cocksuckers," Marta said, under her breath as she lifted another shovelful of dirt out of the fighting position she and Maria were building. She meant the corporals, sergeants and centurions, of course. "How many fucking holes do they fucking think we have to fucking dig to know how to dig a fucking hole?"

Not more than two hundred meters away both Franco and Garcia, along with five or six sergeants and corporals, were clustered around a big bunker, a real concrete bomb shelter. A couple more corporals stood to either side of the platoon position. These corporals, likewise, were just lounging around. The cadre were leaving the women pretty much alone, just watching quietly from a distance.

Later, all the women would curse themselves for not catching the hint that something *really* special was planned. In fairness though, most were too tired to think about much besides the blisters on their hands and their aching backs. These were much more significant than some holes, maybe eight inches in diameter, that dotted the ground they were digging into. Even the heavy-duty cables that ran from the big bunker to the holes remained unremarked.

The women were supposed to be preparing to defend against an attack by tanks, supported by artillery. They'd even been issued antitank munitions and mines—training types that wouldn't really kill a tank but made a flash and bang and some smoke—and some dummy satchel charges.

With a grunt Cat and Maria dropped the log they'd been carrying next to Maria's and Marta's fighting position. They would much preferred to have chopped up their "pricks" for the overhead cover. There was no chance of that, though.

Maria had heard Marta. It would have been hard not to have heard. She took a labored breath before answering; "How many? I guess until we do it right."

Cat and Maria then turned back towards the woods to get another log for the hole Cat shared with Inez.

"Cocksuckers," Marta repeated.

Over her shoulder, Maria called, "That's no big secret, Marta... and this distinguishes them from you and me precisely how?" Cat giggled.

Marta just grunted with the strain of another load of dirt.

When Maria came back, she took Marta's place on the shovel while Marta and Inez went for more logs. The women spent the better part of the day like that, switching off digging and cutting and carrying. Eventually, they had all built pretty fair fighting positions. They even had solid overhead cover.

It was just after an early evening chow that Centurion Garcia blew his whistle and called them together.

Marta figured that it would be just another ass chewing for not building their positions as perfectly as Garcia thought they should be.

Marta was wrong.

"We have a special treat for you today, *ladies*," Garcia began. All the women shivered when he said it. "Ladies" meant something very bad was in store.

"In about ten minutes you had better be in those holes you dug, and you'd better pray your overhead cover is good. Because we're going to shell you silly and then some tanks are going to try to crush those little logs and bury you alive... of course we'll dig you out if there's time but..."

He blew his whistle again and those corporals on either side of the platoon began to run through the area. A couple of jeeps followed. The corporals were pulling igniters and tossing charges to either side. Some of the corporals were placing smaller charges— maybe one pounders, or a little more—on top of and around every fighting position the women had built. Some charges were on fuse delay, others they hooked up to leads running from the thick cables.

"No," Garcia answered the unasked question. "I said 'shell' and I meant with real artillery. The other stuff is cheaper, though, so we're supplementing the shells with regular demo charges. Now get to your holes. And remember what you've been taught about taking out tanks." Beckoning to his followers, Garcia began to walk nonchalantly to the big bunker.

Maria and Marta exchanged wide-eyed looks. Then the women ran for their lives.

"And *don't* move my demo charges," Garcia called to their fleeing backs.

Maria and Marta were almost to their holes when the first shells landed; maybe one hundred and fifty, maybe two hundred meters to their front. There were only three of them, three shell bursts spewing ugly, ragged columns of earth into the air. Even though muffled by subsurface detonation, the blasts made Maria's insides ripple in a way that was both indescribable and very, very unpleasant. The sensation made Marta want to throw up, and she was used to having her internal organs pushed around some.

By the time they had squeezed through the rear entrance ports and fallen in a tangled heap at the hole's muddy bottom there were another six explosions—closer; they could feel that. Then came nine more, closer still. After those three volleys, each one getting closer to them, a different firing battery took over. The women neither knew nor cared who was pounding them. In fact, the first had been 85 millimeter guns. The ones who took over fired 122 millimeter shells, nine per volley. These last were also firing on delay fuses: they went off after sinking a few feet into the ground. If one had actually been permitted to land near one of the women's holes the dirt sides would have been blown in on them, which would probably have proven fatal.

The cadre did this to give the women the illusion of fire coming closer and closer. In fact none of the guns ever fired any closer than seventy-five meters. Which was still dangerous. Part of the danger was mitigated by having the guns fire from the side, parallel to the women's line of fighting positions.

Unseen, Garcia nodded to Franco. Franco turned a safety key in a large metal battery box and began flipping little switches. With each flip of a switch one or a number of demolition charges started going off around the women. In their holes they cried and quivered and vomited and—more than a few—shit themselves. Marta screamed when a one-pound charge atop the little bunker went off. So did Maria.

Once the demo charges had almost all been fired the guns

split their fire so that half was falling behind the women, half in front. Then, as the last of the demolitions, the ones that were on slow burning fuses, were going off, all the fire shifted to fall behind them.

By then Marta had started to cry, great hopeless wracking sobs. She blubbered a lot of things, too, that she probably wished she hadn't... private things. She took a sniff and sobbed too about the smell of feces wafting up from her soiled uniform.

The really bad part, though, was when she tried to run away.

Marta didn't just have bigger breasts than most; she was big in general, strong, too. Maria saw her start to scramble out of their hole. For a minute—it seemed like an eternity but may have been only half a second: a minute is fair compromise—Maria just froze. Then she grabbed Marta's combat harness and held on for dear life: Marta's.

Marta fought, she struggled. She called Maria just about every name in the book.

Hanging onto Marta's combat harness, Maria screamed, "Stupid bitch, I am NOT letting you go out into *that!*"

Finally, Marta just collapsed, sobbing again, saying over and over that she was *sorry.* And the two held each other, there in the bottom of that muddy stinking hole in the earth, as the "barrage" seemed to roll on past them.

Between blasts Maria bantered in Marta's ear, "You know how time flies"... KABOOM... "when you're having fun? Well"... KABOOM... "it can really drag when"... KABOOM... "you're having no fun at all"... KABOOM... "This barrage *can't*"... KABOOM... "have lasted as long as five minutes, maybe six at the outside"... KABOOM... "but it seems longer, doesn't it?" Marta paid no attention.

Then Maria heard the tanks... barely.

Tanks are impressive, no doubt about it. And any soldier who wants to die in her sleep will treat them with a healthy respect. But they can be beaten. The women had already been taught how.

"Yes," that instructor had told them the previous week, "tanks are bigger than you. They're faster than you. They've got more firepower than you. And they've got a lot more protection than the shirts you girls are wearing."

"But let me tell you a little secret: tanks—their crews, I mean—
are as afraid of you as you are of them. Trust me, I'm a tanker.
I know."

The instructor looked over the platoon and singled out Inez;
it was always a great entertainment for him to see how it was
the little ones who liked tanks the most. "Come up here, young
lady." All the others gaped in disbelief when he reached a hand
down to help her up. That was something *their* usual instructors
would never do, implying as it did the possibility those girls really
were human beings.

"Young lady," the instructor asked, "how thick is the armor on
top of this tank?"

Inez looked at him uncomprehendingly.

"Well, reach in through the hatch and try to feel how far apart
your hands are when the armor is between them." She did and
then announced that the top armor was no more than a half inch
thick. He had her do the same with the side of the turret, which
was several times thicker, but still not all that thick.

"That's the first weakness: our real armor is only in front. On
the sides, the rear, the top deck; the armor is positively *weak*.
Oh, sure; it's good enough to keep shell fragments and bullets
out. But a shaped charge in the hands of a good grunt will blow
a hole right through, causing our wives and children to receive
a 'With deepest sorrow' letter from *Presidente* Parilla. That's why
we *insist* on having our own infantry in close support; to take
care of enemy grunts; at least keep their damned heads down."

"That should give you a hint. What's the first thing you have
to take care of to defeat tanks? You, girl." He pointed at Maria.

"The enemy's infantry?" she ventured.

"Right in one. But why?"

"So they can't shoot us when we go after the tanks."

"Almost right, *chica*. But your answer implies that it's their
guns that protect the tanks. That's only partly right. I'll give you
another hint. What's the most important part of your body when
using your rifle?"

He gave her a few seconds to think. She went down the list
of organs and senses but rejected most of them outright. Finally
Maria had it narrowed down to her trigger finger and her eyes,
then decided that eyes were more important. She said so.

"Just so, Private . . . ?"

"Fuentes, Centurion. Maria Fuentes."

"Private Fuentes. You are just right. Because that is the big weakness on the tank. We can't see *shit* from inside those things. Strip off our infantry; cut out most of our eyes; cut out the ability to get precise fire in small doses to protect ourselves."

She didn't really pay perfect attention to what he said next; she was marveling that a man in uniform and authority had just called her something besides bitch or twat, or *lady* in a tone that implied the same thing.

"...are particularly vulnerable. That's something that hasn't improved a bit since the Great Global War. The same charge—satchel or land mine—that would break the treads on a tank of sixty years ago will do the same to a tank today.

"And the engines? We aren't submarines. Tanks require oxygen in vast quantities to keep the engines going; oxygen that has to come from the air around us. Cut that off; we stop dead. Then you can kill us; because a tank that isn't moving is dead meat to good infantry.

"Okay, move into the classroom behind you."

Maria hesitated...which the centurion saw. "Something bothering you, *chica?*"

She stood to attention, hesitated, then asked, "Centurion... how come you are so...ah...polite to us? No one else has been."

He smiled briefly, then answered, "You aren't going to my unit, girl. So I have nothing against any of you. So what does a little politeness cost? It might be different if there was some chance that you women might be mixed in with regular, male organizations. I understand that in the armies that have tried that there is often a vast resentment of women soldiers on the part of the men, partly because the men end up doing nearly twice as much heavy work, and partly because some women will...ah...sell themselves, frankly. But you girls? You're not going to harm me or mine any."

"Oh...I see."

"Yes. Now trot your cute little buns into the classroom."

"*Si, Centurion.*" She smiled fetchingly; the habits of a lifetime die hard. The centurion smiled back until a warning glance from Garcia, standing nearby, turned his face to a scowl.

"Now GO, girl." Maria went.

In the classroom the women were shown a film, *Hombres*

Contra Tanques. Men Against Tanks. This work showed a number of interesting ways to earn a medal for valor, most likely posthumously. Then the women had to go through a number of those ways themselves, using small charges, gasoline bombs—they were told those were called "Molotov cocktails"—mines and more formal antitank weapons.

Inez had taken considerable interest in the film. Cat had said, "Uh, uh." Perhaps she thought she had a choice.

The girls waited in holes for tanks to run over them, then leapt up to toss satchel charges on their decks. Yes, they were very, very small satchel charges, with several pounds of dirt added to make them as heavy as the real thing. As the charges were heavy, it took a fair amount of practice to learn to swing them just right by their straps.

In pairs they used ropes to pull practice mines back and forth across the ground to line them up on a tank that was moving forward. They manufactured and then tossed live Molotov cocktails on towed tank hulks' back decks. This usually didn't work.

This was, by no means, the toughest drill taught them.

Franco, serving as coach, squatted in a ditch by the side of a dirt road.

Next to him, Inez Trujillo lay panting. A pair of tanks waited around a bend in the road, a few hundred meters away, revving their engines menacingly. She was scared nearly witless.

In her hands, clutched in front of her, she had a twelve-pound sticky satchel charge. It, too, was mostly dirt, not explosive. Tanks are too expensive to blow up as training aids.

She reminded herself, *The trick is that the tank can't see* mierda. *So the hunter waits until it's within twenty meters. Then, in the three seconds you have between the driver losing sight of where you will be and the tank crushing where you have been, you leap into the middle of the road and lie down right in front of the monster. Timing things carefully, you pull the igniter, stick the bomb to the underside or suspension of the tank, let it finish rolling over you, then, covered by the dust cloud, roll back to the ditch before the following tank can see you.*

Then: BOOM!

Franco made a call on a small radio he carried. The menacing mechanical roar around the bend picked up and was joined by the squeaking of treads, worse than an infinity of nails on an infinity of blackboards. Inez spotted the long barrel of a tank pushing past the trees. Her tremors grew worse, exacerbated by the shaking of the ground from the metal monster's roll. She saw the barrel swing over towards her, roughly parallel to the road. There was still more squeaking as the tank pivot-steered at the bend. And then the barrel—all she could really see—was moving in her direction.

As the tanks neared, the little pebbles by her dirt-pressed face began to jump up and down. That vibration grew steadily worse. Then the muzzle of the tank's cannon was about twenty meters from her position. Inez braced herself for her leap.

Franco slapped her ass and shouted, "Go!"

Inez made a nimble, quick jump onto the road, then flopped to her belly and rolled. The roll was uneven, deliberately so, to get her in line with it and with the tank's movement. She ended up on her back, precisely as she should have. Frantically, she tore away the tape that covered the sticky part of the satchel charge. By the time she had that off, the tank's treads had enveloped her, grinding the dirt to both sides. She pulled the ring of the igniter and was rewarded with a crack more felt than heard, followed by a small puff of smoke. Shaking, she slammed the charge, sticky side first, against the hull. Then the tank was past her and, gasping for breath, she made another leap for the ditch, hitting and rolling into its warm embrace. A few seconds later she heard the muffled *boom* that said her charge had gone off.

Franco patted her shoulder. Leaning down next to her ear he shouted, "Good job, girl!"

Exhaling, Inez thought, *Damn; that was fun.*

Standing atop the tank, Garcia had seen everything but what had gone on underneath it. He thought, *Fine, character-building exercise this is. Though as a combat technique it strikes me as barely better than nothing.*

Gloria couldn't do it. She wouldn't get out into the road. Once, even, Garcia had to rip the sticky bomb—it *did* have half a pound of trinitrotoluene in it—from her hands and toss it away, hunching one shoulder against the blast as he fell back to earth.

Few noticed that Garcia threw his own body over Gloria's

before the explosive went off. Then he hauled her to her feet and slapped her to the ground with a curse.

Long after the rest of the women had passed the test, Garcia was still working with Gloria. Exasperated, he finally ended up having her lie right down in the road, with him standing on her back, while the tank rolled up on them. At the last second he would jump aside.

She still wouldn't, or couldn't, ignite the bomb and stick it to the tank.

Time ran out before Garcia gave up.

The best part was when the instructors let the women ride the tanks on the inside. That centurion-instructor had told the truth, they saw: Tankers were *blind* compared to infantry. Sure, the latest ones might have been able to see right through fifteen feet of sand to spot a hot tank engine. They couldn't see a cool foot soldier behind a tree or a wall, or in a trench. The women learned; the women *saw*. And when they had to use those little vision blocks? Once a foot soldier got within fifty or sixty feet of a tank, or it got that close to them, the tank *couldn't* see them. It was as if the tank were like a man, a quadriplegic, whose head and eyes are locked straight to the front and on the level.

And they learned that even if a tank could see them it couldn't depress the main gun or the coaxial machine gun.

An instructor said, however, "Don't get too cute, girls, because it can still run you over in the open, and the muzzle blast from the main gun can kill or maim, knock the hell out of you, any-way. But even a small hole in firm soil—the smaller the better, actually—can protect you from that somewhat."

The roar of the tank engines grew noticeably louder. "Marta," Maria shouted, "Marta, come on. Get ready! The tanks are coming."

Marta looked blankly for a moment, then asked, "Tanks?"

"Tanks," Maria shouted again, then slapped Marta's face.

That got through to her. Her face came alive. She reached for her rocket launcher and started to stick her head up to fire.

"No! Wait! Let them pass. You can take 'em from the rear."

Marta nodded her understanding, whispering, "*That* would be nice for a change."

Both women crouched down in their hole with the roar of the

tanks' engines and the squeal of the treads drawing ominously nearer. The tanks began firing their machine guns—at the ground between the positions, but also right over their heads. Some girls later swore they had heard bullets strike the berm in front of their hole! They were right.

The 125-millimeter shells from the tanks' main guns buried themselves in the dirt between positions before exploding with gut crunching force. The sound grew so loud the girls could barely stand it. It wasn't as loud as the artillery had been, but it was somehow much more personal.

Then the hole became very dark. "God, the damned thing's right on top of us!" Maria gripped Marta to give her a little comfort, and perhaps to take some, too. "You would never have gotten a kill with a frontal shot! Let it pass," Maria shouted again. Why not? The tank couldn't hear her.

But it didn't pass, not right away.

"We're right on top of them, Sergeant," announced the tank's driver over the intercom.

"Good. Pivot steer! Let's give 'em the time of their lives."

With a chuckle, the driver began twisting the tank back and forth, side to side, grinding Maria's and Marta's position in on them.

"Teach them to be a little more careful about camouflage in front of their position, won't it, Sergeant?"

"Yeah...teach 'em a few other things too."

"Sergeant?" the gunner asked.

"Yes, Gunner?"

"If they had been better camouflaged from in front I couldn't have fired the main gun without maybe killing them."

"*I* knew where their positions were, Pablo," the tank commander said. "We watched as they were building. I wouldn't have let you hit a hole, or even get too near one. The grinding is punishment for bad camo."

"Oh...I see."

Beneath the thrashing treads, dirt and bits of wood filtered down onto Marta and Maria. They coughed in air made suddenly rank with diesel fumes and dust. When a log fractured, it made a crack they could feel in their bones more than hear with their ears.

After another eternity of terror the tank moved on, more dirt flying from behind the treads and splattering down on them.

"Now, Marta! Now," Maria screamed. Marta hesitated not a moment, she wanted *revenge* for what they'd just been through.

Marta risked a quick look to their front. (Yes, *risked*; bullets had been flying overhead.) Maria guessed there hadn't been any more tanks or supporting infantry, because Marta turned around and fired almost immediately. The boom and flash of the backblast was followed by a shriek of frustration. A miss.

Maria handed over another rocket from their little store of them. Marta twisted it onto the front of her launcher and took aim again. The backblast sent more crud and smoke into their position.

"Give me another one," Marta demanded. Maria passed over the last rocket. This time Marta was *very* careful; Maria could see that from the deliberate way she loaded and the deliberate firing stance she took. This gave Maria time to join her, just her head sticking up from the hole. They saw the tank that had just savaged them moving away. It was firing its machine gun off into the distance.

"Easy and careful, sister," Maria shouted in her ear. Marta nodded, took a deep breath, let some of it out, and fired.

The rocket sped straight and true. It hit the tank right on the back grill. A big column of orange smoke filled the air behind it.

From the command bunker Franco noticed the tank had been hit. He radioed the crew to tell them so... and to tell them how.

The tank slewed to a stop, the hatch flying open. One by one the turret crew emerged. Then they were joined on the back deck by the driver. Marta and Maria, and the tank crew, just stared at each other for a minute, a degree of disbelief on all five faces. One of the tankers—Maria guessed he might have been the TC, the tank's commander—began to applaud. The rest of the men joined him. Marta blushed scarlet when they shouted out, "Well done, girls! Well done." The tank commander threw them a ragged and friendly salute. Then, with a wave, the men reboarded their tank, cranked the engine, and drove off.

Just about then the centurion's whistle blew. Marta and Maria ran to where the platoon was assembling. Before they fell in on Garcia they heard a sound—again, barely—that made them look behind. Inez Trujillo was sitting on Gloria, slapping her repeatedly, back and forth, across the face, while Cat looked on with disapproval on her face. It was sort of funny; this little thing beating on someone more than a head taller. None of the cadre interfered in the slightest.

Heart doesn't come easy.

That night Marta approached the girl who had saved her life. "Maria, I'm sorry for what I said to you. And...I'm sorry for collapsing like that."

"It's okay, Marta. Everyone has their...little moments. And your vocabulary was certainly...ah...enlightening."

Marta said nothing for a while, just kept staring down at the ground.

"I learned the vocabulary in the biggest and best whorehouse in the capital of La Plata," she said, eventually. Then it all came out in a rush. How she'd gotten pregnant at fourteen, been thrown out of the house, met a pimp. Done *everything.*

"I lost the baby, the ability to have a baby, when a customer beat me up, but by then it was too late to do anything else. I was...contaminated. Maria, I learned to hate myself even more than I hated my customers.

"I learned to loathe every part of me. Drugs? Oh, yes. *Huánuco,* mostly. Some marijuana and hashish. Opium. A *lot* of alcohol. When I was twenty I tried to figure out how many people had had a piece of me. It was over seven *thousand.* I wondered what could be left of me, with so many having taken a little away each.

"Then a recruiter came from the *classis.* He wasn't looking for sailors, not where I worked, but for sea whores to service the fleet off the coast of Uhuru, during the antipirate campaign the Yamatans paid for. I went with another girl, my special lover, Jaquelina."

Seeing the confused look on Maria's face, Marta added, "Yeah, I can go both ways. But I wasn't in love with Jaquelina because she was a girl but because of the person she was. We both signed up because we figured we could get away from the pimps; make a bundle; and maybe we could start over fresh somewhere.

"Anyway, they needed some girls who were really *obviously* girls to be bait on a small boat. Jaquelina and I signed up, mostly for the bonus they offered.

"We ended up fighting, because our boat took a bad hit. We got a couple of medals..."

"You've got a *medal*?" Maria asked. Marta just nodded.

"Anyway, eventually my lover was killed." The woman's voice broke for a moment. She swallowed to get control of it. "I tried to stick it out with the *classis,* but the memories were just too bad. So, when this came up, I volunteered for it to get away from those memories.

"If I'm killed here it won't be so bad. Nobody will miss me. But I can't fail. Thank you, for helping me not fail."

Marta started to cry again. Maria began to gather her into her arms, saying, "Marta, I would miss you. I'm going to hug you now. If you yell at me or push me away, I will punch you in the face and *then* hug you. Understand?"

Marta stiffened at first at being pulled into Maria's shoulder. Then she relaxed, softening into the other, while continuing to cry.

What the women needed wasn't just individual heart; they needed something called *esprit de corps.* Men get it; develop it easily, in fact. After all, the boy gang is one of only two spontaneously occurring human organizations.

And that was one area where the *Gorgidas* cadre couldn't help much. They knew how to build it in a male unit, straight or otherwise. It's pretty easy for them. Take any average group of males (well, Franco had once told them not *any* group; in much of the world men usually couldn't develop real *esprit de corps*; most of them were not capable of even conceiving of loyalty to someone or something who isn't a blood relation or a body of blood relations); put them in positions of fair equality, give them competent leadership; add stress, misery, danger and excitement to taste: *voila—esprit de corps.* Having them compete against other groups of men helped quite a bit, too.

"The big advantage," Franco had said, in one of his frequent, informal lectures, "that men have is that they're much more emotional, far less coldly rational, than women are.

"*Women* don't really like to compete at, so to speak, manly things. What does conquest mean to them? What does being better at something than someone else mean, if it isn't innately *womanly*? How does it make any of you more of a woman that you can march, shoot, destroy? Not your job, so to speak.

"And it isn't," he continued, "that women are incapable of loyalty to something besides themselves. They *are* loyal: To children, almost always, husbands, usually, parents, generally, societies and nations...that's slightly less common but by no means unheard of.

"Most modern feminist literature tends to ignore the whole question. Instead, feminists—like Sylvia Torres, for example—want to concentrate only on individual achievements, abilities, and strengths. Which is why those views are useless...to you. Note they *never* seriously talk about women's weaknesses. It's as if they can't even conceive of the difference between battle and peacetime pursuits. Perhaps they really can't understand that battle is a social event, conducted by groups, and in which the cohesion of groups matters much more than individual prowess.

"Worse, it's as if they—like many of the men in the world—can't even conceive of the benefits and need of that peculiar form of semi-insane groupthink: *Esprit de corps.*"

Not all lectures were informal.

The women sang with feeling, "*Miseria, Miseria...*" as they filed into the dank and musty shed. Under its shade, buttocks pressed down uncomfortably into the rough wood chips intended to cushion the fall of the women as they learned to fight hand to hand.

Franco spoke. "You girls know a little more now about battle than you did once. Let me tell you some more.

"A man is not *braver* than a woman is; 'She who faces death by torture for each life beneath her breast.' The Catholic Church has lists of female martyrs *miles* long."

He made a hand signal and a picture of a young girl, hanging, neck broken, frozen with shirt ripped off and breasts disfigured, shone from one wall.

"Rather more recently, there was this girl. We don't know her name. We do know she was hanged by the Sachsens, during the Great Global War, for sabotage. She was captured, tortured, and then hanged because she wouldn't give any up information. That was bravery equal to any man's.

"Tsk-tsk.

"But, unfortunately, she proves not a damned thing about women's bravery in battle; in *groups*.

"None of you have been to war," Franco observed. "I have. Twice, actually, against both the Sumeris and the Pashtians. So trust me in this. Imagine a battle between a group of women and a group of men. Remember this is *not* a drill. Bullets are flying; shells scattering razor sharp shards of steel in all directions. People are screaming; some in anger, more in pain.

"There are a few individuals—men and women both, transcendentally motivated—who ignore all that, fight on despite danger. There are also some who cower and hide; and you can't really blame them, though you just might have to shoot them later. For the rest, though—the relative sheep, like most people—they *only* stay the course because they care about their comrades, and their comrades' good opinions, more than they care about themselves."

Franco turned and pointed to Gloria. "*Chica,* when was the last time you cared if somebody thought you were brave...or tough... or disciplined? Do not answer. Just think about it. Women are far less likely to care about someone's opinion of them when that opinion does not concern something that is essentially womanly."

He concluded, "More than lack of physical strength, more than health, far, far more than courage; it is this that is your greatest obstacle."

To give the cadre credit, they did try to find the key. And they did run off any girls who seemed incapable of eventually making their unit their primary source of self-identification. They also, naturally, dumped those whose lack of competence could degrade the unit, thereby making it considerably more likely that the rest of the women would develop *esprit.* They let stay none of the slackers, nor that one thief, nor those who couldn't or wouldn't learn to shoot...nor those who were too afraid.

Once, the cadre even let the girls see a male infantry training maniple at close range, just for a few hours. They wanted them to see how things were supposed to be.

That was very strange to the women. The men were jocular, content with themselves and with each other. And they exuded a sense of mass *brotherhood* the girls had never seen or felt before. They *knew,* in a way that the women didn't yet, that any man in that maniple could count on any other to fight by his side, and never to desert him.

The cadre tried all sorts of things, some quite bizarre, to help the women learn the way things were supposed to be. Once, for example, they showed a movie, entitled *Kirti,* dubbed into Spanish, about a tercio of Hindu soldiers in the Federated States Army during their Formation War.

The girls—most of them—thought it was a pretty good movie, actually, though very sad at the end. A number cried when all the great characters they'd learned to like as the movie progressed were killed in a hopeless, desperate attack, an attack they'd volunteered to make. The story, they were told, was mostly true.

That evening, after chow, they had discussed it with Franco.

He said, "It was, in fact, the battle actions of this mostly Hindu regiment that had led directly to massive opening up of military service to Hindus, which had gone a long way towards winning the war for the side that did so. Of course, the world being the way it is, the Hindus remained in their own units for nearly a century after that."

Inez commented, "Seems kind of unfair, Centurion...keeping them apart like that. Bound to lead to worse treatment. The movie showed us that."

"Yes, Private, so it seems. Would the world have been a better place, would even those Hindus have been better off, if they'd been integrated with whites from the beginning, but had failed in battle because they didn't like or trust one another? Would a statement in favor of racial integration have been worth maybe losing that war?"

He answered his own questions. "I suppose that depends on whether an aesthetic principle is more important than the success of an ultimate good."

Interlude

Gloria Santiago sat miserable and alone on the front steps to the barracks. Other soldiers passed without speaking. The last of her "friends" had been downchecked by the rest of the platoon on a peer evaluation the day before. That woman was already on her way to a non-combat training unit.

Gloria's eyes were bloodshot, her body sore and bruised. Her once fair skin was dry and scratched. Worst of all, her spirit was very nearly broken.

I just don't understand it, Santiago thought. *This world is so different, so strange. And I'm no good at any of it. Even those damned little bitches Trujillo and Fuentes can beat me up. It's so unfair . . . nothing ever prepared me for this.*

Santiago stood up and began walking away from the barracks to the nearby woods. She wanted to be alone in fact as well as spirit.

From a hundred meters away Corporal Salazar saw her slinking, spiritless walk. He began to follow her to the woods.

CHAPTER SIX

May all our citizens be soldiers,
and all our soldiers citizens.
—Sarah Livingston Jay

Maria:

They couldn't give it to us; it had to come from inside; inside ourselves.

I can't speak for everybody; not for all the *Amazonas*. I can only tell you what I felt; what happened to me.

You remember how Centurion Garcia had made a bunch of us "pregnant," making the rest of us carry their gear. Well that was imposed; we hated him every step of the way. And most of us, by this stage in our training would almost rather drop down dead than "get knocked up." Certainly we wouldn't ask to see the medics over little discomforts, as we might have if some other women hadn't had to carry our load for us if we did.

I wonder, though, if we'd have been so reluctant if there had been some young men around to carry our gear for us. It's just possible they wouldn't even have minded, stupid boys. I sometimes think that men are overgrown babies whose spoiling of us often keeps us from quite growing up ourselves.

Or maybe we keep each other from ever quite growing up.

One impossibly late night after another impossibly long day I went to bed (not a real bed, of course, just my tacky air mattress under a strung out poncho). I was feeling a little poorly, nothing definite, just a general feeling of inner rottenness. But by morning I really *was* sick: dizzy, throwing up, a fever, too. I still don't know what it was that got me, influenza, bug bite, or reaming rod of randomness.

Unfortunately, we had another road march—heavy packs—scheduled for that morning. To add injury to insult, *I* had to carry the machine gun. I *couldn't*; I just couldn't.

The cadre had been dropping girls right and left of late. Less than half of those who had started were still with us. The rest were, like me, pretty much at their limit.

Curiously, again like me, it had also become extremely important to all but a tiny number of those remaining to complete training. Whatever it was: unwillingness to go home as failures, a real need for the benefits that went with service, some stirrings of pride in being soldiers, I don't know.

In my case I *had* to finish training...for Alma's sake.

I think Marta noticed me first, throwing up outside the perimeter. She came up and asked me, gently, what was wrong. I threw up again and started to cry for Alma; and for the life I'd hoped to build for us. I knew I'd never make the march. I'd be a failure. And they'd boot me out.

She held me a minute or two, kissed my forehead. She told me it would be all right. Then she took my machine gun, throwing it up on her shoulder with a grunt. In a few minutes Inez Trujillo came up, she and the rest of the squad. With hardly a word they took my pack apart; splitting up my gear among them. They hung the empty pack on my back. Trujillo told two of the girls—Isabel and Catarina—to help me. They got on either side of me and put my arms over their shoulders.

If Garcia even noticed or cared he never let on. He just called us to attention, gave us a "left face," took his position at the front, and ordered us to march.

The first few miles were bad, but I still had a little strength in me; just enough to keep going. The next nine or ten miles were worse, because I didn't have that strength left by then, but I couldn't drop out after having let the other girls put themselves through hell having to carry me for the first few miles. Funny thing, pride, no?

I don't like to think about that march too often. It was bad. Half the time I was nearly delirious. Most of the rest I was puking. The girls helping me didn't say a bad word even when I threw up right on them, though the stench made them start to gag, too.

Now you might say those women did nothing special; that if they hadn't taken my gear willingly, Garcia would have made them. That's true, they had to carry my equipment if I couldn't.

But they didn't have to carry *me*. That they did on their own. It's hard not to love a group like that.

There was a funny upshot of that incident. Without a word of explanation Garcia had us turn in those miserable poles, the "pricks," the next day. They were carried away on a truck. He never reissued them. We never gave him cause to.

Fortunately, we spent the next four days in the same general area, learning how to conduct raid, ambush and reconnaissance patrols. We did make some cross-country moves, but they were fairly short moves; without heavy packs.

Mostly, they left me behind to help secure the Objective Rally Point, or ORP. That's the last position where your patrol—usually squad or platoon sized—stops, short of the actual place where you set up the ambush or do the recon or raid.

If I hadn't been sick, it might have been fun. I know most of the other girls thought it was. Though, by then, they would probably have to be considered a little weird. Being in the ORP wasn't so bad. Still, I was usually alone.

Actually, I hoped I was alone. There was always the chance of a snake showing up to keep me company. I hate snakes. And the *antaniae*? The moonbats? I am frankly scared to death of them. The thought of one crawling into my sleeping roll with me is enough to pull me to my feet, shivering, no matter how tired I am. As soon as I was remotely able to keep up I insisted that I not be left behind in the ORP anymore. If the other girls thought that was because I was tough, I did nothing to disabuse them of the notion.

It was early one morning, following a less than fully successful ambush and while we waited for chow, that I cornered Trujillo. The others, especially Marta, Cat and Isabel, I'd already expressed my gratitude to.

"Inez…thank you," was all I said.

She just shook her head, as if she didn't quite understand.

"For carrying me. For getting the others to carry me." I looked down at the ground, ashamed, actually.

"Wouldn't you have done the same for us?"

I don't know if I would have before, I really don't. But I nodded, as if I was certain I would have.

"So what's to thank? We're in this together. We help each other."

The subject was a little uncomfortable. I changed it. "Why are you here, Inez? I mean . . . I joined to try to build a better life for myself and my daughter. But why did you join?"

"I thought it was the right thing to do," was all she said.

"There was a man," I reminded her, "back when we first got on the hovercraft to come here. He was something special to you? A boyfriend? A lover?"

She looked confused for a minute, then started to laugh. "Lover? Ricardo is my *brother*! He's in Third Tercio. He's probably at Centurion School now."

"Are you going to try for that? Centurion, I mean."

"I'll take what they offer me, if they offer me anything," she answered.

"They will. You're different from the rest of us, different from me, for example."

"Maria," she said, with a subtle smile, "do you think we carried you and your gear because we thought you were worthless?"

I really didn't know what to say to that.

Somewhere nearby artillery was falling and exploding. Garcia paid it no mind, though it made the rest of us pretty nervous.

He said, "Many armies spend an inordinate effort, I understand, on limiting the effects of friendly fire. We don't spend much. We're soldiers. We're there to be killed if the country needs us to be killed. We're there to win, even if doing so gets us killed.

"You might not expect it to be true, but it is true, that the infantry only inflicts twenty or thirty percent of all casualties in battle. We take, on the other hand, about ninety percent of the casualties. Who kills us? The enemy artillery. Who among us does the killing? The machine guns. What kills or suppresses the machine gunners? Your own artillery."

Garcia pulled a tetradrachma coin from his pocket and flipped it to illustrate. "Now you have a choice. You can stay so far behind your own supporting artillery that there is no chance of any of your own being hit by it. If you do, the enemy machine gunners will be up and firing when you attack. Two years into the Great

Global War, there was an attack. Twenty-five *thousand* Anglians were killed, as many more wounded, on the first day alone, by a few dozen machine gunners that hadn't been suppressed or destroyed by the Anglian artillery."

He flipped the coin again. "On the other hand, you can follow your own artillery so closely that you take some losses in dead and wounded from your own side. Quality control at the factory—or lack thereof—ensures that if you follow a barrage closely, some shells will fall short among your own troops. But then, you can be on top of the machine guns, shooting, stabbing, hacking and blasting before they have a chance to mow your people down."

His face took on a somber, serious cast. "How sad for those killed by their own side's artillery." The frown disappeared, replaced by a rare and ghastly grin. "How *grand,* however, for those likely much larger numbers *not* killed by the enemy machine guns. And the dead don't really care what killed them.

"We go in for the second approach, taking losses to 'friendly fire' somewhat more philosophically than the world norm. It takes a lot of discipline, though, and that means a lot of training. Some of that can be inferential training, general discipline building. It's better, though, if the training is a little more direct and pointed. Move out."

I was scared to death. Garcia wasn't just flapping his gums about following a barrage closely. He wanted us to *do* it.

"*Madre de Dios!* Did you see that?" Marta stopped short, slack-jawed, to see a woman sail about fifteen feet into the air, arms and legs fluttering. The woman landed, stunned, it appeared, but otherwise fairly whole, a few meters from where a delay-fused shell had gone off not too far from under her feet. The woman was lucky the shell had missed her head before burying itself in the ground.

"Don't think about it," Cristina Zamora shouted. "Just keep marching forward. Forward!" Zamora was acting platoon centurion for the exercise.

About seventy-five meters ahead of where Marta and I stood, a wall of flying dirt moved relentlessly up a steep hill. They were firing delay fuses, but that was the only safety measure I could see, that kicked up a visually impressive amount of dirt and rocks with each burst.

We resumed walking forward, firing short bursts either from the hip or, shoulder held, aiming with the F- and M-26's neat little integral optical sight. Look, *anything* you can throw at the enemy to keep his head down is worth the effort. Besides, walking is a lot faster and less exhausting than doing little three second rushes. In battle, an exhausted *Amazona* is a fear-filled and useless *Amazona*.

As we neared the top of the hill, the shell fire shifted a last time and redoubled in intensity. Zamora spoke into a radio, then shouted, "Wait for it!"

The delay fused high explosive was replaced by a dozen rounds of white phosphorus. A cloud of smoke enveloped the hilltop.

"*Adelante las Amazonas!*" We charged, screaming and firing all the way.

For whatever reasons, and each of us probably had her own, we did develop something like *esprit de corps*. Or, rather, most of us did. A few couldn't. Life for them became very hard, because, as the overwhelming bulk of us still remaining bonded together, the others were left out in the cold. Some were encouraged into the group by that. Others just shut down before being washed out.

Probably no one suffered more from this than Gloria. I guess she was so used to being the center of attention that she just couldn't take being cut out. Cut out, however, she certainly was. Oh, she tried to pretend that she felt what we felt. I'll tell you something, though; we women are much better judges of character than men are. Gloria fooled no one.

She took to hanging around one of the corporal-instructors, Corporal Salazar. Salazar's partner, Sergeant Castro, noticed, eventually. I remember a screaming match that ended only when Centurion Franco knocked them both silly.

It was about that time that Gloria stopped being put on shit detail.

I guess Salazar wasn't entirely gay. Eventually, he and Gloria were caught engaged in...shall we say...an indiscretion. Maybe the worst part is that Castro's the one who caught them. Maybe, if Castro hadn't been so upset, he might have kept it to himself. He was a good man, ordinarily, a lot kinder than most.

Some of us were selected to sit in on the courts-martial, just to witness, not to sit the board. Salazar just sat, mute. Gloria kept begging for the chance to resign. It was too late. Castro wept a lot, as quietly as he could. I felt sorry for him.

The two were each charged with mutiny and aggravated fraternization. Salazar was further charged with aggravated abuse of office (improper sexual relations) and adultery; Gloria with conduct tending to contribute to the demoralization of the legion and adultery. (Did I mention that the partnerships in *Gorgidas* were treated as legal marriages in the legion?)

The evidence was pretty damned overwhelming. Castro had seen them. There was some semen from Salazar on Gloria's uniform. It had obviously not been rape, though Gloria tried to claim it had been. I think what ruined that defense is that Gloria still had her teeth and, under the particular circumstances, could have been expected to use them to considerable effect, had it really been rape or, more technically, forcible sodomy. Besides, we were supposed to be real soldiers, ready to fight and die. How could one of us hope to claim rape if she'd been conscious but hadn't fought to death or, at least, incapacitation or been physically overwhelmed by sheer brute force? What was true of civilian women could never really be true for us.

Mutiny? When two or more soldiers combine to suborn good order and discipline in the armed forces, that is mutiny. Salazar and Gloria made two. They were certainly...ah...combined, at the time. The predictable effect of sexual relations between people of substantially different ranks is to suborn good order and discipline. We are responsible for the predictable effects of our actions just as if we intended them. There was no evidence put on that Salazar or Gloria had any defensible reason to believe this would not be the effect if discovered, nor that they would not be discovered (though disbelief in discovery was no defense anyway). So: Mutiny.

The penalty is death. As a matter of fact, failure to report or suppress a mutiny by any means—including summary execution— is also punished by death. I guess poor Castro didn't have a lot of choice. If he'd shot them both on the spot he'd probably have been commended.

Unfortunately, he didn't. When the verdicts and sentence came back they were, "Guilty on all counts" and "Death by Musketry," respectively. It took less than twenty-four hours for Carrera to confirm the sentences. There was no appeal, certainly not to an ignorant civil court. The president of the Republic could have intervened, had he so chosen. He did not so choose.

We made up the firing squads ourselves, for Gloria, while the *Tercio Gorgidas* provided the one for Salazar. They were picked, not volunteers. None of us would have volunteered, even if we didn't like Gloria. We couldn't refuse the order, either. Some tribune from *Gorgidas* that I'd never seen before commanded both. The firing squads stood nervously in ranks as the prisoners were marched out of their cells. I understand that of the twelve rifles, two had only blanks in them. That was so the girls and gays who'd been picked to execute the sentences could console themselves that—just maybe—they hadn't really been shooting.

The sky was that shade of deep blue you see just before sunrise. Many times in training I had thrilled to wake up, stand and stretch, and feel the planet come alive around me at just that hour. I didn't feel any thrill now, though. Those of us not in the firing parties stood in formation to one side to witness. I shook. I doubt I was alone.

Salazar took it fairly well. He marched out to the wall under guard but also under his own power. He stumbled, once, but that was just the darkness. Salazar shook his head "No" when he was offered the blindfold (a mistake, by the way; people who are going to shoot you in cold blood get nervous if you're looking at them. Nervous people don't shoot well.).

Gloria had to be carried, tied, and screaming all the way. While Salazar was allowed to stand, and given a cigarette to smoke (yes, we really do that for these things), Gloria was trussed up to a stake. She kept squirming, though. A sergeant pasted aiming markers over each of their hearts, after bending his head to listen for the heartbeat. Salazar shouted out to Castro, "I'm sorry!"

Some large flood lights were lit on the order of Tribune de Silva. The *Gorgidas* tribune shouted, "Ready," and the firing squads lifted their rifles parallel to the ground... "Aim," and the muzzles shifted imperceptibly... then "Fire!" There was a sound like a single shot, but longer.

I saw fluid (blood, I suppose) and bits of flesh shoot from out of their backs to spatter against the wall behind them. Salazar was thrown back against the stake, then fell to the ground. The impact of the bullets twisted Gloria halfway around her stake. She slumped against the ropes that bound her to it. They were both still breathing; we could see that by the flood lights. Salazar seemed unconscious but alive. Gloria was trying to scream, but only blood and an occasional faint "coo" that was probably her best effort at a shriek, came out of her mouth.

The junior tribune ordered the firing parties to, "Order arms." Then he marched to Salazar and shot him, once, in the back of the head, behind his ear. Unlike the members of a firing squad, there are no blanks for the officer commanding them. If you can't kill you have no business being an officer. Salazar convulsed, then stopped breathing. The tribune walked a few more steps, took aim, and shot Gloria the same way. Her body shuddered violently but the cooing that passed for shrieking stopped. It was a mercy.

Garcia marched us away. We didn't sing as we marched. I know I felt sick. I doubt I was alone in that. That night Marta cried herself to sleep on my shoulder.

Castro hanged himself from the limb of a tree a week later.

Was it right, what they did to those two? I've asked myself that question for many years now.

It was such a small thing in itself; what Gloria and Salazar did, I mean. Oh, sure, one or two of us might have pulled an extra shit detail because Gloria had been selling herself for consideration. (Or maybe it would be better said—more charitably said—that she'd been given consideration for giving herself. Didn't matter, the effect was the same in either case.) Still, I'd have gladly pulled an extra detail or two if it would have spared me having to watch their deaths. I didn't like the bitch, not even a little bit, or Salazar either. But I sure didn't want them dead.

Franco called us together after Castro hanged himself, to talk to us. He was ready to puke himself; you could see that. Maybe he was talking to convince himself; I wouldn't know. But there were tears in his eyes. I am certain of that.

"I remember an old line," he began, "something about military justice being to justice as military music is to music. It's both true and false. For one thing, military music can be of a fairly high artistic order, if art is that which causes emotional catharsis. Listen to Beethoven's *"Yorckische Marsch"* sometime, if you don't believe me; or *"Boinas Azules Cruzan la Frontera"* played on war pipes.

"The saying is true, though, in another respect. Military music serves primarily the cause of battle and so does military justice. It is concerned with the rights and privileges of individuals only to the extent that they may also serve the cause of battle. Battle in turn serves the cause of the country. The country, too, has an interest in winning as cheaply as possible, in terms of human life. Next generation's quota of cannon fodder has to come from somewhere, doesn't it?

"Well doesn't it?" He sounded imploring. I think maybe Salazar may have been a friend. Or Castro...maybe both.

"So maybe the question isn't whether it was just to have shot those two for such a trivial affair. Maybe the question is whether it would have been injustice to the country—which is to say, injustice also to the country's soldiers, which is to say *you and me*—*not* to have shot them.

"Maybe you think the Court should have been lenient. Let's suppose the court-martial board had been lenient. Suppose—despite the evidence—it had not found them guilty of mutiny. They could have received sentences of between twenty-five years, for Gloria, and forty years, for Salazar, on the other charges alone; all of that, by the way, being at hard labor, or until they died of it. Prison in this country is roughly analogous to state slavery, after all."

Franco paused, as if not sure to continue. He did continue, though.

"Well, maybe Salazar wasn't the only one of your trainers capable of having an interest in a woman. Hell, I used to have a girlfriend myself. Yeah, it was a long time ago. These things are often relative, not absolute. And maybe Gloria wasn't the only one of us who might have...given herself for consideration. So, don't you see? We *had* to shoot them. We had to."

I thought about that then...I do so still. Truthfully, I don't know that I wouldn't have done what Gloria did. Yes, it was that rough sometimes. In fact, the only ones in my platoon I am sure wouldn't have were Inez Trujillo and Cristina Zamora—they were just too completely soldierly and decent—and Marta. Though she had her own reasons.

"Does it matter," Franco continued, "if a leader is sleeping with a troop? Does it make a difference to an armed force that its leaders are treating some of its troops unfairly because they are sleeping with others? Will those troops being discriminated against have equal faith in their leaders when they suspect that those same leaders care a lot more for some other troops than they do for them? When we're talking about instincts and feelings, does it even matter if the suspicion is valid or merely conjecture?

"There is some justice in equally shared dangers in war. How does a soldier take it when she might be going on an exceptionally dangerous night patrol so some other troop can warm his or her squad leader's bed that same night? How about the third or fourth time they have to go on a really bad mission that ought go to the squad leader's playmate?

"Oh, yes. *Of course,* once a war starts we'll forget all the unofficial lessons we learned in peacetime about our leaders and the way they do business. *Right. Of course.*

"And I'm the Queen of Anglia." Franco shook his head.

"No, Salazar betrayed you and us, both. It was maybe a small betrayal, but it was real. And you would have lost faith not just in him, but—to an extent—in all your leaders, then and in the future, if he'd gotten away with it."

I suppose he was right about that. No, I know he was.

"And the woman? She was actually fairly capable in a lot of ways. She was quite bright. Her political instincts were obviously pretty high, too. She'd sure known where to give—or sell—herself to the greatest effect. Imagine if she'd actually made it past training. Imagine a unit of the tercio led by her. Who might have been next on her list of acquisitions? What would the rest of the girls have felt if Gloria had made high rank based on de facto prostitution while they struggled along just trying to be good soldiers? How long would the rest of you have kept trying, do you suppose?

"Then, too, she'd also betrayed Castro, another soldier; a comrade, who had a right to expect loyalty from any other soldier in the legion. Forget about Castro killing himself a week later. Even if he hadn't committed suicide, he would never again have been the same soldier he had been.

"A pretty good one, by the way. A decent human being, too."

I think about those executions quite often, even now. I'm sorry they had to be done. I'm not sorry they were done.

Of course, the legions have nothing against sex, per se. I have it on pretty reliable authority from a woman who knew *Duque* Carrera in much his younger days that he was something of a satyr. *Presidente* Parilla was worse. Most male leaders are married and many keep a mistress, too. There's no law against it. Most Amazon leaders are married or living with someone of an appropriate rank. And the legions absolutely only care about adultery that really is to the detriment of good order and discipline; with a comrade's spouse or partner, typically, or an underling. A trooper can screw the world and the legion won't care unless it hurts the legion.

Get caught screwing someone you oughtn't, however, and go to the wall. No excuses.

And if there's no chance of your ever going to go into a battle, you have as much right to comment on that as a man does to comment on a woman's right to an abortion. Some, not much.

So, yes, we can play, more or less like real people. That doesn't mean someone can play with us without permission, though.

Last of all the clothing issues they made to us, we were issued our parade dress uniforms. The uniform is still the same, even after all these years. Kilts.

I've always thought that made sense. They're warlike. It can't be said that kilts are really either masculine or feminine. They look good on both sexes. And they are distinctly more flattering to women than shapeless skirts or baggy trousers. I understand Carrera (one of his aides, I imagine, on his—our—behalf) applied all the way to Taurus for a particular tartan—that's the pattern of plaid—for us. Carrera even went ahead and changed our unit name from Thirty-sixth *Tercio Amazona* to Thirty-sixth *Tercio Amazona (Montañera)* in case the Highlanders might object to kilts on other than highland troops.

We did, by the way, get *some* mountain training, though we honestly weren't anything like as capable as Fifth Mountain Tercio. I'm sure there are women out there who could match the *Montañeros,* or even outdo some of them, in mountain climbing, just as there are women who can run, ski, swim, what have you, better than the average man. Do you have any idea how much time those world-class women athletes, or any women who excel at some physical activity, have to spend on their sports? Even the naturally gifted ones we like to hold up as examples spend most of their waking hours in exercise. That just isn't practical for a soldier; there's too much else to do.

The other thing is that kilts—light ones, like ours—are very practical and healthy for women in a hot, muggy climate like we have. The uniform included all the other items of regalia that go with kilts, basket weave handled dirk high among them.

Towards graduation from Basic we were allowed a couple of

thirty-six-hour passes. It isn't generous and isn't intended to be. What it really is, is a half reward and half reassimilation into civil life for those not going to go on to a leadership school. None of us knew, as of yet, who would be going on- and upward, though we made some educated guesses.

A thirty-six hour pass doesn't get you much. You're not allowed to leave the island, even though you could make it to the City and back in theory. But you can catch a movie that isn't either propaganda or training, you can eat a civilized meal at one of the three or four little towns on the island, you can visit the museum at the main cantonment area. You can go swimming or sunbathing on one of the beaches. You can even go dancing, there are a couple of clubs for the recruits, beer only. You can phone home, if you're willing to wait an hour to get to a pay phone.

I called Porras to speak to Alma.

She asked me in her little voice, "Mommy? Is it really you?"

"Yes, Baby," my heart leapt, "Yes it's me."

We couldn't talk long, there being a long line of women behind me waiting to phone their own loved ones. But I did get to find out that Alma now knew her ABC's, could add up to five *plus* five, and really, really wanted to know if the Gonzalez children could live with us when I came home.

A half dozen of us elected to go dancing one Saturday night. Trujillo was somewhat reluctant, but went along to keep an eye on us. She was like that.

We boarded a bus—one ran around "Perimeter Road" every fifteen minutes—and headed for Main Post, near the airfield. It stopped probably thirty times outside one or another of the little camps, like Botchkareva, that littered the island. The bus dropped us off right outside the Enlisted Club there on Main Post.

There was a kilted *Amazona* that I didn't know except by sight waiting outside. She wasn't in tears, but you could tell by the sound of her voice that she really wanted to be, and might have been but for her training. Inez asked what was wrong.

"I came here by myself," she said. "And they . . . grabbed me"— she pointed to her buttocks and breasts—"and laughed about it. Bastards."

"I see," Inez said, without inflection. "I see."

She turned towards the main door to the club, took a deep

breath, and walked forward. We followed her in. She must have known we would.

Do men really act that way with a little beer in them? There were two long lines of staggering drunkards, one on either side of the hallway. Through some wide doors I could see a number of privates lined up along the top of the bar. They were making gestures and echoing commands that, I'd guess, were what troops about to jump out of airplanes did. Not far from the bar someone had pushed together four tables in the shape of a shallow 'T', a chair sat on the leg of the 'T' and one really inebriated sot—he was probably eighteen or nineteen—was waving napkins in his hands. One by one a bunch of the others, arms outstretched like airplane wings, would run up to the long top of the 'T' and either do a belly flop and slide along it (someone had thoughtfully poured beer over the surfaces of the tables to make them effectively frictionless) or veer off and rejoin an almost unbelievably stupid looking circle of others, all of them likewise imitating planes.

I really shouldn't criticize those boys. I once, years later, took my girls to a male striptease. Women can be, if anything, at least equally silly under the right circumstances.

I'd guess that the word had gone out that the *Amazonas* were on pass. The boys along the corridor were waiting for us. I won't repeat their comments, they were demeaning and, under the circumstances, very, very unlikely.

The boys began to chant and clap their hands in time. Unfazed, Trujillo walked forward as if they weren't even there. She walked, that is, until one of them tried to reach a hand under her kilt. (Old joke: Is anything worn under a kilt? Answer: No, everything is in perfect working order.)

I'm pretty good with a knife. Inez was something else. She had drawn her dirk and slashed the boy's arm nearly to the bone in far less time than it takes to tell about it. One-armed, she pushed the gasping boy against the wall, then pinned the offending hand to the paneling with the dirk. Then she stood there in the middle of the hallway, arms folded and calm as could be, and asked, "Who's next, boys? You?" she pointed at one with her chin. "How about you two? Why not all at once? Come on, you're big and strong, you can take on little ol' me. Of course, it might get a little *messy*."

By that time the rest of us had our dirks out, stroking them, and were standing close behind Inez.

I have never seen so nonplussed a group of slack-jawed, bug-eyed men in my life. It must have come as quite a shock.

Finally, one of them, maybe a little less drunk than the rest, said "Cortizo, get an ambulance for Hernandez. Don't call the MPs."

To us he said, "You are obviously not who we were waiting for. Pass, Ladies." His voice added the capitalization.

Inez pulled the dagger from the wall, cleaned it on the boy's uniform, and resheathed it. He fell to the floor when she released his shirt. Then we walked into the dance area unmolested.

Barbaric, no, having to actually fight for one's dignity? Why shouldn't Inez have left it to the law to preserve minimal respect for our persons? Weren't we *entitled*?

Sister, in this world you're not entitled to *anything* that isn't bought and paid for, and then only if you can defend it. I have no doubt that we could have called the MPs. I also have no doubt that we could have ruined the lives of some young men whose only fault was stupidity and immaturity. (I'm glad we didn't. A number of those boys gave all they had, later on, for our good and the country's. You can forgive a lot in someone who died for the country... and for you.)

Then, too, if we had, they would have despised us for it. Maybe that boy Inez slashed and pinned hated us afterwards. Or maybe not, men are funny about wounds. They often don't mind a scar or two. And they've got a sense of justice, most of them, that can accept being slugged when they deserve it. But hated or not, those boys at least knew we were like them, soldiers, warriors.

I think Inez did more for us in that moment than anyone ever had or would.

The dancing itself was pretty uneventful. Only a few boys had the courage to ask one of us. I can't recall that any of us declined. But, much like them, we were mostly too bashful to ask. Silly, no?

Some of them had a drinking contest going on, off in a corner. They didn't invite us and we had no interest in joining. We did, however, watch as—one by one—the boys passed out, semi-comatose. I didn't envy them their hangovers in the morning.

Though the spirit of the competition I found intriguing. We didn't do that sort of thing.

Interlude

"I'm telling you, Balthazar, I quit. I've had it. Santiago was the last straw." Franco's eyes glistened with tears.

"Up yours, *cueco*. Up yours, *cueco,*" the trixie shrieked from its perch.

Franco glared at the thing with hate.

Garcia said, "Oh, stop whining about it, will you? She's dead, Salazar's dead . . . worst of all, Castro's dead. But they're dead. There's nothing you can do about it. It's over."

"No, it isn't. It will never be over. I knew, Balti. I knew before they were caught. And I did nothing. It's my fault."

Garcia shrugged, irritably. "Okay. Fine. Have it your way. It's your fault. I can't for myself see how, since if you really did know, then they were already guilty and just waiting to be caught, tried and executed. But, if so, so what?"

It had been a rhetorical question. Both men knew it. No answer was needed. To cover the silence Garcia pulled a bottle and two glasses from his desk drawer. He poured for both of them, then pushed a glass to Franco.

"You know, in a way, I knew it, too. Oh, no, not that anything had happened. But I knew it would, that something would." He reached into a different drawer and pulled out a mid-sized file.

"These are the last peer evaluations from before the executions. Read them. No, no, forget the rule. Just read them."

Franco read. "My . . . the girls really didn't much like Miss Gloria, did they?"

"Nope. I should have realized they're a pretty sharp crew, some ways, taken the hint and dropped her then. But I didn't."

"Why not?"

"Because I had hope for her, that's why. Or maybe, since I'd already put a lot of time into her, I didn't want to lose my investment. Or perhaps I thought there was a chance to return the lost lamb to the fold. Maybe all those things; maybe something else."

"I don't care," Franco said. "I still want out."

"Permission denied. If you did fuck this up ... or if I did ... we owe these girls something now. And we are going to see they get it. Now drink up, then go walk the barracks."

It wasn't until after Franco had left that Garcia poured another drink and downed it quickly. He wasn't the kind to cry but, *God, if ever I had reason to...*

CHAPTER SEVEN

Ladies do not do *that sort of thing.*
—Victoria I, *Regina Imperiatrixque*

It had begun to feel so *good* to be an Amazon, a sister among sisters. Family.

By the time the women were being given passes there were a bit over two hundred of them left, out of nearly six hundred who had started. That represented pretty heavy attrition, and a heavy expense on the part of the legion. What were left, though, were pretty much pure gold. All the dross had been removed though, naturally, only after first being carefully crushed.

The eight remaining cadre in Maria's platoon, Sergeant Castro and Corporal Salazar being dead, didn't let up on them even a little bit. But, so it began to seem, they didn't have to apply much pressure anymore, either. And, with eight of them for the twenty-seven women left in the platoon, the troops were given personal attention probably unequaled in any army, for either men or women.

They had become quite sharp, those girls, very clever. They knew they were, too.

Each one had gotten to the point where she could navigate in a pitch black jungle, alone—with no one and nothing to guide her beyond a map and compass—and still find her way to within a few meters of where she was supposed to be. Some of them could adjust an artillery or mortar shell almost into a enemy's *lap* in three rounds, often two. They could—because they did— keep the same frozen position under a little bush so perfectly that once someone actually took a leak on one girl's back and never knew she was there. (She knew he was there, though.) All but the very least graceful could slip between two alert sentries without either of them hearing her. They had become very good at emplacing and camouflaging mines and booby traps. They could also shoot, strangle, stab, chop, blow up, burn...destroy; all the womanly skills.

Many restrictions had been relaxed. Still the troops were absolutely *not* allowed to have alcohol in their tents or—when they were permitted to use them—barracks. It became a challenge, of sorts, because there was a beer machine not two hundred meters distant from Maria's platoon's hut. The entire area, to include around the machine, was patrolled by *Gorgidas* privates and corporals, day and night. One whole platoon had been given eight hours' hard duty for trying to get some beer from the machine and into the barracks. Getting at that beer machine had become a matter of pride.

It was arguable whether the Seventh Platoon girls had ever put as much planning into a tactical mission in the field as they did into the mission to raid that beer machine. Eighth Platoon, the pure lesbians, found out what they were planning and insisted on joining in.

"Fine," Inez said, when the two representatives from the Eighth had shown up unannounced. "We needed a distraction anyway. You're it." The two girls from the Eighth just nodded. They were Sonia and Trudi who had formed a pair bond and would be, effectively, married upon graduation.

The women had built a terrain model, an earth, moss and stick representation of the compound, not far from the barracks, in the woods and out of sight of the cadre. The leaders of the enterprise, and the two lesbian girls, had crawled on their bellies to get to it the night before the raid. Four ponchos were snapped together and lay over them to keep in the meager light from the red-filtered flashlights.

It could, and did, get awfully hot with nearly a dozen people crammed in like that. This was the final rehearsal.

"All right," said Inez. "One last time...the time is 0210."

"H-Hour. Teams A and B are down in the pits," they chanted softly. "Pits" was slang for *under the barracks*. "We crawl like worms to the drainage ditch...Team C digs the hole!" They had seen something like this poetic mnemonic technique in one of the war movies the cadre showed them in a steady diet, usually with snide comments for spice.

So what if it wasn't good poetry? They were soldiers, not poets.

Inez pointed with a stick at a couple of twigs laid over a long indentation in the model. "0222?"

"We're under the bridge that spans the ditch." Earlier the girls had, in fact, timed how long it took them to low crawl to the ditch—twelve minutes—under the guise of practicing their craft on their own initiative.

Sonia and Trudi whispered together, "Eighth Platoon begins to brawl, a lovers' spat that breaks some walls."

"0227?"

From everybody: "*Gorgidas* runs to break up the fun."

"0230?"

"Inez and the chicks await in the ditch. Maria and Marta head for the switch. Security!" Maria's job, and Marta's, was to cut the lights in the compound. There was a breaker box on a light pole not far from the footbridge. They also had an extra lock to make sure the cadre couldn't turn the lights back on any time soon. The rest of Team A, Cat and Isabel, had left and right look out: "*Security.*"

"0235?"

"The lights go out. A new fight breaks out. Eighth can't tell among friend or foe. *Gorgidas,* sadly, takes many a blow." The women giggled a little over that line.

"0236?"

"Inez and crew charge for the brew."

"0246?"

"The suds are stowed in the laundry bags. Who says the Amazons are just young hags?" Yes, poetry was not their forte.

"0251?"

"Marta, Maria, Inez and crew are back in the ditch with a beer for you. Pull in security!"

"0253?"

"Crawl away home."

"0307?"

"The beer in the bags goes down in the pits. The girls go to bed while the cadre have fits."

"0310?"

"Mission complete 'til next we meet." They planned to leave

the beer under their barracks overnight, then drink it when the cadre weren't expecting anything.

Inez smiled. "Good. Very good. But there's one last thing. You know how revenge isn't so sweet if the person you rape doesn't know he or she has *been* raped? Well..."

0210. H Hour. No plan ever survives contact with the enemy.

It started well enough. Faces painted black and green, all the raid team crawled without problem, though not without effort, to the ditch, then hid themselves in a tight cluster under the footbridge. A funny thing, adrenaline; they reached the footbridge almost ninety seconds early, then waited nervously for Eighth Platoon to begin their part.

From the direction of the barracks, "You lying, cheating bitch!" reverberated through the camp. That was Sonia! This was followed by a scream and the sound of breaking glass. The volume quickly rose to a crescendo of violence.

Marta snickered, "Say what you want about those girls; they can act!"

The raid team heard the pounding sounds of men's feet on the little footbridge. The guard had abandoned the area near the machine. So far, so good.

"Come on, Maria. Isabel and Cat, go!" Marta tugged Maria to her feet, quite unnecessarily. While the other pair split to right and left, Marta and Maria sprinted for the breaker box. Maria carried an iron bar in her hand. Marta had the spare lock.

The sound from the Eighth Platoon was just beginning to die down as the pair reached the box. Not a lot of time left. Maria pushed the bar part way through the lock and twisted. It held until Marta threw her weight into the problem. Both hearts thumped when the metal of the lock split with an audible crack.

"Do you think they heard? If they did, we're screwed," Maria commented.

"Not likely," Marta answered. "And not by *them*."

The two had never seen the inside of the breaker box. It had two levers inside. Marta reached into it and flipped both of them. All the flood-lights died, but so did every light in the camp, including the lights emanating from the beer machine.

"Fuck!" Marta returned one of the levers to its upright position. The floodlights came on; the beer machine sat dead. Marta fumbled and brought the machine back up; but the floodlights were still on. With a curse she turned the floodlights off again.

What had sounded like a fight in Eighth Platoon's barracks turned into a riot. Men's shouts were intermixed with women's.

"Sounds like a lot of fun."

Inez and her crew padded past, almost silently heading for the beer machine. Marta and Maria dropped to their bellies and watched as best they could by the dim light of the beer vendor. Everything seemed to be going according to plan, when they saw Inez start thumping her head against the machine.

Maria had a sudden blinding flash of the obvious. " 'Exact change,'" she said. Marta looked at her quizzically. "Inez's team only has single note bills to feed to the beer dispenser. If my guess is right, we're fucked."

"No we aren't." Marta grabbed the iron bar and began to sprint to join the other team. Maria followed.

"Screw it," Marta announced when they reached them. "Like Inez said, the point is to get the beer and get away with drinking it, not to avoid being punished later on. We can prop the door shut for long enough to do that."

The machine was secured shut by another lock, no better than the one on the breaker box. Into this Marta pushed the end of the bar. With both girls leaning on it, the lock split. The door swayed open.

Inez thought about it for a moment. "As for the lock...that lock is cheap. We'll take six less beers than we planned on and leave the extra money to pay for a new one."

The other grunted their assent. They were sneaks, and proud of the fact. They weren't mere vandals or thieves.

To Maria, Inez said, "You and Marta go back per the plan. We can handle the rest...and, Marta, good thinking."

As it turned out breaking the machine open saved them a lot of time over feeding bills into it one by one. It was much quieter, too. All the raiders reassembled in the ditch nearly three minutes early. Then they crawled back to the "pit" under their barracks where a hole was ready made to throw in their soiled uniforms, along with the all-important beer, and bury them. Team C, Zamora's girls, with ponchos laid to keep the tell-tale dirt off, buried the loot while the rest of the raiders cleaned up—quietly—and crawled back to bed, to pretend to sleep.

✧   ✧   ✧

It was daylight before anyone else figured out even a part of what they had done. The cadre hadn't figured out quite who, of course. It could have been any platoon, or even all of them together.

Unfortunately, it was pretty obvious that Eighth Platoon had been in on it up to their ears. They were given a mercilessly shitty day, one harking back to the first days in training. But—good girls—none of them ratted.

About noontime, some one of the cadre found the broken lock for the beer machine. They found the money that had been left, too, and duly reported it. Everybody else's day rapidly became miserable, too.

The *Gorgidas* searched high and low. All of the barracks were ransacked; the troops' personal effects also, such as they had. The cadre looked in every nook and cranny of the place. Zamora's people had camouflaged the stash well, however. The cadre didn't notice anything amiss. Perhaps part of the reason that they got away with it was that their stash was in such an obvious place.

The cadre did find the terrain model on which they had done the planning out in the woods nearby. (Inez: "Shit! Big mistake. Forgot. Damn! *Always* erase your terrain model before going on a mission." Zamora: "Don't sweat it, Inez; everybody makes mistakes.") The diagrams on it led almost straight to the guilty platoon, though it could have been any of three others, plus the Eighth.

Oh, did the cadre torture the women from those five suspect platoons. Grass drills, pushups, running laps with their rifles held overhead...and that nasty trick where the women got in position for pushups and, when the sergeant blew his whistle, threw their arms to the side and head back, thereby letting gravity beat their tits against the gravel...over and over and over again. Ouch.

This lasted till long after midnight. Finally, the cadre grew tired of it and sent them to sleep.

Of course, some of the women didn't go to sleep. After lights out, and with aching muscles, Zamora's team crawled below to retrieve the beer. One bag went next door to the Eighth, while the others were divided out among the raiding platoon, one beer per girl. They had a few to send to each of the other platoons, too. Six of them crawled on their bellies to deliver the beer. An apology? More of a victory statement.

They had the beer. They had won. But then, go figure, they were all too afraid at first to open them. Maria's sat on her chest, unopened, while she lay in bed.

"Fuck 'em," someone finally called out. "They can only kill us; they can't eat us."

Marta bellowed, "Too tough! Besides, *they* wouldn't like it if they could."

Some other girl yelled out, "Hell, they wouldn't know what they were doing if they did!"

From Eighth Platoon, across the maniple street: "None of *them* do, gay or straight!"

Then someone else, yelled, "In Caaay-dennnnce...Pop!"

There was a barrage of beer tabs being pulled, escaping gas, and giggles. (Well...men giggle, too, sometimes.) It seemed like hundreds of pops; though there were only about two score left between both platoons by then. Maria popped hers with the rest; then laughed for many, many minutes. The beer was too warm, but more delicious than any she could ever remember, then or after.

A pleasant woozy feeling engulfed Maria; half beer, half victory. She saw something, something she would never be quite sure of. Still, she thought she saw a shadow on the window by her bunk, a shadow that looked a lot like Centurion Garcia. The shadow seemed...somehow...to be smiling.

Inez had told them, "It wouldn't be *right* for us to hide what we've done. It would be...*cowardly*. So every one of us is going to leave her empty can at the foot of her bunk, precisely centered. Zamora, you stand at one end and line them up by sight, just like it was a parade field. Then we'll take whatever unopened cans are left and place them in a neat pyramid just outside Garcia's office, a gift to our trainers."

It was an article of faith to the women that Garcia never really smiled. And, indeed, they'd never seen him really smile with mirth, not once. But he came in the next morning, took one look at the empties, another at the pile outside his door, then went into his office. But even with the door locked, and despite what sounded like his best efforts to strangle himself, they could still hear him laughing 'til he nearly cried.

When he finally emerged, stone-faced as usual, he held a lock and key in his hand. Swinging the lock around his index finger, he announced, to no one in particular, "I happened to notice, as I came in this morning, that the vending machine over by headquarters needs a new lock. Take care of it ... and ... tidy up the barracks, filthy girls. Meanwhile, I have a small wager to collect from Centurion del Valle." He dropped the lock and key to the floor, bent to pick up two cans, then left, whistling some martial tune.

Maria thought then, as she was to think later, *damned shame he's not straight; he'd probably make a fine father.*

But Garcia was to die, too, and all the children he ever had were the Amazons, that first crew and the sisters who followed. But then, they were pretty good kids, who followed in their old man's footsteps.

Graduation exercise ... "the wringer."

Oh, that wasn't the official name. No one ever called it by its official name. To one and all, male and female, it was simply, "the wringer."

It began about one on a rainy morning. The Amazons stood in the rain, covered only by their wide-brimmed jungle hats, helmets slung by their straps on their canteens. Ponchos were really superfluous: they could be wet from the rain, or they could be wet from sweat and then stink besides. Just plain wet was better. But the training schedule had said: "Uniform: Field with ponchos." So thus it had to be.

Garcia, similarly clad, called the roll. It was a ceremonial thing. He called, "Fuentes, Maria?" She answered, as she had to in order to take the test, "Private Fuentes; willing and able, Centurion."

No test, no graduation. No graduation and she could either resign or do the whole damned last month and a half over again. Worse, she would have to do it with some girls she didn't even know.

On their backs the women carried a scaled down load: full water and ammunition, but only minimum essential equipment and only one ration apiece. "Food would be provided," they'd been told. They had also heard through the rumor mill that "food would be provided" really meant that *some* food would be provided ... intermittently ... maybe ... if they did well.

The first part of the test was a march, thirty miles in twelve hours, combined road and cross country. No big deal, really, especially with a reduced load. They could all do that, they figured, if not quite standing on their heads.

A training unit's own cadre wasn't allowed to lead them on the march. It was a test of how well the cadre'd done as much as it was of how good the recruits were. Instead of the usual cadre, the School of Infantry on the Island had a testing board. They would set the pace, noting any who fell out.

Before turning the platoon over to those SOI men to lead the march, Garcia told the platoon to, "Stand at ease." Then he said, simply, "Good luck, troops." He hadn't ever called them "troops" before, never before called them anything but in a tone of voice that *meant* "twat"—and *that* unusually pejoratively. Perhaps it meant something to him when he finally did. It surely meant something to the girls.

Garcia then called them to attention, did a smart about face, reported to the testers, "Seventh Platoon, Training Maniple, *Tercio Amazona,* 'willing and able.'" Then he'd marched off to the side.

The tester—his stick said he was a senior centurion though under the poncho no one could see his name tag—showed them a map of their route. It wound through the Island then stopped near the ocean on the east side. When they'd had a chance to see their route, the tester ordered them to, "Right ... Face," then, "Forward ... March."

The first few miles weren't bad. Maria noticed, though, that her socks were wet with the falling rain. No problem for the first few miles, but, when the testers inevitably picked up the pace, she began to blister. Within the first ten miles, her feet were just areas of bleeding, oozing pain. Every new step was an agony.

She had a chance to change her socks midway through. She had to peel them off carefully because almost all the skin and callus of her feet had been torn off. Dried or tacky blood stuck the socks to the open flesh. Each little toe was deeply abraded. It made her a little sick. It was one thing to see someone else bleed; she'd gotten used to that. But to see the damage to her own body? Yech!

She wasn't the worst off among them, either.

It was a horror to pull new socks on over the wounded flesh. The foot powder she put on in a vain effort to control the damage burned. There was neither time, nor materials, for more than that. She screamed out loud in pulling her boots back on.

Struggling back to her feet was pure hell, every muscle in her legs screaming in protest.

The next fifteen miles represented roughly thirty thousand individual steps for each of them. Each individual step meant effective vivisection of uncountable raw nerves as the material of the socks (even the dry socks they'd put on were soon soaked with blood and crud) and the boots rubbed against their poor tortured feet. Then the long drawn out flash of burning pain as they set one foot down was followed by pain of a slightly different quality as they lifted the trailing foot for the next step. Like crucifixion, hard marching varies its agonies so one can never quite grow used to them.

Unlike their own cadre, the men leading the march did apparently feel sympathy for them, did see them as real women, real people. They couldn't slow the pace; a standard had been set they were under compulsion to have the Amazons meet. Nor were they allowed to help the females carry anything; that would have been a violation of training regulations so gross as to call for a court-martial. Instead, they—some of them—suggested the girls give it up, fall out and fail. "It's better than what you're going through," they said. There was a truck trailing the column to carry those who couldn't make it.

Couldn't make it? The *Amazonas*? Oh, no. They could and would, bleeding or not. Just as they'd called encouragement to each other, they heaped scorn on those men who suggested they drop out.

They were proud of each other that none of them took the testers up on that truck. They all knew pain by then, some them knew the pain of a long and difficult labor. All pain ends, in time.

Inez whispered, "But pride... pride lasts forever."

In time, the road march portion of the test ended. For so long as she lived each woman would always recall the joyful cries of the leading ranks as they shouted, "The sea! The sea!"

It took rather longer for the pain to go away.

There was food, water (blessedly cool) and medical care waiting for them as the march ended. The medics did what they could to bandage the damaged feet. But, when the entire foot is wounded, bandages can't help much. Still, the antibiotics they layered on were probably an aid in the longer term. Infection in tropical Balboa could be dangerous.

The women slept well, more or less dead to the world, before beginning the next phase. That wasn't so bad; a lot of tests of individual skills and small unit tactics. They did as well as an equivalent group of men, perhaps a bit better. This phase took three days, time for their feet to partially heal. Then came the next-to-last phase, the "sickener." The "sickener" was weighed very heavily in selection of leaders but failure to complete it wouldn't cause failure in the course. It was almost optional.

That, too, was a march, only across country. The Amazons went by hovercraft to the real jungle, a godforsaken place near the western border, in the *La Palma* jungle. The trip across the bay was really wonderful, very fine. Everyone was in great spirits, singing and laughing. Why not? It was almost over. And they *had* graduated.

They didn't know how long this "sickener" was to be, or how fast they had to go. *Still*, they thought, *it couldn't be as bad as what we'd just been through, even with our feet still in ruins.*

They'd have thought right, too, except for one little thing or, rather, one class of little things. Those sat on the ground in front of each Amazon. They were steel, four pointed, and big enough that they couldn't be fit into a rucksack.

Each weighed about thirty pounds. It had sharp edges, designed to dig into the shoulders. It was also uneven, cleverly designed so that there was absolutely *no* way to carry it in a reasonably comfortable and balanced position. Just to add insult to injury, the son of a bitch had loose pieces of steel inside to rattle around and make a most annoying racket. Its official name was "Nausea Inducer, Steel, Four-point, Projecting, Class B (female)."

They each had their own, to carry and to name. Trujillo called hers a "bitch."

They picked up the "nausea inducers" and moved to the start points. Each of the women had a map and a compass. They also had a point in the jungle, two to three miles away, to which they had to navigate. No two girls both began at, and had to find, the same points. There wasn't any company on this one, no one to help them in mind or body. Each girl was on her own, for most of them in a way they hadn't been in their lives.

"You ready to go, *chica*?" the sergeant asked Inez when she reported to her start point.

" 'Private Trujillo, Inez, willing and able,' Sergeant." she echoed.

"Very good, Private Trujillo. From this point you will navigate on your own, without assistance or encouragement, carrying one 'nausea inducer,' to a point on your map as marked. There, you will be given a new map with a new point to navigate to. I can't tell you how many points there are to your course, so don't ask. I can't tell you how far the course is, so don't ask. I can't tell you how fast you have to go, so don't ask. Any questions?" He smiled, not precisely evilly.

"No, Sergeant. That pretty much covers everything."

"Yes, it does. Private Trujillo, I mark the time as 06:48 hours. Good luck. Go."

Between the condition of her feet and that horrid chunk of steel on her shoulders, she couldn't run. She moved out as quickly as she could while still keeping her balance. The "bitch" ensured that she would not always be able to keep her balance.

It wasn't all that hard finding the first point. She fell a few times; her "bitch" cut into her shoulders continuously. Still, it wasn't too hard.

At the first point, another sergeant checked Inez's name off of a roster, then handed her another map, taking back the old one. "A bit slow, Private Trujillo. I don't think you're going to make it."

Inez didn't bother to answer. Throwing her bitch back on her shoulders, she half-trotted even farther into the jungle before slowing down to a more practical speed.

Even before reaching the third point—of who knew how many?—her bitch had actually succeeded in taking her mind partly off the puffed up bloody terror of her feet. The way it cut into her shoulder, wore down her arms, dug into her back or chest when she lost control of it (which was happening with increasing frequency)—above all, the goddamned rattling of steel on steel right into her ear—she began to really feel sick to her stomach with frustration.

Nausea Inducer? Oh, yeah.

At the third point the grader, this one was a corporal, said to her, in a voice dripping with concern, "Girl, you look like you've had about enough. Why don't you knock off and take a break? There's some coffee here, food. You can rest your feet and back for a bit and think about whether it's worth keeping this shit up."

Inez answered, "With all due respect, Corporal, please give me the next map and please, please ... Fuck Off!"

She didn't know it at the time—wasn't thinking all that clearly, anyway, actually—but troops were allowed a certain latitude of expression on a "sickener."

The corporal laughed, not unkindly. "Here you go, *chica*. But it won't get any better."

She looked at the map. It showed her she could follow the very ridge she was on for two and a half kilometers, then descend two hundred and fifty meters to a creek. From the creek she could go a very short distance north to a small bridge. From the bridge she could shoot an azimuth—take a direction with the compass—and walk, maybe run, less than four hundred meters to the next point. She re-shouldered her bitch and took off.

"Oh, the dirty, dirty bastards," Inez muttered.

The ridge was fine. The creek had been there. She had, in fact, followed it for a while, frankly not paying enough attention. There was *no* bridge. They'd given her a doctored map. She didn't know anymore exactly where she was. She'd been *counting* on that bridge.

Trujillo suddenly felt sick, sick, so very sick. *I am going to lose time. I might fail. I don't even have to be doing this.* She sat by the side of the creek and wept for a while.

Great things, tears. A man might not have wept. He also might have given up right then; no outlet for frustration. Inez didn't give up. She dried her face of tears and sweat, picked up that horrid chunk of steel, and walked as quickly as she could back to the last place she'd really known where she was, a spot beside the creek at the base of the ridge. Then she inflated her rubber air mattress and paddled herself and her "bitch" to the other side of the river.

As Inez was sitting her tiny frame on the air mattress to deflate it she had a borderline brilliant thought. She got off of the air mattress immediately and blew a little more air into it. Then she took some cord and tied the mattress so it cushioned the bitch.

Oh, it was hot and sticky after a while. But it dulled the sharp edges and—blessed relief!—dulled the damned noise. She took another compass bearing and began a fast walk uphill to the fourth point.

At the fourth point two sisters from different platoons sat with hanging heads and downtrodden expressions. The sergeant there offered them some cool water. They refused.

"Why don't you join them, Private...Trujillo?" he asked. "They've done the smart thing. You look like a smart girl. You should join them, give up on this shit."

The girls wouldn't meet Inez's eyes.

She didn't trust herself to say much of anything to the sergeant beyond, "Map, please, Sergeant."

The next two points, numbers five and six, were uneventful. She took the piece of map that led to point seven and looked at it. *There is no way I am going to reach it—even near it—before sundown.* She didn't mind sleeping in the jungle, except for the snakes, and the unthinkably nasty *antaniae*, but she'd never been out there completely on her own before. She was pretty sure she didn't like the idea.

The corporal at the point tossed her a single ration before she departed. As he did so he said to her, "You're doing okay. Don't listen to the ones who tell you different. And don't tell anyone I told you."

"Thank you, Corporal," she said, and meant it. "I won't."

She made it about halfway to point seven before night fell, pushing on to use every last bit of daylight available.

Inez didn't bother putting up a poncho to sleep under. She put up the net against the mosquitoes and the moonbats. She also had a can of bug spray and doused herself liberally with that, then rolled up in her poncho to go to sleep.

Snakes and moonbats notwithstanding, the jungle is really not an especially dangerous place. But it can sound that way. Between the howling monkeys, the occasional splash in any nearby body of water, the cries of all manner of wildlife, a person can lie awake all night with worry. And, while the septic-mouthed *antaniae* gathered, with their cries of *mnnbt-mnnbt-mnnbt,* they rarely attacked anything that wasn't terribly young and weak.

As Inez was starting to drift off she felt a certain warmth at the corporal's few kind words of encouragement.

Then she sat up with a start. She *knew.*

The son of a bitch had just said those things to lull me into complacency. I'm not doing "Okay." No one in my shape could be doing all that well.

She was up in a flash, stowing what little bit of her gear she'd broken out. Her compass she set by the filtered glow of her flashlight. Then she shouldered the whole stinking load and began to weave her way as close to point seven as she could, given the fact that she tripped about every third step.

She remembered something Garcia had once said just before a much shorter navigation exercise, "By the way, did I mention that, while you're safe enough in the jungle at night—if you stay in one place—there are any number of things out there that will kill you if you blunder into them?"

Trujillo was scared to death at each step she took. Every time she reached a hand out to grab a vine it was an act of will to make herself touch it; snakes hang from trees, too.

I don't like snipers or snakes.

The sun arose the next day to find one terrified, exhausted, scratched and generally bruised Inez. Nor did she dare to take a break. A few hours later she came to point seven. There was a centurion manning that point.

"Private Trujillo, this is not bullshit. Your next point is seven and one half kilometers away. It is probably not your last one. You are moving too slow to meet the standard. I suggest you hurry."

"Just what the hell do you think I've been doing, Centurion, dawdling?" She just took the map without another word. *God, it really is nearer to eight klicks away.*

Inez alternated walking and semi-jogging with only the briefest of halts to check her bearings. The heat and humidity were nearly unbearable. *How does the weather god know when it is most miserable to rain, most miserable to shine? He must read our training schedules.*

With the pace, the load, her previous exertions—and some blood loss, too—she began to feel faint. She kept pushing on but she only barely kept on course.

Finally, she saw it, off in the distance and in the open; a jeep with a couple of troops lounging around. She fixed that image in her mind and concentrated on putting one foot in front of another. She staggered; she fell. But she just kept getting up to push onward. The jeep seemed impossibly far away.

As Trujillo drew closer she saw that were more people there, lying on the ground, unmoving. Closer still and they showed as girls, more than half a dozen of them. She couldn't help thinking that whatever it was they said or did to the women at that point it was enough to make a large number of them quit. She began to cry again. But she kept walking.

Inez fell to her hand and knees. The damned bitch came loose from the air mattress to gouge her back and make a long ugly scrape down one arm. She stopped briefly to pick it up, then staggered back to her feet. She held the bitch by one hand, the air mattress by the other. Still weaving from side to side, she barely discerned that the girls that had been flat on their backs were sitting up. Some dim part of her mind might have registered the fact that *they* didn't look defeated.

She fell again and crawled.

At the edge of a little clearing she got up on both knees, then swayed to her feet, and said, "Private Trujillo, Inez. May I have the next map, please?"

Cristina Zamora came up and put an arm around her, holding her up and squeezing her tight in shared triumph. "No more maps, Nezi. You made it."

Not everybody did. Almost two thirds had given up before reaching the end, or let someone convince them that they were doing just fine and slacked off thereafter. They would graduate. They had missed an honor, though, and the chance to become leaders.

Not everyone who didn't make it quit or failed. Three were dead. One fell into a ravine and broke her neck. One died of heat stroke. Another . . . well, they never found her body, though they found her pack and *nausea inducer*. She probably drowned, or was eaten. Or both. Most likely, both.

Some time later, when Inez was in charge of a group of fighting women, when she was all alone, scared, tired and miserable, when she had to win a fight first with herself to make herself go on before she could make anyone else do so, she had cause to remember that "sickener."

The test wasn't quite over. They spent two days searching for the bodies though they only found two of them. Then, after a few hours rest they moved to a broad river and waited for transport. The same hovercraft came back to take them back to the island for their graduation exercise. This was nothing much, a series of platoon attacks on an "enemy" strongpoint, using live ammunition. The only reason they did it was so the president and some of the Senate, plus *Duque* Carrera—and, via TV, the rest of the population—could watch them go through their paces.

After that they went back to barracks, cleaned up, and turned in such of their gear as belonged to the training base. The uniforms, rifles, and individual equipment were theirs to keep forever. They even had a full two days to recover and rest; that, and prepare for graduation parade.

In the old days, before the legions had begun transforming themselves from a regular force of mercenaries or, depending on one's definitions, auxiliaries, into a national army, the *Isla Real* had been home to approximately fifty thousand soldiers and their families. Now, the bulk of those regulars had moved to the mainland to provide the cadres for reserves and militia formations, and even the numbers of troops present had shrunk to under twenty thousand, mostly people in training plus maybe five thousand regulars with their families present.

Even so, a large percentage of those that were there had turned out to watch the official formation of the *Tercio Amazona* and the graduation parade of its first members. Carrera was there, along with a select committee from the Senate and his wife, Lourdes. The president was not there.

"And so," Carrera asked of Senator Cardenas, chief of the select committee, seated next to him on the reviewing stand, "will the Senate pay for the two tercios? Now that you've seen them?"

"We'll . . . pay for them," Senator Cardenas agreed, with bad grace. "But the special uniforms and the statue are on you." He pointed with a chin at a bronze, life-sized statue of a woman. The work suggested a beautiful bone structure but with skin roughened by the chisel. She sat atop a rock, clad in partial abdominal armor of an extremely archaic design. The woman was grasping weapons—bow, spear—in her hands. Her upper body was exposed, leaving her breasts bare. Except that she didn't have *breasts*. One of them, the right one, was excised, as if by a rude scalpel and fire. Only the bronze simulacrum of scar tissue remained.

"Very good," Carrera said genially. "I wanted the kilts and the statue to be my personal gifts, anyway. My thanks to the Senate. And now—"

He stopped speaking as the pipes and the drums of the training base band marched out from the right as the reviewing stand faced and onto the close-cropped, emerald green parade field. The band was followed by eight tiny platoons of about twenty to twenty-four women each.

The women were dressed in kilts, with white ruffled shirts and light waistcoats above. Their feet were encased in heavy shoes, with hose held up by garters over their calves. Atop their heads each woman wore a Glengarry, cocked to the right, ribbons hanging down free behind. It had never been made a part of their dress uniform, but each of the women had, apparently by mutual agreement, posted a large red flower over her left ear.

Lourdes bent her head to whisper something in her husband's ear.

Carrera nodded, looked at the flowers and smiled, mostly to himself. *Good, very good.* Then he stood to receive the report.

The band counter-columned off to the left as the platoons of women left-wheeled to face the reviewing stand. The adjutant for the training base took the report from Tribune de Silva, then turned and reported to Carrera, "*Duque,* all present for the induction onto the legion's rolls of the Thirty-sixth Tercio."

"Post the orders," Carrera said, then stepped away from the podium.

"Pursuant to Legionary Headquarters directives of..."

While the adjutant was speaking, Carrera stepped off the reviewing stand and looked around at the front of its base. There, carefully tended, were some extensive flower beds. He ignored what was going on around him, while he selected out a particularly large and beautiful red blossom, then plucked it, leaving six or more inches of stem.

He walked to the statue, and waited, listening for the adjutant to say, "...the Thirty-Six Tercio of Mountain Foot, *Amazonas,* is formed and called to the colors."

On the word, "colors," Carrera stuck the red blossom behind the statue's left ear.

Then, still smiling, he walked back to the podium, took it over from the adjutant. He gave Lourdes a wink and began, "My beautiful bitches..."

Interlude

"Are you happy now, Patricio?" *Presidente* Parilla asked. "You've proven your point. At ridiculous expense you've gotten—what is it?—maybe a maniple of women who might, just might, be able to do something besides scrub pans, type, or change bandages. Now what? Shall we turn them into a ceremonial unit?"

"These girls deserve better than that, Mr. President," Carrera replied. "You saw them, too. I know you were watching. They're remarkable. And you *know* they are."

Parilla shook his head. "What I know is that they're a colossal waste. But they might look good for propaganda's sake; guarding some monument, say. Or swirling those silly kilts you gave them in a parade."

Carrera hesitated, trying to find the words. *I could threaten to resign. That would get his attention. He knows there's a war coming and that he can't win it without me. But, no. He may need a commander ... but I need a president ... even more than I need the Amazonas. If I threaten to resign, and he knuckles under, he won't feel like a president anymore. Shit!*

At length, Carrera said, "Make a wager with me, Raul. The girls have done everything we ask of a foot soldier. Let's see what else they can do. If they can't crew the heavy weapons found in an infantry tercio, I'll back off. We turn them into parade troops ... but not pay the girls off and disband their unit."

Carrera's voice grew impassioned. "I'm not telling you they'll be better than men. They may not be as good. But they deserve the chance to try. Just let them try, won't you?"

Parilla looked at Carrera intently for a moment, then said, "Sweeten the pot, Patricio. If these women fail to be able to use

every weapon found in an infantry tercio, I want them turned
into a ceremonial unit. And then I want your goddamned queers
disbanded. If your bitches can't do it, to include shitting their own
leaders, I want *Tercio Gorgidas* to go away. Then maybe I can forget
about the shame of having 'married' the bastards. And don't tell
me it isn't fair. *Gorgidas* trained them. They've had their chance."

Carrera slowly nodded. "Agreed. Every weapon in an infantry
tercio." *Fifth Mountain Infantry Tercio,* he silently added.

Before Carrera left, Parilla asked a question. "Patricio, why do
you even care? What do you expect to get from these women?"

"More men!"

"Bah!" Parilla answered. "And what is this about wanting to
create a new nongovernmental organization for the care and
feeding of refugees of war?"

"All part of the plan, Raul, all part of the plan."

CHAPTER EIGHT

Every experiment is like a weapon
which must be used in its particular way.
—Paracelsus

Maria:

Basic may have been over, but they were far from finished with
us. There was still a tercio to build. Carrera came to speak with
us shortly after graduation and laid it all on the line. Yes, we'd
done well. Yes, he was *very* proud of us. Yes, we had to learn to
use every weapon in a mountain infantry tercio, and demonstrate
that we could use them under combat conditions, or we were a
footnote in history.

At least he was honest.

Life, however, became much, much better. For one thing, they
moved us out of Camp Botchkareva—which was needed for the
next group of girls to be trained—and into a really nice little
caserne, one the Legionary Housing Directorate had renamed
"Camp Penthesileia," a couple of miles down the road and right
on a small beach. This was, I gathered, an old senior tribunes'
housing area from when the entire legion had been on the island.
It was a lot bigger than we needed but there was a housing glut
out on the island anyway.

Each squad had its own house, not plush but certainly nice,
and infinitely nicer than the tents and huts of the old camp. There
was a common mess, or maybe it had been an officers' club at
one time, as well as kitchenettes in each squad hut. The officially

provided food didn't improve, but then, it had always been pretty decent. And not having to choke it down with barely enough time to chew was a definite plus. Nice, too, was not to be surrounded by barbed wire. And we guarded ourselves, for a change.

Well, why not? We were real soldiers by then. And I'm sure I would have pitied anybody who came in uninvited.

Best of all, our FG's brought our kids out to those of us who had kids. They stayed right with us in our squad huts; sleeping in our beds or rooms. The sweet, sweet smell of my baby in my nostrils as I drifted to sleep was . . . well, no words.

Over the next few days Marta grew a little sullen. I wasn't sure why that was so but, acting on a hunch, I sent Alma to sleep with her one night when I had guard. Poor Marta really needed a baby so badly. Within two weeks, Alma was calling her "*Tia* Marta."

The FG's cared for them while we were working. I sometimes remember those days as the best times of my life. I had my kid, all my best friends still, useful—even important—work to do.

Not that it was all work. We used to have beach parties about every third night. Did I mention how cheap shrimp and lobster were on the island? We pooled our mess rations and supplemented those from our pay to eat and feed our kids like royalty.

We rotated with the cooking in the huts, though we usually had breakfast in the common mess and packed a lunch. There were a half dozen civilian cooks for that. Eventually, the *Tercio Amazona* would have its own regular cooks but, for now, we were too rare and—just possibly—too valuable to detail any of us to those duties permanently.

On the other hand, Cat was one fine cook; maybe better said, First Cook. She took charge in the kitchen of whoever was detailed to evening mess duty and *showed* them how to do it.

Except me. I can almost burn water, frankly, so I did my share by helping prepare the meals and cleaning up afterwards.

Occasionally we'd have men over, though not to stay. Group living and individual sex just don't go together—too much noise for the others to sleep (at least if the parties know what they're doing. I really didn't, frankly, but then I didn't try to have anyone stay over with me either). Besides, for those girls who just had to, there was a very romantic beach a stone's throw away.

Before going any further, I probably should tell you a little about a legion infantry tercio, since that is what we were to become, or to try to become. Its name comes, in part, from an old Spanish word that means, essentially, regiment. We didn't take it merely for that reason, however. A *tercio* also implies a third, *tercer*. Ours are divided up into three, oh, echelons: Regular, Reserve, and Militia. The regulars of a tercio are one third the number of the reservists. Regulars and reserves together are about one third the size of the militia. That is to say, about six percent, plus a little, are regulars, full-time soldiers. About nineteen percent are reserves on call at any time, but owing only seventy-seven days service a year in time of peace. The rest are militia who are also on call, but only owe twenty-five days a year unless called up for war or other national emergency.

It was a variant on Zion's militia system, I learned later.

It would be many years before we would be large enough to form a real tercio, so what I will describe is the size and shape of a fully mobilized tercio of men. As I do, remember that the cohorts and maniples of our tercio were to be thirty percent bigger in field strength, to give us more bodies to do the physical work, and that one hundred and thirty percent strength would be augmented by an additional, compounded, thirty percent to allow a portion of us to take maternity leave. So we would, eventually, be one hundred and sixty-nine percent the size of a male tercio, assuming there were enough really tough and willing women in the country. Or in Colombia del Norte, since we recruited from all over.

In a tercio there are three infantry cohorts, each consisting of three infantry maniples, a (heavy!) weapons maniple, and a headquarters and support maniple. The infantry companies have three infantry platoons, each with three rifle squads and a weapons squad, and a weapons platoon with three mortars, six medium antitank weapons, another two .34 caliber medium-heavy machine guns, plus a small headquarters.

The weapons maniple had heavier mortars, 120 millimeter as opposed to 81 millimeter, either eight recoilless rifles or eight light armored vehicles for antiarmor work, an antiaircraft section with light surface to air missiles or antiaircraft guns or a mix of both, a reconnaissance platoon, sappers, forward observers to call for and adjust artillery and mortar fire, or air support, on the unlikely chance we should have any. There was a small headquarters there, too.

The headquarters and support maniple had the cohort headquarters section and the two staff sections. These were I: Operations, which includes a section each for operations, logistics, and intelligence (entitled Ia, Ib, and Ic respectively) and II: Personnel administration. There were also a communications platoon—messengers, radios and field telephones—a medical platoon, and a platoon each of cooks, mechanics, and truck drivers, a couple of whom drove fuel trucks. The HSM commander had a tiny little section to help him command.

Beyond the three infantry cohorts, there was a combat support cohort that had an HSM, either a Cazador maniple or an armored cavalry troop for reconnaissance, an engineer maniple, a light tank maniple, and an antiaircraft battery. (A maniple and a battery are basically the same thing, but artillery is always in batteries. The armored cavalry, but not the armor, call their maniples, "troops." Yeah, I think it's silly, too.) If it was a mechanized infantry tercio, there was no light tank maniple, but there was a full cohort of medium—forty-five or so ton—tanks.

At legion level—most other armies would have said "division level"—there was also an artillery cohort available to be attached to each tercio (though ours would instead be an organic part of the *Tercio Amazona*). It could have three batteries of either *very* heavy mortars (160 millimeter!), mostly for the Marine tercios, 122 millimeter self-propelled guns for the mechanized infantry, or light, auxiliary powered (they had a small engine mounted to move them short distances) 85 millimeter guns for the infantry. These made excellent antiarmor weapons, at least against medium armor, too, by the way. The artillery cohort had a headquarters and support battery, as well.

The headquarters and support cohort of the tercio had companies of personnel administrators, military intelligence pukes ("self-propelled oxymorons," we called them), communications soldiers, medics, mechanics, truck drivers, supply rats, and a headquarters detachment. The recruiting maniple, training maniple, and band were also assigned to the headquarters.

If a tercio was to be reinforced by its share of its legion's heavy stuff, it would pick up another engineer maniple, along with companies of medium tanks, heavy (forty-two ton) self-propelled tank destroyers, and a heavy antiaircraft battery. Possibly it might also get a cohort or two of heavier artillery pieces and rocket launchers.

All in all, it came to about forty-one hundred soldiers for the men, without being reinforced by legion or with their normal artillery cohort, a bit under seventy-eight hundred for us. That includes having our own artillery cohort. Maybe sixteen hundred of those could be expected to be on maternity leave at any given time.

That was if, and only if, we were ever to be allowed to expand to a full tercio. Carrera had made clear that this was a matter of some doubt in some important circles. Sure, we had been trained to be pretty damned good light infantry. This said precisely *nothing* about whether or not we could handle other weapons and pieces of equipment. It was a great looming question mark hanging over our future.

About a third of us had been picked to go to Cazador School. That was the *sine qua non* of being promoted to centurion or officer rank. Only one girl who hadn't completed the "sickener" was picked for Cazador School, and she had crawled three miles dragging a broken leg before passing out just short of the finish. Not everyone who *had* finished was picked.

Some of the others had to be trained on different jobs for the tercio, clerks to cooks, medics to mechanics. We had anywhere from three weeks to three months to wait for those schools to begin. The legion kept us on active duty for that time. The rest had been "asked" (*sure* we were!) to volunteer to take part in some experiments to see what, besides infantry, we could and could not do.

It was something of a shock, after the sheer brutal meanness of our training cadre in Basic, to be treated so... *pleasantly* by the men who taught us how to use, to the extent we and they could, the heavy weapons. I think this was because of three different factors. One, we really were soldiers now; part of the team, albeit an uncertain part, so there was no real need for condescension or reason for contempt. Two, we were sharp, alert, and on the go, more so than an equivalent group of men usually were. The instructors probably appreciated that. Three—let's be honest—we were damned cute after all that exercise, and with our hair beginning to grow back and our skin to heal. And *these* instructors were straight.

They sent us a female tribune. There were still a few holdovers from the days when political connections could get you a commission and the old Civic Force had been less selective about commissioning people than the legion was. She wasn't a real soldier, though. She knew it, we knew it, and she knew we knew it. Her name was Claudia and, I suppose, for the merely administrative crap she had to do she was adequate. To be fair, I understand she also wasn't a bad Intel analyst, not to say that kind of work takes a real officer or anything. But we never respected her at all; she wasn't one of *us*.

Someone we *did* respect was the temporary first centurion they sent to keep us in line. He was a straight male, seconded to us from the *Tercio Santa Cecilia*, the place where the disabled and mentally retarded did their service. Centurion Robles had lost the use of the lower half of his body in a training accident, smashed spine. That's how he ended up in the TSC. Despite that, and even bound in a wheelchair, he kept us on a tight rein. He divided us into the groups that would rotate through the various experiments the legion wanted to run on us and managed the whole thing.

They began my group on medium and heavy mortars. Curiously enough, it wasn't the heavy 120 millimeter mortars that gave us trouble. They were too heavy for *anybody* to really carry any distance. So was their ammunition. That's why the 120's were all truck- or mule-borne, with extra trucks and mules for the ammo. While the chunks of the mortar were heavy, we could and did find techniques that let us set them up and use them quickly enough to meet the legion standards.

The lighter mortars—the 81 millimeter jobs—really were a problem, though. They were light enough, barely, for a group of men to backpack along with their personal equipment. And a maniple of male infantry could carry enough ammunition to make it worthwhile to have the mortars on hand to support them.

The men could also carry the mortar's forty-two pound bipod, even with all their other gear, without too much trouble. We just couldn't, not indefinitely. We tried having two of us carry the bipod. That didn't work; it wasn't big enough to allow two of us to get under it and still walk. We tried switching off between two of us very frequently. That didn't work either; with everything else the load was just too heavy even for the brief time someone had to carry it. The 81's turned us to rabble fast.

We could, and did, sling the bipods on a pole, just like we'd

slung our sick sisters' personal gear during Basic. Like then, it was
a misery. It was also much slower getting the mortar into action.

Inez asked one day, "Well, why not dispense with the 81's and
just have us use 120's?"

Our instructor answered, "Don't be silly, girl. The reason they
don't give trucks for the 81's is that they are *supposed* to be back-
packed; to go into places, firing positions, where a truck wouldn't
reach; to support their rifle platoons wherever those platoons
might go. 120's can't always do that; and their range isn't all that
much better than an 81's. And *forget* the notion of giving you 60
millimeter mortars. You would be the only ones with them and
supply would be too much of a problem."

Carrera had given us a solution, though it was a solution not
without its costs. The legion gave us mules, the only mules on
active service outside of Fifth Mountain Tercio, to help us carry
the damned things. They could march almost anywhere we could;
almost anywhere the men could. The cost? About four hundred
drachma an animal, plus feeding and caring for the surly critters.
The *Tercio Amazona* became one of only three tercios to need a
veterinarian on its strength.

(I later heard that there was something of a tiff between Carrera
and Parilla over the mules. But, since Parilla had approved—or
been tricked into approving—our being designated as a mountain
tercio, he could hardly complain about our having the same mules
the Fifth Mountain had. Yes, Carrera *was* a sneaky bastard.)

The last mortars they tested us on were the 160's, both versions,
Zion's and Volga's. The legion has both, though it is slowly phas-
ing out the Volgan ones except in fixed fortifications. Both were
flops, as far as we were concerned. The Volgan gun was too heavy
for us to hope to set up in action, though once it was set up we
could load it without too much trouble as it was a breechloader,
with the breech low to the ground. The Zioni gun we could set
up, barely, but we simply could not lift those ninety pound shells
up to the muzzle to drop them down. Christ, a number of us
weren't *tall* enough to reach the muzzle, not even on tippy toes.

We could use both the mortars found in a cohort, the 81's and
120's. That was something.

We also found that the recoilless rifles used by male tercios
were too heavy for us. The solution: more mules. That really

wasn't so great a solution, though. It's tough when an enemy tank stumbles up on you and you have to spend extra minutes trying to unpack your gun and ammunition. Well, we could hope they would be gentlemen and give us time. Fat chance. Well, it was our own chance we were taking, wasn't it?

The next experiment was in artillery. We started on the 85 millimeter guns. It's funny, but *firing* the guns is the easiest thing about them. Digging them in, camouflaging them, above all carrying and breaking down the ammunition for firing, were much, much harder. But, with crews of eleven women (nothing less would do) instead of the usual eight men, we could manage quite well, really. You *know* they were not going to give us any men to do the heavy work.

I understand that one of the world's major armies did an experiment on using women to crew artillery pieces, but actually had men do all the setting up, digging in, camouflaging, carrying and breaking down of ammunition, etc. The women just loaded and fired the guns, which were mostly the lightest ones available. I can't imagine what that proved, other than the ability of any army to make a bad idea look good, through sheer weight of effort and duplicity practiced routinely and on a heroic scale.

We also found we could serve the self-propelled 122 millimeter guns. That was the outside limit of our ability, though. The 122 millimeter rocket launchers were impossible, we could not lift the rockets high enough to reload the launchers. They weighed more than some of us did, even with the extra muscle we'd put on. The towed 152 millimeter guns were beyond us for the same reason the rockets were; the ammunition was too heavy. The guns were too heavy also, really. The same proved true of the 180s.

We could *use* the 152 millimeter self-propelled guns just fine; they had flick rammers and so did most of the work themselves. It was decided, rightly I think, to call that experiment a failure because, while we could crew the things perfectly well in action, we could not lift the ammunition into the stowage racks inside the turrets. Fat lot of good a gun is, after it's run out of ammunition, if its crew can't reload more. And, after one woman had to be invalided out of the tercio line and made into a clerk because she kept trying until she ruined her back (tough girl!), the powers that be simply wrote off any further attempt to turn any of us into medium gunners.

The Force has three kinds of tanks. We still call them Ocelots, Jaguars, and Pumas, even though the latest ones don't bear an exact resemblance to what we had way back when.

The Ocelots are light amphibious "tanks." Really, they were not intended to be used as tanks, even light ones, having been designed as infantry fighting vehicles. They're a Volgan design, modified by us. Every standard infantry tercio has a maniple of them, twenty tanks. Even with the armor we've added on, they weigh less than twenty tons, about the same as a Great Global War medium tank. Ocelots could move pretty quickly across the land, and at a respectable speed in the water. They mounted a 100 millimeter gun, which can fire a useful antitank missile as well though, because of terrain factors, we didn't use the missile much. With a full crew of three women, we could fight those things just fine. Maintenance was tougher, but still possible.

Don't get the wrong idea; when an Ocelot ever meets a real tank in battle, head on and in the open, what you will have is a dead Ocelot and three dead Amazons. But, for the other work of supporting the infantry with machine gun and cannon fire that can't be easily suppressed, or the odd antiarmor ambush, they are superb.

There was something the instructors told us that you might find interesting. We were *better* tank drivers than the men. They were head-shakingly emphatic on that point.

Why? In our country, most men know how to drive a car. That means they have already acquired a mindset of fairly civilized driving habits before the legion gets them. Most of the *Amazonas,* on the other hand, didn't know how to drive a car before enlisting. That meant that we were in no way as restrained as men tankers were. We also didn't have habits that, while quite appropriate to driving a car on the highway, were equally inappropriate in driving a tank across broken ground with people shooting at you. We could, and did, put those tanks through paces that turned some of our male instructors white to see. Provided you don't break your neck, it's a lot of fun jumping a tank over a ditch... or doing one's bit to prevent forests.

On the other hand, when the first thing you learn to drive is a tank, it can have adverse effects on your driving when you finally do learn to drive a car. Check the statistics: *Tercio Amazona* tankers are the bar-none, absolute *worst* civilian vehicle drivers in the country, possibly in the world. Not one has ever gotten a job as a heavy truck driver, though some of our non-tanker women have.

The Pumas and Jaguars should have been even easier than the Ocelots. All three have automatic loaders, so even though most ammunition for the 125 millimeter cannon weighs about one and a half times what an Ocelot's does, it didn't make any difference, for loading purposes. But the Ocelot's missile, as opposed to the high explosive round, had to be hand loaded, which is a bitch.

The auto loader does have a distressing tendency to load arms, shoulders and heads instead of shells. Ah, well, there's a price for everything.

It is a pity, don't you think, that tanks crews have to do more than fight their tanks?

Problem number one: Automatic loaders—like all other pieces of complex machinery—break down regularly. For whatever reason, tank autoloaders broke down a lot more often. When that happened, we could not load the main gun, the cannon, by hand, as quickly as the men can and sometimes must. This was true even though the ammunition comes in two parts, projectile and propellant, that are loaded separately.

Problem number two: Automatic loaders, again. They are called robust. That just seems to mean they are heavy. When one broke we couldn't lift or move the things we had to in order to get at it to fix it.

Problem number three: The tracks on which the tanks moved. When a set broke, or the tank threw one off—both of which happened with frightening frequency—the crew had to fix it. This is, even for men, a difficult operation. What three average men could, just barely, do, three unusually strong and robust women could not.

Why didn't we add a fourth crew-woman to the tanks? Honey, where do you propose we put her? The inside of those things is already cramped beyond belief. I doubt, too, that even four women could fix the track on a Puma or Jaguar. Six sometimes could, under ideal conditions.

Yes, I know, I know. We *did* use the crews of two or three tanks when we were in the motor pool. Sadly, tanks throw their track at other times and places; times and places where the rest of the tanks can't stop to help one. Battle.

So, although it had been proposed that the *Tercio Amazona*

have a maniple of heavies as well as lights, that thought died a richly deserved death. For the same reason, we were never given any of the heavy self-propelled tank destroyers, the SPATHAs. Well, Fifth Mountain didn't have any either. So?

Could we have combined the *Gorgidas* and *Amazona Tercios* to make a small brigade or division which could use all those weapons? Yes... probably, but there would have been a price to pay. Could we have dispensed with the idea of a segregated regiment and had men crew the heavier weapons? Just maybe, but at an even greater price.

You've got to understand the ideology of a regiment. It isn't a sausage casing, a dead animal's intestine, into which one grinds up and stuffs people to make them fit a mold. Besides, anyone so lacking in character that you can make him or her fit a mold isn't worth the effort. All you've got is the appearance of something and then only under pressure. Apply a different pressure and you'll get a different appearance. Apply the pressure of a line of enemy tanks and infantry with malice in their hearts coming towards that woman and the appearance you'll get is of the woman's—or a man's!—back as she runs away.

Franco had lectured us on this in Basic, at length, in one of our relatively few formal, prepared lectures.

"A regiment is a home, a family," Franco had said. "It is the largest real family of which mankind is capable. It has its own religion: Courage, fortitude and the traditions of its past feats. It has its own martyrs and saints in the always remembered spirits of its brave, honored dead. Its members look toward *its* future as their guarantee of a kind of immortal life after death.

"The regiment is selective as to who it admits as family members. Not everyone can fit. At a bare minimum, those who are allowed in must be such as will not disgrace the regiment. That is why the regiment is initially brutal to those who would join it, to quickly and efficiently drive out the weak and the meek who might some terrible day bring down the regiment.

"But from those who can fit into the regiment, much can be tolerated, as any family tolerates its own eccentrics, to include those whose eccentricity is to be unusually creative, courageous, and good. Armies which have no true regiments, being fragile things, held together only by the weak forces of law rather than the insuperable ties of habit, custom, and genuine emotion, cannot tolerate eccentricity in any meaningful and useful form. Without a natural binding force, a special base to hold their members together, these armies must impose an artificial, unnatural and mindless order that stultifies the best in their members.

"A regiment must have a special base for its existence. Among professional, long service armies, that professionalism can provide that base. For others there must be something else.

"Most of the regiments in the legion are geographically based. To take the Second Infantry Tercio as an example, nearly every *Rio Abajano* naturally thinks his *barrio* to be the best in the world, however poor in monetary terms. So, too, must be its regiment. And he will certainly try to make it so. Also, one cannot run and hide from one's roots so easily. Disgrace in his regiment will follow him so long as he remains in that neighborhood. Disgrace in the regiment amounts to internal exile for life.

"For my regiment, the *Tercio Gorgidas,* our base of existence, our unique quality, is our gender orientation. Whatever you may think of it, whatever anyone may think of it, to the soldiers of the *Tercio Gorgidas* it is natural, normal, and preferable. And when we are together in our regiment we need neither hide it, nor be ashamed of it, nor defend it against others.

"And because that is important to us, indeed the most important thing to many of us, it is extremely important to each of us that we do everything in our power, every day we may do so, to make this thing which legitimizes our lives, this wonderful family home, our regiment, a shining pillar of military virtue. We simply want our family, our home, to be the best.

"By the way, deep down, most of us consider you others to be somewhat perverse. Certainly distasteful.

"Other regiments have other bases. For the *Tercio Santa Cecilia* the base is composed, partly, of their handicaps but, more importantly, of their overcoming of those handicaps.

"For you, your base will probably come partly from your sex; probably more importantly from overcoming what many consider the traditional limitations of your sex. Also, in a way that neither a geographically based regiment like the Second, nor a regiment like mine, can hope to be, yours is to be a truly elite regiment, excluding not merely those who might someday fail, but taking in only those who are certain to be great.

"It *is* possible to mix and match, to put people into any regiment or any position in any regiment that some bureaucrat or social engineer thinks is a good idea. From a strictly military point of view, however, to do so is not preferable, at least when one's army is composed of other than long service professionals."

Franco paused here, contemplatively. "Social engineering can work, of course. The problem is the social engineers. Compared to any decent maniple commander—or especially a good first centurion!—they are, wherever in the world you find them, utterly arrogant and contemptibly incompetent. To say that they are also mindlessly doctrinaire would be an excess of praise.

"We, too, could use the legion for that kind of social engineering. We could mix up you women, the men of *Gorgidas,* straight men, the handicapped, women less capable than you . . . ad infinitum."

He gestured at one of us, Isabel, as I recall. "What would happen then?"

Snapping to a rigid attention, Isabel answered, "Why, I imagine we'd all get along and work together, eventually." She ventured a query. "Wouldn't it be a good thing, Centurion, if all people, everywhere, looked past superficial differences and just learned to accept people as they are? Wouldn't mixing us up do that?"

"Sit down, girl," he said, not unkindly. "Do you know anything of the history of social engineering in this century?"

From her seat, Isabel shook her head "No."

"Whenever you throw two different types of people together, and the difference can be amazingly tiny, you tend to get a ruin. People who have lived and worked side by side for decades will rob, burn, rape, and butcher each other with gleeful abandon. Look at the former Volgan Empire where, despite powers of coercion to change people beyond even Centurion *Garcia's* wildest dreams, people are recognizing their differences, throwing off ties decades and centuries old, and often butchering each other."

Isabel raised her hand and, recognized, stood up again. "Centurion, what about the Gallic Foreign Legion? They're as racially and culturally mixed a group as you could find, anywhere. And they are, I've read, very good soldiers."

Franco smiled. "In the second place, there have traditionally been no majorities in the Foreign Legion. Even the Gallic members, and they are not usually—quite—a majority, are often forced to hide their citizenship. Therefore, there is no group with which a legionnaire can identify with so well as the Gallic Legion as a whole.

"But in the *first* place, what the Gallic Legionnaire identifies with—and probably in most cases has since childhood—is not any cultural or ethnic group, but the identity of 'soldier,' in this case expressed as 'Legionnaire.' To him, this is what makes a human being. And all who cannot claim that title are not even people, unless they're closely related by blood or marriage. The Legionnaire accepts the men of the legion, primarily because he has rejected the human race.

"Moreover, having now had some time to study integration, the sociologists are leaning towards the view that integration does not always increase tolerance, acceptance, and understanding, but often just the opposite. Which shows that even a monkey—or a sociologist—can learn. Why, some of them are even beginning to realize that racial intolerance exists in all races. That's one of the major reasons integration fails. People who haven't a shred of prejudice to begin with will soon learn some if they're put next to people of different races who reek of it."

Isabel, still standing, gave it one last try. "The Federated States seems to have done well with integrating their military and using their integrated military to better race and gender relations in their entire society."

Franco smiled coldly. "Have they? Why then does their army still need a large and intrusive bureaucracy to continually preach for better race and gender relations? Why special days, weeks, and months for every little group? Why do those who most fervently believe in social engineering insist that their society is as racial strife torn—and gender strife torn—as it ever was after fifty years of tearing it apart and rebuilding it, or trying to, in accordance with the social engineers' prejudices?

"Oh, I'll agree with you that, among their real military professionals, race is a non-factor. But that's because, like the Gallic Legionnaire, the real military professional down south has accepted other soldiers as brothers—whatever their race—only because he has rejected the human race!"

Franco raised a quizzical and cynical eyebrow, matching it with an even more cynical smile. He looked over us with something approaching amusement, and what I think was contempt directed at the Federated States.

"Be it noted, however, that our Federated States Army professional has not really accepted most of his female peers as sisters, also quite irrespective of their race. This is reasonable, because, unlike you, they are not being turned into equivalent professionals.

"Of course, under the stress of actual war, it is by no means uncommon for people of different backgrounds and beliefs to become as one. This is especially so because the soldiers are faced with an enemy who is always, *always* felt to be something other than quite human. The problem, however, is that armies exist in peace and prepare in peace for war. Without that other-than-human enemy to focus attention away from their internal differences, the soldiers cannot entirely bond as they should if there are real, however trivial, differences between them. This may well get fixed after the first *overly* bloody battle, but I wonder how many more of them die than have to because their regiments were subject to principles of social aesthetics rather than sound military ones."

Franco chuckled. "You know, if a research doctor of medicine tried to do with research subjects what the social engineers want to do with soldiers, fair minded people would be protesting in the streets. They would demand—at a bare minimum—informed consent on the part of the subjects before those subjects took part in health- and life-threatening experiments. By God, a doctor who did something like that without consent would be vilified, called a Fascist, hounded from office!

"But let a social scientist—and isn't that an oxymoron?—conduct experiments with the lives of mere soldiers and no one cares. Except in our country, of course. We really do care."

Franco smiled slightly. "Let's go back to the social scientists, shall we. In fact, let's just consider their impact on an armed force. Better still, let's contrast them with *Duque* Carrera.

"The social scientists love people like me. *Duque* Carrera does not, especially. The social scientists dislike soldiers. *Duque* Carrera loves soldiers. The social scientists have done precisely nothing enduring for people like me, except to make people who otherwise wouldn't give me a second thought actively despise me. *Duque* Carrera has set things up so I can be married, with all the benefits that go with marriage. *Duque* Carrera has put me in a position where I needn't hide a thing. Indeed, I can be proud of it *because* it is the mark, the stigmata, if you will, of a very proud regiment. *Duque* Carrera has made a military organization of my people that will, I am certain, if we're ever called on to fight, prove our worth to our people in a dramatic, memorable way. Social scientists would have us scattered, irrelevant, powerless, unremarkable.

"So who's done more for me? For you?"

So, no, while we could have been mixed up with others, we could never have been as effective as individuals, and the groups—the tercios—we formed could never have been as effective as we were on our own, or they were on their own. It was a simple fact: as *Amazonas* we could be proud of ourselves and of each other. As mere sexless numbers filling a space in the table of organization, we could hope, at best, to be proud of ourselves individually, and then only if the fact that we were the physically weakest members of our units didn't rob us of that pride.

Maybe it is true that integration makes a better civil society. I wouldn't know. Our society is really pretty homogenous, compared to some others. But I have wondered, from time to time, why it is that those who most insist on the celebration of diversity are also those who seem to most wish to make everybody as alike as two peas in a pod. And fail to do so. Miserably.

Interlude

The legion's *Escuela de Cazadores* had moved around a bit over the years. Currently, it was split between four locations, for the four phases of the school. Two of these, headquarters at Camp Gutierrez and Camp "Greasy" Gomez, had been relocated to be not far from the legionary base at *Lago Sombrero*. The mountain camp, Camp Bernardo O'Higgins, was up in the mountains, between Hephaestus and Boquerón, in *Valle de las Lunas* Province, not all that far from Camp Spurius Ligustinus. The last, once simply called, "Jungle Camp," and now known as "Camp Mitchell" was far to the west, deep in the jungles of *La Palma*.

The base at *Lago Sombrero* was bisected by the east-west running highway. The highway, itself, was bisected by an airstrip that ran approximately north to south, with the northern end hard by the cantonment area. It was at that end that Carrera's Cricket came to a halt and it was at that end that a tribune, Thomas Broughton, met him.

Broughton was of average height or slightly above that, compared to the Balboans. For a retired veteran of the Federated States Army, he would have been considered a bit on the short side. He was also a prick, though that didn't derive from his stature, but just came naturally. Carrera had hired him more than a decade before, to run the legion's leadership selection course, "Cazador School."

Carrera dismounted from his Cricket, a high-winged, single-engine, monoplane with amazing short-take-off-and-landing abilities. He pointed the pilot to a spot where he'd meet the plane when his business was done. The spot was just a little grass plot, a few hundred meters away and pretty much out of anyone else's way. The pilot nodded, but waited for Carrera to get well away from the plane before beginning to taxi over.

Broughton met the *Dux Bellorum* at the edge of the strip and led him to his vehicle, parked on the other side of a dividing barrier.

"How far is it to this briefing?" Carrera asked.

"Mile, maybe," the tribune answered.

"Let's walk then; fucking Crickets are cramped. We can talk while we walk and, who knows, maybe we can skip the fucking slides. Besides, you sent my aide the packet and I've already been through them."

"Your call," Broughton agreed, then stepped off to lead the way. The driver of the vehicle pulled in behind them and followed up the road at a walking pace.

Carrera spoke as he walked. "The key question, Thomas, is how you are going to make this thing possible for some of them, while not making it so easy that any of the not-quite-good-enough get through."

Broughton shook his head doubtfully, then answered, "It's going to be tough. It's going to be very fucking tough. Ever since you laid this thing on us we've been wracking our brains. And we don't have a perfect solution. I'm not sure there even *is* a perfect solution."

After a brief hesitation, Broughton continued, "We don't want this to be like what the FSC has done; sending policewomen to a short, nearly stress-free patrolling course run by the Ranger Department at Fort Henry, then letting those women live with the illusion that they've somehow gone to Ranger School."

Carrera scowled. "No; it's got to be real. It may not be the same as what the men do, but it *has* to be real. And the problem is that we really don't know what these ladies are capable of. No one knows. We expect you to find out, actually."

Broughton nodded again, saying, "Yeah, but we might find out it can't be done. Or not very well.

"We apply four stresses here: Starvation, sleep deprivation, hard physical work, and fear, both of injury or death and of failure."

Carrera rolled his hand to indicate, *Yeah, yeah, I knew that. Get to the point.*

Broughton understood the gesture. "Right. We believe that sleep deprivation will affect the women about the same as the men.

"Starvation is trickier. The women will be smaller, with less need for food and greater fat reserves to begin. We are either going to have to starve them more, or starve them longer for the same effect. Or load them more to make the starvation come quicker, though I *strongly* recommend against that. Right now we're leaning towards starving them longer, giving them a longer course.

"That, by the way, sir, is going to play hell with our schedule.

"The physical work? We know they won't be able to do as much; it's silly to expect they could. Their basic training cadre was very clear to us that these women are great . . . but they cannot do what even an average group of men can do in the strength department. And this school is for men who are far above average."

"Mules," Carrera answered.

"Sir?"

"Let them use mules, one per squad, to help carry the load."

"If we do that, sir, we are going to be getting very close to what they do up north, creating an illusion of equality that will shatter as soon as people find out the difference."

"Then crank up the other stresses. You can make the course longer; tough luck for the schedule; work your cadre harder, task the Fourteenth Tercio for some bodies. Cut the girls' food even more. Cut their sleep even more. Make the live fire exercise at the end worse. Grade them harder . . . Kill a few.

"And don't forget this. The purpose is to select the best women. If you can chop their numbers by more than half on more food and sleep, you can give them more. If you have to shoot at them, starve them, or deprive them of sleep more to get rid of half we don't need, then do that.

"This is an art, not a science," Carrera concluded. "Or maybe not even an art but a crap shoot. Some people make a decent living throwing dice around."

CHAPTER NINE

Bent double like old beggars, under sacks
Knock-kneed, coughing like hags, we cursed through sludge
'Til on the haunting flares we turned our back
And toward our distant rest began to trudge.
Men marched asleep ...
　　　　—Wilfred Owen (KIA, 1918), *"Dulce et Decorum"*

The hovercraft to take sixty-three of the women to their next phase of training, Cazador School, had come hours early. Why not? Today's schedule wasn't that tight, the girls were reputed to be rather attractive, to hold really great beach parties, and—what the hell?—the hovercraft crew was male. Straight male, as a matter of fact.

With a whine and a lot of foam-churned surf and flying sand, it settled down between a short, straight line of piled duffle bags and other individual equipment, on one side, and a life-sized bronze, nicknamed "Hippolyta," with a freshly cut red flower stuck in behind her ear, on the other. As the engines growled down, a different sort of whine announced the lowering of the boarding ramp. A few minutes later, five men emerged, the apparently oldest of whom asked, brightly, "Did you ladies call for a taxi?"

Marta, not wanting to be pulled from her friends a moment early, started to shout, "Fu—" when Inez Trujillo stopped her.

"Two of them are wearing Cazador tabs," Trujillo said. "Intelligence is always worth gathering."

"Ah ... right," Marta agreed, then called out, "We can toss a few more kebabs and some lobster on the grill. Come on over, boys. Grab a couple of plots of sand."

Catarina took the hint and, grabbing one of the other girls, walked briskly in the direction of the kitchen.

"I thought most warrant officers didn't go to Cazador School," Inez said.

The chief pilot of the hovercraft stopped gnawing on the kebab he'd been given, tore his eyes off Marta's ample chest, and answered, "We don't, most of us. The procedures for warrant officers—doctors, lawyers, chaplains, some pilots and other technical specialists— are a little different. People with special skills—lawyers, doctors, nurses, chefs—just need to have their professional certifications and complete Basic, and a not-so-very-hard warrant officer candidate course, and they're in. Some, though, people who have both the technical skills and independent command of a combat force, which, as a matter of fact"—the warrant waved his kebab in the direction of the hovercraft—"*that* is, do have to do Cazador first. Us, pilots, submarine crews. Also doctors, lawyers, nurses, and chefs that want to be in charge of groupings of their specialty do, as a prelude to OCS or CCS. A few others."

His attention reverted to kebab and kabosom.

His copilot, a younger sort, left off picking at the lobster tail he had on a paper plate balanced on his lap, and added, "The road to authority takes a sharp uphill bend with Cazador School. That's true whether you end up leading infantry, overseeing trucks, or driving a boat."

"What's so hard about it?" Cat asked, from her post by the grill.

"Cazador School?" the younger warrant asked. "Imagine going for about three months on a ration that the World League High Commissioner for Refugees would sneer at. Then add to that a tremendous load of hard physical work and fairly continuous pain. Almost no sleep. And you're *always* uncomfortable."

The older one gestured at Marta's breasts and said, "Kiss those goodbye, honey. Everyone's going to lose about twenty to thirty percent of body weight. You won't have an ounce of fat left."

"And the sleep deprivation," said the younger. "You're going to be zombies, the walking dead." He looked up at Catarina, hopefully. She, nodded, smiled, and then deposited another lobster on his plate.

"You can expect," he added, "to have under two hours per night. That's average; it's possible to get none at all for two or three days at a time."

One of the other crew, one without a Cazador tab, said, "That's what got me. I washed out; I just couldn't take the lack of sleep."

"No shame there," the younger warrant said. "Only about half the men who go make it. And they're already a pretty select lot."

"Did they send you guys here to discourage us?" Marta asked suspiciously. She remembered the "sickener."

"You girls asked us for the unvarnished truth," the senior hovercraft driver said. "Since you're feeding us, we're not going to lie to you. It's *hard,* hardest goddamned thing I ever did in my life, bar none.

"And throw in, for good measure, danger. Sometimes it's only apparent and you won't know it is. But sometimes it's real, too. You can get killed or crippled there. Happens all the time."

"And you're going to be afraid of failing," said the younger. "I think that's the worst fear of all."

Trujillo already had an answer from her brother, but she wanted a second opinion. "If it's that bad, why do it? Why make it such a choke point in leader selection?"

"Will you settle for a personal opinion?" the senior warrant asked. "Okay, then. Mostly, because it works. Part of that is that only the tough, smart, dedicated, and competent make it through. But that's only a part. The school builds character; the tough became tougher still.

"It will also tend to teach you a lot about yourself, about your personal weaknesses and limitations.

"An ancient Zhong general, on Old Earth, said, 'Know your enemy and know yourself and in a hundred battles you will never be in danger.' You *will* know yourself when you're done, to include a lot of things you would probably rather not know."

Inez went silent for a moment to contemplate that.

"But you'll learn some good things, too," the younger warrant said. "Up to a point, the more you face danger the easier it becomes to face. You'll face a lot of danger and you'll learn to deal with it, to make yourself go on despite it."

The elder warrant then said, "It isn't about the learning or the training though. I went to the school with people who said, 'I'm only here for the training.' None of them made it. After the first month or so there really isn't any new training; it's all an endurance test. So they dropped out. See, Cazador School isn't about skill. Oh, sure; it will teach a little of small unit tactics, but it isn't all that important. Then, too, what it teaches tends to be pretty simplistic."

"Okay," Inez asked, "if it isn't the people who are there for the training who make it through, then who does make it?"

The warrant chuckled, "Mostly the last people you would expect; the people who are there for the sheer bloody *glory* of the thing. When all else fails, girl, when you think you can't keep your eyes open another minute, can't walk another step, and can't take another second of your stomach's complaining... remember the *glory* of the thing."

All thing pass. Good things just seem to pass more quickly. That final party on the beach passed more quickly than most.

With the sun setting to the west, two of the moons, Bellona and Eris, arose in their quarters. The hovercraft crew disappeared up the ramp, with many thanks to the women for a free feed. A line of Amazons formed and, with strained grunts, began moving the baggage across the sand, up the ramp, and onto the hovercraft's deck. No one had to tell them to do it; they knew teamwork now. Others among those staying behind plopped small metal covers onto tacky tiki lights ("Hey, they're tacky but they keep the bugs off.") to smother the flames. A few grabbed buckets and began hauling water from the sea to dump on the fires.

With many a tear, the girls remaining, temporarily, at Camp Penthesileia bade farewell to those who were leaving now, the sixty-three slated for Cazador School. Over the next week, others would be going to different places, ranging from the field medical course to the mortar course.

Cat was going to a short machine gunner's course and then home. She didn't mind that, in itself. She was already in charge of a family. That was personal responsibility enough, she had told the ones moving on and possibly up. But she wept over little Inez like it was her own baby being torn from her.

Inez took it very hard, too, being split up from her best friend in the course, her substitute mother. They'd been best friends all through Basic. Now Inez would be alone.

"I'll write, I promise," Cat told her.

"It won't be the *same*," Inez answered, in a voice breaking with sorrow.

Spontaneously, Cat took out a picture of herself and her family.

"This is all I have to give you, little one. Take it. Maybe it will help. And remember, I'll be thinking of you...of all of you."

Sometimes the mountain must come to Muhammad, when, say, Muhammad is up to his chin in a sea of paperwork. Thus, while Carrera had made time to visit the *Tercio Amazona* several times in the course of their training, he just couldn't make time now. So the girls got off the hovercraft on the same landing platform from which they'd left for the island, unloaded their crap, then promptly reloaded it on the buses designated to take them to *Escuela de Cazadores*.

An officer—Maria recognized him as the aide de camp Carrera had sent her to—boarded and said, "Ladies, you have one stop to make on the way. I'll be leaving you there and someone else will be giving you a little talk."

The buses took off with screeching airbrakes...

...to pull through well-guarded metal gates that fronted on the main highway leading east along the coast road.

Inez, sleeping in the back and startled awake by the turn, glanced at her watch. *Hmmm...ninety minutes, give or take. I wonder what's ninety minutes west of...oh, shit.*

Even as Trujillo thought it, a whisper went down the bus from front to rear, "They've brought us to the *Duque's* house."

Lourdes, Carrera's wife, had both taste and the money to indulge it. The legion's birthplace, the *Casa* Linda, a huge old stone mansion overlooking the coastal highway on one side and the sea on the other, had long since been transformed, at least in its family areas, from a barracks *cum* headquarters into something resembling a real home. Oh, sure, it had its military attributes, still; some trophies, a certain amount of statuary, weapons on some of the walls, and such. And there were some barracks and offices on the grounds, as well.

Wearing her senatorially awarded *Cruz de Coraje en Acero* pinned above her left breast, she met the girls at the buses, thanked the aide who had brought them here, and said, "I'll take it from here, Ricardo."

"The *Duque* wanted me to pick up some paperwork from him," the aide said. Lourdes shrugged. *Your business and his. Not mine.*

Lourdes de Carrera was tall, as tall as Cristina Zamora. Small breasted, she had a well-shaped rear end over very long legs. The thing that really caught people's attention, though, were her eyes, as large as a deer's, shaped like a Bedouin girl's, and a warm brown. All on their own, those eyes smiled.

From the paved area where the buses had stopped, her eyes joining her lips in a friendly smile, Lourdes led them around to the front of the house, through the wide doors there, and into the central hallway. The hallway was paneled in rare, iridescent silverwood, a native species. The wood was more bronze than silver in color, though a pattern of silver rings ran through it.

Holy crap, Trujillo thought, *this crap is* expensive.

"I'd offer you the grand tour," Lourdes said, "but Patricio is waiting downstairs and he told me there's no time. If you're ever in the area, though, just knock. Rather, just tell the guards on the gate I said you could knock. You'll always be welcome, any of you. If I were younger ... but who am I kidding? I'm too soft."

Inez looked at the medal and, knowing some of Lourdes' history, said, "Maybe not, ma'am."

Lourdes blushed and asked, "Now if you'll follow me?"

She led them past the stairs, then through a door that led to another set leading down to the basement.

"I wanted to have this area finished," she said, "but Patricio said, no, it reminds him of our, of the legion's, rather rough and humble roots." She shrugged, "I suppose he's got a point."

From the foot of the stairs she led them through the basement to a conference room, built into one side. This had been expanded since the early days, but there was still only just enough seating for about two thirds of the Amazons. The rest would have to stand.

Carrera sat at the head of a long table, scrawling his name across a document and muttering imprecations. Inez, last out of the bus but first into the conference room, thought she heard him say, "I never really imagined that when I gave them the money they'd actually make *me* account for spending it. Shit. I *hate* paperwork."

He looked up as the girls assembled and said, "Give me a minute, please, ladies. Some things just won't wait."

After perhaps two minutes, he closed the folder he'd been working on and looked up again. All the women were still standing. He lifted the folder in the direction of the aide and said, "Take this to Kuralski, in the City, please, Ricardo."

The aide took it, nodded, and without another word turned and left.

Once he was gone, Carrera waved a hand and said, "Please, girls, take seats if you can find them. If not, don't be formal; the floor and the table both work for my purposes."

Lourdes, who'd come in last, giggled, covering the lower half of her face with one hand. This earned more giggles from the other women and a dirty look from her husband. That caused more giggling, though it had a nervous quality to it.

"Okay, okay," Carrera agreed, rolling his eyes and rocking his head from side to side. "I suppose it was funny. Now if only I could learn to be funny when I intend to be funny. Sadly…

"All right; to business."

As he spoke he looked around from face to face, seeking eye contact. He smiled broadly at seeing Maria Fuentes, but that was the only special recognition he gave anyone.

"It's an article of faith, among us," Carrera said, "that there is no better group of combat leaders—officers, centurions, and non-coms alike—anywhere in the world than ours. Sure, maybe the Zionis and Sachsen can claim to be as good. But *nobody* is better.

"It is also—and absolutely—true that no group of leaders pays as uniformly high a price to earn that status."

Carrera reached under the table and pulled out a bottle of whiskey and a stack of paper cups. He poured himself one, a pretty stiff one, then passed bottle and cups on to the woman on his left, saying, "Share the wealth."

While those were making the rounds, he continued to speak, stopping occasionally to sip from his own. "There are a couple of ways to become entrusted with a position of authority in the legion. The regulations permit a tercio commander or higher to promote someone to brevet—if you're not familiar with the term, that means 'temporary'—signifer and even junior tribune, or brevet optio or junior centurion during war."

Sip.

"This has happened, too, a few times. However, as soon as the campaign was over, the brevets had to go through the same quali-fication procedures as did anyone else in peace. If they made it through that, their brevet promotions became permanent, with the permanent date of rank of their original brevet promotions. If they did not succeed, however, they went back to their previous ranks.

"Some think it's silly to send to a selection course someone who has proven they have the ability to lead in combat. But the philosophy has this much going for it: That within the leadership corps, the officers' corps and the centurionate, there are *no* outsiders, no second-class citizens. Rather, there will be none once the last of the holdovers from the old Civic Force leave or retire."

Sip.

"The procedure is, of course, the tough part.

"Ordinarily, the road to a commission as a signifer or being awarded a centurion's baton begins in basic training. There the recruits are, by graduation time, lumped into one of two sets: Leader or follower. This is confirmed or rejected during a not-too-long, six or eight months, period of service with their tercios. If the soldier has shown leadership ability *and* good character in Basic, and has that status confirmed by the tercio, the new private gets assigned to the reserve echelon of the tercio. Otherwise, he goes into the militia."

The militia was machine gun fodder, though it was well-cared-for machine gun fodder, for all that. They were also fairly well trained in their technical duties, as much as lengthy basic and advanced courses could teach them reinforced by twenty-five full days a year of refresher training.

Carrera made a sound that was almost a sigh. "The militia are made much more effective by their leaders. All the leadership and real talent are in the reserves and the regulars who draw their numbers from the reserves.

"Mistakes are sometimes made, of course, in selection. Status can change, and occasionally does.

"For men," he continued, "in the next few months to few years another decision is made for those who are reservists: 'Do we try to make this soldier an officer, a centurion, or a noncommissioned officer?' Intellect and character are rated about evenly in this selection process, though there are minimum levels of IQ required for officers and centurions. Education, per se, we count for little and connections we count for nothing at all.

"A lot of the jobs that are done by *very* senior noncoms, often even by officers, in other armies, are done by centurions in the legions. We also try to turn troops with leadership potential into centurions before age twenty-five, or signifers before age twenty, so they'll still have some energy when they become senior.

"We couldn't follow all that process with you ladies," Carrera explained. "You don't have an *experienced* cadre of your own to do the selection. *Gorgidas* has had to do that job for you. You haven't had time to get assimilated and evaluated in your own tercio, because you *are* that tercio."

Sip. Sip.

"Still, the *Tercio Amazona* will need combat leaders. When you reached full planned strength, you will need one hundred and sixty-eight officers and two hundred and sixty-five centurions. Yeah, that's above the normal tercio strength, but the increase was only to allow for maternal leave slots and for some units you'll have that other regiments don't, your own light artillery, for example. The extra man power—rather, woman power—you are authorized, to make up for less physical strength, does not allow you any more leadership. You will have the smallest percentage of officers of any military organization since Twentieth *Valeria Victrix* stepped off the boats at Rutupiae. Wherever that is. Somewhere on Old Earth, I gather."

Sip.

"It will not only be harder to become an Amazon than a regular soldier, it will be harder to become a leader of Amazons than to become a regular, male, leader of male soldiers.

"Unfair? Possibly. But then, can't the Amazons reasonably expect to have even better leaders by being even more selective than the men are?"

"Now, as to what you have ahead of you..."

"Maria. Goddamit, Maria! Wake up."

Fuentes started to sit bolt upright, heart beating a tattoo inside her chest. She had to stop inches from her position of rest; the straps of her rucksack held her down by the shoulders. Groggily, she said, "I wasn't sleeping, Centurion."

"Save it for the instructors. It's Marta."

Maria breathed a heavy sigh of relief as her heart began to slow down. Falling asleep on patrol (except in accordance with the appointed leader's sleep plan) could get one in quite serious trouble. Though lying about it, as she just had, could make things a lot worse.

"Marta...right," she muttered, almost intelligently.

"Hon, ruck up. We're moving out again."

Maria didn't have to put her rucksack on; she'd fallen asleep lying on it. Tiredly and groggily, she forced herself over to all fours, then, ever so slowly, rose to her feet. Marta put out a hand to steady her tottering form. She was swaying enough to be noticed even in the dark. The women had been marching almost continuously for a day and a half.

Marta patted her shoulder, turned away and followed the girl in front of her. Maria followed Marta or, rather, the two glowing pieces of tape on the back of her hat. A light rain, light for that part of the world at that season, began to fall. They had many hours of marching ahead. They didn't even know quite how many. The instructors never told. Even when they thought they knew, the mission could change mid-stride and, often enough, did.

It wasn't the loss of sleep that got to them. It wasn't the physical activity. It wasn't even the starvation or the fear. But all four of those things, working together, were enough to make anyone a wreck. And they were all rapidly becoming wrecks.

It was a slightly different course from what men underwent. Whether it was easier was deliberately made hard to say. Although the school had reduced the lengths of the cross-jungle moves the Amazons had to do in comparison to the men, and lightened the load they had to carry by giving them mules to help and increasing the size of their squads, the school had also chopped their rations below even what the men were given and added several weeks to the course.

Was the school trying to be harder on them? No, though that knowledge may have surprised the women. But if they had not added a matching hardship to offset every item, event or phenomenon that had been made easier, then to men who had graduated *their* version of the course, the women would have been second class citizens, so to speak. Not quite good enough; not quite equal . . . inferior.

No doubt many thought it unfair. Others understood.

"If a woman, or a man, ever graduates from a Cazador course that wasn't as hard as mine, I'm going to think that he or she is a wimp," said Inez. "Tough."

"Come *on*, you miserable, quadruped son of a bitch," Marta cursed, trying to drag a mule over a log fallen across the trail. The mule was having none of it.

"No good, worthless, shit-eating motherfucker," Marta said, giving the bridle another yank. "Not only don't they feed us *shit,* but we have to carry food for *you*! When we get a chance to fucking sleep, do we sleep? No, we have to make sure you're all nice and comfy first."

She stopped tugging for the nonce, then looked at the mule contemplatively. Marta leaned over and whispered something in the mule's ear. Its long ears jerked up. With a loud bray, it bounded over the fallen log, then stopped, trembling, on the far side.

"What did you say to it?" Inez asked.

"Mules are smart animals, the instructors said. Well...I told it that if it didn't get its furry ass over the log, we'd *eat* it."

Because the female squads were slightly larger than the men's they didn't have to be in charge of a mission—a "leadership phase"—quite as frequently. So another reason the course was made somewhat longer was to give the women even more stress from being in charge more often than the men had to be.

Some time later, in Officer Candidate School, Trujillo was told by a man that she could never have made it through "real" Cazador School. She was able to answer, "That may be true. It is also true that you could *never* have lived through *Cazadora* School. You'd have died of starvation, or folded up and collapsed two weeks before graduation from lack of sleep."

He could not dispute that.

Men lose the ability to have an erection for the duration of the school. With the women, they didn't have their periods. This created quite a panic among the few who had "celebrated" their graduation from Basic in a particularly enthusiastic way. When they talked among themselves about it, a wave of relief washed over those women's faces as they realized that they were not pregnant. Yes, they had contraceptive implants. No contraceptive is one hundred percent reliable.

After losing their menses, their breasts were the next things to go. Marta's became two flopping obscenities. Halfway through the course even the less well-breasted girls had nothing but lumpy bags of skin sagging lifelessly against slack chests. Then their posteriors shriveled away. Marta's hip bones were laid nearly bare by the loss of her arse. Those bones then rubbed the skin over them against her rucksack frame until she had two weeping sores just above where her buttocks had been.

An additionally unpleasant side effect of this semi-starvation was that minor wounds, scrapes and cuts would not heal. Marta had those two sores over her arse for the last two months of the course. She would carry the marks there to her grave.

Some had it worse than others. Marta kept plugging away, but it was easy to see that it bothered her.

Soldiers at war dream of peace, home, comfort, safety . . . family . . . sex, too. *Cazadores* dream of sleep and food. Even Alma, disturbingly, didn't enter Maria's thoughts quite so often as the thought of a well-fed rest.

Maria announced to Marta one day, "I have discovered a funny thing. Dreaming about unlimited food is very unsatisfying."

Marta, larger and more starved than Maria, answered, "I don't know. Dreaming about some goddamned fucking food is about the only satisfaction I have here."

"Try this instead," Maria said. "Give yourself an imaginary twenty drachma and go shopping in your mind. Buy no more than that twenty drachma will buy."

Marta looked skeptical but agreed to try. After a period of eyes closed, daydreaming, her face took on a smile. *Will I get the half gallon of ice cream or the whole roasted chicken? Hmmm . . . that bottle of rum will have maybe seven thousand calories. That, or the box of chocolates?* Little by little her mental shopping cart filled up. Sometimes she put things away in order to buy something better. *But I simply* must *save out five drachma for a couple of burgers with fries . . . greasy, wonderful, fries . . .*

When she opened her eyes she agreed, "You're right, Maria. It *is* better that way."

"Better," Maria said, "than hallucinating that a piece of tree bark is a hamburger like that one girl did."

"Well it *did* look like a juicy piece of bark."

Occasionally the women were well fed. They ate a real meal, an amazing three or four thousand calories' worth, in a real mess about every seven or eight days, which was slightly less often then the men did. Part of this was because of the mules. The decent feeds tended to coincide with returns to base camp from the field. The mules let them stay out longer. It was planned that way.

But when they *were* fed out of a real mess?

Ecstasy! Marta swallowed, looked at the remains of food on her tray and moved her fork to pick up just one more mouthful of mashed potatoes. She lifted the lump halfway to her mouth, then realized, *One more bite and I'll puke. And they won't give me another meal to make up for the lost one.*

Reluctantly . . . regretfully . . . she lowered her fork and took the tray to the turn-in window.

As she walked back to the little hut she shared with a dozen other women—they were allowed to walk after eating in the mess, though that was the only time in camp that they were—Marta mused on the sheer idiocy of the thing. Whatever she'd been told in explanation, it just made no sense to her, the starvation and lack of sleep.

I just don't get it.

We're disoriented most of the time. We make the most appalling tactical mistakes over and over and over.

It's the same with the lack of sleep. We're so tired we're outright silly most of the time. We're slow, stupid, and dull. When we've got a leadership phase, like as not we'll lose control.

Nope, I just don't get the reason.

The small airplane circled twice overhead, then flew on, With it, it took seventy rations, enough for the thirty-five women remaining to survive, if that was quite the word, for another two days.

Trujillo was in charge of the supply mission. She looked at the departing plane, and said, "I don't understand. What's wrong?"

The Cazador instructor, a Centurion Ramirez, seconded from Third Infantry Tercio, looked on, apparently without sympathy, and said, "You never specified an air drop, *Cazadora*. The plane came by, saw no landing strip, was not equipped to drop the supplies you requested, and continued on its way."

"But . . . but."

"No 'buts'; you fucked up, girl."

Inez rocked back and forth, arms about herself, eyes closed, repeating over and over, "It's all my fault. It's all my fault."

The others tried to comfort her, though after more than two days with exactly nothing to eat, they had a hard time of it sounding sincere.

It was a trick, of course. All the times before when the *Cazadoras* had to request supply, a parachute drop had been presumed; their leader of the day hadn't needed to ask. The purpose of this exercise in pain was simple.

Inez learnt it well. *I will never, never, never again fail to tell the deliverer of supply how to deliver the beans and bullets. I will never again assume it is taken care of.*

After two starving days, their missions brought each squad to the shores of a very lovely lake. The cadre called it a secure area and let the women sleep for an entire four hours. Still they were not fed. Going to sleep hungry is better than staying awake hungry. They slept like the dead.

Marta dreamt of nothing.

When she and the others awoke, each pair of them was issued a snow white bunny, an adorable thing.

Remembering Maria's daughter, and her own de facto niece, Marta thought, *Alma would love to have this bunny as a pet.*

There was also a large pot of black, bitter coffee for them—no sugar, of course, that would have meant giving them calories. The instructors wanted the girls absolutely ravenous.

Not mentioning the rabbits, one of the instructors began a lengthy lecture on how to prepare a meal for themselves under adverse conditions. He said, "Now, remember, *Cazadoras,* with small animals in particular, it's a good idea to cuddle it, pet it, and generally calm it down before breaking its cute little neck. Scared meat is tough meat."

Getting the message before most of the others, Marta had blanched and clutched her rabbit protectively to the remains of her breasts.

While the instructor was speaking, a lamb on a leash placidly munched grass a few feet from where he stood. It was so simply lovely that, bad as their condition was, all the girls smiled at seeing it.

About halfway through the lecture, the instructor pulled out a pistol and shot the lamb dead, right in front of them. It collapsed in a spray of blood.

"See?" said the speaker. "That animal never knew what hit it. You'll find the meat's fairly tender.

"Now remember, when you cook it up in an ammunition can, make sure you remove the rubber grommet that seals the can..."

It didn't matter what he said. The women could not tear their eyes away from that dead lamb, its pathetic body cooling in the shade.

The instructor pulled out a knife so sharp its edge seemed to fade off into a silvery mist. "Now gather round, girls," he said, "and I'll show you how to divvy up a lamb to feed thirty or more..."

The farm girls took the butchering in stride. The city girls mostly turned their eyes away. Even so, they didn't turn down the food when each two-woman team was given a few ounces of the meat, along with a handful of rice, a moldy potato or two, a carrot, an onion, some unidentifiable greens, a little salt and a metal ammunition can.

They hadn't eaten for two days. If they were to eat, they had to cook their own meal. Sadly, however, what they'd been given— excepting the rabbits—wasn't enough to keep body and soul together. That was why they had been given the rabbits; those wonderful, cuddly, lovable little bunnies.

They had to kill them to live, or at least to stop the hunger pangs.

Marta just couldn't. She tried. She'd pet the rabbit to calm it down, then try to deliver a killing blow to the little thing's neck. But she couldn't really follow through with the blow. She just succeeded in scaring it *almost* to death. Eventually, she fell to her knees, crying.

Maria had to eat. So did Marta. Maria took the rabbit from her friend's arms. The rabbit looked up at her with terror in its eyes. Even so, she took it by its feet and said, "I'm sorry, but it's you or us." Then she smashed its little head against a tree. It took her three swings to kill it, poor animal. That's how weak she was.

Marta wouldn't speak to her as she skinned it and cut it into pieces. But, once that was done, she took over the job of preparing the stew.

Marta resigned from the school shortly after that. Though Maria said she thought Marta was being premature, she understood.

As tough and miserable as the school was in general, the really hard times were the leadership phases. That was when you could really screw up and have it matter, exactly as Trujillo had.

As soon as a squad finished one mission—or a part of a mission, they couldn't really predict the instructors—the old leaders would be taken aside and evaluated on their performance. While that was going on the new instructors would let the rest hang for a bit, hearts pounding and sick at the stomach, then announce who was responsible for leading the next mission or the last half of the current one.

It was always a tremendous relief when someone else was chosen. That meant they only had to be miserable, which took little talent or effort, but didn't have to worry overmuch about failure, humiliation, or hurting their sisters through their own incompetence.

Sometimes they had to plan a mission for someone else to carry out, sometimes they had to carry out a mission someone else had planned. Sometimes a leader was relieved on the spot and some other girl inherited her mess. Whatever sort of mission it was, the only constant they knew was that it would really, really *suck*.

The women had to pass leadership phases to graduate the course, at least fifty percent of them overall and at least one in each of the three field portions of the course: Primary Cazador, mountain, and jungle.

Most were uneventful; some were passed, some were failed.

The instructor announced, "*Cazadora* Campestre, you are relieved. *Cazadora* Fuentes, take charge of your squad."

Crap. "Yes, Centurion."

Maria trudged wearily to where Inez was trying to bring order from chaos. Two other squad leaders were already there by the time she arrived and sat down.

"Maria, your squad cleans its machine gun last in order," Trujillo said. "Don't start until the other two are done. Must keep two thirds of our firepower ready."

"Sure . . . okay," Maria answered wearily.

"Meanwhile, I need you to make me a terrain model of this area here, from this point to this." Inez's finger traced a route on the map.

"All right. Sure."

"Maria? Maria? Wake up, Maria!"

"Sorry. Just so damned tired. Sorry."

Maria dug into a pocket, pulled out a small packet of freeze dried coffee, and ripped it open. She tilted her head back, opened her mouth, and carefully poured the contents under her tongue.

Inez's look of distaste matched the sour expression on Maria's face. "I don't know *how* you can do that," she said.

"Me, neither." Maria stood to return to her squad.

Concentrating on the sand table, utterly exhausted, dried coffee or not, Maria never noticed that the time had begun for her to have her squad start cleaning the machine gun until it had already nearly run. By the time she was able to order hers taken apart it was already time to put it back together and move out. Her squad's gun didn't get cleaned properly.

The instructors caught that. By the expressions on their faces she knew they were going to fail her at the end of the mission. How she hated those condescending, contemptuous looks.

Morale at a low ebb, Maria did little more than keep her troops in formation for the march. They were moving forward in a column of squad wedges, her squad last, through a very green glen.

I am so toast. They're going to fail me. Worse, I deserve to be failed. I am low, loathsome, a piece of . . .

Suddenly, from behind and to the right, came the rattle of massed fire from machine guns and rifles. The first two squads had missed the ambush completely.

Maria and her squad dove for the dirt, automatically. She was confused, and more than a little annoyed at the other two squads and Inez.

Fuck, fuck, fuck. She risked sticking her head up just enough, and just long enough, to see who was shooting her people and from where.

Feeling a rush of anger that quickly turned itself into energy, she began shouting orders to her squad. "Alpha Team. Four o'clock. Suppressive fire! Bravo Team. Twelve o'clock. Move fifty meters then halt to support Alpha's withdrawal."

As soon as she heard fire coming from behind her, she knew that Bravo was in position. "Alpha Team, machine gun, follow me!"

She and the five Amazons from Alpha, plus the two-woman machine-gun crew, scampered forward, in the direction of the other squads of the platoon. Ahead, she could see Inez chivying the other two squads into position.

"Alpha, down." She waited until that team was firing on the enemy, then called, "Bravo, up and *move*!" even as she leapt to the machine gun to direct its fire personally.

It worked . . . perfectly, through three bounds, a textbook breaking of contact with the enemy. This allowed the entire platoon to
withdraw and regroup without loss. She might have been pleased
with herself, except for that damned dirty machine gun hanging
over her head. She was still very sure that she would be failed
on the leadership phase.

Nor was she doing so well that she could afford to fail one.

Continuing the march, Maria argued with herself. *Unfair,* she
thought. *Not my fault. What could I have done about another
squad's tardiness in cleaning their gun?*

Then another part of her mind realized, *It really doesn't matter
that it might have been unfair. War is unfair and sitting and crying "stop being so mean to me" gets you either nowhere or dead.
What I should have done is gone to one of the other squad leaders
and said, "I'm having my machine gun cleaned in five minutes. If
yours isn't done by then, I am going to come back here and beat
you to death. I'll try, anyway."*

That was almost precisely what the instructor told her during
her evaluation at the end of the mission. Then he surprised her
speechless. He said, almost reluctantly, "On the other hand, the
machine wasn't so filthy that it didn't work. And you did a truly
superb job of breaking contact and covering your platoon when
you were all ambushed from behind. We're not looking for perfection; just for lots and lots of very damned good. For this reason,
Cazadora Fuentes, you are a pass for this mission."

It's considered impolite and unprofessional to thank an *Instruc-
tador de Cazadores* for passing one on a leadership phase. Maria
just nodded, looked up at the sky, and said, very quietly, "Thank
you." The instructor could think she was thanking God if he
wanted; that was permissible. She was thanking both.

The other leadership phase she would always remember was
the last one, the one where they really shoot . . . to kill.

It was a fixed rule of the legion that no son or daughter of
the nation would be led into battle except by leaders who have
been tested in battle. They had seen what it was like when some
of your small unit leaders turn out to be cowards. They had seen
it during the Federated States' invasion, years before.

Battles being somewhat infrequent and unpredictable, however,
Cazador School gave them one real one.

Robles, the wheelchair-bound centurion from the *Tercio Santa Cecilia,* still served as the women's administrative leader for Cazador School. He had gone through the school some years before losing the use of his lower body. The girls had seen him regularly, as individuals, throughout the course. This had been for performance counseling, mostly. Four days before graduation, he called them together as a group to explain the next, and last, problem. There were twenty-seven of them left.

"Ladies," he began, "the hardest part is over. Each of you still remaining has passed all the requirements of the course but one. That one, however, makes the difference between a real combat leader and an almost ran. The next one they shoot at you with the intent of hitting."

They'd had a number of live fire exercises throughout the course where school personnel had shot in their direction. But it became fairly obvious after a while that they were deliberately shooting to miss. It was still nerve-wracking to hear a bullet whiz by one's head, but after a time it had stopped being terrifying.

They were going to shoot to *hit?*

"You've gotten to be a substantial investment for the legion by this time. For this reason, you will wear torso armor, ceramic, to reduce the chance of your being hit fatally. Of course, if you take one in the head, you are probably deader than chivalry. And the statistics say that at least one of you will be shot during this exercise. More likely two or three."

That was both true and false. It was true in the sense that most every rendition of this particular exercise saw someone shot. It was false because it was usually a rather large maniple of men going through. The odds of even one of the twenty-seven remaining women being hit were actually fairly poor.

"If anyone wants to resign now, I'll understand. Dismissed."

They *were* going to shoot to hit!

Almost no Cazador students actually quit at that point in the course; they'd already paid too high a price to just give up. But they all thought about it . . . continuously.

And, for a change, the women were given time to think. Once they came to the assembly area for the graduation exercise, life became remarkably sweet in comparison. They were fed as much as they cared to eat, most of them wolfing down ten or twelve *thousand* calories a day while they prepared for that last mission.

There was even a small alcohol ration, served with dinner, the legion having no truck with any silly puritanism that forbids soldiers the few comforts that *can* conveniently and cheaply be provided. And a bit of grain alcohol doesn't take up much space or weight. Best of all, the time to prepare allowed more than ten hours sleep per day. Before they crossed the line of departure into the live fire area they were relatively fat and positively happy.

Why throw away life under those circumstances? Why, indeed? No one, perhaps could understand, unless they too went through the rest of the school. But of the twenty-seven of them left, no one quit. No one quit even though the road to the range led past a memorial that listed the names of every single legionary ever killed there.

"Fuentes! Fuentes! Maria!"

"Over here, Inez."

"What you got?" Grammar tends to go by the boards when people are shooting to kill.

Maria shouted out, "Turret. Three o'clock. Two hundred and fifty meters. Machine gun only. It's got us pinned!"

As if to punctuate, a burst of fire came from the old redundant tank turret and swept above the little depression into which Trujillo had led herself and her radio operator. The bullets cracked the air overhead with their passage. Two of them actually hit the dirt and bounced above them. The sound they made was quite different; less a crack and more of a screech. It then traversed to do the same to the group led by Maria.

No way we are going to be able to crawl out of that hole without someone else distracting the machine gun. She shouted the same to Trujillo.

"Hang on, Fuentes. I'm calling for artillery."

Artillery. Right. Maria crossed herself for the fourth or fifth time that morning.

Ignoring the fire—since they weren't shooting at *him*—an instructor made notes from about fifty meters away from Maria's squad and not on line with her squad and the turret. His body armor was painted white so the turrets wouldn't shoot at him by mistake.

The machine gun kept pattering the dirt and breaking the air.

The school wouldn't really fire live artillery at the turret, though at the time Maria thought they had. Instead, they fired shells the fuses for which hadn't been armed and, even then, only at a distance offset from the turret. Then they detonated underground charges around it. Much like the time the women had been "shelled" in Basic, it looked real to them.

The fire from the turret's machine gun stopped.

It might a trick to lure us out. Sooo...up to me to find out. Maria cocked her right leg and moved her arms to a close analog of the pushup position. Her arms popped like springs even as her leg shot her forward. She ran about twenty-five meters and flopped to a low spot in the ground. When she wasn't hit, she figured it was safe enough for the rest of the squad. Between squeezing bursts at the turret she called for them to advance to join her. They did.

Then they alternately rushed and crawled to a low berm. Inez Trujillo must have been watching because, after about one hundred and fifty meters of advancing, the artillery lifted. Maria got the squad on line at the berm ahead.

She glanced left and right to make sure she had everybody, then shouted, "On three...one...two...three!"

On her command, all the women with her popped over the edge, presented their muzzles to the target, and began to put a really vicious fire on it. Perhaps only one in fifty shots actually hit, even though all of the students' rifle and machine gun ammunition was live, the men shooting at them being behind armor.

While the turret was being hit, the crew ceased fire as if they were genuinely suppressed. In that safe time, Trujillo, bringing behind her her radio operator and another girl serving as a runner, bolted to Maria's berm. Panting with the effort, Inez flopped down next to Maria. Both her RTO and her runner kept low. There wasn't really room along the berm for them anyway.

"Inez," Maria shouted between bursts, "I can keep the bastard suppressed, but that's all. I can't tell whether that position is destroyed, suppressed, or just waiting for us to expose ourselves. But there's a shallow ditch over to the left. I think you can get a squad up it with no one to see."

"Got it," Trujillo said, then turned to the runner and ordered her to go back and order forward the second squad. The squad leader was to use the ditch to get into the "enemy" position and make sure the turret was KIA, killed in action. They caught occasional glimpses of a skinny rump or a thin F-26 barrel as Second moved up the ditch.

"Maria," Inez shouted over the din, "the signal to lift fires will be a green smoke grenade!"

"Got it. Lift fires on green."

A storm of fire thundered from the left front as girls began to spring forward and across the objective area. Maria saw the green smoke begin to waft through the air. "Cease fire and report," she commanded.

"A team, no casualties. All equipment okay. Down to thirty rounds per troop. Not much water left."

"B Team, no casualties. Less than twenty-five rounds per rifle. Shitty on water."

"Machine gun okay. Only fifty rounds left. Out on water."

Maria turned to Trujillo. "We need ammunition badly. Water, too."

"Right; the whole platoon, I'd suspect." Inez began issuing orders to form a hasty defense. Then she ordered one of the mules brought forward, one that had another full load of ammunition, and ten gallons of water.

The rest of the platoon assembled, setting up a hasty defense in the area of the turret they had taken. Its hatch was locked from the inside just in case one of the women had a grudge against the crew. The men under the hatch, mission over, played a game of spades inside its protection.

"Movement! One tank. Two o'clock. Eight hundred meters." Whoever made that report, no sooner had she spoken than the students heard a freight train going by, almost overhead, followed by the sound of a blast. This was followed by a fairly large explosion to their right rear.

"Fuck! Fuck! Everybody down!" Trujillo gave this order just in time, as the tank began to pelt the general area with machine-gun fire. Looked at another way, though, the order was unnecessary— they had all hit the dirt immediately.

Was the tank trying to hit them? Yes...but.

It can take anywhere from several hundred thousand, up to a million, shots to kill one soldier in battle. There are many reasons for that, though the big one is that everybody is pretty much scared out of their wits. There are few, if any, people in the world who can deliberately hit a target with a rifle or machine gun when their hands are shaking like leaves in a strong breeze. It can't be done, except by a fluke. Nor does marksmanship training really help all that much as one can never train someone to shoot accurately under conditions of being terrified. The most that can be hoped for is to train them *not* to be terrified. Scared? That was fine. Terrified was right out.

On the other hand, the students really couldn't hurt the tank approaching or the turrets they used for machine gun positions, they were invulnerable to anything carried. Besides, the women only had simulated antiarmor ammunition. So the "enemy" gunners didn't have any reason to be afraid, as they would have had in war.

The tanks would have murdered any class of *Cazadores* if something hadn't been done to reverse the imbalance of fear.

What the school did was make the turret and tankers' bullets plastic, except for five rounds in ninety-three which were tracers. The plastic would only sting like hell unless the person hit was very close, in which case the shooters were under orders to either aim high or surrender. The five that were tracers, on the other hand, not only sounded real and could really kill, the students could actually see them under some circumstances. It was terrifying.

Even that wasn't enough safety; the legion wanted live leaders, without paying more than the minimum required in dead meat. So they had mounted the machine guns in more or less vibrating mounts. It was actually very, very unlikely that any given burst would both have a real bullet, be properly aimed, and not shake away from that point of aim.

All else failing, the students wore armor that protected all of their vitals except for their brains.

"If we'd had any brains we wouldn't be here in the first place," commented Trujillo. "But at least we haven't lost anybody."

They did lose someone, sort of.

The tank was rolling slowly toward them, firing the odd burst to keep their heads down. The girl in charge of the mule was trying desperately to get it to take some kind of cover. The stupid animal ignored her.

Then the tank noticed them. It fired a long burst—Maria saw

that it included a tracer—that went wide. The girl dove for cover. Then the tank fired an even longer burst, fifty or sixty rounds, two or three of them tracers. The mule went down in a shower of blood and gore.

By this time, the tank had rolled close enough for the women to have a chance with their rocket launchers. At Trujillo's command, all three of them fired. One hit the tank with a bright flash. The tank stopped short. In seconds, another three rockets went out. Two hit the tank. Someone inside then popped the red smoke that indicated a kill.

The women cheered, mule quite forgotten.

At that point the instructor called a freeze in place. He picked a new group of leaders. Then the women made ready to attack another position.

Only one Amazon was hit that day. The bullet went through the leg muscle. She didn't let out a tear.

The next day was graduation. Carrera himself came out to watch. The commandant of the school, a foreigner named Broughton, made a short speech. Robles wheeled himself out, pinning the *Cazadora* tabs on their shoulders. He pushed the pin into flesh before withdrawing it and clasping it shut. No one winced or complained. Then they ran, in formation, past the reviewing stand.

Interlude

Once upon a time, and not so very far in the past, the president of "the legitimate, democratic, popularly-elected government of Balboa"—which was precisely none of those things—would have stood in respect and fear as the Gallic commander of Tauran Union forces in Balboa, General Janier, entered the conference room. That president, and his entire government of self-interested and corrupt oligarchs, was dead. Now Janier, without any deeply felt respect and certainly with no fear, stood for the ambassador of United Earth and the Tauran Union's commissioner for the Balboa Transitway.

Rather, Janier felt no respect or fear for the one man, the Earther, and one woman, the Tauran, he was there to meet. He had fears, though. As if to punctuate those, a brace of jet fighters, old, rebuilt but obsolescent, from Balboa's Legion Jan Sobieski screamed over the building, causing not only the windows to rattle but the very glasses on the conference table to shake and move.

"Can't you do something about that?" the commissioner asked. She was named Unni Wiglan, and was a leggy blonde well into middle age, but looking younger. Like most of the Tauran Union's semi-hereditary aristocracy, she rotated from job to job, each a sinecure where the holder was expected to produce little but high-sounding statements and expansive budgets. Though she was the commissioner for the Balboa Transitway, she had come in on the morning's airship from her home near Pousse, one of the capitals of the Tauran Union. Certainly she had little interest in actually living in the austere Transitway Zone, a roughly one thousand three hundred square kilometer strip, eighty by sixteen, carved out of the surrounding jungle, a place of little enlightenment and no culture, and surrounded by a virulent military dictatorship.

"No," Janier answered, simply, shaking his head. "I can't do a damned thing about them. And they do this every day, at this time, daring us to try and exposing our impotence. I chose this time and this place to show you."

"To show us what?" asked the ambassador from United Earth.

Janier snorted, taking a seat. Formalities were one thing and, as a soldier, he tended to live by them. But actually continuing to stand? That might have given these bureaucrats the very false impression that he held them in any personal regard whatsoever.

Snorting again, he said, "To show you just how willing the other side is, how eager to drive us into the Transitway and the sea. Seas, rather."

Janier smiled mirthlessly, asking, "And do you know what the worst part is?"

Wiglan shook her head. The Earth ambassador didn't answer at all, but then he paid attention to his morning briefings.

"The worst part is that my army here is unreliable. The Castilian battalion, under that greasy wretch, Muñoz-Infantes, has all but officially defected. They train with the Balboans. They have an officer exchange going. They feed the Balboans intelligence, or did before I cut the Castilians off.

"And, while I have my doubts that the Balboans have let them in on their operational plans, I know to a certainty that Muñoz-Infantes has his staff planning to assist them in any of a number of contingencies. He's even preparing to marry off his daughter to one of their officers, a Volgan émigré.

"It is not clear that, outside of my own Gauls, my army will even fight, except perhaps in point self defense."

"I've spoken to the high admiral about your problems," the UE ambassador said, "since she returned from Earth. She cannot provide ground troops."

Janier shook his head again. "I don't expect her to. The intelligence she provides, that your fleet provides, is aid enough from space."

He turned his attention back to Wiglan, the commissioner. "I need all my troops exchanged, and new battalions sent out, battalions that aren't contaminated by close contact with the Balboans. I need the Castilians recalled and not replaced except by non-Castilian troops. I need people who can't communicate with the locals, who can't be propagandized by their radio and television."

Wiglan had had little contact with soldiers in her life. Indeed, except for sleeping with a number of them to entice them to provide some aid to the previous high admiral of the Peace Fleet, she'd avoided them like the plague. She didn't understand them, any more than she understood Janier.

"Why?" she asked.

"Because this is a soldier's paradise," he answered. He sighed. "They don't respect you, Commissioner. They don't respect people like you. They don't respect the Tauran Union. They don't respect United Earth. This political system suits my men to a T, and they would be loath to attack it. For that matter, on any given day up to half a dozen of them defect."

"It's actually worse than that," the ambassador said. "This place is a menace, greater than its population, greater than its limited wealth, greater than its position dominating trade. This place is a menace because of an idea, an idea in opposition to everything we believe in."

"Huh?" Wiglan asked.

Janier's respect for the ambassador went up a notch, even as Wiglan's clueless "huh" caused his respect for her to drop to the same degree.

In these confines, with these people, Earth's ambassador could speak freely. "In the first place, you must understand that real revolution, internal overthrow, of this kind of government is effectively impossible. We tried it when they were weaker than they are now and failed.

"Right now virtually everyone in Balboa who has sufficient aggressiveness and is of age is already a member of the legions. They even take cripples... if those people are willing to risk their lives for it. So suppose that there is someday a good reason for some young people to want to overthrow the government down there? Why should they? They can get a vote out of all proportion to their numbers by joining the legion and training to fight you rather than actually fighting their own people. They don't need to rebel for twenty years... which it might take... and then fail... which they certainly would. Not when they can have the vote in ten. They can get control of the government peacefully. And everyone who is not willing to do that probably... no, certainly... lacks the motivation to fight against it.

"Which wouldn't matter but for one thing. They're going to

have a government of soldiers, and—with all respects to the general—propaganda aside, soldiers are not by nature peaceful men. Maybe peace is their profession but, if so, war is an all-consuming hobby. Worse, Balboa is set up to have a government that will have no moderating influences in it. Few women, few or no pacifists, probably very few genuine intellectuals. If it has anyone who believes in the rule of law—our kind of law—over the rule of power it will be a fluke. There will be few lawyers in the electorate, I imagine."

Janier smiled again, still without mirth, adding, "And it will appeal to all those everywhere who wield the real power, the soldiers."

"But you're..." Wiglan stopped.

"I'm a soldier, yes," Janier said. "But I'm also, like you, Commissioner, a member in good standing of the growing and solidifying aristocracy of this planet. We want what he"—the Gaul's head inclined toward Earth's ambassador—"and his people have. Rule by us and ours, in perpetuity, an end to rule by the mob, good living, security, culture."

"For us, and ours," added the ambassador, "democracy is just a means to an end. The masses of people don't reason. We drive them like animals through a mixture of fanaticism and hysteria. Balboa has found possibly the only way to avoid that, to have popular government that doesn't ultimately end up handing all the real power to us and people like us. And they have the means and the will to expand.

"They have to go," the ambassador finished. "Please get your government to give the general whatever he asks for."

CHAPTER TEN

Beauty without Vanity,
Strength without Insolence,
Courage without Ferocity,
And all the Virtues of Man,
without his Vices.

—Byron

A dog is a good citizen.

—Plato

Maria:

They gave us six whole weeks to recover (eat, sleep, and *heal*) from Cazador School before we went to the next course. For that time they sent us back to our little beach caserne on the island. It wasn't the same, though.

Again Porras brought Alma out to stay with me. Though full to bursting, the place seemed awfully empty to me as most of it was filled with girls from the second class. The ones from my class who had finished their initial training were back home, many of them learning new jobs for the civilian market.

It was lonely, being mostly among strangers. On the other hand, the look of amazement on the other girls' faces when they saw my Cazador tab was priceless. I missed Marta and the others of my class very much. When Marta wrote me, she said that the legion had her in a civilian school to learn computer programming. She said she would be going to the primary noncommissioned officers' course sometime after that.

When the six weeks was up, seven of us, including Inez Trujillo, went to OCS, Officer Candidate School. The remaining *Cazadoras,* which included me, went to CCS, Centurion Candidate School.

What was the difference among those so selected? I truly don't know. Some of the difference had to have been our relative performance in our training so far. Then, too, I'm sure they looked at IQ to a degree. I was pretty smart, but so were we all. Only the very brightest went to OCS, and then only if they'd done exceptionally well in training.

I might have refused OCS if I had been picked; centurion looked to be responsibility enough to me and maybe more fun, too. Besides, I had hardly ever seen an officer so far. As near as I could tell, centurions were the gods of the legion.

In any case, I was pleased enough. There is a lot of prestige that comes with making the centurionate, true, but that wasn't what pleased me. The difference in benefits and pay between an officer and a centurion is minimal, at least up to field grade officer ranks (legates and such). Being a centurion would help me provide for Alma almost as well as being a signifer or tribune would have. Not that I'd start as a centurion, of course. Just as officers get a probationary period as signifers, we have to spend a time as optios.

What *is* a centurion or optio? He—or she—is the strong right arm of the officers. They plan, they coordinate. They lead, too. However, the real push behind the force, the force behind the officers, are the centurions.

We're trained differently, officers and centurions. They worry about tactics, grand tactics and operations, logistics, administration, intelligence, and, at higher ranks, strategy and grand strategy. We worry about combat leadership at the worm's eye level. *We* take care of day-to-day training, operations, and discipline. Without us, the soldiers would be rabble. Without us, the officers couldn't command.

We listen to the officers, obey and—especially—enforce their orders. Those are the rules. Besides, they're generally smarter than we are. Morally, however, we are at least their equals. They know it; we know it.

The officers in a maniple come in three different types. You typically have a commanding officer, Christ's vicar on Terra Nova or near enough. He or she is usually a middle ranking tribune.

Then you have an executive officer, a junior tribune with enough experience and talent to be worth listening to. Lastly there'll be a signifer serving as a platoon leader, having the finishing touches put on her by the CO and XO, by her *very* experienced platoon centurion, and with added touching up from the maniple's first centurion.

Centurion Candidate School is at Camp Spurius Ligustinus, a picturesque little spot in a high valley in the mountainous eastern part of the country. It's not all that far from the Mountain Cazador Camp, Camp Bernardo O'Higgins. Being up in the mountains, CSL enjoys a relatively cool climate, one which I came to appreciate during our twice weekly "death runs." They called them fun runs. It was a lie; there was no fun in them.

Anyway, it's cool up there. Sometimes, at night, one even needs a sweater. Yes, we were each issued a sweater that we could either return or buy when the course ended. Since none of us were issued used ones, I suspect that, like us, every centurion candidate bought theirs as a momento.

It is also a very well appointed camp, given the size. There is a small movie theater, post office, exchange (read: store), commissary (read: grocery store), library, gym with pool, chapel; in short, every amenity to include the beauty salon that was more than a little useless to us. In comparison with Cazador School, or even Basic, it is nearly Heaven on Terra Nova.

I've wondered if that's part of why the legion gives us even more miserable living conditions in Basic than really necessary; so we'll appreciate what it *can* afford to give us later on.

Instead of barracks, we had bachelor(ette) centurion quarters, BCQs. No, they weren't private rooms. We each shared small apartments with three other women. Within close walking distance we had two centurion clubs. One of these was for the newer candidates. That was pretty Spartan. But about halfway through the course, candidates were invited and required to join the real—and might I add, quite plush—centurions' club. I suspect that half the reason for this was to allow the real centurions, the cadre who ran the place, to teach us a bit of decorum, informally. We took all our meals, when we weren't training in the field, at one of the clubs.

We could drink if we wanted to, whatever we wanted to, duty status permitting, once we were allowed into the real centurions' club. We could also drink as much as we wanted to; no one would say a word. I never lost the feeling though, that they allowed this to see if we could handle our liquor. At the vote taken by the cadre on whether a candidate would or would not be allowed to join the hallowed ranks of the centurionate at graduation, I do not doubt for a minute that one's habits with alcohol were taken into account. Not everyone who meets all course requirements is awarded his or her stick, the centurion's sole badge of office.

There was only a single officer at Camp Spurius Ligustinus, the poor bastard. He was there merely for administration, legal discipline and so forth, and, though he bore the title "Commanding Officer," the real boss was the Camp and School sergeant major, Sergeant Major Martinez. I wouldn't even know the CO's name, Cherensa, if it hadn't appeared on my final orders.

There were two sergeants-major in the Force that were hand-picked by *Duque* Carrera. The first of these is the *Sarjento-Major de la Legion del Cid*. When I joined we didn't have one of those, the old one having been assassinated and not yet replaced. It was whispered that the time lag was Carrera's way of mourning.

Martinez was the other one.

He was an unusual character; a stocky little fireplug of a man, or maybe better said a brick with arms and legs. In all my months there, and even after, I never saw, never even heard of, him raising his voice. He was never emotional; though there was a sort of very subdued enthusiasm about him that was frankly . . . engaging. The man clearly loved his work. Even when he whacked you with his baton he did it impersonally, with no hard feelings on either side.

On parade he was splendid; robotic precision meshed with style and grace. Under stress—occasionally under fire, we did a lot of training with live ammunition—he was unflappable. If he ever hesitated about a decision, it was for about as long as it takes in our country for the driver behind you to beep his horn once the light ahead turns green. That, in case you didn't know, in the shortest measure of time in the known universe.

He had short little legs—even shorter than mine—that still seemed able to run any of the candidates and most of the cadre into the ground.

SGM Martinez seemed to know *everything*; not just what was in the books. I mean, I have never known someone who had so much military knowledge crammed into his or her head.

It wasn't any great leap for me, my sister Amazons, too, to want to be like Martinez.

A casual observer might assume that discipline in the legion is entirely imposed from above. That observation would not be remotely correct. Certainly, a centurion or sergeant won't hesitate to flatten an insubordinate troop. (Officers do *not* sully their hands; that's *our* job). Curiously, a leader almost never has to do so.

Why? Oh, partly they don't have to because it's manifest that they probably can. But that's only part of it. There are always a few soldiers who are just naturally talented scrappers. But even these will rarely challenge a centurion's authority.

The law, of course, authorizes the death penalty—immediate and summary—for assaulting a centurion or officer. But I can't remember the last time that particular provision was used. The law is a fragile thing, you see. It's never there to help you in combat. That's why we try not to rely on it overmuch.

Sure, we're trained to fight. Still, as I mentioned, there *are* naturals who could take any centurion on. And they know it as well as we do. And they don't do it anyway.

They don't do it because, unlike them, we don't care much anymore if we get hurt. That makes us far too dangerous to scrap with.

We'd already had the more or less administrative training in hand-to-hand combat, the punching, the tossing, the rolling and landing. We knew all the places to strike to hurt or kill. Just knowing *how* to do it, however, the legion didn't think was quite enough. They wanted to be sure we *would* do it. There's a world of difference between the two, a difference usually lost on civilians.

All the hand-to-hand training took place in a sawdust pit on the north side of the camp, overlooked by what the cadre called, "Mount Motherfucker." That's because we ran to the top of the thing at least once a week.

Our primary instructor was a large, very light-skinned type named Quiroz. Even his muscles had muscles. Like Marta, he was an immigrant from La Plata and had the odd Tuscan accent. I'd heard, but never had it proved to me, that he'd been an officer in the Army of La Plata before shifting over to us. I also heard some other things about Quiroz, in Pashtia, that were a mix of admirable and scary. I mean, really, dumping mines on someone to hold them in position so you can shoot them one at a time and they can't get away? That's just cruel. Then again, I've heard than a man from La Plata was just a Tuscan, who spoke Spanish, thought he was an Anglian gentleman, and acted like a Sachsen.

"Two ranks, candidates," Quiroz said, that first day of serious hand-to-hand. In the pit, the twenty of us formed up in two lines of ten, facing the instructor.

"First rank...about...face." I put my right foot behind and to the left of my left heel, then twisted on my left heel and the ball of my right foot to change the direction I was facing by one hundred and eighty degrees. Doing this on sawdust is tricky, by the way. The instructor then extended the formation to double arm intervals, about six feet between each of us.

"*Very* often, ladies," he said, "leadership boils down to no more than the ability to inflict a beating...or take one. You're going to learn to do that. You'll practice on each other. At my command, you and the person in front of you will fight. There are no rules except that you may not gouge eyes. You *may* bite and scratch. The last one of a fighting pair left standing is the winner. Losers will be matched again against each other and will fight again. This will continue until there is only one woman left in the pit standing...and one lying down, hopefully comatose."

"Unfortunately—for you—you are both a small number, compared to a male class, and an odd number for me to use straight line elimination. So, of your ten pairs, only the first four winners will be released. The remaining sixteen of you will form eight pairs, who will fight again. The eight winners of those bouts will be released. Then four pairs will fight. Then two. Then one."

The self-satisfied swine chuckled out loud. "That means that the worst of you will be beaten five times this afternoon. Tough shit."

"However, the legion loves you all. Losers of the first set of matches get an additional one and a half hours remedial hand-to-hand combat training this evening, in lieu of dinner.

"You are lucky in another way, too. Men only do this two or three times a week, and we wear them out first with physical training to cut down on the damage they do each other. However, because there are fewer of you, and therefore less fighting and beating to take on any given day, you—unlike the men—will do this *every* day until further notice. Moreover, because you are not as strong as men in your upper bodies, you will not be worn out with exercise before you fight."

He looked pointedly at Zamora, probably because she was the biggest. "If I catch you throwing a match to save the others some pain, girl, you are history."

Zamora's eyes widened at being singled out. "I understand, Centurion." The other girl, her partner, gulped. Cristina gave the other girl a look that was, more than anything, a deep and profound apology, in advance.

Cristina was such a nice girl, really. She never hurt anyone for her own sake that I ever saw.

"Now fight!"

They only gave us nose protectors after our noses were broken, and then only so long as it took for them to heal. Mine was broken nine times throughout the course, counting multiple and repetitive breaks. After a while, I stopped being afraid of being hit. I'm still not, as one ex-boyfriend discovered to his dismay. Once he woke up. But that's another story.

We studied and practiced small unit tactical operations a great deal. We could not make a full platoon in the field ourselves, so they supplemented our ranks with about twenty-five more Amazons who had finished Basic successfully, but had not been picked for Cazador School. Those sisters did scut work around the camp when we weren't using them as training aids. This was a big training advantage for us. The male candidates had to use each other, which limited their opportunity to learn to lead by leading. We had just over twice as much time leading as they were given.

This was, by the way, a very good thing.

Ever think about geometry as a vital aspect of combat leadership? Probably not; I hadn't. It is, though. Every battle, every skirmish, ever fought hinged, in part at least, on the question of shape. Shape affects everything in war. (That's why the legion has added Shape, along with Attrition and Annihilation, to its list of the Principles of War.) Sometimes the shape concerns a time and space relationship: "Will I be able to achieve a decision at X, in order to move to Y, quickly enough to ensure the enemy can't either get in position to block me at W or successfully attack me himself at Z?"

Sometimes it's as simple as whether or not the slope of a hill is shaped in such a way that a machine gun can get grazing fire (that means the bullets never get above waist level and therefore "graze" the planet's surface).

For whatever reason—genetic, environmental, or simply because they spend so much time watching *our* shapes—men seem to have a better innate understanding of the irregular shapes and time-space relationships found on the battlefield than we do. They think that way and we—most of us, anyway—do not. (And if someone says a word about that being because men lie to us all our lives; telling us that something is eight inches when it's really six, I *will* paste them. Though, I admit, it could be true.)

So the extra practice leading troops came in very handy; learning to understand and use that for which we, generally, had less innate . . . feel.

I learned something else from using those sisters as training aids: knowledge is also power. By the time they came to us, we had far more knowledge than they did. They obeyed us without demur.

Managing training is a big part of a centurion's job. Martinez taught most of those classes himself, in a classroom that was way too big, about five times too big, for the twenty of us. I remember listening carefully to one such, while holding a rag under my nose to catch blood from that morning's slugfest.

"There are five, and only five, reasons to train," he told us. "These are selection, development, conditioning, skill training, and testing of doctrine and equipment. Of these, skill training is the easiest, and possibly the least important. Still, the best training does all these things at once.

"When . . . if, you become centurions, you will be in a position to select among the troops you lead. What do you select for?" He looked straight at me.

I sniffed the blood back, stood up, and quoted from the book, which was actually a doctoral thesis funded by Carrera, so I later learned. "Sergeant Major, we will select people for three considerations. Firstly, we select who will be made a leader. Then we select—and get rid of—those who ought not to be retained in uniform in *any* capacity. Of the remainder, the bulk of your troops, you select who should do which jobs, get which training, be assigned to which of your subunits."

"Good, Candidate Fuentes, good." He turned his attention back to the class as a whole. I sat down.

"Now it is impossible to do a proper job of selection in a peacetime environment, unless your training in peace simulates war very closely. The things many other armies use—connections, wealth, degrees, to some extent IQ scores, and so forth—are not merely poor indicators of the ability to lead in combat, there is reason to believe that some—connections and degrees, especially— are adverse indicators. I tend to believe that.

"So your training *must* be hard, painful, miserable, and—to a degree—dangerous. At the bare minimum, your training must have the appearance of being dangerous. Your soldiers must *believe* it is dangerous."

Martinez gave a tiny smile, then pulled out from under his podium a whip. He rotated it in his hands, to show it to us, while continuing to speak. "Based on the above, it would seem that simply flogging your troops once a day with a cat-o-nine tails would meet the requirements. Obviously, this is not so. Training must be exciting, interesting, more fun than pain filled, and—and this is *very* important—it must give your soldiers a sense of having accomplished something, of having won a victory or—if they lose—at least of having given a worthy effort. Besides, we want and need conscientious adrenaline junkies, not masochists."

I raised my hand. When Martinez waved the whip at me, I stood to attention. My voice sounded funny even to me as I asked, "Sergeant Major. Does that mean that we should take our troops out for . . . oh, adventures; white water rafting, scuba diving, things like that?"

He dropped the whip back underneath the podium, then nodded as if he agreed. Somehow, I didn't think he did. He then said, "Good question. No. That sort of activity doesn't hurt, precisely. But it doesn't help all that much either; certainly not enough for the effort and expense. And there is a danger that, if you try to do these things, you may well lose sight of your responsibility to make all of your training exercises adventurous."

I wasn't quite satisfied. "What about team building, Sergeant Major?"

"If you can't build enough adventure to aid team building into normal tactical training and social affairs, Candidate Fuentes, I suggest you find another job. And stop dripping on the floor."

I sat down, wiping my red-stained face as I did.

"Development," he continued, "is concerned with building upon those conscious intellectual and moral factors a soldier must have. I speak here of judgment—human, technical, and tactical; of determination and courage—physical and moral. I mean all those things that are, or can be, consciously learned.

"Remember, though, that while you can teach a *monkey* to load an artillery piece, you will never teach him to stop picking fleas off his body and eating them. You cannot make a silk purse from a sow's ear; you cannot make an idiot a genius; you cannot make a coward a hero, except in the newspapers and in some other nations' high political offices."

That got him a laugh.

"Conditioning is closely related to development, in some ways almost a subset of it. To some extent, they overlap as equals. We condition our soldiers—leaders, too—in the unconscious attributes of a soldier. This includes conditioning him to accept pain and discomfort, generally through physical training and harsh field training. We condition them to obedience, being very careful not to overdo it. We condition their bodies to health and strength. We condition against hardships by chopping off food, water, and rest without notice.

"One area where conditioning and development overlap is courage, where we first condition against fear by repeatedly placing the soldier in apparent or real danger, then *develop* the ability to use that reduced vulnerability to fear to allow the soldier to willingly place himself in greater, quite likely avoidable, danger, the better to do his combat job.

"Discipline is another area where conditioning and development overlap, though differently from courage. We could impose discipline purely from above. This would be conditioning. It would also destroy initiative, one of the few areas where our poor country enjoys an advantage over her likely enemy. Therefore, we partly condition discipline: 'Don't do this'; while developing self-discipline through encouraging initiative: 'Do what needs doing, as best you see it, *now*.' It's a tricky art; one that will probably take some time and practice for you to master."

Martinez pulled a knife out from under the podium and threw it at the back wall. We all turned to look. Sure as hell, the thing was quivering almost dead center of a bull's-eye target there on the back wall. It was at least fifteen meters away.

He looked at it, shook his head, and *tsked*. I guess he wasn't quite satisfied with the throw. He muttered, sotto voce, something about, "getting old."

"Skill training." Martinez sighed, still shaking his head. "A great general of Old Earth, Napoleon, once observed, to paraphrase, that moral factors are three times more important than material ones. Skills are material factors.

"I think this is mathematically suspect. At one level, every one of the five factors that go into first class training are equal. That is to say, if your troops are effectively zeros in any one area, then they are zeros overall. This is because the factors and attributes cannot be added up to find the truth, as a statistician might. Instead, they must be multiplied by each other. Soldiers with absolute, even suicidal, courage but zero military skills have little value except in giving their enemies useful marksmanship training by becoming targets. Look up the Zulu *impis* at the Battle of Ulundi. On the other hand, soldiers with perfect skills but no courage would run away long before they have a chance to use their superior technical skills. I can't give you an example of this because I have never found a case of an army being so stupid as to put all its faith into its people's skills.

"However, Napoleon was right in this: moral factors are three times harder to *develop* in the troops than mere physical and mental skills are. They are, therefore, only about a third as likely to be adequate in a given military force, unless three times the effort is expended on them.

"You can, to some extent, develop moral faculties through skill training. Teaching a soldier how to blow through barbed wire with explosives is skill training. Having him do it while cringing nearby in a shallow crater, as the explosive goes off, builds his moral faculties, too. Training a soldier to rush from position to position quickly is a useful skill. Having a sniper shoot very near him as he does so also builds his moral power.

"There is also a useful moral power that comes simply with being able to do something important properly, like shooting and hitting what you shoot at, for example. Self-confidence, if not entirely misplaced, has its value. Take that with a grain of salt, however. All the courses and books in the world on building *self*-esteem are largely exercises in learning how to be a bad judge of character.

"Testing of doctrine and equipment? Simply this: if your peace-time training doesn't identify weaknesses in both, you and your soldiers will bleed in war. You might even lose. For this reason, again, your peacetime training must simulate war as exactly as you can make it do so."

Most of our time was *not* spent in lectures. Lectures are a nice adjunct, but they're not enough in themselves. Instead, we learned to do by doing.

One of the major jobs for a centurion is to manage time, find time, create time. This is a problem in any army. It's even tougher for us, with so little time to train the reservists and militia compared to how much training they really needed. Maybe one of Joan of Arc's pikemen didn't need a lot of training. Our riflewomen would.

You might think that this is all very easy: make a schedule and stick to it. We do make schedules, of course, sometimes quite elaborate ones. The next time I see one of those work out as planned will be the first time. It's the merest truth; the more carefully you plan, the more effort seniors put into supervising, the less efficient the use of time.

So, amidst everything else we had to do in Centurion Candidate School—classes, physical training, beating the crap out of each other, inspections, field exercises, in short, right in there with every eighteen hour day—every one of us had to teach every other one about one new skill, technique or trick every week. We first had to teach ourselves, of course, skills like emplacing and recovering mines (tricky, that last), identifying friendly and foreign tanks, first aid, what have you. God help the candidate who failed to reach and teach everybody. And no time was scheduled for it, we had to find our own in every trivial bit of slack in the training schedule. Mandatory Opportunity Training, or MOT, they called it.

This was, by the way, about twice the MOT burden men had. Oh, they had to do the same basic thing. But each man only had to deal with his own squad, nine or ten other candidates. I, on the other hand, had to hunt down all nineteen of the others every week, using every spare moment.

If I failed, if the cadre found just that one candidate that I hadn't managed to get to, we all got punished. Severely.

Though the worst punishment was in failing your sisters.

Unfair? Maybe. Then again, maybe it's the straitjacket put on us by society, maybe it's genetic, but we—women, I mean—are much more comfortable with order and rules, law and regulations, schedules and such. Men chafe under rules; are much more at home with chaos and disorder than we are. Men loathe regulations. Since war is chaos and no one has yet found a way to change that (and no one *ever* will), we were potentially at a grave disadvantage compared to men.

MOT wasn't a big thing, really, though it was a big pain. It wasn't even about teaching or learning the tasks. It was all about learning to make time, deal with chaos, and watch out for each other.

Though we run most of our own training now, we've never stopped using this technique. In some ways, number of tasks to teach, for example, we've made it even harder.

We had no great number of feminists left in the tercio. It was funny, but, while feminists had volunteered for the *Tercio Amazona* in larger numbers than their representation among the populace, they had not succeeded in anything like the same ratio. Whether this was because they objected to the harsh treatment, or they were strong only in their wants and not in their wills, or—and there had *maybe* been a couple of these—they had joined not to make the legion stronger for battle but weaker, I don't know. Suffice it to say that most of those who made it through Basic, and all but a handful of those who had made it through Cazador School were actually more traditionally minded women, country girls, most of them, used to hard work and few amenities. I was almost the only pure city girl to have made it so far.

Even so, it was hard not to have picked up some of the viewpoints of modern feminism, the women of our country are not that old fashioned. All of us believed in equal pay for equal work, for example. I rather suspected that the few real feminists among us would not have accepted the corollary; that unequal work should receive unequal pay. I'm not sure I did myself. By that logic, because our units were larger, we ought to have been paid less. Work isn't everything, though, to a fighting force. As long as we would fight equally, I thought, and still think, we should be paid equally. I believe that was *Duque* Carrera's viewpoint as well.

He came to speak to us, once, as our training neared an end. Sergeant Major Martinez introduced him. As if he needed an introduction. I remember that he smiled at me warmly, and gave me the smallest imaginable wink, when he entered our classroom.

"Ladies," he began, and when he said "ladies" he seemed to mean it, "it does my heart much good to see so many of you still here, still in training. I am going to speak to your officer candidates tomorrow. I wanted to speak to *you* first. You're frankly more important.

"To begin, you have been kept somewhat in the dark regarding the details of raising your tercio. That was deliberate. There was no sense making promises that I could not know if I could keep. This was a good thing, as I now know I cannot keep to everything I might have wanted to promise.

"All of you here today will—almost unquestionably—graduate CCS. That's the good news. So I have been told that six of the officer candidates will likewise graduate OCS. The bad news is that there are too many of you future centurions for the number of officers: seventeen to six. There are also too few troops for that much leadership. That remains true even with the two hundred and ninety-three new Amazons that have finished Basic since your class and the several hundred still in the fourth class.

"We also have the problem that none of you is truly an *experienced* leader. And experience, at your level, counts for a good deal. So . . . while you will graduate, and while you will receive your centurions' sticks, you will not be accessed into the force, most of you, as full optios."

He raised a hand then to quiet the muttering. "Be patient. We are going to do with you what we do with most of the men, but in a slightly different way. You will—again, most of you—return upon graduation as sergeants and corporals to the six new casernes the legion has built for your tercio. You, like the men, will wear those stripes and a small cloth stick sewn on the sleeve to indicate your status. You will assume your rank as optios and centurions only when your tercio is large enough to justify it. And that will take a couple of years.

"Tough, isn't it? Well, if you really are soldiers now, as I've been told, then you won't be complaining so much about your personal perks. If you are going to complain and put yourselves above the country and the legion then you are not soldiers at all. Which will it be?"

As the question was obviously rhetorical, none of us answered. The muttering died away even so. He had touched a nerve when he suggested we might be selfish about this.

"Good. What we will have then is six of the most junior officers imaginable, nineteen of you qualified to be—in theory—optios, several score extremely junior NCOs, and about three hundred trained privates."

Carrera singled me out, I suspect only because I was the only one with whom he could attach a name to a face. "Candidate Fuentes, do you know everything you need to know to lead a platoon?"

It was a trick question, of course. If I said I thought I did, I'd being showing far more ignorance than if I admitted, truthfully, that I did not. I sort of ducked the question. "I imagine I know as much as any man in my position."

Carrera nodded. "Yup, I have no doubt you do. What would a man in your position, returning to his tercio, have that you do not?"

I thought furiously for a moment. Then I made a joke, of sorts. "Adult leadership, sir?"

Carrera nodded with great seriousness. "Yup. A man would leave here, or OCS, with all the tools he needed to begin ... *provided* that he was in company with experienced officers and centurions to teach him the fine points. We don't have *any* experienced female officers and centurions to give you, not one. I wish we did. But everything has to start somewhere, and you are the somewhere.

"Tell me, do you think I should put you under the command of that leftover female tribune ... what's her name?" His fingers wriggled in the air as he searched his brain.

I offered, "You mean 'Claudia,' sir?"

"Yes, that's the one."

I couldn't believe he was serious. "Sir ... she's no kind of officer at all. An overpromoted bureaucrat. It isn't so much that she doesn't know the right way ... sir, she's spent a lifetime learning all the wrong ways. By now she's just too old to relearn. Sir, you *can't*! It would be"—I struggled for the right word—"It would be ... sabotage!"

"Can't and won't," he agreed. "But you must have experienced leaders. And I can't—well, I don't—trust any straight men in the Force to do that for you. I wouldn't even entirely trust myself."

Oh, shit. I knew what was coming even before he said it.

"Therefore, the *Tercio Gorgidas* will provide your command and staff for the next few years."

We all groaned.

"I thought I ought to tell you that myself. *Gorgidas* has been ordered to provide you with five tribunes of varying grades, a sergeant major, and four centurions. They will form the cadre for the first maniple of *Amazonas.* That's not counting those who will continue to run *Amazona* basic training for the next several years, until there enough of you to do the job.

"I said maniple, but it will be a different sort of maniple. It will be organized to be able to expand to a full regiment in time. Each of those six soon-to-be OCS graduates I mentioned will start as a platoon leader for one of the platoons. Six of you will become platoon optios. The rest of you will become squad leaders.

"None of this is your fault, by the way. We...I...made a mistake. I really didn't expect nearly so many of you to get this far, so I didn't plan for it.

"Platoons? You'll have six in that first maniple: three infantry, one combat support, one artillery, and one headquarters and support. They'll run about forty to seventy women each to start with.

"In time, as we recruit and train more women, the platoons will expand to maniples, then the maniples to cohorts. Shortly after that point I—or more likely my successor—will pick the tercio commander and some of her key staff. That's when you all will see the last of *Gorgidas,* except maybe on parade or in the field. Your tercio will owe a great debt to *Gorgidas* when you are finally able to pay it."

One of my sisters raised a hand and stood to attention. "How long will that be, sir?"

"About ten years, I think. Though you here in this classroom can expect to assume the rank and duties of centurions in a much shorter time. If recruiting and training keeps up as it has been, there should be enough Amazons for you to take over platoon centurion and platoon leader positions within, maybe, two years; at least for full mobilizations. Most of you can expect to be first centurions or cohort sergeants major within five years or so.

"For whatever it's worth, no man could expect such rapid promotion. Then again, after you fill the big positions, things will slow down radically for the women who follow behind you.

"There's one other thing before I go. Even though you won't be able to wear your rank for a while, and even though we'll pay you at the rank you wear, the benefits you were promised for coming as far as you have already will be yours, for schooling and such. What the hell, there's a little extra money in the budget." His face took on a contemplative look. "For that, and some other things."

He turned to go, but turned back suddenly. "I guess there is one other thing. I'm damned proud of all of you." Then he left.

We had a lot of combat leadership training and under circumstances where we were a lot more conscious than in Cazador School. We had, as mentioned, some lectures. The gist of one of those has stayed with me through the years, possibly because it was very near graduation. We were talking about motivators that affect a soldier at different times and levels.

Though it was billed on the training schedule as a lecture, it fact it was a discussion. Martinez led it. We were far enough along that it really was a discussion, too. Martinez and the others had accepted that we really were going to be equal. It made a difference in how they acted towards us. The level of formality dropped quite a bit. One measure of that is that he held the discussion not in a classroom, but at the club, over drinks.

Martinez passed me a beer; I went to find a seat. He grabbed his own drink, a dark amber sipping rum of some kind, then walked to the table he'd had set up for us. It was actually two big tables, placed long ends against each other, and covered with a white tablecloth. It didn't have any flowers, but then we weren't all that flowery a force.

At the table he took a seat. "Why are you all here?" he asked, then added, "No, don't answer. It was rhetorical. A lot of you probably think you're here for reasons of patriotism. Some may think you're here for narrow self-interest or family interest."

I thought that last pretty much described me but Martinez shook his head, doubtfully.

"You know," he said, "it really doesn't work that way. Altruistic patriotism, or even factors of narrow self-interest, may get a civilian to volunteer to become a soldier. When the going gets tough, however, as it does in war—or basic training in preparation for war—patriotism and self-interest become very, very weak motivators. What do you suppose keeps them at it then, Candidate Zamora?"

"Fear of punishment, Sergeant Major?" she answered, uncertainly, one finger twirling a short lock of her pretty red hair. "That certainly helped me get through Basic; at least initially."

Martinez gave a rare chuckle. "Not if they're worth a shit, it doesn't. Oh, sure, sometimes, early on, we apply a little bit of the stick to help someone over a hurdle. But if they haven't acquired the ability—better say, the character—to go on, all on their own, by the time they finish Basic, they're pretty useless. There's nothing too awful that we can do to them that the enemy can't do more of, and worse. If they're that afraid of what little we do, how can they ever have the strength to resist what the enemy can do?"

Another candidate asked, "Pride, Sergeant Major?"

"Close," he said. "Pride helps, but there's something more powerful."

I was willing to give it a shot, and I thought I knew the answer. "Shame, Sergeant Major."

Now he really did smile. "Precisely. The young soldier in Basic is ashamed to go home a failure. If it wasn't for that, our failure rate would be intolerable. There are some differences between men and women in this, however.

"One: A prospective Amazon is doing something no one expects of her, and which most people will feel is beyond her. So what shame is in it for her if she quits? Two: For the immediately foreseeable future your new recruits will have to be trained by men. I have read a report from your training cadre which suggests very strongly that you are relatively immune to being shamed by men, though you are quite good at shaming each other. This is something that probably can't be fixed until there are enough of you with enough experience to take over running basic combat training for your own tercio. That's one reason, the main one, actually, that more fear was used for a longer time in your basic training. I suspect strongly that when you all can run your own Basic, you'll actually be able to lighten it up, and produce a better soldier because of it.

"In any case, shame—maybe with a little admixture of fear and pride—gets the soldier through Basic. What keeps him in the line under fire?"

Someone answered, "Love, Sergeant Major."

"Yes. But not just any old love. It has to be love of the group. If it's not, if it's the love of just one, then the only logical thing to do is hit the one you love over the head and drag them away from danger."

"Sergeant Major," I said, "the *Tercio Gorgidas* is made of what you just said couldn't work in battle, pairs of lovers. They are some tough *hombres*."

He nodded his head. "I know. That bugs me a little, too. It might work, if they can figure out how to have both loves. I'll tell you, too, that I think *Duque* Carrera made a mistake turning them into infantry."

I asked why.

"Because if they fight as infantry their casualties are going to be pretty random. That's how battle is these days. Nearly every dead *Gorgidas* trooper is also going to mean another one who's just lost everything he cares about. Some are going to be morally crushed by that. Others are going to go wild. Carrera should have made them tankers, or—better—light tankers, in Ocelots crewed by pairs of pairs. That way the poor bastards could live or die together. Now? If we changed them to tanks I think they'd be insulted. And they're adults. If they're willing to take the risk, who am I to complain?"

Getting back to the subject, he continued, "So love of comrades keeps soldiers on the battle line. All the sociologists seem to agree. And patriotism counts for little or nothing in battle. What's the trap? I gave you a small hint."

Zamora answered, "I . . . suspect, Sergeant Major, that after a while you get tired of seeing your friends die."

He answered as if he knew. "Yes . . . yes, you do. This is especially true when you can't understand *why* they have to die . . ."

I had a sudden blinding flash of the obvious. "It has to be worth it, doesn't it, Sergeant Major?"

He nodded very seriously. "Yes. The cause has to justify the expense. And that brings us right back to . . . patriotism. Maybe no one really fights for their country. But if they really don't believe in or care about their country, the time will come when they won't fight at all."

We saw Carrera one last time at Camp Spurius Ligustinus. He came to present us our regimental eagle at graduation.

Of course, the eagle really belonged to the entire tercio— commissioned officers, centurions, warrant officers, sergeants, corporals, privates and discharged veterans alike. But it exists in a special relationship with a tercio's centurions. Officers come and go. They spend more time away from the eagle on higher level staffs and in school. They also have to think more about those higher units and sister tercios. Sometimes they even get sent to a different regiment, if it comes from an area that has trouble producing officer material.

Centurions almost never leave their tercio, certainly never more than a few years in a career. We may go run basic training, or do recruiting, but even those are just different parts of the unit.

You can get very attached to the symbols of your home, tribe or country, when you never really leave those symbols. Most armies seem to have forgotten this. We haven't.

You've seen a tercio eagle, of course: metal plated bird of prey—a stylized harpy eagle, if you didn't know—with wings upstretched as if for takeoff, the bird itself on a carved wooden perch and the perch attached to a spiral-carved seven-foot pole, with the pole decorated with awards and honors. Pretty, no? I don't think you can imagine how beautiful it is to one of *us*, as long as it's our own. The silver cohort eagles are nice, too, of course, but they're not quite the same.

Carrera and Martinez both made speeches. Carrera spoke of the eagle and the nation; Martinez of the role and sacred duty of the centurion. Then we marched, single file, across the stage. As we did, Carrera and Martinez shook each sister's hand and passed us our batons.

I took mine and stepped off the stage. Once at floor level I looked it it, held in both my hands and felt something course through me I don't think I'd ever felt before and still don't have words for. It was more than just pride, though.

Interlude

On the surface the governments of the Tauran Union and Balboa were really quite alike. Both were apparently federal democracies, though Federalism was waxing in Balboa even as it waned in Taurus under the continuous assault of semi-aristocratic bureaucrats who were beyond the rules and beyond control. Both had three branches of government with the legislature being bicameral; which is to say, split into two. Balboa also had a sort of popular assembly which had the power to nullify any legislative acts and reviewed most of them. Both had written constitutions and both were ruled in accordance with law, though since the bureaucrats of the Tauran Union made most of the law to suit themselves, this was a marginal similarity.

In theory, the Taurans could use military conscription. In practice they didn't. In theory, Balboa did use it, though still not in practice.

An election in Balboa was probably more dignified. An election in the Taurus certainly involved more citizens. This was unsurprising as, since the Revolution, relatively few Balboans were allowed to vote. Most of them could have, of course, had they just complied with their draft notices and the law. It was their choice, whether or not to assume all the responsibilities of citizenship.

The centuriate assembly began with a parade, of sorts, on a flat area of mowed grass not far from the *Mar Furioso*. Second Tercio, including its cadets and discharged and retired veterans, marched onto the parade field to the regimental pipes and drums. The tune was "*Boinas Azules Cruzan la Frontera*." The oldsters came first, in centuries, followed by the still serving men and women, in their maniples, then the cadets. The mass formed up in blocks in three lines; the retired and discharged in front, their centuries well spaced out, then the main tercio behind. The cadets formed up to the rear.

At the last note of the pipes, the drums flourished. That was the signal for the former troops of the first line to sound off with, "We once were young and brave and strong." Immediately after, the main tercio shouted, much, much louder, "And we're so now, come on and try." The thousand or so junior cadets, half their voices breaking, answered, "But we'll be strongest, bye and bye." Witnesses tried very hard not to smile at the boys' breaking voices.

After some ceremonial legerdemain the colonel-in-chief of the tercio, a seventy-three year old retired tribune with a seat in the Senate, ordered, "Bring your units to open ranks. Stand by for inspection."

While the serving regular cadre inspected the second line, the political leaders inspected the oldsters. This was more symbolic than real. All they checked for were that each voting member of a century present had his or her personally engraved, government issue pistol, rifle, light machine gun, or submachine gun, that they were serviceable and clean, and that the oldsters carried a full load of ammunition. The firearms weren't needed, of course, at the election; the *Tercio Amazona* was pulling security for the affair. (It didn't have any voters, yet.) If the inspection had a purpose, it was to reaffirm the truth that political power grew from the barrel of a gun.

They stacked all arms prior to beginning the vote, in any case. It was enough to know and to show that arms *were* there, to legitimize the vote if necessary.

Following the inspection, the few hundred officers and centurions were ordered out of the formation to form smaller blocks of their own. The troops and cadets were marched away under their sergeants. The centurions and officers remained mainly to answer questions and see to the care of the honorably discharged or retired.

The first order of business was a plebiscite on some few laws enacted by the legislature. This came in three parts, the first being on whether the bill was in understandably plain and unambiguous Spanish. If not, it was automatically rejected if enough centuries across the country agreed it was incomprehensible. The second was to identify which acts had annoyed someone enough to want to have them voted on, and the third the actual vote for any laws which had failed the second criteria. Laws which could not garner sufficient support of a majority of the nation's political centuries were automatically overturned.

This was done by open roll call and voice vote; no secret ballot. There was a disadvantage to this, of course. It was a way for someone to ensure a bought vote stayed bought. It was felt, however, that there were some things a person ought to be ashamed to vote for.

Despite the name, the centuries had fewer than one hundred living members each. They had one hundred names, but that included the dead who had been accessed into the centuries early. Some of those dead hadn't even graduated Basic but had been killed in training. Still, their names were there and the living voted, in effect, on their behalf. It hadn't happened yet, but the day would surely come when one old man or woman, the last of his or her century, cast, in effect, one hundred votes.

Once the plebiscite was completed, the results were sent to the colonel-in-chief. It was his duty to report the votes by centuries to the national government.

Next there was an election for the "at-large" seats in the two legislative houses. These were reserved for discharged members of the legion who had earned certain awards for valor in battle. What that kind of courage had to do with good government may have been debated. Nonetheless, in forming their new constitution, Carrera and Parilla, and the legion's chief ideologues, Jorge and Marqueli Mendoza, had thought that it was precisely the lack of courage that has made so many societies rotten from the top down.

After the at-large seats were voted on, the centuriate assembly voted on the local, which was to say, regimental seats. There were the usual speeches, none allowed to last longer than five minutes. Everybody who was voting knew everybody who was running, so it wasn't obvious why they should waste much time.

Afterwards they had a great party, the leaders of the tercio and its voters.

CHAPTER ELEVEN

Cried all, "Before such things can come,
You idiotic child,
You must alter human nature!"
And they all sat back and smiled.
  —Charlotte P. S. Gilman, "Similar Cases"

The problem is, Maria thought, sitting in the counselor's office in a blank office building not far from the center of the City, *that I really don't know what I want to be when I grow up.*

The legion was willing to help the Amazons to do or to learn to do almost anything for which they were qualified. A low interest loan to start a business? No problem. A *beca,* or scholarship, for higher education? Easy. Any one of a number of jobs in the defense industry or government? Absolutely.

They could have anything, that is, if the needs of the country indicated an opening. Towards that end the counselor had given Maria and some others a battery of tests. The first set had been more concerned with what they might like to do than what they might be good at. These were followed by others designed to measure raw talent. Between the results of those two, the counselor and Maria finally decided that she could be a good teacher of elementary or high school children. For that she needed college.

Scribbling some notes on a pad, the counselor said, "Time won't be that much of a problem. You spend what?... one full weekend a month, Friday night through Sunday night; a bit over two weeks annually training the militia..."

"Actually, sir," Maria told him, "we aren't big enough yet for a militia echelon. So we spend five to six weeks at year at the

Centro de Entrenamiento Nacional; the big training facility, gener-ally by maniples attached to one of the male infantry regiments."

"Well then, no real change. That leaves a lot of time for edu-cation."

"I suppose," Maria answered doubtfully.

The counselor sighed, the sigh composed of equal parts of frustration and exasperation. "Others have done it," he said. "You can, too."

"It's not what you think," she said. Then she confessed, shame-faced, "But I didn't even finish high school."

"Ohhh," he said. "So that's it. You did, actually."

"Huh?"

"Don't you remember taking an equivalency test when you joined?"

"I remember a lot of tests," she answered. "I don't remember *that*."

"Never mind," the counselor said. "Trust me; you did. It says so right here in your record. Decent scores, too. And you already have some college credit from your military training; about two and a half semesters' worth."

Seeing the disbelieving look on her face, the counselor added, "Don't you think you learned some things in Cazador School no college can teach? And you've got two semesters' worth of military history from Centurion Candidate School all on its own. To say nothing of three credits' worth of sports and athletics, a semester of management, one philosophy course...a semester of military law...civics..."

Maria thought about the course structure of the training she'd completed and answered, "Well...put that way..."

"I *did* put it that way." He drummed fingers on chin for a moment, thinking, rather, savoring the feeling of doing good for a fellow soldier. "So, Maria, we are going to enroll you in the university. All your books and tuition will be paid. You must, however, return the paper books or buy them when a course is finished; the legion isn't rich."

It still seemed impossible. She said, "On that subject, neither am I. I get three months' pay a year for my military duties. That isn't quite enough, really not *nearly* enough, to live on and take care of my daughter."

"Hmmmm. Let me see." More scribbling. A couple of phone

calls. The counselor took a quick trip to the fax machine, then returned with a smile.

"How does a part-time job sound? Say twenty hours a week? You'll be working with a shipping firm that gets a lot of business from the legion on condition that they hire a lot of members of the legion. The job requires a security clearance but you already have that. You have a substantial credit in the bank from your training. You and your daughter should be able to get by on that much. What do you say?"

Maria looked down and shook her head ruefully. "Where was all this aid when I *really* needed it?"

The counselor's face lost its helpful, friendly grin momentarily. "You didn't deserve it then," he said. "Now you do. This help and, so I understand, something else, too."

With the money withheld and saved for her while she was in training, Maria found a small but cute apartment in one of the older but nicer parts of the City. It was a safe and decent place for Alma to grow up. The apartment was furnished, though not grandly. This was just as well as that saved money would only go so far.

Alma? For the first two or three weeks Maria was home, the baby missed Lydia Porras more, perhaps, than she'd missed her mother while she was gone.

"It's only natural, child," Porras chided, one day during a visit. "She's been here now for months. Give it a little time. She's still your daughter."

Maria hoped so. She said, "She's become such a little lady, Lydia. Your influence, I am sure. I never had time to teach her much."

"She's just older, Maria, nothing more. By the way, when are you going into the hospital for restoration?"

"For *what*?"

"You mean they haven't told you?"

That was the "something else" Carrera and the counselor had hinted at. For the Amazons were to be *restored* to the way they used to look, better even, if desired and possible. It seemed only fair. By the time they were done with training, their breasts and bottoms had shrunk to nothing, no soft feminine curves, just bone and muscle. Even the extra poundage some had put on after the forced starvation of *Cazadora* School had not gone to the best places, aesthetically speaking. Moreover, among the to-be centurions, their noses—Maria's more than most—were generally pretty badly deformed, even pulverized. If they were not quite ugly, they also were not very pretty anymore.

So the legion paid to rebuild them, to make them approximately as pretty as they'd been before they began, or perhaps slightly more so in Maria's case. She, just as an example, was given a rhinoplasty—a nose job, and a breast restoration, plus a little sculpting of her jaw line. The surgeons also removed some scars and gave some limited liposuction for the poundage she'd put on after *Cazadora* School. Basically everything that could reasonably be done to improve appearance, they'd done for all the women who'd gone the distance. Carrera even brought in special plastic surgeons from Santa Josefina and Maracaibo for some of the work.

"Unfortunately, they couldn't do much about my height; I'll die short," Maria told Marta and a few others one day over coffee at a little sidewalk café just off of *Via* La Plata. The others were Trujillo, Gonzalez, Galindo, and Zamora. In theory, it was against the regulations to socialize like that. In practice, Inez called it a "training meeting" and ignored the spirit of the law. They were all in mufti; after all, there was no sense in advertising that they were ignoring the spirit of the law.

"Don't worry, dear," Marta answered. "You're kind of cute, short. And wasn't that the damned nicest, *kindest,* most *generous* thing Carrera ever did for any of us?"

Marta must have been feeling warmhearted; there wasn't a single "shit" or "fuck" in the sentence.

With a laugh, Inez answered, "Kindness and generosity? Don't you believe it, Marta. Carrera—and I'm sure it was his personal decision—isn't quite that sweet. If he'd thought the money was better spent on something else then there would have been no plastic surgery for us. I don't mean either that he doesn't care about us, or about giving us a fair shake. In the big scheme of things, however, the happiness of a few individuals just doesn't count all that much with him."

"Then why'd he do it?" Marta asked.

"Recruiting," Trujillo said, "the same reason he formed our tercio in the first place."

"What!" Marta gasped. "No way. I didn't go through all that you did, I know, and I would still not go through half of what I did just for a nose job."

"No," Trujillo said. "I don't mean recruiting of women. Only the few of us who've gone to one of the candidate schools were badly messed up enough to really justify the money he spent on restoration. Carrera wants us—all of us—*beautiful*... to shame men who hadn't volunteered yet into joining up. It makes sense, too, if you'll think about it a minute."

Marta did. "Are you trying to tell me the legion doesn't really *need* women infantry?"

"I don't know, Marta, if they need women, period. There aren't too many of us who are both suitable and willing. We cost a lot more to train than men do. We've got some limitations they don't have."

"You mean we're just things...means to an end...not important in ourselves? That's disgusting!"

"Marta, dear," Inez said, "everybody in the military is just a thing to be used. If you can't accept that, maybe you'd better find something else to do. Carrera needs men for machine gun fodder, and lots of them. Men, however, have started to grow a little scarce. There are still quite a number out there, but they are not volunteering readily enough. So he's shaming them, the bastard, using us to do it. Women doing difficult and dangerous jobs shame men just by being. However, attractive women can shame men more readily and thoroughly than can unattractive ones. So we were made pretty again; not for ourselves, but to shame the men. What do you want to bet it works, too? Gloriously?"

It was glorious, the first time Maria reported to a class at the university. Girls clustered around to ask questions. The citizen-soldiers and veterans were very polite and surprisingly respectful, especially the women soldiers doing their time in the non-combat branches. But the draft dodgers? Those men nearly crawled away from her, they were so ashamed. They wouldn't even meet her eyes. She found it simply delicious.

Though it wasn't as delicious as when she first saw Juan, and knew he'd seen her. Juan was still quite young, of course, only a few years older than Maria, but he'd gotten a little fat. She could see, too, that he'd begun, ever so slightly, to lose his hair. And he hadn't joined up, of course, wrong social class and outlook. Juan cringed when he saw her. Maria ignored him, naturally, and enjoyed doing it.

Eventually, Juan worked up the nerve to approach her. He had picked a Friday when she had drill that weekend, so she was attending class in semi-dress kilts. It was a non-jungle drill; inspections and inventories, mostly. Those were rare but any armed force has a certain amount of necessary administration.

"Hello, Maria," Juan said. "It's been a long time."

"Not so long," she answered, thinking, *Is that lame or what?* "But then, time flies . . ." She turned to go, the very picture of disinterest.

Juan *harrumphed* and reached to stop her. He didn't quite have the nerve to touch her, but he did reach out before stopping himself. She turned back anyway.

Juan said, "I'm . . . well, I just wanted to say; I'm sorry. You know, for . . ."

She cut him off with a chopping hand and a contemptuous sneer. "For what? For giving me a chance to grow up free and strong? For saving me from the life my parents had planned? For giving me a wonderful daughter? Juan, I don't hate you. I don't respect or like you, of course. But I don't hate you. You've served your purpose in my life, that's all." She laughed, but pleasantly, thinking that would hurt just a bit more.

Just then another student, a reserve junior centurion, walked up. "Maria, dinner tonight?"

"Not tonight, Manuel. Sunday. Seven, sharp," She answered. "And I have to be home by ten. Test on Monday." Then she sauntered away, leaving Juan in her figurative dust.

Maria slept with that fellow reservist, Manuel, that Sunday night. Marta watched Alma, as she often did. That was only the second man—if you could call Juan a man—Maria had ever willingly been with. But Manuel's sense of timing was too good to let go unrewarded. Besides, at the time Maria felt like being rewarded, too.

Classes were hard. Work was hard. Taking care of Alma was hard. Toss in the one day in four Maria spent as a soldier in any given year and life was sometimes *very* hard, and very often tiring.

But every night she wasn't in the jungle or on the caserne,

or on a rare date, she had Alma. When the baby fell asleep in Maria's arms, she knew that everything she had done had been worth it. It took a while but, eventually, Maria even reclaimed her place in Alma's life as her mother, Porras being relegated to a favorite grandmother.

Grandmothers? Maria's own mother did not visit anymore. Perhaps she was frustrated—her daughter thought it likely—that Maria had not been driven by poverty into returning to her control. Whatever the case, Mrs. Fuentes hadn't had anything to do with Maria or Alma, in fact, since Maria had joined the legion. She wouldn't let the little sister visit either. Maria's guess was that Mrs. Fuentes was too afraid her little sister would join up, as well.

Mother made a mistake though. She forgot about the younger brother, Emilio, he of the baseball glove. A few days after Emilio's eighteenth birthday he came to see his sister and niece.

Maria heard a knock on the door, opened it, and the next thing either of them knew she was giggling happily, had picked Emilio up bodily, and was dancing him around her small apartment. From a soft-faced boy, Maria's brother had grown up to be a larger, harder version of herself.

Mom and Dad did good work, after all, didn't they, she thought.

"I didn't remember you being quite this beautiful," Emilio began, once she'd put his feet back on the floor. "Then again, I don't remember you being that *strong* either."

He took a folded envelope from his pocket.

"Maria . . . I've gotten a letter from the government. You know; my draft notice." He handed it to her to read.

"Funny," she said. "I never received my own draft notice. Where I was living, I'd been too far out on the fringes of society to receive mail before I'd joined up anyway."

After reading, Maria said, "Well, Emilio, you don't have to go. It says so right here. All that happens if you don't go is that you can't vote, sit on a jury, hold public office, or have some jobs that are reserved, or any government aid. But if you are like Daddy you'll never vote or run for office anyway. And Daddy is going to leave you so much money you won't ever have to work outside the company, and then only if you want to. They won't change your tax status and no one can mention military status in a court of law—unless you are a veteran and there is a motion in court to strip you of that. What's the problem?"

Emilio smiled ruefully. "You are, *hermana*."

"Me. What do I have to do with this?"

He put a hand to her shoulder and squeezed. "Come *on*. Do you think I could look at myself in the mirror to shave with my sister being a *centurion* and me being a draft dodger?" Emilio shook his head, adding, "Father and Mother don't see it that way, of course."

"Of course," she echoed, sighing. "They wouldn't."

Just then Alma walked—she didn't toddle anymore—into the tiny living room of the apartment.

"*Tio Emilio!*" She rushed into her uncle's arms. He picked her up and swung her around in a full circle before pulling her up to his arms and kissing her on her head. They conversed in serious five-year-old-speak for a while.

When they were done, Alma nestled nicely in Emilio's shoulder, Maria asked, "So what *are* you going to do?"

"I was hoping you might tell me."

"Brother," she said, "this has to come from inside you. I can't tell you—no one can tell you—what you ought to do."

Emilio started to look just a bit...maybe...frightened.

Relenting, Maria continued, "But maybe I can help you think about what you ought to do. Tell me, besides not wanting to be outdone by your big sister, why *might* you want to join? Or not?"

He thought about it. "Honor? Glory? They don't mean much. Mostly, I'd guess, I want not to be inferior—to feel myself inferior—before any man, or woman."

" 'Every man thinks meanly of himself who has not been a soldier, or gone to sea,' " she quoted from a social philosophy class at CCS.

"Something like that," Emilio agreed.

"Fair enough," she continued. "So why don't you just go to another country? Father would pay for that, I'm certain. Maybe some country that doesn't care about the difference between a soldier and a civilian. The Federated States, for example."

Emilio shook his head. "Nah. Wouldn't make any difference. I'd still know about all the others; about you, too. I can't run from my own mind and memory...even if I were willing to run from my country."

"The country then," Maria asked, "it means something to you?"

"It means...something. I don't know what. Sure, all my—traceable—ancestors are buried here. And though that means something...but, hell, I didn't know most of them."

"Still fair enough. What does 'means something' mean to you, when you say it about the country?"

Emilio sat silent for a while, but she could see wheels—old, rusty, and unused ones to be sure—turning in his head. Finally he answered, in a sad and hopeless voice, "Everything—everyone—I know and love is here. And where else could I go and still be *home*? I might pass for a...oh, say, a Santandern, somewhere else, to other people. People who wouldn't know or care that I'd run out on my duty." He pointed to his heart. "But would *I* ever belong in such a place?"

It was Maria's turn to remain silent for a moment, thinking, parsing the words he'd said for meaning. "Duty? That means something to you, too?"

"Maria, if I knew what my duty was it might mean everything to me. So tell me. What's my duty? And look, knock off the Socratic Method, would you? This is your brother you're talking to."

"All right," she agreed. "No more Socrates." She parroted from CCS. "'You have several. There is the duty to God; which is also duty to the gifts of God: liberty, justice and right. Then you have a duty to humanity. You have a duty to your people, your nation. There is duty to tribe and family, that includes Mama and Papa, children as well...'" She gave him a hard and dirty look, "Though you had better not have any, at your age..."

At Emilio's broad, sardonic, smile, she sheepishly admitted, "Okay, so I was being a bit of a hypocrite there. You're still my little brother and you're too young to be a father."

"Oh, I agree," Emilio answered, with a tone that suggested it had been possible at one time or another. Maria let that go.

She said, "Anyway the very last thing is duty to self. Somewhere mixed in there is duty to your immortal soul. It's the only thing to guide you when duties conflict.

"Mathematicians and statisticians, philosophers, too, can argue—quite uselessly—about the relative weights of these duties. I'd suggest that you ought to follow your own soul. It's as good a guide as any, and better than most."

✧　　✧　　✧

Emilio joined. He wrote her from the *Isla Real* a few months after they'd talked:

Queridisima Hermana,

Hello, Maria! Greetings from the pearl of islands and the armpit of the world. How *did* you stand this place? I'm at 10th Tercio's training caserne (excuse me, "The *Glorious* 10th's," a serious slugging for forgetting that. Let's hope they don't check the mail) on the Royal Island.

(Uh, oh. They *do* check the mail. Please excuse the delay while my platoon centurion beats me vigorously about the head and shoulders—"in an approved military fashion"—as I write on the blackboard: "I will never call my tercio anything but the Glorious 10th. I will never call my tercio anything but the Glorious 10th. I will never call my tercio anything but the Glorious 10th. I will never call my tercio anything but...")

Okay, the beating's over. Please excuse the bloodstains on this paper; a whip is *such* a sloppy instrument. (I'm kidding. We both know that whips are reserved for the marginally more serious offenses.)

This place sucks, of course. But, I feel closer to you than I ever have before. Camp Botchkareva is just down the road a mile or so. It's even uglier than our caserne. I feel sorry for those girls every time my maniple marches by. (On the other hand, I'd rather be with them, in their camp, than here—alone in my bunk—in mine.) Again, how *did* you stand it, Maria?

Good news! I've been picked for a leadership track. I don't know yet whether it will be centurion or officer (centurion, I think). Of course I won't know until after Cazador School. Will you come to my graduation, *Cazadora*?

Sister, I want to thank you for your advice. This was the right thing to do.

Love,
Emilio

Maria folded the letter and pressed it to her breast. She was very proud that Emilio had done the right thing.

✧   ✧   ✧

Dodging cars and fighting their way through the crowds, Marta, Cat and Maria went shopping one Saturday, on *Via Hispanica*. Porras was watching the children, even though she had no obligation to.

The girls weren't looking for anything in particular, or even paying much attention to where they were going. Mostly they were just out enjoying each other's company. That, and Marta's jokes.

"... So one of the talking male trixies turned to the other and said, 'Put away the Bible; our prayers have been answered.'"

Cat bellied over with a loud guffaw. Maria just shook her head, saying, "You are *such* a dirty bitch, Marta."

"You're just jealous," Marta answered, with heavy tone of false self-righteousness.

"True, true," Maria agreed, good-naturedly.

"I'm hungry," Cat announced.

Marta sniffed and agreed, "Ahhh. Sumeri food. Yum."

Maria shook her head, doubtfully. "You two might be up for something composed of a mix of Holy Shit peppers, some Joan of Arc peppers, and a small admixture of Satan Triumphant. But I think I've suffered enough with the legion."

"Ah, don't be such a baby," Marta said. "It only hurts for a while. Like, say, taking it up the ass."

"You *are* a dirty bitch," Cat said, smiling.

"Oh, come on," Marta chided. "You don't mean to tell me you never ..."

"Not even once," Cat said.

Marta's face grew serious. She said, "Good for you."

Maria stopped suddenly and went ghastly pale. Her eyes were fixed on the second floor windows of an office building on the other side of the street. Every wretched moment came back to her in a flash. She felt anew every humiliation Piedras had inflicted on her. She began to shake and before she knew it, she was throwing up on the street.

Marta asked, "Maria, what's wrong with you?"

"Nothing," she answered, shakily. "I'm all right." But then she started to cry; unable to help herself. She felt like a helpless, stupid, eighteen-year-old *thing* again.

They were nearly at the Sumeri restaurant by then; the overpowering smell of hot spiced lamb and chicken said as much, as did the scent of freshly baked chorley tortillas (the grain made a lousy pita). Cat and Marta pulled Maria upright, then led her into the small café.

"What is wrong?" Cat demanded. Maria just shook her head.

Marta signaled to a waiter and ordered a bottle of sipping rum, some ice, and three glasses. The first one she poured herself, neat, then force-fed it to a sputtering Maria. She poured another, dropped in a couple of cubes of ice, and stuck the glass into Maria's hand.

"Tell us what is wrong, dammit!"

It took half the bottle, not all of which went into Maria, before they got the truth out of her.

One of the university courses Maria signed up for was given by Centurion—or, rather—*Professor* Franco. It was billed as a history course but turned out to have heavy elements of social and political philosophy. The main text was written by a legionary, Warrant Officer Jorge Mendoza, and his wife, Marqueli. They also studied Thucydides' *Peloponnesian War,* along with Orwell's *1984.* The students read all of Machiavelli's major works, as well as some by Aristotle and Xenophon. Franco even took the time to peruse some of the sillier social philosophies of more modern times.

If asked why she took the course Maria would probably have answered that it was half out of curiosity about what a *civilian* Franco would be like. He turned out to be quite...*civilized,* actually. Then again, compared to some others, he always had been.

Much of the course was concerned with the subject of societal change and reform.

Franco began one class quoting Machiavelli, "'There is nothing so difficult to take in hand, more perilous to conduct, or more uncertain in its success, than to take the lead in the introduction of a new order of things.'"

Franco turned and pointed casually at Maria. "Why does reform of human society fail, Miss Fuentes?"

She started to stand to attention, then remembered that this wasn't the legion. Her posterior had barely lifted from her seat before she forced it down again.

Paraphrasing the text, she answered, "The problem is just too complex, Professor Franco. The interrelationships among the people of the society that a reformer wants to change are *unknowably* complex. You can't change the society without knowing how it exists as is, and no mere human can hope to know all that. Many, too, refuse even to try to see it as it is."

He agreed, "That's true enough, as far as it goes. But it isn't quite enough, Maria. Let's narrow our inquiry down to one particular aspect of attempting reform, using the armed forces as your agent of change. It's a very popular technique, in some circles.

"Tell me, why use armed forces to effect societal change? You, there in the back. Tell me why?"

The woman he called on was a non-Amazon reservist, a private first class who had taken out a legion-backed loan to pay for college on her own ticket.

"The armed forces can *make* people change, Professor. They do it all the time. Naturally, when someone wants to change society, they go to those who know how to make changes to do it. That's the armed forces."

Franco let a small smile form. "Is it really? An interesting supposition. They changed you then, so you claim?"

"Well, of course. I'm stronger, healthier, more self-disciplined. I take more care with my appearance. I'm a lot different than I used to be."

"Are you more honest, forthright, and truthful than you used to be? Or are you less?" Franco asked.

The woman thought about it, then said, "I'd have to say I'm the same, as far as those things go."

"And you are perfect in these areas?"

"Nobody's perfect, Professor. I'm pretty good."

"Are you ninety percent perfect? Ninety-nine? Let's give you the benefit of the doubt and say you're ninety-nine and forty-four one-hundredths percent pure . . . and—as you say—always were. That's fair, even generous, isn't it?"

Franco continued, "That being the case, isn't it pitiful that the legion couldn't give you a lousy half a percent and change more to make you perfect? By God, what are they to do with someone who comes to the colors ninety-nine and forty-four one-hundredths percent rotten? A hopeless task, is it not?"

Franco called on someone else, a civilian boy. "What if you did know *all* of the complex relationships among people? Never mind that you can't, exactly, it *is* possible to know a useful amount; maybe even enough to get started."

The boy—Ishmael was his name; he was a foreign student, in Balboa under some exchange program set up between Carrera and Sumer's ruler, Adnan Sada—thought for a few moments before answering. "Well, Professor, you run into the problem of active resistance or damnation by faint support. The very people you're trying to change will resent it and—depending on their level of courage—either openly resist or pretend to go along while privately resisting. I think something like that happened to Tsarist Marxism, though it took years for the failure to become obvious."

"'Something like that,'" Franco echoed. "The Volgans are, in fact, an interesting case. Think about it: Using powers of compulsion and persuasion far beyond our apparent ability, even beyond our wildest dreams, with three full generations to make the change in, and with the decided advantage of having a series of external enemies to focus people away from their petty domestic concerns, still, the Tsarists failed miserably. Tell me why," he demanded of another boy, this one a reservist.

"It's similar to what Ishmael said. They tried to change the inner nature of the mass of the people, and very profoundly. They couldn't do that; nobody and nothing can actively do that. But they did succeed in driving it underground, for a while. Then human nature came back with a vengeance."

There was a Volgan in the class, a senior tribune named Chapeyev who had once fought with Carrera in Santander and now taught at one of the junior military academies. He still wore decorations from the old Volgan Empire, along with a bronze-colored cross for valor on his chest.

"Professor," he began when he had been recognized. "I remember when I was boy, back in old Folgan Empire. It was never ending, the propaganda: Life of Great Red Tsar, marfels of Folgan industry, efils of capitalism, efils of birth control, marfels of Imperial agriculture. Then more Life of Red Tsar and more efils of birth control.

"They had complete control; you got no other official messages."

The Volgan shook his head. "When I was boy, was easy to believe. But you would catch, sometimes, your elders smirking about it when propaganda was on TV. And you wondered. Smirks didn't mean anything, of course, even in Folgan Empire smirking wasn't against law. But you grew up and saw: Corruption, decay, bad management, hypocrisy, shoddy goods.

"I was soldier. In my case ... saw many shoddy weapons. Then the smirks of olden times came back with full power. Of course the adults had smirked. It was all lies, lies suitable for children only."

Franco asked the question, "But what about using the army? Didn't the Volgans try to use the army for reforms?"

Chapeyev snorted in derision. "Army is good for many things, in change of society. You can teach skills: Reading, writing, mathematics, some use of machines. You can get dirty Trypillian peasants to wash regularly, though it not as easy. All this you can do, because army can focus attention on other things, the efil enemy and the dangers of battle, need for teamwork, soldierly ideals. All make sense, even to dumb Trypillian peasant. But that limit of army's power. You talk to recruit of social systems, justice, proper political falues? Army lose power to persuade. Those things are not of army."

"I think that's right, Tribune." (First names in the classroom *unless* you outranked Franco, apparently.) "But what if you change the army's values, make it more political an instrument, less military?"

"Worse. Convince soldiers to be political, soldiers take over government very quick. Quick, quick. They hafe guns and tanks. What are fotes, compared to that? Even if not, army gets power over troops only from foreign enemy, outside threat. Maybe better to say, army gets only power troops willingly *give* it, and troops only give willingly because of outside threat. Make army less military, make army more socially ... conscious—is right term?— good ... eliminate outside threat, and army can do nothing, loses power over troops' beliefs. It can still affect open behavior, but only while troops are being watched."

"Are you saying, Tribune, that an army can only be used to make a society *more* military, and then only if the army is more military than civilian oriented, but that if you make the army less military and more civilian, then it can do no good in any way?"

"*Da,*" Chapeyev answered, then concluded, "But can do much harm."

Maria asked, seeing that Franco agreed with Chapeyev, "But we are using the legion for social, nonmilitary change, aren't we ... Professor?"

Franco smiled and agreed, "Yes, we are, Maria. But look at the details. Sure, the view of *your* regiment, by the legion, is changing. And, since the legion has become by far the most important element in society, one could say that it has therefore changed society's view. In a way. I haven't noticed that that's done anything much for women at large.

"The legion is being used to identify those people who are worth spending some money and effort on to raise up, economically and socially. And this matching of opportunity to ability and worth is plainly helping our economy despite foreign efforts to sabotage us. But few in the world approve of the legion being the center of our society. You might also have noticed that democracy—old style democracy, which in our case was just a corrupt oligarchy with the forms of the thing—died in the process.

"And were the legion to be anything but what it is—an illiberal, nonegalitarian, undemocratic, harsh, brutal, vicious and almost conscienceless machine—whose sole direct purpose is killing people and breaking things, it could not do even so much as it does.

"But societal change outside of the legion? As far as society's values are concerned? No, that hasn't happened in any way that the legion is directing. Nor will it, because there is no military utility in social change that cannot be directly related to the ability to wage war.

"One could try—and it's been tried elsewhere, though without any noticeable success—to convince soldiers that acceptance of nonmilitary values is a military plus because we need all those different people mixed in, happy and accepted. And it's true, we do, but only if there's a real threat. Maybe if it were equally true in both stable peace and in war it would work. But militaries don't usually need the really tiny minorities at all in peace, so they certainly don't need them happy. The militaries would be much better off without them, actually. Since the reverse isn't true, the message doesn't get accepted. Note here that war in the offing is effectively the same as war being conducted for this purpose."

"Then why does anyone try?" Maria asked.

"Arrogance, just arrogance. A lot of fairly unintelligent people, who obtain degrees that convince them they are in fact intelligent; no *brilliant*, they must be brilliant to have these wonderful degrees from such wonderful schools. They see the basic problems usually; that's not too hard. And since they don't see all the subtle problems, and since *brilliant people* like them couldn't possibly miss anything important, then those subtle little problems must not exist or are, at least, unimportant. Then these *brilliant* people barrel ahead, foolishly. They tear down all that went before. And, when their reforms fall flat on their foolish faces, they must find scapegoats, since their solutions are too *brilliant* to have failed without active sabotage. That way, by the way, leads to the reeducation camps. Ask Tribune Chapeyev."

Franco glanced at his watch. "Okay. That's it for today. For your study assignment I want you to read about Sedgwick-Green. It's a South Columbian low-income housing development, and you'll find it covered beginning on page two-thirteen of your text. When you come back to class on Wednesday be prepared to discuss how it is that this drug- and crime-ridden horror, unsightly, unsanitary and unsafe—in every way worse than what it replaced—could ever have come to pass. Pay particular attention to the breakdown in human relations, the knowledge and esteem of one's peers and neighbors, that took place when the old neighborhoods were destroyed and people moved willy-nilly into new 'homes.' Be prepared to discuss this in relation to declining property values. Note, too, how the people of that place are willing now to give up dignity and liberty for a little safety. And ask yourselves who is to blame, and why."

While waiting at the bus stop to go back to her neighborhood, and hopefully to be on time to pick up Alma from preschool so the child didn't have to wait inside, Maria paid to download a newspaper to her legion-issued electronic slate. She opened the folder up and scanned the international news first—*Bastard Tauran Union!*—then scrolled to more city-specific things.

She was on page three by the time the bus came. She dropped her tenth of a drachma into the box and went to find a seat. She ended up sitting next to a middle-aged man who was also reading from his own, civilian, slate. The man *tsked* and said, "I don't know what the city's coming to. Poor man."

Maria looked over and saw something about a street crime near *Via Hispanica*. She couldn't see more than that. She tapped in a query and searched her own "paper." When the query was answered she began to read.

It seemed that someone named Piedras, Arnulfo Piedras, had been assaulted and brutally beaten the previous night while on foot between his office near *Via Hispanica* and his auto.

The simple fact of there being a street crime in the city would have been newsworthy. What really made this particularly newsworthy, implied the column, was that Piedras claimed to have been attacked by four people, at least one of whom (possibly more) had been a *woman.*

These four, all their faces covered, had, he claimed, struck out of nowhere, knocking him to the ground, then beaten him with short clubs. Two had held him down while a third, very tiny one had carefully and deliberately smashed in most of his teeth with the butt of a dagger, leaving just two ragged lines of broken, bloody stumps in his mouth.

Not content with that, one of them—this was the one he was certain, based on her shape, had been female—had kicked his crotch so repeatedly and viciously that it was doubted he would ever be able to perform as a man again.

Then that one, accompanied by a really tall person, had swung Piedras back and forth by his arms until those had been dislocated. They'd dropped him to the ground and broken his collar bone and several of his ribs. Two of the attackers had then taken their clubs to his fingers and thumbs. Somewhere in that process the poor man had passed out.

Based on where and how he'd been found, apparently before leaving him the attackers had dragged his semi-conscious form to the street, put his feet on the sidewalks, then jumped on his knees.

The police were stumped. The viciousness of the attack, without Piedras' wallet being touched, left little obvious motivation, few clues.

Wonderingly, Maria closed the file and turned to look out the window at the passing scenes.

You don't suppose?

Towards the end of the school term, the *Tercio Amazona* held its first Centurions' Ball. This was traditionally a major event, a high point of any tercio's social season. (Officers had a ball, too, but there just weren't enough officers in the *Tercio Amazona* to make a good party. The centurions invited them, specially, to theirs.)

It was a little difficult for the Amazons. For one thing, just about all of them loathed civilian men as a matter of principle. Hence, they couldn't ask any civilians to escort them. Even if one of the women had been of a mind to, the disapproval of the others militated against it. Of those women centurions who were married, most had married other centurions. The one who was married to a full-fledged civilian was getting divorced. Perhaps there was too much strain on a marriage when the wife is more of a man than the husband.

To make matters worse, higher and lower ranking men were quite off limits to them. No male officers, no warrants, no sergeants, no troopers. Between those two factors rather more than ninety-nine percent of the men in the country were either off limits or unacceptable. Moreover, a large number of the male centurions were married. While they might not have minded escorting an Amazon centurion, their wives were likely to.

The women were all scrambling for dates.

Maria solved the problem by asking Franco one day after class. He laughed and said Garcia was unlikely to be jealous of *her*, so, "Sure. The term's effectively over. Your grades are already in; no chance of someone whining 'favoritism.' Why not?"

It really was a big event. The tercio cooks—they had some dedicated cooks, by then—had gone all out to make the food something really special. ("Rank Hath Its Privileges.") The centurions' fund paid for decorations and a band. The tickets (attendance was optional, tickets were *not*) paid for additional raw food and the booze.

"You, Professor—sometime Centurion—Franco, are a *great* dancer." A breathless Maria sat down heavily, using her napkin to wipe some exuberant sweat from her face.

Franco laughed, "It goes with the territory."

A bleary eyed Zamora, sitting opposite, asked, "What territory?"

Franco raised one eyebrow as if to answer, *That was a dumb question.*

Zamora nodded, *You're right, it was.* Then she said, "It must be very difficult for you. I wonder how you manage."

"Oh, well enough, I suppose." He looked at her knowingly. "How do you?"

" 'Well enough, I suppose' "

Maria, concentrating on regaining her breath, missed the byplay.

Signifer Inez Trujillo, a guest in the mess and sitting at Franco's right, did not miss it. She deliberately changed the subject.

"Centurion, I was reading recently an article arguing that we should get rid of our medium tanks and change to nothing but light Ocelots, even in the heavy brigades."

"Well, ma'am," he answered—Inez now outranked her former trainer—"it seems to me that this would be a foolish move..."

Another centurion, male and straight—married to one of Maria's classmates, joined in, "But think of how much easier to keep the Ocelots supplied and running."

Soon a half a dozen men and women were gathered around, hashing out this important question as profoundly as any similar group of inebriates would have been capable of.

Zamora left the table dateless and alone and rather sad.

Alma had her birthday not more than a few weeks after the Centurions' Ball. That was the sort of occasion when a certain amount of cross rank socializing was permissible and desirable. Maria's entire reserve squad and their kids were there. Catarina came over early to help with decorations. Marta made the cake. Porras spent what must have been half her monthly stipend on Alma's present, then put Maria's name on it; perhaps so Maria wouldn't think she was trying to steal Alma back. It was warm, homey. All Maria missed, all Alma missed, were that her family didn't come. Alma especially missed Emilio, but he was off to Cazador School. He had managed to call and ask his sister to get something for Alma from him. She did, of course.

Emilio wrote Maria again, once, while on a short break. When she answered she told him that she certainly would go to his graduation, stick, kilts, and all.

She did, later, go to her brother's graduation. Their parents didn't. Emilio wasn't there, anyway. The legion had let Maria know, through channels and in advance, as gently as possible, that he wouldn't be. The letter the legionary chaplain had hand-delivered said that a rope up a cliff had broken, no fault of Emilio's. He had fallen several hundred feet to his death. At the ceremony his entire class answered "Here!" when his name and honorary rank were called. It wasn't until then that Maria started to cry.

Emilio was buried at Camp Bernardo O'Higgins in the mountains, not so far from Camp Spurius Ligustinus. His headstone was marked, "Centurion Junior Grade Emilio Fuentes, CCA: *Todo por la Patria.*"

He had left his insurance to Maria, but she put it in the bank for Alma's future.

She went to visit his grave sometimes. She missed him a lot.

Interlude

Carrera and Parilla sat in the private theater of the legion's head-quarters. There came a whirring of a video player being loaded. As the projection screen flashed to darkly colored life, Parilla said, "This had better be worth my time, Patricio."

Carrera smiled, cryptically, and said, "Just watch, Raul."

The screen showed a dusky shot; that perpetual semi-twilight of the real jungle. The scene lightened to show the backs of a group of miserable trainees under ponchos, struggling through the muck, heads and bodies bowed under the weight of helmets and overstuffed rucksacks. The sounds of the jungle—insects, *antaniae*, monkeys, parrots, and trixies—were lessened as an unseen woman began to sing to the accompaniment of a guitar. The song had been partly plagiarized from a civilian hit down in Southern Columbia.

> "On an endless muddy tank trail on an island out
>   to sea
>   You can hear the jungle growing, you can hear the
>   small birds sing."

Then the scene shifted enough to see that the poor critters tramping the muck were women. They had put some real effort into looking almost incredibly wretched.

> "And your mind turns back in time, back to the
>   girl you used to be."

The scene flashed to a well-dressed high school girl, young, pretty, a party dress on, laughing—probably flirting—with some

269

boys. Flash again to the same girl. Fatigues, rifle, helmet, pack. On screen she pulled herself up a steep, jungle-grown bank— slowly, with difficulty—using roots for handholds. Then she was over and walking again.

> "But my memories are fading from the pain down
>   in my boots
> And I'll march for twenty miles today, there's noth-
>   ing else to do.
> I'm not asking for a free ride, though I wish the
>   march were through.
>
> And here I am..."

With a face that radiates confidence and worth, the girl turns and looks almost directly into the camera...but a little past it. Maybe as if she were looking into the future.

> "...I'm on the march again.
> There I am, I'm leavin' today.
> There we go, so far, so far again."

Back to the girl with the boys. The camera backs up. The scene with the boys plays on the page of a book, like a scrapbook or photo album. Then:

> "*Aqui soy yo.* It's another day."

Still the book, but the scene freezes. The page turns and it's a still shot of the muddy trail again. The girl, the Amazon, is now looking directly at you. The picture moves again. She smiles.

> "We near the place to overnight. We pass a group
>   of men."

That was the scene, a tired maniple of girls trudging past a tired maniple of boys.

> "I can feel them staring at me though I haven't
>   slept since when.

So I act like it's all nothing even though I'm near
    my end...
I can just make out their whispers 'Are those girls
    or are they boys?'
And impossible, silly fantasies of home and hearth
    and joy.
And for just a little moment I can feel I'm one
    with them...

And here I am, I'm on the march again.
There I am, I'm moving today.
There we go, so far, so far again
Aqui soy yo. It's another day."

Again the scene shifted to a group of women soldiers moving at night under fire. A parachute flare hung in the dark blue. Tracers arced overhead. There was no sound of artillery, but flashes lit the night sky in the background. The flashes were demo charges; more predictable than artillery; safer as well.

"Underneath the burning sky-flares; God, I want
    to get away,
But I know my sisters need me so I hold on until
    day
And the sweat drips down like rain drops while I
    try to hide my shakes..."

The sun arose on the screen. Spilling mud behind themselves, a few Ocelots showed up. The Amazons began to load aboard them.

"Don't think of rest, don't think of food, there's
    duty to attend.
The ears will soon stop ringing and the pounding
    in the head
For there's always one more mission 'til we're dis-
    charged or we're dead."

One of the girls commanding an Ocelot turned, again, to look into the future, past the camera. She was wearing a T-shirt that was about to break under the strain of her breasts. The camera panned back and a squad of Amazons, hand-picked for looks, was staring directly into it. With an irregular lurch, the tank moved out onto the road. The girls swayed with the rocking of the tank over the uneven ground, but they never took their eyes from the camera. "Why aren't *you* here?" those eyes asked.

> "*Aqui soy yo*. I'm on the road again.
> *Aqui soy yo*. We're rolling today.
> *Aqui soy yo*. Who knows how far again?
> *Aqui soy yo*. Another day."

Carrera killed the video. He said to Parilla, "Raul, we began showing that two weeks ago in movie theaters. We show a shorter version on TV. Recruiting for the *Tercio Amazona* has dropped by seven percent since that video first was shown. It's equally true that male recruiting has jumped by sixteen percent in the same period."

"Go figure," Parilla conceded, with bad grace.

"That means a gain of almost two hundred men over an expected loss of one point four Amazons actually making it eventually into the tercio. Over just two weeks, Raul."

At hearing those figures, Parilla conceded, "All fucking *right*, Patricio. You were right and I was wrong. Don't rub it in."

"I won't," Carrera answered. Handing over an intelligence report, he said, "We have too much to worry about now without arguing between ourselves. Read."

CHAPTER TWELVE

For the warrior there is nothing more blessed
than a lawful strife.
Happy the warriors who find such a strife coming
unsought to them as an open door to Paradise.
—*Bhagavad Gita*, II, 31, 32

Maria:

Within just under two years we had reached a size that allowed us to have all three echelons: regular, reserve and militia, albeit at much reduced strength. It was then that all the first class of centurion school graduates, and a few of the second class, were allowed to actually take off our stripes and carry our batons, at least when the militia was called up to train. At other times, we were merely sergeants and corporals. I still had a year to go to finish at the university, so I stayed in the reserve echelon for the time being. It was made pretty plain to me that if I wanted to become a regular, a full-time soldier instead of a teacher, upon graduation, I would be welcome.

When the militia was called up, the batons, or "sticks," were our sole insignia of rank. Only the tips would tell someone what that rank was; black for optio, black and bronze for centurion, J.G. (junior grade—the lowest class in the centurionate . . . me), bronze for senior centurion, silver for first centurion and gold for sergeant major. We also were paid at those ranks whenever we were on duty at them. I'll admit, I didn't think that was overgenerous.

The thing that amazed me, on those first days when we began calling up the militia echelon, was the way some of them seemed to expect us to be quite a bit different from the *Gorgidas* soldiers who had run their basic training. I'm not sure those women understood that we had been put through the wringer by the same schools, Cazador, CCS and OCS, that had trained *Gorgidas.*

I remember one young trooper with something of a chip on her shoulder. No, I won't mention her name, she turned out well enough in time. (By the way, we didn't really mind little chips; we all had them ourselves. There's a point of intolerance, though.) Inez Trujillo, now Tribune Trujillo and our commander, was walking the line, conducting a simple in-ranks inspection. She looked one girl up and down, listing her various deficiencies of dress in rather humiliating detail, possibly made more humiliating by the fact that Inez showed no personal animus in her comments, just professional observation. She walked on.

I was following Trujillo through. Marta followed me, taking notes. Softly, out of one ear only, I heard this girl mutter "bitch" after *my* commander had passed.

I didn't even stop to think about it. Furious, I just swung my baton across the stupid girl's face, knocking her to the ground, stunned but not quite unconscious. To Marta, I said, "Seven days confinement, unpaid, hard labor, bread and water...and get her slovenly carcass back at attention." Writing that down, Marta then picked the girl off of the ground, shook her twice, slapped her, and let go. She didn't fall again.

Trujillo pretended not to have noticed. If she had noticed and had admitted to it, I would have had to have given that girl a much more serious punishment.

You are probably confused now as to how the troops could tell what rank we were at any given time. Really, it was very simple. I wore stripes pinned to my collar whenever the militia wasn't around. When they were, or when there was a social or other event that required or suggested the higher rank, I took off the stripes and picked up my baton. I was "centurion" with the baton, "sergeant" otherwise. The only ones who could have gotten confused were the other reservists who saw me in both configurations. They got used to it pretty quickly, though. After all, they were privates for the most part normally, but sergeants and corporals when we called up the militia.

The legion gave some of us the opportunity to star in a recruiting video once. Marta and I both did it, her in the hatch of a light tank though she was not a tanker. The video played on TV *Militar* and in most of the movie theaters in the country.

Even as she took the pay for it, Marta complained extensively about our being used.

The money from the video paid for me to get Alma into a better school than she'd been going to, a Catholic School, actually. She liked it. She liked it especially when I came to pick her up in kilts.

Ever see small children with a soldier? If you ever do, watch carefully. The soldier isn't just a big person in a funny suit to a child. They'll gather around the trooper at a respectful distance, and just stare up at her with big wondering eyes. Then one of the braver ones will come forward and try to touch the uniform, hesitant and afraid. When the soldier doesn't object—we never do—they'll all gather closer and every one of them will touch that uniform, or the skin, if they dare.

You see, to a child, a soldier is magic. I doubt that the country or culture much matter; soldiers are *magic* to anyone who isn't too blind to see. Children, I've noticed, see some things more clearly than most adults do.

I'd felt it myself, many years before. When I was out shopping with my mother on *Via Hispanica,* and Second Tercio had marched by, I'd felt that magic, too. I didn't quite understand back then, though. I guess I was too old already to see clearly.

Of course, to Alma, I was magic in a different way. I was "Mommy." So she'd just stand away and let the other boys and girls have their brief touch of *mana.* After all, she got to walk home, hand in hand with this person who was magic to all her school friends. I suspect that was *mana,* too.

"Mama, do you have drill again?" Alma asked me when she saw me checking my rifle and other gear. I hadn't put on the armor yet. That could wait until I was out of sight.

I answered, "No, baby. It's an alert. Now run over to the Rosales' apartment and wait for *Abuela* Lydia to come and get you. It shouldn't be long." God, that hurt.

"*Si, Mama.*"

I don't think I've mentioned how it came about that we ended up at war. It didn't make sense to me at the time. It still doesn't, not entirely.

When I'd joined the thought of our actually having to fight never entered my head. Would I have joined up if I thought war was a real possibility? I doubt it, not the way I was then. Now? I've got less standing between me and my brain than a guy does. I wouldn't go eagerly. But...I'd still go. After all, I went, didn't I?

You remember that helicopter that got shot down the day Alma and I met Carrera? For a while that looked like the end of our problems. Everything calmed down for several months afterwards. A calm before the storm, I'd say it was.

While I was at training, things got much more serious. I've heard a lot of different rumors, more than a little propaganda, too, concerning why. Be that as it may, right around the time we were dividing up the beer in our barracks at Camp Botchkareva, the enemy started provoking us again.

They'd alert a few of their troops, roll or helicopter them to an assault position not far from one of our casernes, and wait for us to go on alert. Sometimes it was just a few troops; but sometimes it was everything they had. You never knew but that one of those alerts would turn into an actual invasion.

So naturally, our side had to respond. For the cost of anywhere from a hundred to about ten thousand of their troops having to delay their sleep by a few hours, our boys—maybe a couple of hundred thousand of them, sometimes—would have to get out of their beds, leave their families, and report to their units. Remember that we were mostly citizen soldiers. Except for the six percent or so that were full-time regulars, everybody had a civilian job. Sure, this gave us an awful lot of combat power when everyone was mobilized. But every time the enemy forced us to call up the troops it hurt our economy...and our troops' paychecks or businesses, most of them.

We never knew if it was real or not. It was nerve-wracking. It was intended to be.

I've heard that this time Carrera and Parilla sent them a tacit ultimatum: stop this crap or we will fight.

They had to send them that ultimatum. If they'd just let it pass the troops would have taken matters into their own hands... unwisely. They'd grab some enemy female civilian, maybe rape her, maybe just rough her up. They'd shoot some civilian-clad enemy soldier while he was reconnoitering for a later attack. They'd take a potshot at any foreigner who happened to be passing by. It had happened that way before. And we'd been invaded before...and lost...badly. Carrera had already hanged some numbers of our own people who had engaged in just that sort of unofficial reprisal.

But, eventually the hangings would fail. One of our troops— sick of being dragged out of bed in the middle of the night and wanting to make someone pay for it—would do something really outrageous. Then, the enemy would have enough excuse to attack with popular support. Picture the headlines in the enemy's press: "One of our boys killed while on pass!" Never mind that he was "on pass" making sketches or photographs of an area for use in a later attack.

Truth surely is the first casualty of war...or of preparation for war.

I can't imagine why, but the enemy didn't believe the ultimatum. They sent one maniple across the border. Carrera sent one cohort—if I remember correctly it was Second Cohort, Second Tercio...yes, Second of the Second, it was—to fix, fight and destroy them before they could get away. Although the television said the enemy had started the shooting, it really doesn't make any difference who started it. They were merely peacefully provoking us when we had the temerity to provoke back. As a result, there was a god-awful battle between 2nd of the 2nd, that enemy company, and, later on, the rest of that enemy company's battalion.

I'd studied that fight while I was in Centurion Candidate School; required reading, so to speak. If even half of what I was told 2nd of the 2nd went through is true, I'm so glad I wasn't there. Those boys—good boys, they were—took over fifty percent casualties, a frightening number of dead. One of our platoons started the fight with seventy-seven men, including attachments. When it was over there were twelve, not all of these unhurt, who could even stand. It seems nobody on either side was all that interested in taking prisoners.

The enemy had it almost as bad and their dead were an even higher percentage of their casualties. They'd have had it a lot worse except that they had tanks we just couldn't meet one on one. We destroyed a number of their tanks, mind you. It just cost too much to get them.

Our side would likely have been creamed except that Carrera informed the enemy commander early on that if he escalated hostilities beyond a certain point we would attack holding nothing back. Since we outnumbered them about twenty or thirty to one, in country, once our militia and reserves were called up—and we were calling them up fast—this was no idle threat. Even their air force didn't interfere. Well, we did have about five hundred artillery pieces aimed at their main air base.

So it became, instead of a general war, a minor contest of wills and willingness to bleed. We won that contest.

Everything became unnaturally quiet for months after that incident. Sadly, the quiet didn't last.

Why did they want to provoke us? Why did they want to fight? It was our system of government. Rather, it was the way they viewed our system of government. I suppose they were right, in a way. Our two systems were said to be incompatible, inherently hostile.

I ultimately came to believe that was true. One example: My government had the courage to raise a real regiment of women infantry. That was more courage than anyone anywhere else in the world had shown so far.

Still, beyond procedure, what was the difference? Maybe it wasn't so much. They let everybody vote who wasn't a criminal. When they exercised their draft, one could become a criminal by avoiding it, losing one's vote. One could also become a legislator or even their chief executive if one could avoid a criminal prosecution for avoiding the draft. They'd always had generous provisions for legally doing so. That this was decidedly ungenerous to the poor slobs drafted didn't seem to bother anybody who counted.

We sent everybody a draft notice, then didn't do a damned thing to enforce it. It was a friendly reminder, nothing more. If you didn't go, your political rights would be suspended, no vote, no election to public office, no power. But that's pretty much it.

(Of course, later on, Balboa *did* have cause to take some hundreds of thousands of unwilling people as forced labor to dig fortifications. That service was creditable towards full citizenship . . . if those people then volunteered for training and finished their ten years, minus, of reserve or militia time. Some did, some didn't.)

A lot of countries do this, or something like it: Sachsen, Gaul, Zion, Helvetia, all those mostly frozen Southern Tauran states. The major difference is that with us there is no exemption for women. Even Zion only drafts unmarried women, and then only for really noncombat jobs.

The net effect of this was that we were not a *liberal* democracy. Our government wasn't run by lawyers. Our electorate were all people who had given up some time, endured a little exposure to danger, and experienced a lot of misery. And not a one of them had had to. Or got all that much for doing so, certainly nothing like the price they had paid in otherwise avoidable misery.

Of course some people, including myself eventually, like the kind of life we had to go through before we earn political power. That's half the trick to our system of government. The people who liked that crap tend to stay for a full twenty-five years, even more for some of them. By the time they're discharged—assuming they're not killed—they're too old to vote or hold office for long. They... We couldn't screw up much that way, or for long.

The system was plainly skewed towards people who tended— and it was possibly no more than a tendency—to think of the whole country first.

The tendency, though, was enough. You see, liberal democracy *almost* works. It's a great system of government provided that the people with power—voters, in other words—won't just vote their narrow self interest and narrower emotions, won't balkanize into selfishly competing factions. Eventually, though, they will do just that. Then all elections go to whoever promises to rape the treasury and the other taxpayers of the largest amount of money for the greatest number of people or gain the most in extra rights for the most interest groups, future be damned. Being more or less good looking seems to help a lot too.

Looks didn't matter much in our elections, though the decorations a candidate wore on the lapel or around his or her throat counted for something. And, while our electorate is capable of looting the treasury, it is just that much more likely to balk at something that's good for them personally but not so good for the country. They'd also be ashamed to vote that way, in public as we do, with no secret ballot. It isn't perfect, but it seems to be enough to work...a little better...enough better.

What damned us most in the enemy's eyes, or at least his propaganda, were the effects of this on women. I, personally, would have found this funny if it hadn't been so damned tragic.

Women in Balboa only went into the service in about one sixth the numbers that men did (though we obtained a disproportionately large number of foreign volunteers, mostly from other Latin states). This changed our politics radically from what was the democratic norm around the world. As I said, we were not a *liberal* democracy.

Of course, no woman with a father, brothers, husband or sons can be said to be entirely voteless. That would be as silly as saying that children don't get a vote. But how else does one explain the growing concern with children's issues around the world except by the vicarious representation of children by adults, and especially by women? So, as long as they love some woman, and even men of the *Tercio Gorgidas* had mothers, men won't let anything too terrible happen to us politically, no matter what the appearances of the political process. That's how we got the vote in the first place.

If men were the terrible creatures portrayed by some, we not only wouldn't have the vote, we wouldn't have *shoes*.

It makes one wonder, though. If we not only have our votes, but men's votes as well, do men even get a vote? Maybe it's true what that Old Earther said, that women have so much natural power men can't afford to let us have more.

Still, without the compassion—sometimes misplaced—that results from a huge number of women's votes, my country spent hardly a cent taking care of the unfortunate, though we spent a fair amount helping the unfortunate to change their fortunes. In practice, that meant taking them into the legion . . . if they just had the heart to make it, even to try hard. Some places the handicapped are shut out of sight and away, objects of pity. In my country they serve in the armed forces in somewhat higher proportion than the national norm. And, because of that, they get all the respect and benefits that go with it, job training, education . . . care from a government and people that are *grateful* for what they've done.

We even have a few pacifists in the legion. And the legion tries to assign them to noncombatant duties. However, the preference for the pacifists is to assign them to rather life-threatening duties as combat medics. Or, say, Explosive Ordnance Disposal. In any case, we don't let pacifism be a cover for cowardice or weakness or indifference to the nation.

Those whose religious and moral views don't permit them to serve in any capacity are simply shut out. And they are completely incapable of doing anything about it. Revolution within the legion and the veterans remains a possibility, though our election processes make it absurdly improbable. Revolution by outsiders, successful revolution anyway, is impossible. But, as their last military duty before discharge, to ensure that they know how to revolt if they ever have to, the veterans go to a month long course in conducting revolutionary warfare before getting their walking papers. And they keep their weapons. Yes, even the machine guns.

Our criminal code? Don't commit a crime in my country! If you're caught and convicted, punishment will likely be quick in coming and severe. Drugs? Death, often by drowning. Armed robbery? Death, usually by shooting or hanging. Extortion, corruption, grand larceny? Death on a rope, with a long drop. Rape? There's a sharp upright stick waiting for you. Espionage? Slow death on a rope...or wire, no drop. Treason, murder, or kidnapping? You don't even want to hear about that degrading and painful a death. It tends to involve nails.

Actually, rape is a strange case. We impale or hang people for it, true; and even if, in the victim's choice, hanging will do, it's a slow, choking hanging where the culprit takes maybe fifteen minutes to die. But, because the penalty is so severe, we also require real proof. Someone swearing "so and so raped me," without physical evidence that says "rape" very strongly—generally in the form of black eyes, or broken bones and teeth—or without other eyewitnesses, is unlikely to result in a conviction provided the defendant denies it. One person's word against another does not constitute proof beyond a reasonable doubt. The simple presence of semen in a vagina is not considered adequate physical evidence on its own.

On the other hand, it is very likely that even without that evidence the woman's husband, father, or brothers will hunt down the guilty party, give him the chop, then take their not-too-bad chances that a jury will find it to have been justifiable homicide. *Doing society a favor,* I've heard it called.

The victim might do it herself, for that matter. If the victim is an *Amazona,* she and her squad mates are very likely to hunt down and eliminate the guilty party, once she gets out of the hospital. I say that because no *Amazona* has ever been raped without putting up such a fight that the rapist or rapists had to beat her unconscious first. Though, even then, she's more likely to have her throat cut afterwards.

Illiberal? We have a criminal law on the books called "Linguistic Matricide." This is defined as, "(1) the conscious attempt, by someone in a position of state or state-sponsored authority, to reduce human freedom of thought by forcing those subject to that authority to acquiesce or participate in the artificial manipulation of the language for a social, political or philosophical end or (2) the attempt to hide or distort truths to alter the perception of reality by the same state or state-sponsored parties." Conviction carried up to fifty lashes, a hefty fine, and two years at hard labor. I'm not sure of the last time someone in my country tried to substitute a value-laden, multisyllabic bit of nonsense for good, plain Spanish. It was either a law professor who tried to make his class ignore the fact that Spanish words have masculine and feminine genders, or that time some government spokesman attempted to call a battle a "limited objective exercise in the application of military force."

Somewhat similarly, we had a "Truth in Taxation" amendment to our constitution which required that no taxes that were actually paid by the common people be hidden under misleading labels and concepts like social security, "cost sharing"—where there was no real sharing, corporate income tax, or inflation. Every wage and earnings statement in Balboa shows as exactly as possible what the wage earner really pays in taxation. That's why we have no corporate income tax and social security has been changed from an eleventh annual payment allegedly paid by an employer to the government to a seven percent flat tax taken right from salaries.

That also explains, maybe, why social security taxes and benefits have remained unchanged for these many years gone past.

My country was decidedly illiberal in foreign policy, too. Years before some Santandern drug lords had tried to terrorize us into acquiescing in the passage of drugs through our land and waters. They thought better of it shortly after we attacked those men's homes in Santander, killed their workers, guards, and most of their relatives, then brought the main culprits back here for torture and a really, really bad death. (*Nails.*) Same thing when some of our troops on peacekeeping duty in Uhuru were shelled and sniped at. A number were killed. Our troops took the hill the artillery fire was being directed from, and sniper fire coming from, and they killed every living thing on it, no prisoners.

But we had no street crime to speak of. We'd pretty much ended corruption in public office. (Rope; no drop.) Our schools were safe and disciplined. Our economy was thriving despite official embargoes. Our urban literacy rate was rather higher than our antagonist's. And we thought we were strong enough to resist outside attack.

I think even the *Taurans* would have agreed that much of this was good. Perhaps if we'd somehow been able to package the whole deal in an aesthetically pleasing way they wouldn't have tried to interfere. Aesthetics, however, were not our strong point.

Human rights were the big issue to the enemy, so they said. We were ruled by a military dictatorship, so they said. ("Bullshit," say I.) We were a threat to world peace and world trade ... so they said.

Maybe they were right to have feared us. In fact, in time we could have become a threat to them. Actually, by now, we and our confederates and allies have become something like the threat they'd feared. Of course, we wouldn't have those confederates and allies if it hadn't been for the war. A self-fulfilling prophecy?

Our system worked pretty well. There were already grumblings in some other Latin states to imitate us. From the enemy point of view, several hundred million Latins, with the ability to raise a mass army of fifty or sixty million soldiers, or a much higher quality army of twenty million of so, was just too big a potential menace to let stand. We had to go.

Of course, we claimed that, like Santa Josefina, we didn't even *have* a real army. This wasn't quite true, though. We were nothing like Santa Josefina. We were more like Helvetia, or Zion, which also don't have armies. We, and Helvetia, and Zion, didn't have an army because each country *was* an army.

I got home from the alert much later that evening, just in time to catch the news on the television. It seemed some foreign women, Taurans, four of them, had been kidnapped, raped and murdered by some men wearing our uniforms. Then whoever did it had released a tape of the whole nasty, horrible mess to the news stations.

I wasn't looking forward to what might happen the next day or two.

Interlude

The *Curia* was subdued. There were at least a dozen spots that were vacant now, senators the Taurans had tried to arrest in their homes and who decided not to go gently, or others who, ignoring their years, had grabbed a rifle or machine gun and gone to find the regiments that had elevated them. Carrera wasn't back yet. He was somewhere in the Transitway Zone, more specifically at Fort Muddville, watching a cohort burn out the last Tauran defenders of Building 59.

That didn't matter; he and Parilla were long agreed that the war could not be permitted to turn into one of those interminable Zion-Arab things that just went on and on. No, this would be fought to a finish, either the destruction of the Revolution in Balboa, and the legion that had brought it about, or the discrediting, humiliation, and casting off of the new hereditary aristocracy of the Tauran Union... and with it, United Earth.

A screen on the wall of the *Curia* showed a long tongue of flame lick out to splash against the brick wall before finding its way through a blasted out window. Smoke began to pour from all the other windows at that end of the building. The hundred and eleven senators so far assembled watched the scene with grim satisfaction.

The senators stood in front of Parilla's dais and curule chair, rather than in their wonted marble benches. They'd had to vacate the space; those benches were now full of people in formal dress, mostly, though a few wore the battle dress of the legion. Further down, towards the great bronze doors, still others in similar clothing held musical instruments.

Parilla stood at a podium that had been wheeled in for the

occasion. He was flanked by the statues of *Balboa* and *Victoria*. The latter had been ready for some months, but Parilla had thought it better to wait for the victory that gave the statue her name.

"So I'm superstitious," he'd told the Senate. "So sue me. We wait until we *have* the victory before we proclaim it."

A cameraman at the far end, on the aisle by the doors, gave Parilla a high sign.

He began to speak:

"This morning the Republic of Balboa was suddenly and deliberately attacked by ground, air and naval forces of the Tauran Union. The *excuse* given for that attack were certain crimes allegedly perpetrated by members of Balboa's armed forces upon Tauran citizens. The real reason for the attack was to force upon Balboa a traitorous clique of puppets who would do the will of the Tauran Union even against their own country and people."

Parilla stopped speaking to take a short drink of water.

"In any event," he continued, carefully placing his glass back on the podium, "the criminals who caused this war—those, at least, who are in our hands—have been punished. Some few remain at large in the Tauran Union. They, however—being elected officials or unelected but well-connected bureaucrats—appear to have a certain immunity to criminal action at law. Still, do not be fooled. The war the Tauran Union began is not yet over.

"We currently hold some eighteen thousand Tauran prisoners of war. Many of them are wounded. We also have some thousands of Tauran civilians, former workers in the Transitway Zone. We are not nearly done with counting the dead and wounded, ours and theirs. So many were lost at sea that we may never have an accurate count.

"In the interests of possible peace we will, in three days, begin transferring prisoners of war, at the rate of one hundred per day, back to the Tauran Union. First we shall return the wounded, in accord with the severity of their wounds. Then we'll return the civilians. Then, if there are no further hostile acts, the Tauran Union will be given back her military personnel. This is contingent upon several factors.

"First: the conditions of permanent peace. We insist upon absolute renunciation by the Tauran Union of any interest in and over the Balboa Transitway and the Republic of Balboa. After all, the Tauran Union can hardly claim any longer that Balboa is incapable of self defense, can they? We also demand the repatriation of any and all Balboans held by the Tauran Union. Lastly, we demand reparations for the damages we have sustained, to recompense our wounded, to pay for property damage, and to care for the orphans and widows this artificially provoked invasion has left without a provider. We think a million drachma for each prisoner we hold should be sufficient for *that*.

"Further, Balboa demands that all hostile actions on the part of the Tauran Union's government, to include the unwarranted 'drachma embargo' and all other interferences with Balboa's trade, cease.

"Return of prisoners and detainees will be through the port of Cristobal, by ship. We will march and truck them there. It is up to the Tauran Union to have transport waiting.

"And now, a final word from *la Republica de Balboa* to the people and bureaucrats of the Tauran Union."

Parilla smiled broadly and pointed at a formally dressed man holding a little stick, the conductor of the Balboa City Philharmonic. The stick tapped a few times, then pointed. A male singer, in battle dress, his head wrapped in a bandage, sang out. His voice was a deep baritone:

"O Tauran Union, den of iniquity."

A hundred voices raised themselves: "INIQUITY!"
The lone baritone continued:

"Odiferous fief of a corrupt and unelected
    bureaucracy."

"BUREAUCRACY!"

Almost instantly, the hall was filled with music, more specifically the Old Earth composer, Beethoven's, "Ode to Joy." The words had been changed a bit, though. Balboa's granite senate house rang with the lyrics:

"Fuck the filthy Tauran Union!
    Fuck their courts and MTPs!
    Fuck their rules and regulations;
    Their whole vile bureaucracy!

Asshats, Bastards, Cowards, Dimwits,
Excrement-Feeding Gallows-bait.
Hang the swine Higher than Haman,
Ignorant Jackasses, Knaves!

Watch them purge the bent banana.
See your taxes rise and rise.
See your nations fall to ruin.
Watch as every freedom dies.

Lick-ass Morons, Nincompoops, Oh,
Pity the Quagmire these Reds made.
Sycophants and Thieves, the whole crew,
Underworked and overpaid.

Friday mornings they will sign in
To ensure their holidays
Are paid for by lesser people.
Free men call those people, 'Slaves.'

Green on the outside, red on the
Inside, Watermelons, black of soul,
Xerox copies of each other,
Yahoos, Zeroes, one and all.

To the lampposts, Tauran People.
Tie the knots and toss the ropes.
Fit the nooses. Haul the free ends.
Stand back; watch your masters choke."

With a complex wave of the stick, the singing and music ceased. Every man and woman in the Balboa Philharmonic was smiling, perhaps smugly. Smiling more smugly still, the maestro turned to the cameras and bowed.

"And that pretty much sums up our feelings about *you*," Parilla said, also smiling. The smile disappeared. He raised his arms above his head and shouted for the cameras, "*Viva* Balboa! *Viva* Anglia *Libre*! *Viva* Sachsen *Libre*! *Viva* Gaul *Libre*! *Viva* Castile *Libre*! *Viva* Jagelonia *Libre*! *Viva* Tuscany *Libre*! *Viva* Lusitania *Libre*!

"Death to the Tauran Union!"

CHAPTER THIRTEEN

There could be no honor in a sure success,
but much might be wrested from a sure defeat.
                                        —T.E. Lawrence

"Ah, you're awake," someone said in a warm female voice. It was the voice of a stranger. "The doctors thought you would come out of it sometime today. There's someone here to see you."

Maria blinked her eyes against the sudden light of consciousness. Her first sight was a shifting, swimming Zamora, standing over her. Zamora's arm was in a cast and sling. She wore a big smile, even so.

"I was so worried about you, Maria," the tall redhead said, obviously meaning it. "You can't imagine..."

"Alma?" Maria gasped out with a dry throat. First things first.

"She's fine," Zamora assured her, then passed her a cup of ice with a straw. "Porras is bringing her by later today."

Maria slurped down the little bit of icy water in the bottom of the cup, sipped a little more, then asked in a more natural voice, "My girls?"

Zamora hesitated for a moment. *Good news first.* "Arias is up and around. Marta's still in intensive care; collapsed lung, a lot of tissue damage, blood loss, some nasty kind of infection. Most of the time she's unconscious, but... she'll probably be all right. Most of the rest..." Zamora shook her head sadly, then came closer and held Maria, one armed, while she cried for a very long time into Zamora's neck.

After that long time, Maria sniffed, "Did we...?"

"Oh, yes." And Zamora smiled broadly, a wicked smile, showing fangs. "Kicked their asses right out of the country. Chopped 'em up good and ran 'em out," she said, with a satisfied look on her face. "All but a bunch—a *big* bunch—of prisoners. Sank a chunk of their fleet, too."

"Who did else did we lose?"

"Dead? Almost half. Of the rest... most of us are here now... in better shape or worse. Outside of the mortar platoon there's maybe a couple of dozen or so unhurt from the whole maniple. I've heard that our maniple took higher casualties than any other in the legion except for *Gorgidas* boys on our flank. Both we and they got unit citations for our eagles. If that helps any."

Maria didn't start crying again but... it hurt. She asked, "Why did the Taurans shoot the wounded?"

"I can only guess," Zamora answered, "but my guess is that some one of us took a shot at one of them and hit, then hid among the bodies. They may not have felt they had much choice but to make sure everyone who looked dead actually was dead. By the way, after Second Tercio had seen what happened to us, they killed every living thing they could get at on top of that hill. The only prisoners they took there were a few hundred that stayed safe underground until the Second cooled off. That and maybe a couple of civilian women. No men."

Maria remembered something from a law of war class from Centurion Candidate School... "feigning death or wounds to gain an advantage." Then she remembered the historical examples they'd been given, from the Battle of the Somme in the First World War, on Old Earth, and the *Mar Furioso* fighting during the Great Global War here, to the experiences of the legion in Sumer and Pashtia; all instances where killing the enemy's help-less wounded became routine because perfectly healthy soldiers were pretending to be wounded to gain an advantage, shooting then ducking back among the bodies.

Maria could picture some poor *Amazona*, half out of her head with pain, trying to strike one more blow before losing conscious-ness and falling down among a bunch of wounded.

Shaking her head, Zamora continued, "You and I are in better shape than most, Maria. Which is good because... um... I don't think it's over."

"How can it not be over? You said they were gone, kicked out."

"While you were still under I caught the president's broadcast on TV. He was pretty harsh. To the enemy, I mean. They've got to swallow some serious shit before we'll give them back their people we're holding."

"Shit," I said. "What have we got to fight *them* with? Besides bodies, I mean. We were lucky this time."

Zamora disagreed. "It wasn't all luck," she said, holding up her cast. Soldierly pride was plain in her voice when she added, "A lot of it was guts, and I don't just mean the guts we spilled in the attack."

Porras brought Alma by later, just as Zamora had promised. She also brought along all of Catarina's kids. The eldest one, maybe, understood that his mother was dead. The youngest didn't really know the difference. It was the middle one that broke her heart. She knew Mama was never coming back, but she had no understanding of why. She did have enough sense of cause and effect to ask, "But...what's going to happen to *us*?"

Maria was in no shape to make any promises but, even so, she promised that she would take them in. (Which, *if* her side won, would be no financial hardship. The legion took care of its own.)

Alma thought that was a great idea. "Oh. *Really,* Mommy? Promise?"

"Yes, baby. It's a promise." *Besides, I know I'll never have any more children of my own.* The doctor who'd treated Maria had been gentle but firm on that. Reproductively speaking, she was ruined inside.

Porras just raised an eyebrow, saying, "That's all in the future. For now you'll be staying with me."

Maria visited Marta every day she could. Sometimes Marta was awake, sometimes not. She didn't say much, usually. She didn't cry much either. That was worrying.

The speaker on the bus played:

> "For chainless wave and lovely land
> Freedom and nationhood demand,
> Be sure the great God never planned
> For slumbering slaves a home so grand..."

"Can you change the station?" one of the women in the back asked loudly.

"Wouldn't make no difference," answered the uniformed driver. "Every station got the same things."

Maria looked out the bus window next to her and Zamora and saw a column of short, dark, armed men marching up the coastal road. Their uniforms and helmets were not Balboa's. Neither were they any of the nearly-as-familiar Taurans. Beyond the column of men another one, this of well-spaced-out tanks, moved in the opposite direction. The tanks looked new.

"Who are they?" Maria asked Zamora. "And where did those come from?"

Zamora smiled and pushed red hair off of her face. "Apparently, Carrera has been expecting and preparing for war with the Taurans for better than ten years. For ten years he's been buying and secreting arms, sometimes in country, more often aboard ship. For the last couple of weeks he's been calling his lost children home. Twenty-six freighters, I understand, half a million tons or more of supplies and equipment that nobody knew we had. Enough to put everybody up to strength and then some.

"As for the men; something like forty thousand volunteers have come from all over Colombia del Norte, along with a few hundred Castilians, about a thousand from the Federated States, and even several score each from about half the states of the Tauran Union.

"Most of them, about two thirds, seven full tercios' worth, came in organized units, mostly in cohort strength, though the entire Atzlan *Paracaidista* Regiment is here. A few places sent companies, all they had that were up to real combat. The rest are individual volunteers, mostly untrained or, worse, badly trained. Their motivation's good, though. We could have had a lot more but Carrera limited it to those we'd have time and facilities to train."

"No shit?"

"No shit," Zamora answered. "Damned good thing, too, because it looks like the Zhong Guo are kicking in with the Taurans."

"So we're outnumbered five hundred to one rather than a hundred and fifty to one?"

"Something like that," Zamora agreed.

"You don't sound too distressed at the idea," Maria observed. "Cristina?"

"Yes?"

"Do you like to fight?"

"No."

Zamora and Maria had expected the bus to take them to legion headquarters, so they were a little surprised when the bus stopped at the circle fronting the *Iglesia de Nuestra Señora, Ciudad* Balboa's largest and grandest church.

"Doesn't miss a trick, does he?" Zamora asked.

"Huh?"

"The church. Maybe we had to meet somewhere besides headquarters if it took some damage in the fighting, which I imagine it did. But why a church? Why *this* church?"

Maria didn't know and said so.

"Holy war," Zamora said. "Catholic us against atheist Taurus and pagan Zhong Guo. He's brought us here to remind us there's another reason we fight besides patriotism."

"He's got to be the most cynical bastard in the history of the planet," Maria said.

"Cynical or realistic," Zamora countered, with a shake of her red head, "who can tell the difference?"

More buses pulled up to the circle as Maria, Cristina, and the crew of walking wounded from the hospital dismounted. More women began to fill the open space between pavement and cathedral. Their voices became a hubbub of recognition and occasional sobs as they learned of the dead and wounded. A cassocked priest appeared at the front door and motioned for the women to begin to file in. As the lines formed and entered, the hubbub died amidst the awe of bright icons, fluted marble columns, relics, and statuary. Even the roughly ten percent of the women who were other than Catholic—and there were in their number Mormons and Moslems and Sikhs and Jews—were moved to silence.

Zamora and Fuentes were near the front of the mob. Maria's head and eyes turned to take in all the art on the walls. Zamora was, as usual, more tightly focused. About halfway up the nave, she nudged Maria with an elbow and then, once she had Maria's attention, pointed with her chin at a uniformed man and a teenaged boy, likewise in battle dress, the both kneeling at the altar, hands clasped and head bowed in prayer. A couple of tall turbaned men, armed and in legionary battledress, stood behind them and two more to the sides, all facing out. One had to look closely to see it but, oddly, Carrera wasn't in the center; the boy was. Behind those guards was a medium tall woman in foreign robes. When she turned to look behind at the Amazons filing in, Maria saw she had bright green eyes and an extraordinarily intelligent, to say nothing of beautiful, face.

"Carrera," Maria announced, softly, in deference to the holiness of the place. "Is he being devout, do you suppose, or cynical?"

"They're not necessarily mutually exclusive," Zamora replied. "That boy's his eldest son, I think, and he's offering him up on the altar, too.

"So, Maria, was Abraham a cynic?"

Eventually—it only *seemed* like forever—Carrera and the boy crossed themselves and stood. Carrera tousled his son's hair and directed him to a seat in the front row, not far from Maria and Cristina. The tall woman with the green eyes sat next to the boy. The guards, too, moved to cover their apparent charge.

Now that, thought Maria, *is a beautiful boy. He's got his mother written all over him, too. I wonder what she's feeling about now, with her husband taking her boy off to become machine-gun fodder.*

Carrera wasn't the sort to waste a lot of time. "We've won a battle. The war's not over. It won't be over until we are destroyed or the Tauran Union is a footnote.

"We're giving back their most useless prisoners to buy time, time to offload the equipment, time to dig in, time to assimilate our new volunteers and allies—bet you never guessed that the International Rifle Platoon Competition was intended to gather allies, did you?—time to get in position and ready for what's coming.

"It's going to be really bad, what's coming."

Carrera's finger pointed skyward. "Assume the United Earth Peace Fleet is against us, in spirit and, to the degree they can without drawing a violent reaction from the Federated States, materially, as well.

"The Zhong are coming in against us, though I can't really see them being able to move and support more than maybe two hundred to three hundred thousand men across the sea. The Tauran Union has already dispatched ships to help move them.

"The Taurans are fragmented. Indeed, some of them stand with us against their own bureaucracy. But we can expect anything up to a dozen modern divisions, equal to ours in manning, superior in equipment, with a tremendous air superiority. Assuming they can grab a port, of course.

"Bring out the map, please," Carrera shouted to somebody. He went silent then, while a large mounted map was wheeled out in front of the altar. On the map's mount was a laser pointer. This he picked up. He flicked it on and circled the *Isla Real* with the red marker, repeatedly.

"That's the strongest fortress in the world," he said. "Nothing else compares even remotely. In training, you saw your own little camps. You didn't see—or didn't see much of—the roughly one point one million cubic meters of concrete we poured, the hundreds upon hundreds of guns, the minefields just waiting to be activated, the tunnels, the rails, the trenches. Trust me: One hundred and fifty thousand men couldn't take it if they had one hundred and fifty thousand years to try. And if they can't take it, no ships can sail past it. If ships can't sail past it, then no landing at or near the capital can succeed; they'd just starve to death. I'm not worried about the north."

The laser moved to the west, wriggling over the undeveloped jungles of *La Palma*. "They're not coming through here in any strength, though I'll put a few tercios down there—foreign volunteers, generally, plus the *Tercio de Indios*—to make sure they can't distract us or put the government into a panic. But there are no ports worthy of the name, no roads, only one airstrip that isn't just muck most of the year, and that one's short. And, wearing loincloths or not, the Indians are good in *la jungla*."

Carrera flicked the red arrow over the port of Cristobal, at the southern end of the Transitway. "The Taurans will be coming here," he said, "though they're not going to limit themselves—not if they have two brain cells to rub together—to the old borders of the Transitway Mandate. And we'll meet them and beat them." He gave a little shrug and added, "You're going to have to take that on faith."

He stopped speaking for a moment while he physically wheeled the map board one hundred and eighty degrees around. On the other side, the women could see, was a better scale map of the eastern portions of the country.

"Here's where our danger comes from," he said. The red marker flicked from spot to spot to spot as Carrera called off the names of a dozen or more little ports dotting the northeastern coast of the country. "None of those, alone, could support an army of a size to matter. Taken together, however, and with the kinds of improvements a modern army, or one—like the Zhong's—with a lot of manpower, can create, they can support an army. More-over"—the laser traced the long coastal highway—"from there they've got a highway into our vitals. And I don't have the force to meet it, not so long as the Zhong and the Taurans are attack-ing to the north and south.

"Worse,"—the red light settled on Capitano, a good sized port to the southeast—"from here a full corps could come over the mountains, link with a force along the northern coast, and make that drive into our guts deadly.

"What is necessary is to buy time in the east until we have a decision, north and south. That's where you come in; you, Fifth Mountain Tercio, a chunk of Fourteenth Cazador Tercio, the mountain cohorts from Lempira and Valdivia, and a few others. And a few hundred thousand others besides that.

"I am going to half evacuate the city—we don't have bomb shelters for more than half, anyway—and move more than three hundred thousand civilians to a big 'refugee' area around and along that highway and some of the ports. The 'refugees' have a purpose of their own. While we, the legion, will feed them, and the more permanent residents of the area, as long as the enemy hasn't occupied their area, once they do come in—and they will—the food stops. Thereafter, the civilians will suck up as much as one thousand truckloads a day of enemy supply in food, medicine, etc. World opinion will *demand* that those people be fed and cared for. That will hurt them, children. It might even make a western attack a logistic impossibility all on its own.

"However, I cannot be absolutely sure about that. Give the devils their due; they can move supplies.

"So the civilians aren't enough. I need that road kept closed. I need the ports kept closed or, at least, marginal. I need the feeder roads kept closed.

"Using the 'refugees' to hide among, you and the others are going to close off invasion from the east. Of course, as in any partisan war, the regular forces could destroy you if they are willing and able to spread out in little packets to do so. Fifth Mountain is going up into the mountains as a regular organized force to threaten the enemy and keep him from spreading out enough to find, control, and annihilate you. Also to block the road from Capitano.

"Think about it," Carrera said with a smile. "Hiding among those civilians you are going to be an intelligent, self-aware, self-replicating, mobile and undetectable minefield that the enemy won't be able to destroy in place, move, or clear permanent lanes through. To add insult to injury he's going to have to protect you, feed you, shelter you, clothe you, and provide medical care for you every moment you're not actively shooting at him." Carrera laughed. He had a nasty laugh, sometimes.

"And you are *perfect* for the job. You're women. You just don't look like a threat, little 'helpless' things that you are. You'll be able to go places, see things, get information from the enemy's soldiers in a way nobody else could hope to. You'll be able to hide in plain sight; coming out only to fight."

"It won't last forever, of course. Eventually they'll catch on to you. Until they do, though, you'll have a field day. Even after they do ... you'll still be able to fight them."

Zamora raised her hand. "Uh ... *Duque,* what about uniforms? Those'll give us away."

Maria thought, not for the first time, *Cristina, for all your virtues, you can be a little dense, sometimes.*

"The Taurans claim to follow, and have in fact ratified, the Additional Protocol the Earthers inflicted on many of us some decades ago. So there's no need to wear uniforms except for immediate action, by the enemy's own rules.

"On the other hand, the Zhong don't follow the Protocol. If you get caught by them ... well, you'll be subject to execution under the law of land warfare. On the other hand, before it becomes an issue we'll be holding some of *their* POWs. And we're holding a fair number of Taurans that we caught not only out of uniform but in our uniforms. They've already been court-martialed and sentenced to death. The enemy tries to do anything to any of you for being out of uniform, I'll hang those people ... in a heartbeat.

Anyway, if you don't want to do this, I'll understand. This is for volunteers only. Show of hands."

Better than no protection, I guess, thought Maria, raising her own hand.

The women volunteered; all that were left. Carrera had known they would.

"Now there's one other problem," Carrera said. His eyes went up, toward the church ceiling and past that, to the skies and space. "The Earthpigs are going to be feeding the Taurans and the Zhong all the intelligence they can gather. We've got reason to believe they can pick up a lot...a lot more than they used to be able to. We're still trying to figure out why the change happened.

"In any case, among the things they'll be able to see from space is electronics and especially anything electromagnetic. So all your neat do-dads, the night sights on your rifles, your Red Fang communications systems, your light-enhancing goggles, and global locating systems, all have to be given up or stored deep against a rainy day. You'll be fighting primitive. So will the other units in and around your area and in *La Palma.*

"And, no, that's not true for the forces I'm keeping in the center and on the island. They'll be in so great a density that we couldn't hide them anyway. There's nothing to be learned by the enemy except that they're generally there. Each one will be like a lit match held against the sun. But an electronic thermal sight could pinpoint you girls for a rock from space or, at least, a bomb from a plane.

"I'll be able to give you some Yamato-made radios, a few, we don't think the Earthers can sense. And we've got a fair field telephone system you can get some limited use out of. Oh, and Legate Fernandez has had the Signal Tercio get some carrier pigeons trained. But that's about it.

"Sorry."

Maria was sad, not so much for herself, truthfully, as for Alma and Cat's kids. If she was sad, though, Porras was angry.

"It isn't right," Porras said. "You have done enough."

"Lydia," Maria answered, "when we are going to use everything and everyone to defend ourselves—thirteen-year-old boys, the crippled, the mentally retarded—I can't see why *we* should have been exempted. Besides, Carrera's right. We *are* the best choice for the job."

Porras's bright eyes flashed, "But you are women! Some hard training and hard living are one thing. But where will we all be, all of us, if there are no more young women to bear more children?"

Maria answered carefully, first having to fight down her own grief that she would never bear another child. "Oh, sure, Lydia, maybe there is a limit to the number of women we can afford to lose. Too many and *adios patria; adios pueblo.* We are, after all, the bottleneck in the production of the next generation of cannon fodder."

"Exactly!" Porras shouted. "It takes up so much of our time to have a single baby; so much more time than a man needs to spend on his part of the process, the bastards!"

Maria shook her head. "A thousand or so of us? No, Fairy Godmother, we won't make any difference to anyone but ourselves and our families."

"And to me? And to the children?"

"I don't want to talk about that. It's bad enough I have to do this, Lydia. Leave me a moment's peace about it for now, will you?"

Before they left, Carrera decorated a number of the women. That included Maria, with a CCA, a *Cruz de Coraje en Acero*. He also pinned an "I forgot to duck" badge on her blouse. Zamora got the CC in silver for something she'd done on Quarry Heights after Maria was hit; that and a brevet promotion to Tribune.

The commander of Second Tercio was there, as well. He had a kind of informal award to present. To the *Tercio Amazona*, he presented the right to use the Second's own special march, "*Boinas Azules Cruzan la Frontera*," in perpetuity, in commemoration of its charge up *Cerro Mina*.

Hippolyta was there to cover the awards.

Afterwards, the women marched away singing:

> "Said the mother, 'Do not wrong me,
> Don't take my daughter from me,
> For, if you do, I will torment you
> And after death my ghost will haunt you...'"

Prepare for a kind of war they had never trained on in detail! Reorganize! Plan! Move!

Work.

The artillery and combat support cohorts—each of which was rather below full cohort strength, still, even with full mobilization—turned in their cannon and other heavy equipment. Farewell guns. Farewell Ocelots. The women wouldn't need them for what they were going to do. Infantry was the thing. Even if they had kept the heavy weapons they knew the enemy had ways of finding them and taking them away unless some very special precautions were taken. The women were told, and believed, that the Earthpigs could sense a big chunk of metal from up in space. Besides, despite all those ships landing supplies Carrera's plans required—or at least could use—even more. The guns and tanks were reissued to other units.

The women were issued a large number of mortars, though, mostly medium 81's. Maria was not alone in hating 81's. Small arms? More than enough. Several times more than enough. Land mines? Tens of thousands. Anything the country made for itself the women were given in bulk.

Most of the Headquarters and Support Maniple was split up among the remaining five to provide medical and other support. A few cells, intel and commo, were kept pure and hidden deep.

That still left Zamora's maniple very short of troops. A few people were levied from each of the other companies, mostly junior noncoms and a few experienced privates. Then the largest chunk of the latest batch of recruits from Camp Botchkareva were transferred in, geographic recruiting base be damned. They soon had enough to form four platoons again, but a little differently from the way they had originally been set up.

Each platoon had enough for three infantry squads of eleven or twelve each, plus a mortar team of at least eight, and a two girl antiaircraft team. The antitank team was five or six Amazons. Platoon headquarters had twelve or so: the platoon leader or centurion, platoon optio, two snipers, two forward observers for the mortar team, a pair each of radio rats and medics, and a team of combat engineers to help out with the mines and booby traps. The engineers were huge girls, as they had to be to carry the fuel tanks to the flamethrowers they brought with them. The cooks were turned into riflewomen since nearly everybody could cook and the cooks had been trained first as infantry. (Though Maria was still a fairly wretched cook.)

Zamora, being brevetted tribune, was made the maniple commander. Maria kept her squad, now platoon, leader's slot. If she was not as qualified by experience as she should have been, she had the supreme virtues of being alive, available and already in the maniple.

Zamora gave her old stick to Maria to carry. But, "Don't let the enemy see it," she warned, seriously.

Oh, Cristina, it doesn't matter if you're a dumb-ass sometimes. I still like you.

For an XO, her second in command, Zamora was given a still-wet-behind-the-ears signifer right out of OCS. Another one took over one of the platoons. That was it for officers; Zamora and two rookies.

Maria didn't get an officer. That really didn't matter. Her real job, once the enemy showed up, was to ride herd over her platoon, keep the enemy either out of her area or nervous while he was in it, and maybe do a little coordinating with adjacent units. Any centurion could do that.

Maria didn't need an officer. She needed a platoon optio.

About a week after her women had begun their preparations, a truck pulled up. Maria figured it was more supplies or weapons, they trickled in from time to time. Walking up to the truck, she asked the driver what materiel he was carrying.

Before the driver could answer, a familiar voice said from the back of the truck, "I might be a *thing*, Maria, but, by God, I will shoot you if you call me 'materiel.'"

"Marta!"

The two ran into each other's arms. Maria noticed a wince when they hugged.

Marta noticed that Maria noticed. "It's mostly healed. It's mostly gone, for that matter."

Maria looked down. Marta seemed all there.

"A falsie. About half of it anyway. The other one makes me lopsided. I just may take up Garcia's suggestion that I get a reduction...after the war. If it still makes any difference, that is."

Quickly Maria filled her in on what the girls were doing.

"Doesn't seem very soldierly," she commented.

✧   ✧   ✧

The women didn't go out looking like soldiers, no, indeed. Instead, Carrera had had a number of them sworn into a nongovernmental organization he'd had created sometime before, Christian Action, an affiliate of the Interplanetary Red Cross. They went out dressed in civvies and ostensibly in charge of about fifteen thousand civilians per "Relief Team." "Relief Team" was another way of saying, "rifle platoon, reinforced."

They played that part well enough, wiping their share of runny noses, helping the refugees set up their tents, issuing food and conducting medical checks. But when they weren't doing those things they were doing other, more important, things.

Stashing supplies was the first priority. Everybody buried their own individual weapons, uniforms, and equipment within a kilometer or so of where they were staying. Generally the women tried to bury them near—but not too near—where a group of civilians was going to be put.

It became more complicated after that. The leaders—that included Maria—had to try to figure out where the enemy might someday be and where they could hide an arms cache so it would be in a good position for them to recover it later and use it on an enemy nearby. They knew it would be much easier to move without interference if the arms and equipment didn't have to be openly carried or carried far.

"It's perfect," Zamora said, pointing at a hill. "Not only is it perfect, but they'll be here."

The hill at which the new tribune pointed was surrounded on three sides by water. It sat, the very edge of it, right at five hundred meters from a three-way intersection of the main coastal highway, the less well-developed road to a small port to the north, and another dirt and gravel road that led inward to a town up in the hills to the south. Overlooked by the hill, a steel bridge crossed the river that surrounded it on three sides.

"It looks like a likely spot to me, too," Maria agreed. She was there with Marta and a couple of squads of her Amazons. Zamora was alone except for one driver and a couple of older people Maria took to be foreign. Cristina had introduced them as "Mr. and Mrs. Nguyen."

"I'll bury a mortar and—what do you think, one hundred and sixty rounds?—about three kilometers that way"—she pointed generally to the tree-clad southwest hills—"and put some caches in about five hundred meters behind us, enough to support a platoon raid on whoever occupies that hill."

Zamora considered that. "No, not a hundred and sixty rounds of mortar. They'd never get a chance to fire it before the counter-battery came in and turned them to paste. Sixty rounds is enough. They can fire that and still get the hell out of the area before the artillery hits them. Though you might bury the other hundred not too far away."

"All right, sixty," Maria said. "And two more caches of fifty nearby." As soon as she did, Marta took three women and a truck in the general direction in which Maria had pointed. They'd bury the mortar and the ammunition.

"Where else have you identified?" Zamora asked.

Maria pulled out a map and pointed in turn to four other spots where she'd had buried some of the very large issue of light equipment and weapons the legion had sent out.

"What about mines?"

Maria scratched at her ear and said, "I had an idea. You might not like it. Then again, you might."

"What's that?" Cristina asked.

"Mines, particularly antiarmor mines, are big, bulky, and notice-able, right?"

"Sure."

"Detonators aren't. I'm putting in plastic AT mines, pretty much everywhere, and recording the locations. When we want to arm one, we send out one or two girls in civvies and just uncover the mine, insert and arm the detonator, then cover it again and camouflage it. Nothing's a mine unless we want it to be. Every-thing is mined where and when we want it to be."

"See, and I *knew* there was a reason you're in charge of a pla-toon," Zamora said, smiling broadly, and patting Maria's shoulder. "I'll pass that trick on to the others."

"There is one thing that bugs me, though," Maria said. "Where did all these mines come from? I mean, we *did* sign that treaty after all."

There was an engineer with Maria, a big husky girl named Ponce. She answered, "It seems that whoever drafted the silly document hadn't bothered to ask about what a land mine really was. So... while we couldn't stockpile the mines in advance, legally, instead,

Carrera stockpiled *millions* of empty metal and plastic casings, more millions of pounds of explosive that just happened to be cast in chunks the exact shapes and sizes of those casings. Oh...and detonators and bouncing charges, of course. They were all stored separately so they weren't mines until we put the parts together..."

"Cynical or realistic?" Zamora asked Maria. She had no answer.

Ponce continued, "The process of assembly takes about thirty seconds or so, each, and can be, and is being, done by little old ladies in tennis shoes in a couple of warehouses near Arraijan. It actually takes longer to record where we put the mines than it did to put them together.

"Kind of makes you wonder about the minds of people who try to ban certain types of weapons because of aesthetics, doesn't it? I guess their delicate sensibilities make it just too, too distasteful for them to really try to understand the weapons themselves. So they fail."

"Yes," Zamora replied, "and a good thing for us, too."

"We're not just setting them up for harassment and road and area denial," Maria said. "Sergeant Ponce's putting in some fairly dense fields between places we think we'll want to attack and places where we can hide. There'll be paths through, paths we'll know and the enemy won't. We hit them; we run; we run right through the mines. If they follow, they'll regret it."

"You do that a couple of times," Zamora commented, "and they'll probably stop trying to follow."

"That's what we thought," Ponce said.

"There are also some other places where we're putting down just a few mines, along with a bunch of metal fragments or tiny magnets—"

"I know about the 'Dianas,'" Zamora said. "It'll make clearing those few a real chore, since it's effectively impossible for a magnetic mine detector to tell the difference between a 'Diana' and a real mine.

"Okay, I'm satisfied, Maria. I'm going to go check out First Platoon. The Nguyens will be staying with you for a week or two. Treat them nice. They've got experience in this area and a whole *bag* of tricks."

It turned out that Mrs. Nguyen preferred to be called "Madame." Her Spanish was fair, though her husband's was wretched. They both spoke excellent French. Maria had high school French, a couple of years' worth. They got by.

"Recruited girl...name 'Han,'" Mr. Nguyen said, in the Spanish he was still working on. "She marry one you people...or maybe white round eye. Not sure. She recruit bunch us. We help."

His and his wife's ages looked to be anywhere between seventy and one hundred. Gradually, in mixed and broken French and Spanish, it was revealed that they had something like a century's worth of fighting as guerillas between them. They were a great help.

"You got sleep," Mr. Nguyen said. "You got eat. You got...stand down...plan...prepare...rehearse. Enemy use that. Come in when sleeping...quick-quick...helicopter...no warning."

"We could mine all the open areas," Maria offered. She thought about that for a minute and said, "No, no we couldn't. We have a lot of mines, not an infinity."

"Got better trick anyway," he said. "Need little air legion... you call, 'ala,' yes? Anyway, need little help from thems peoples."

The engineer squad, under Ponce, was straining and groaning to roll a two-thousand-pound bomb into a hole they'd dug the night before. The hole—about twelve feet long and two wide—was centered in an open area about three hundred meters on a side. Fast growing vegetation in fertile Balboa's soil and clime would cover the thing in less than a week. They had some fast-growing progressivine cuttings they intended to transplant to help camouflage along.

Ponce cursed aloud as the bomb plopped into the hole. Upset by that and by the squad's activity, a bright gray and green trixie leapt from a tree at the edge of the wood line and flew across the open space, making its trixie cawing sounds.

"Trick with Zhong," Mr. Nguyen said, "is threaten face."

Maria shook her head. "Like...threatening to punch them?"

Frustrated with the difficulties in communication, the man said, "No...no...threaten..." Then he stopped for lack of the right word and concept. "What you call what show to world? Appearance?"

"Like...honor?" Maria asked.

"That it. You call 'honor.' With us—Zhong, Yamato, all us—we call word translate 'face.' With Zhong, must be able to make commander lose face."

"What's that have to do with putting a bomb in a field?"

"Big shame," Nguyen said. "Okay lose helicopter once, maybe. Maybe twice. After that, commander enemy look stupid if lose a third. Won't take risk."

"Ohhh."

"Yes, make lose face. Helicopter come...wind bend tree...tree has wire...wire runs bomb. Bomb go boom. Helo go boom. Do once. Do twice. Enemy lose face. After that, you sleep sound. Plan easy. Secure."

"Ohhh."

"You good girl," Nguyen said, reaching up to pat her on the cheek. "Remind me own daughter."

"How is your daughter?" Maria asked, quite sure that the daughter was a grandmother herself by now.

Nguyen looked very sad for a moment. "She dead," he said. "Killed young...planting bomb." Then he added, with a note of pride, his chin lifting, "In war against Zhong."

If Maria needed easy communication, she really had to go to Madame. She found her standing in a hut in a village, lecturing a group from Maria's platoon.

"Since your enemy," Madame said, "has so very kindly given you so many, *many* bombs—*such* generosity!—during and after their last invasion, surely someone ought to get some use from them."

Maria waited until Madame had announced a break, then called her aside. She scratched her head. They were putting in a lot of bombs, but, "Madame Nguyen, what about magnetism from the bombs. Won't they be found? What about radar from the air?"

"Well, naturally, child, you should de-gauss them, if you can."

"Degauss?"

"Ah...eliminate the magnetic signature. I've shown your Sergeant Ponce how to do it. And bury the bombs with a radar scattering shroud over them to keep the enemy from finding out which landing zones were so trapped and which weren't.

"Then too, some places, you can put the bombs in underground but don't wire them to the saplings. Just like you are doing with some of the antipersonnel mines. That way, so you see, the enemy gets accustomed to using a particular landing zone, or trail, or road until some night you ladies pay a visit to the place and the next day—or the next, doesn't matter really—it goes boom right in their overconfident faces. On the other hand, all you must do is get to the area and assemble the mines. You need not even carry detonators with you. Just bury them nearby. Then even a strip search would reveal nothing."

Marta smiled, tentatively, as if she were long out of practice in smiling.

"I've got to ask," she said, "and I hope you won't think I'm prying, but where did you and your husband come from, that you know all this?"

Madame sighed, "The colonel and I?"

"The *colonel*?" Maria asked.

"Yes, he was a colonel. You would say a 'legate.' We're from Cochin. For the last couple of years we've been teaching the Revolutionary Warfare course for about-to-be-discharged veterans.

"He's more a regular who knows how to operate like a guerrilla than an actual guerrilla himself. I was a real guerilla, though some might say a terrorist.

"We fought for our country, between us, for over a century. Then we discovered that Tsarist Marxism wasn't compatible with patriotism. Things got bad for us. We were recruited and came here.

"Listen to the colonel," Madame warned. "I know a lot of techniques, but he understands things like intelligence, communications and coordination, and the consummate importance of *never* letting the enemy think he's doing well."

Madame checked her watch and announced, "Break's over, girls, back to class." Maria stayed to watch.

"Let me show you some of the difference, a trick," Madame said, and beckoned them to follow. Maria did, into a concrete house, even though she wasn't specifically invited.

On one wall was a picture, painted by a perhaps not terribly talented local artist. It was hanging askew.

"What's wrong with that?" Madame asked.

"It's crooked," one of the very new Amazons answered. "So?"

Madame wagged her finger. "Only a fairly senior officer of the enemy is likely to be bothered by a picture askew. Idiocy and focus on mere appearances often increases with rank. So you booby trap the thing so the bomb goes off—so an electrical connection is made—when the picture is righted."

The young Amazon's eyes lit up. "Ohhh."

❖   ❖   ❖

Madame showed them how to pack a bicycle with explosives and a timer, and how to scrounge or make their own munitions when the materiel they'd been supplied ran out.

Marta snorted in Maria's ear, "As if we're very fucking likely to outlast the supplies."

"Hush!"

Madame Nguyen also spoke to them at length about maintaining political control and what needed be done with enemy prisoners of war. None of the Amazons cared much for what she said on those subjects, which didn't mean she was wrong or that they wouldn't do it.

Supplies rolled in almost daily. Keeping track of them, receiving, accounting for, and transmitting them, was Marta's job. One day, each platoon in the maniple received at least one "secret" weapon. It came in an electronics-proof case. When opened, the case revealed a remote controlled miniature tank with just enough armor to protect it from small arms fire and about a quarter of a ton of explosive. The little robots were wire guided and each carried a closed circuit lowlight TV for the operator to see where it was going. There was also a loudspeaker on each one so the operator could make announcements to the enemy.

"What the fuck?" Marta said when she saw it.

"I read about the idea in Franco's class," Maria told her, "in the single science fiction book we read. 'I am a thirty-second bomb. I am a thirty-second bomb. Twenty-nine. Twenty-eight...'"

"Oh, *funny!*"

"How many did we get?" Maria asked.

"Three of the little terrors. They're called"—she consulted the hand receipt—"'Davids.'"

"Okay," Maria said. She pulled up her mental map and said, "Send them to cache areas one...three...and four. And have one girl per squad trained to drive them."

"Wilco, Centurion," Marta answered.

Part of the Amazons' cover was that there were men, from the Fourteenth Cazador Tercio, mixed in their operational area and among them. The leader of the nearest group to Maria's was a Centurion named Cesar Pastora. His platoon and Maria's got along pretty well, helped, perhaps, by the facts that the *Cazadores* were boys, that the *Amazonas* were girls, and that...

"My sister's a squad leader in your regiment," Pastora had told Marta. He told Marta a lot of things. It was just possible that he made excuses to find opportunities to tell her a lot of things. It was also possible that she didn't mind at all. Marta had been lonely for a very long time.

"Let's say that that gives me a certain perspective on the *Tercio Amazona* that some others may lack."

Watching the Amazons dig in one day, Pastora added, "There may be some other things that we lack, too. Have you noticed, Optio Bugatti, that your women are actually quite a bit better at camouflaging things than my men are? No joke."

"Could be," Marta agreed. "Maybe all those years we'd been learning to coordinate colors and patterns had some indirect payoff. Don't know."

"Could I ask for some of your troops to assist mine?"

"Make it worth my while," Marta said.

"I'll cook dinner—which is to say, warm up our canned rations—for both of us tomorrow..."

"Tempting," Marta answered, "but..."

"...and I'll have my platoon dig a dozen bunkers for yours."

"Done."

"The enemy's going to be coming in ignorant," Pastora said, over what passed for dinner. Some cans still sat in the coals, near enough to keep warm but not so near as to scorch their contents. "But he's not stupid. You ladies will be able to live openly but discreetly among the refugees, coming out to fight in secret and only occasionally. But only for a while. Eventually you're going to end up going underground."

While he spoke, Pastora made a show of cleaning out one can thoroughly, then mixing the ration-issue rum with water and the little fruit drink packets that also came in the rations. There wasn't any ice.

"We know they'll catch on," Marta agreed. "We've made some camps in inaccessible places for the long haul."

"Want me to look them over?" Pastora asked. He added hastily, lest Marta be offended by the offer, "I'm sure, based on everything I've seen, that they're fine, but what's a second opinion hurt?" He held out the can of fruit juice and rum, saying, "You can drink this safely; *nothing* can live in the presence of legion-issue rum."

Marta took the can, sipped, and made an oh-Jesus-what-is-that-shit face. Not that she wasn't used to the rum that came with the rations. But Pastora mixed his a little stronger than she was used to. Uncut, the rum was strong enough to use as a fire starter.

"Yeah, sure, Cesar," Marta said, passing the can back.

"How's the charcoal production coming?" Pastora asked. The charcoal was for underground cooking in the messes they'd dug here and there. Under the Nguyens' tutelage, they'd run plastic, while it lasted, and then bamboo pipes a good distance from where the food would be cooked to draw off the smoke, if any, so the enemy couldn't find them by that smoke.

"We've enough—rather, we'll *have* enough—for a couple of months, if we're frugal," Marta answered. She took the can back from Pastora and sipped again, the fiery rum racing to her toes.

"You'll have more than that," Pastora said.

"No, not for all of us," Marta disagreed.

"Dear Optio," Pastora said, shaking his head, "it's not going to be 'all of us.'"

Marta shook her own head. "I don't understand. Sure, we'll take losses but—"

"You'll take losses. We're going to be destroyed." Pastora laughed as if it were actually funny. "You know what they say: 'On your feet or dead; never on your knees.' When the enemy comes, we're going out to fight him. When we're crushed, he'll think for a while that he owns this area. Then you girls have your turn.

"I remember you, you know," Pastora said. "From the *classis*, off the coast of Xamar. You have a very distinctive...ummm... profile."

Marta was suddenly horribly ashamed. She'd been hired as a sea whore, originally. Covering her face, she stood to go.

Pastora stood, as well, put his hands on her shoulders to stop her, and said, "No. I'm *proud* of you, Marta. One woman in a thousand, if that many, can do what you've done, rise as you've risen. I don't think any less of you."

Marta sat again and took a much longer drink from the rum mix. She shook her head. She really *liked* Pastora. He was a nice man, and especially nice to her. Sure, she'd been in love with a woman once, but that was because of the person that woman had been, that, and their shared life and experience. She wasn't doctrinaire about it.

She put the can down, stood herself up again, and repeated back to Pastora, "'On your feet or dead; never on your knees?' Come on, I'm not that doctrinaire about it."

"I am glad we are not alone in all this," Marta said one day, as she and Maria watched a sweating and straining group of *Cazadores* hauling loads that none of the women could have hoped to.

"You're glad? I am ecstatic that I am not entirely in charge," answered Maria. "Speaking of which, how are you and Centurion Pastora getting along?"

"We get along pretty well, actually," Marta said, smiling broadly.

"I know. And that surprises me. I thought you preferred..."

"I'm not doctrinaire about it," Marta answered, primly. "Besides, it's not like I'm the only one who's gotten all gooey."

Maria nodded her own head, sadly, thinking, *Half my girls will cry themselves to sleep when the men march out. And don't march back.*

Doctrine called for using everything to resist an occupation. Besides the Amazons and *Cazadores,* and below them in the military scheme of things, were the refugees, not all of whom were helpless. There were one hundred and eighty-three people in Maria's area whose credentials were pretty much impeccable: Retired soldiers, veterans discharged into the Home Guard, children of soldiers and the widows of soldiers who had been given jobs in legion-owned factories.

The *Amazonas* and *Cazadores* trained those as and when they could. Mostly, though, the civilians were a source of labor. It was expected they would become a useful source of intelligence. The credentialed ones were also a means of controlling the others whom the soldiers didn't know and had no real basis for trusting. Ultimately, they might be a source of recruits.

All the rest, the nearly fifteen thousand otherwise useless mouths without credentials, were also put to work, but on open projects: Communal bomb shelters, sharpening wooden stakes to use for foot traps, making charcoal, drayage and storage. Those with agricultural backgrounds were even put to work growing food.

✧ ✧ ✧

While preparing, the people used small portable AM/FM radios to keep up on the news. It was almost all bad. First the Tauran Union and the Zhong had begun flying over the country on reconnaissance missions despite the government's protests and despite the disapproval of most of the world. So Balboa stopped returning their POWs. At least one high altitude reconnaissance flight had been shot down, too, though that had been something of a fluke nobody seemed to think the legion could repeat.

Then the legion's *classis* began mining the *Mar Furioso* approaches to the Transitway, to either side of the *Isla Real*. That led to the enemy sinking one of the mine-laying ships. Either a flight of Legion Jan Sobieski planes or a battery of the air defense tercio—it wasn't certain, based on the reports—took out two of the enemy's aircraft that were going after another of the mine-layers. Balboa finished up the mining with the two ships they had left.

Then the *Taurans* tried to force their way in with mine clearing ships, escorted by warships, with fighters overhead. The *classis* sank a mine-clearing vessel and damaged a destroyer before the rest pulled back out of range. The radio said reports in the enemy press put the loss at over two hundred Tauran lives. Balboa's didn't count.

One broadcast was directly from Parilla directly to his opposite number, his enemy. It concerned the thousands of prisoners of war still held by Balboa. Those, Parilla announced, were to be split into very small groups, then placed, under guard, in the area south of the City. Maria remembered from Carrera's map that that was where he was putting all the service support for both north and south. Parilla said this was *not* intended to be some kind of human shield. He said that nothing of any military value to Balboa would be allowed within two hundred meters of one of the newer and smaller POW camps, excepting only that the legion might put medical units and field hospitals there. That was, so he said, so that the enemy could bomb with gleeful abandon using their extremely accurate precision guided bombs.

Even as Parilla was speaking, most of the surface elements of the *classis*—one light aircraft carrier, one heavy cruiser, some corvettes—made a run for it to Santa Josefina, to the east, there to be interned. No mention was made of either the *classis* submarine force nor of the shallow draft patrol boats.

Oddly enough, a couple of days later, and for two days after that, a series of convoys rolled by, heading to Santa Josefina, carrying some thousands of troops. Sometimes they stopped by the side of the road to rest, or to ask for water. Maria was there on one of those occasions and spoke to the men, none of whom would say a word of what they were up to or where they were going. She found it interesting that, while the insignia indicated that the men came from nearly every tercio in the legion, every one of them had a thick Santa Josefinan accent.

We always did have a lot of recruits from there, Maria thought. *And, somehow, I don't think those men are going home to escape the war, not on legion trucks and buses.*

In a deep bunker in one of Maria's platoon's little bases, Marta had her head on Pastora's shoulder. Nobody thought the worse of either of them for that. She, Maria, Pastora and his optio were studying the map, going over contingency plans when they heard it, the sound of a jet flying low overhead. It paid no attention to them. It was obviously heading toward the City.

Pastora said, in a subdued voice, "I'll come by later, *Centuriona.* We both have better things to do right now."

Enemy planes flew by regularly thereafter. Neither platoon had television, unless they went to the only major town in the area, so they couldn't see the punishment being inflicted on their country.

But they could hear. Over the radio they heard a mother weeping softly as she and her neighbors dug in the rubble for the bodies of her husband and children. Marta and the others clenched their fists and vowed revenge for that.

They heard a radio announcer give a blow-by-blow description of three of Balboa's obsolescent fighters shot out of the sky by some unseen enemy airplanes. And the pounding the island took? Sometimes they could listen to bombing over the radio and actually see the night sky to the west light up with the flashing lightning of three-thousand-pound bombs.

Listening to that, worrying herself sick over Alma and Cat's kids, Maria couldn't help herself. She began to hate an enemy that, before, it had just been her job to fight. They all did, and yearned for the day of revenge.

Desire for revenge warred with fear and frustration, however, as the enemy made their main landings, Taurans to the south around the port of Cristobal, Zhong to the north, on the *Isla Real.* The landings on the island were repulsed, supposedly with heavy losses to the Zhong, but Fourth Marine Legion was trapped inside Cristobal, holding on to the charred, ruined city by their fingernails.

Then came the news that both *Puerto Armados,* on the *Mar Furioso,* and Capitano, on the Shimmering Sea, had fallen within two days of each other to enemy Marines. Detachments of Fifth Mountain had fought before being driven back, licking their wounds, to their enclave in the mountains between the ports.

One day, a lone enemy bomber limped by, trailing smoke. There was a puff, a lurch, and then another, larger, puff, followed by a parachute. Maria sent four girls under Vielka Arias to round up the pilot.

When Vielka limped back to report, she showed a bullet riddled Zhong body and said, "He tried to escape."

Maria noticed that one of the pilot's legs had been broken but that it hadn't been done by a bullet. *"Tried to escape?" Oh, yes . . . of course.*

Bombs are very accurate. They will always hit the planet they're dropped over.

In the bowels of that planet, Marta sat with someone's girl on her lap. With her in the bunker were half the platoon headquarters and a couple of hundred civilians. Civil or military, they all cowered as the logs overhead shook with concussion, dirt filtering down between them to coat hair and clothing, hands and faces.

Why are they even bothering? Marta wondered. *Sure, we're here to be hit but it's unlikely they even* know *about us. Is it just terror?*

A young woman, eighteen or twenty, Marta couldn't say, shrieked aloud at a particularly near miss. That was understandable. It was understandable, too, that the shrieking went on long after the ground had ceased to rumble.

Understandable, but not tolerable, Marta decided. She lifted the small child off her lap and stood. Bending to the girl's ear, she said, "I'll be right back, honey." Then she strode to the shrieking woman, grabbed her by the front of her dress, and slapped her silly.

"Will"—slap—"you"—slap—"shut"—slap—"the"—slap—"fuck"—slap—"up?"

Wide-eyed, in shock, the young woman bit her lower lip hard enough to turn her chin white and nodded, quietly and very briskly.

"Good." Marta went back to her log seat and picked the child up again.

I swear, *some people just need to be slapped.*

After two days of aerial attack, essentially no harm had been done to either the Amazons' or the Cazadors' ability to fight. Maria didn't lose a single girl to the aircraft, in fact, though a couple of hundred civilians were hurt or killed. Pastora lost one boy who took a shot at a bomber with a shoulder-fired antiaircraft missile.

There is a reason they call them missiles rather that hittiles. The antiaircraft gunner didn't even get a near miss and the bomber's wing man dropped a seven hundred and fifty pounder on the boy's lap.

There wasn't enough left for a decent memorial service.

Not that there was time for a memorial service.

Within a couple of hours of that incident the helicopters started coming in, Zhong troop carriers. While that was happening, still more choppers winged past from over the mountains. These were Tauran, coming from carriers in the Shimmering Sea to help the Zhong ferry troops ashore.

"It's time," Pastora said. Maria nodded her head, sadly, while Marta's shoulders shook with her attempt to keep in her sobbing. Pastora shook Maria's hand, then wrapped Marta in a bear hug. If that made the sobbing worse, and it probably did, Pastora was a big enough man, and strong enough, to dampen the shuddering.

"You don't have to do this," Marta said, in a shaking voice.

"I do, love," the centurion replied. "They will not set foot on my land, nor place their boots on the necks of my people, without me and mine striking a blow against them. It's a matter of honor."

"Move away! Clear a way!" one of the stretcher bearers shouted, as he and another brought a bit over half of Pastora into the bunker. His legs were tourniquetted off, what there were of them.

"He had a . . . a disagreement . . . with an artillery shell," one of the bearers said. The bearer—his name tag read, León, and his rank said "corporal"—looked ghastly white with fear. Maria had the sense that his fright didn't come from the combat he'd just come through, but from the knowledge that he was now senior in his unit.

Yeah, Cazador, I know what it's like to suddenly find yourself in charge of a goat fuck, Maria thought, with sympathy.

"Find the optio," she ordered Ponce, once she saw Pastora's condition. *God, poor Marta. Twice she finds somebody to love and twice she loses them in blood.*

Maria heard heavy steps, booted feet, pounding down the log stairs into the bunker. Marta raced over and threw herself to her knees, next to Pastora's litter.

"On your feet or dead," he said, smilingly but weakly, "never on your knees." He reached up a hand to stroke the woman's cheek, softly.

She reached up to hold held his hand firmly in place, sandwiched between her own and her cheek. "I think I told you," she said, in a near whisper, "and demonstrated, too, that I'm not doctrinaire about it."

"I remember. You remember, too, that I was going to ask you to marry me if we came through this."

Before Marta could form an answer, one of the platoon medics came in, lugging an aid bag slung across her back. She took one look and shook her head. Even so, the medic said, "I'll try."

Marta started to back out of the way.

"No, Optio, stay there. Morale is as important as anything else in these things. Keep his morale up." The medic checked Pastora's dog tags and shouted out, "I need a line of volunteers with Type O Negative blood!"

"I'm O Neg," Marta said.

"Good," the medic answered. "That means you can hold his hand while I transfer blood."

In the limited light of a flaring lantern, Marta stroked Pastora's cold, damp face. Tears ran down her own cheeks.

"Stupid men. Stupid honor."

Interlude

The town of Concepción had once been small, peaceful, even sleepy. No more.

Now it bristled with activity. It bristled, too, with weapons. It might even have been said to have bristled with the sharp points of barbed concertina wire that surrounded it, controlled it, divided it.

Children watched, wide-eyed, as load after load of helicopter-borne men, equipment, and supplies descended onto the open field just outside the town.

Young women watched, too, as those same helicopters disgorged dozens of young men, small even by local standards. If those men were small, they also looked strong, and even exotic. The young women watched with interest. Their own men, brothers, fathers, cousins, were mostly gone elsewhere.

The interest of the young women varied, however. One among them was not looking for large biceps or matching those against larger stomachs. One was counting men and heavy weapons, noting locations for supplies, watching the interaction of the leaders and the led. This one took notes only in her mind; a pen and paper would have been too noticeable, too dangerous.

The young woman who watched with a different eye noticed that the soldiers were, many of them, overage. She saw how they sweated in the muggy air. She observed how the looks on some of the faces suggested that their wearers would rather be anywhere but there.

A very small dozer excavated a long deep pit not far from where the young woman waited, watched and counted. *A protected spot for supplies? No,* she decided, *a command post; there are too many wires and antennae for this to be anything else.*

A lean man, taller than the enemy norm, wearing the uniform of the Zhong, oversaw the baby dozer with the keenest interest, as if his life depended on it. The watching woman could not make out the rank or name of the tall man from this distance. She wasn't sure what to make of him...though she thought making him a corpse would be nice.

A civilian clad man of middle years, his arms tied behind his back, was prodded forward to the taller Zhong at the point of bayonet. A few words were exchanged and the civilian was led away in the direction of the town's small jail.

The watching woman recognized the mayor—the *alcalde*—of Concepción, as he was led away by his guards.

The taller Zhong, he must have been either the commander or his deputy, turned his attention back to the dozer and its work.

Unnoticed, the watching woman turned away and slid through the town. On her way she made mental note of the positions of four mortars, what looked to become a motor pool, and the medics' aid station.

Then she stopped short, at the edge of the town. Half a dozen of her countrymen, all in uniform, had been lined up along a ditch they'd apparently been forced to dig. The shovels were still there, stuck into the dirt spoil. Behind them, a dozen mean-looking Zhong Marines stood easy, rifles in hand. At a command the woman didn't understand, the Marines lifted their rifles to their shoulder. At another command, shots rang out, and the six men along the ditch crumpled into it. An officer, at least she assumed it was an officer, drew his pistol and walked to the ditch. Non-chalantly, he walked along it, stopping to fire a round every step or so. When he was finished he gave another command and the Zhong slung their rifles, walked forward, picked up the shovels, and began to fill in the ditch.

CHAPTER FOURTEEN

Remember that two wrongs don't make a right,
but that three do.
—*National Lampoon*'s "Deteriorata"

Maria:

A tall, rangy black girl carrying a .34 caliber sniper's rifle whispered to me, "Here they come, Centurion."

I risked a peek up though the narrow firing port of the position I'd taken up with one of my two snipers. Lucinda was by far the better of the two, actually. I can't recall ever seeing her miss by mistake; not even once.

Oh, very nice, I thought.

I swept my binoculars along the enemy's line. *Ten men. One radio. Crossing an open field. Call it four hundred and fifty meters.* Remembering a particularly unpleasant patrol in Cazador School, I had an idea... two of them, really. Without taking the binos from my eyes, I whispered, "Can you put one through the radio?"

Lucinda—we called her "Zulucinda," or "Zuli," for shorts—answered, maybe a little miffed, "At this range? With *this* rifle? Me? *Hmmph.* I could put one through the microphone."

"Let's not be overly ambitious," I said, "the radio will do just fine. But let's wait a minute until they're all in the middle of the open field." I took careful note of the faces and bodies. Yes, the one just in front of the radio operator seemed to be in charge.

I thought for a second, then said, "Three shots in rapid succession. Wreck the radio, then two more at random to keep their heads down."

318

We waited.

It had been almost a week since Pastora's boys got chopped up. The Zhong Marines had come, pushed on, been replaced by enemy reservists, and then pulled out for their next mission. The reservists weren't too well trained or led; not in comparison to our reservists and militia.

Supposedly the departed and thoroughly unmissed Zhong Marines were even then making another go at capturing the *Isla Real*. Hopefully, they'd fail again. In any case, not my problem.

I didn't know how much of it to believe, but the radio was quite definite that they were not having a walkover there. I guess the part I didn't believe were the reports of a large—to my mind an incredibly large—number of enemy warships sunk or damaged on the first day of the Marine landings.

In any case, as I suggested, the enemy reservists hadn't proven nearly so formidable as their regular Marines. On the other hand, they were already showing signs of being quick learners. I wanted to make sure they didn't have much of a chance to learn.

Lucinda's first shot rang out and the radio disintegrated in my view. The enemy were diving for cover even as the next two shots lent them encouragement.

"Come on, Zuli. Let's get to the next position." Lucinda was a tall—better than six foot—girl. That, along with her color, lent her her nickname. She rather liked it, I suspected.

We slithered away to our next firing position.

By the time we reached it, the enemy squad had begun to sort itself out. One man, the same one I'd noted as being the leader, was moving low from place to place checking on his men.

"Okay, Zuli, see the one with the big gut?"

"Right."

"Shoot him in the belly."

"I could shoot him in the head!"

"You want a challenge, put it through his spine . . . or his kidney, but leave him alive and *conscious*. Screaming would be nice. And two more random shots to keep them pinned down for a bit."

At the same moment as the next gunshot, the enemy squad leader screamed in pain, flopping ungracefully to the dirt. Zuli fired twice more.

"Let's go," I said. "And head or heart shots after this." The squad leader was screaming for help as we crawled and ran.

It took them a while before one worked up the nerve to go to his leader's aid. Zuli tracked him in her scope for half a second then blew his brains out. I saw it. The man was running one minute and the next he was a headless corpse with a red mist atop his spraying neck.

Zuli finally got the idea and emptied the rest of her magazine, three rounds, in the enemy's general direction. She managed to put in a new magazine as we raced along a dry creek bed, circling around to our next position.

After the next two went down, one more head shot and a heart shot, the others simply wouldn't move. Then the squad leader stopped screaming for help, dead, maybe, or maybe just unconscious.

Did I mention that Zuli was using .34 caliber *armor piercing* ammunition? It went right through their vests and helmets. Despite some myths to the contrary, the nonstick coating didn't help all that much to penetrate the armor. It was mostly to aid in reliable and consistent feeding of the ammunition. It was the armor piercing nature of the bullets—the hardened, sharpened point and dense alloy core—that spun right through the tough fibers of the enemy's body armor. The coating also was good for keeping down wear and tear on the rifle's barrel, which was very important to a sniper.

After a while someone managed to take charge of the remainder. I think it might have been the guy who'd been carrying the radio. They stayed low where even Lucinda couldn't get a decent shot. They were trying to crawl out of our field of fire, I suppose. Couldn't blame them.

On her own Zuli was much too proud to take a shot she didn't think she could make. I had to *order* her to keep up the harassment, to keep pushing them in the direction they were going.

Then we were rewarded with a boom and another scream of pain. Who says mines aren't useful?

The five remaining stood up to surrender, hands in the air. A couple of them were waving white rags.

Oh, oh. Decision time.

I had Zuli cover me while I walked forward, my rifle at the ready. They seemed pathetically frightened and eager right up to where they noticed I had tits. Then they seemed angry. How unfair, being shot up by *girls*. I suppose it was, in a way.

I motioned with the muzzle of my rifle for them to start moving ahead of me. When I had herded them back to where the bodies were (all except for the one whose face had been ripped off and throat laid open by a mine; he was plainly dying), I stopped them and had them lie down on their stomachs in a row.

At my signal Lucinda joined me. She just shook her head and said "Centurion, they've seen who we are."

"I know," I answered. "Start collecting up their rifles. There's another four or five and a light machine gun at the edge of the minefield. Be careful. It isn't marked."

"That's okay. I helped put this one in," she said, leaving.

The prisoners presented me with a considerable dilemma. Sure, we had solid reports, eyewitness reports, of them killing our prisoners. But that wasn't the same thing as me killing theirs.

But, as Lucinda had said, they'd seen me. They could identify me to their side. After that, it would be a very short time before they carted me in. And then they'd shoot me...as they had a right to, I thought, my being a combatant but living out of uniform and all.

I figured Carrera probably would go ahead and hang those other prisoners who had been caught doing the same thing...if he knew they were going to shoot me, or had already done so. I suspected the enemy knew that, too. They'd just do it, probably unofficially. I doubted they would endanger their own people by announcing it.

And I had absolutely no way to hold these guys prisoner for any length of time. I wished I could have. It might have made the enemy a little more reluctant to bomb from the air.

I thought about Alma, about how much she needed me to come home to her. Cat's kids, too.

When Zuli had gone out of sight, I said—though I doubt they understood me—"Sorry, boys, but getting back to my little girl's a lot more important to me than you are. Sorry." Then I raised my rifle and...found I couldn't do it. *Shit.*

When Zuli returned, laden with weapons, I told her, "Put those down and tape these guys. We'll try to evacuate them, when we get the chance, to headquarters."

Once the prisoners were taped up, Zuli and I spent half an hour arranging the other bodies as best we could to look like they'd been killed in a sudden mass ambush. I shot Zuli's victims so the enemy wouldn't necessarily believe that one sniper did all that.

Let them think we were in the woods in droves.

It was a nice haul: Eight rifles with about two thousand rounds of ammunition, two light machine guns with nearly as much, a couple of dozen grenades, a map (unmarked, unfortunately), and a set of radio frequencies for the next week. The radio, of course was useless. I began to regret not letting Zuli shoot the microphone. Maybe best of all, we took a set of enemy-built night vision goggles. They were a little better fit than the Volgan-made ones we normally used and couldn't now. Those I kept for myself on the theory that if the Earthpigs overhead were good enough to pick up night vision goggles, they'd likely be good enough to tell the difference between Zhong and ours and not notice that mine was Zhong but in our hands.

We stripped the bodies of the head-shot victims for their uniforms and equipment. The loot we stashed about two kilometers away in a small hole in the ground, then camouflaged it as best we could in the short time available.

I sent someone back for it later.

We found two of our girls, a couple of days after the night they'd disappeared. We didn't find them where they were supposed to be, but about a kilometer away. The cooing of the *antaniae* and the circling vultures led us to them.

Corporal Martina Espinar and Private Elpidia Sanchez were on mine-arming detail, their job to go to a road intersection and uncover, then arm and rebury, a series of mines we'd previously buried.

How the enemy spotted them I don't know and, likely, never will. They were spotted, though, there was no question about that. And there wasn't a lot of doubt about what had happened to them.

Sergeant Ponce led me there. "I didn't move anything, Centurion," she insisted.

They were lying side by side, a few feet apart. The legs of both were spread wide, their hands tied behind their back and their uniform trousers—because we were still following the rules of the Protocol—had been cut away. Their throats had been cut. That was gratuitous, though, because the tightened ropes around their necks had almost certainly strangled them before their throats were cut.

The *antaniae*—nasty little bat-winged fuckers—that had been chewing on their faces scurried away when we arrived. We had to identify them by their personal effects.

"Why?" I asked. It was a stupid question; I knew why. At least I thought I did.

My guess is that, when they were caught, and the enemy realized they were in uniform and so would not be punished for what they'd been doing, he decided to take things into his own hands. Not that the Zhong were squeamish about shooting people, but they were in the effective hire of the Tauran Union and the Taurans *were* squeamish.

"Stupid of them not to have buried the bodies," I said.

"They were probably in a rush," Ponce answered, her voice gone cold and toneless.

"Yeah. Get pictures. Get a lot of pictures. We can burst transmit them to headquarters with one of the Yamatan radios. Getting them on the wire after that is their problem."

I stood there for a long time, staring at the bodies, steeling myself for what I knew I was going to do. Finally, I said, "Bring me the five prisoners Zuli and I took."

It took nearly half a day to get them there. By the time they arrived, led by ropes around their necks, we had a hole dug for my girls, and the location recorded. We put the prisoners on their knees, in a line facing Sanchez's and Espinar's bodies. They began to chatter in panic as soon as they saw the bodies and understood what I intended.

Little as I am, I was as big as these men, and they were kneeling. I went to the first one, the one on the right, grabbed his hair with my left hand and pulled my dirk with my right. Pulling his head back, I put the dirk to the left side of his neck and drew a deep line all the way to the right. His blood spurted out in a crimson fountain, the spray almost reaching Espinar's corpse.

He went limp almost immediately. Then I walked to the next, still cold as ice. Then the next. The fourth one, I could smell, shit himself before I even grabbed his hair. The last one tried to get to his feet to run, but I wacked him atop his head with the dirk's pommel, then threw myself on him, stabbing, stabbing, stabbing.

I'll always regret we never did find out who'd murdered my Amazons. I'd have paid good money for the chance to have a little chat with them. But killing those five would have to do.

It's called, "Reprisal."

✧   ✧   ✧

Not all our missions to arm land mines went awry, nor even most of them. I remember walking in civvies to one of my villages, ostensibly to check on Red Cross food distribution. On the way there I passed an enemy ambulance. There were already some rescue people around; the enemy's, I mean.

But there wasn't anything they could do. The mine the ambulance had gone over—it had about seven kilograms of high explosive in it, I knew—had literally flipped the thing one hundred and eighty degrees to land on its top. In the process the mine had ruptured the tank and set the fuel alight.

There were four charred bodies in the back of the ambulance, two in the front. I made appropriate sympathetic noises, even shedding a tear or two, before moving on my way.

Thank God my parents had sent me to those acting classes.

We got a helicopter near the town of Concepción almost the same way a week later. I was there to see that.

The Zhong weren't really big on civil-military relations. In fact, in the short period of time since they'd landed on the mainland, they'd demonstrated complete indifference. This, from a Tauran Union-Public Relations point of view, was highly suboptimal. The pictures of Espinar and Sanchez making the rounds of the GlobalNet—the main news broadcasters and papers refused to touch that story—weren't helping them any, either.

So, since the Taurans hadn't yet occupied any area of the country with any substantial civilian population, they had all these redundant civil affairs types that they sent to "help" the Zhong.

Dressed in mufti, with a Red Cross armband on, I was speaking to the enemy battalion's attached civil affairs officer, when it happened. I think we were talking about the vexing problem of condom distribution.

At my orders, and near sunset the night before, Zuli had gone to the perimeter of this enemy-held town to flirt with the guards at the gate that overlooked the landing zone. Zuli was decent looking, but nothing beautiful, except for her body which, even after my plastic surgery, made me feel like a boy. In any case, I counted on her body and her size to attract notice.

While she'd distracted the guards, another girl—I'd have to go to the memorial wall to remember her name; she didn't make it through the war—had crawled out to the helicopter landing zone, or LZ, outside the town. A *lot* of the supplies used against us came through that LZ. To be fair, much of the food the enemy gave me to feed the refugees also came through the same place.

We'd buried a two-thousand-pound bomb—about a thousand pounds of it explosive—in the middle of the open area. There was a small sapling more or less off to one side. The other girl found the bomb in the dark—why not; she'd helped bury it—then connected it by a pull wire to the sapling.

The next morning, while I was chatting amicably with that civil affairs officer—he spoke Spanish, surprisingly enough, and flirted with me outrageously—a resupply helicopter came in for a landing with a big net full of cargo hanging by a strap beneath it. Two Zhong soldiers rushed out to guide it down.

You know, they really could move supply, those people.

I watched the guides out of one eye, the whole time trying not to act like there was anything wrong. It took all my self-control not to flinch as the sapling began to bend in the rush of wind from the helicopter's main rotor. One moment the two soldiers were making hand and arm signals at the helicopter pilot. I actually had to look away to keep from diving to the dirt. The next moment I was knocked on my butt, ears and tail both ringing, and there was a big black cloud on the LZ.

I watched as the enemy helicopter was shoved to an angle then slid sideways to the earth. Its rotor splintered before the whole ship broke apart on the ground. Flames from its ruptured fuel tank roared up.

That civil affairs officer exclaimed, "Those fucking miserable terrorist bastards!" I think that's what I remember him saying. I don't speak English all that well.

Once he collected himself, the enemy officer became very considerate; even helping me to my feet before going to investigate. When the smoke cleared, and that took a while, there was little more than some disconnected parts of the helicopter and its crew. Of the men who had been guiding it to a landing there was literally no sign.

The burning wreck kept the landing zone closed for an entire day. For another day the enemy kept it closed himself looking for more bombs.

I gave Zuli and the other girl the next two days off, along

with a can each of cigarettes and rum to split between them. *I* didn't have the authority to award any medals, though I kicked a request up to Cristina Zamora, who did.

Retaliation wasn't long in coming. The next day the enemy bombed the civilian camp nearest where Zuli and I had ambushed their squad. They did it with artillery ... for two *hours*. When I went to that village with a few of my troops, all of us being in civilian clothes, all we found were bodies and parts of bodies. Some of them were tiny parts, from tiny bodies. There were also some burnt scraps of cloth and a *lot* of craters. The area smelled funny. White phosphorus, I guessed.

The three-person cell of reliable people I'd had there was reduced to one. He came in with about two dozen other adults and a like number of children later in the day and told me about it.

"I should have known," he said, hanging his head with pain and shame, and holding the bandage over what I took to be a bad burn on his arm. It had been white phosphorus, all right.

The man rocked back and forth as he spoke, his voice devoid of emotion. He spoke in phrases, not sentences, as if he were somehow detached from the world. "I should have known ... when the helicopter ... appeared overhead. But I didn't think ... anything ... much of it. It hovered there ... for about five minutes ... before anything ... happened.

"Then ... it left and ... right after ... all at the same time ... there was ... an ungodly racket, like a heavy freight train ... going by. There were ... it must have been ... dozens of explosions ... all around the outside ... of the camp. Almost all ... at the same moment. People ... children, especially ... the children ... started to scream. They stood there ... frozen ... for ... half a minute ... I guess. Then the next ... set of trains and more explosions ... closer this time. We began running ... for the little shelters ... you had us dig by our tents.

"Then it was right ... on top of us. And it didn't ... let up. You couldn't ... ask it to stop ... we tried. We begged ... and pleaded ... and cried. But it ... never stopped."

"Your family?" I asked, not seeing them with him.

"Gone ... all gone." Poor bastard was too far gone himself even to cry.

✧   ✧   ✧

As I'd been taught in CCS, I did a crater analysis on where the shells had come from. It's not too accurate a method, but it was all I had at the time. As it turned out, the battery that had fired on the encampment wasn't even in our area. So I passed on the message to Zamora and asked her to handle it. I understand that artillery unit, and the men in it, received special treatment all the time they were in our country. That probably wasn't fair. I imagine that they were told the camp was a guerrilla hideout and to shell it silly. I really doubt they knew any different at the time.

It wasn't too long, though, before the papers got wind of the bombardment. In the enemy's news it was initially treated as a great victory over us. And for "Democracy," of course. In Latin papers it was reported as an atrocity. Right after that, Santander, which had been trying to stay neutral, set up a few deniable camps at their end of the trail that ran through *La Palma* Province to facilitate the increased flow of volunteers. The camps supposedly provided some initial training to those volunteers.

We got some good use out of the widower as well. Sort of. He asked me for a way to strike back. I had a way. I told him he could use an explosive bike, take it to the enemy, start the timer, and run.

He took the bicycle, the frame and saddle bags of which had been filled with explosives, by an enemy outpost, ostensibly to sell cool sodas. He didn't try to run. He detonated it when he had gathered six of them around him. Though he died where none of them did, I had to call that one a win. All six had to be evacuated out of the country, we later found out. Most of them were missing big chunks of their anatomy.

I've mentioned the one town in my area, Concepción. Oh, no, it was nothing grand. The only monument near the place was that burnt out helicopter. Before the war the town's population had been just under a thousand. What with the refugees and all, it was maybe five thousand now. The enemy battalion had set up its headquarters in the town center. They'd also set up billeting tents, mostly to one side. That's why I'd been there to talk to the enemy civil affairs officer.

Maybe they were there to take advantage of the creature comforts of the place, such as they were. Maybe it was because the town dominated the local road net. I don't pretend to really understand *them*.

The problem with the town was that there, where enemy largess could be most directly applied, the townspeople—some of them—were beginning to go over to the enemy. That could not be tolerated.

There was one man, in particular, who had turned coats. It was the Zhong-appointed mayor of the place. The real mayor, being a veteran of the legion, had been locked up by the enemy the second day they'd been there. He was rotting in the town jail. Okay, maybe he wasn't precisely rotting. The enemy actually took fairly good care of him. So?

Anyway, I sent Zuli to take care of the turncoat. From three quarters of a mile away she put a bullet through his brain while he was talking to the enemy commander. The traitor dropped like a felled ox right there in the town square. I understand his wife was splattered with his bones, blood, and brains. Tough. She should have talked him out of turning his coat.

It took a while after that for them to come up with a replacement.

It was about that time that the enemy, who—as I've said—were already showing signs of being quick learners, began to suspect that the resistance they were facing was more than just random. Life became more difficult for us.

It started with ambushes; them ambushing us, or trying to. Sometimes it worked for them, sometimes it didn't. But, after two of their ambushes had worked, they were no longer in doubt about who they were facing. I lost five girls—dead—before I wised up.

The problem was that I needed to be able to send my *Amazonas* anywhere in my area. That meant the enemy had to be kept in the dark as much as possible. It wouldn't be too long, so the Nguyens had told me, before substantial numbers of our people would begin to defect—helping the enemy mostly by informing on us—unless we kept up a regular presence in their camps and showed willingness to punish. And once that gradual defection began to happen? We'd have no place to hide. Even the ones who wouldn't outright defect would stop helping us out of a sense of self preservation unless they thought we, or at least our side, was going to win. "Buying insurance," Madame Nguyen had called it.

We had one big advantage. I and my troops knew where our mines were...and were not. The enemy didn't at first, and never entirely. I could move anywhere, to include right through the minefields, in places, anyway, without worrying about being blown to kingdom come with the next step. They couldn't.

Eventually, the bad guys started putting in booby traps, simple things like hand grenades on trip wires (no, you don't attach the wire to the pull ring), to keep us from moving around our area so freely. We also found some homemade electric mines, one or two of them the hard way. You know the kind I mean: take a metal can, cut the top off, put the top on the bottom and perforate both with the sharp end of a bottle *cum* can opener. Fill the hollow space with explosive that's been primed with an electric blasting cap. Connect the metal piece that you cut off the top to one wire, the blasting cap to another. Connect the other wire on the blasting cap to the main part. Put the can in a hole. Put the ex-top over the main part of the can with them kept separate by a sheet of paper or light plastic (in our climate plastic is much better). Camouflage. Pray. Connect the wires to a battery. Then, when someone steps on the can, the sharp triangles pointing down punch through the paper or plastic. The metal connects, the electricity flows, the cap goes off, and bye-bye foot. Or leg. Or, depending on size, life.

They were a pain in the ass—errr...foot—to us, sometimes, but not so great a pain as our, real, mines were to them. Still, homemade mines, like other mines, work, even when they don't. Before we were done more than a few of my *chicas* had wet themselves to find they were in an enemy mine field. You know the old joke about the farmer who tries to protect his melon patch by putting up a sign that says, "One of these melons has been poisoned." They were crossing out my "one" and putting in "two."

Far more nasty, they used directional mines. We had them, too, although of a different type. The problem with them, for the enemy, was twofold. A really sharp troop, and most of mine were sharp, can spot the tripwire much of the time. Also, if we spotted it, you can bet we disarmed that mine and put it where it would do *us* more good.

I later found out, though, that when the enemy requested normal antipersonnel mines to do to us what we'd been doing to them they were turned down by their highest political authorities, even though they had *not* signed the antilandmine treaty. I think that was the Taurans' doing. Idiots.

The question even generated some debate in their newspapers.

One set of headlines I saw in a captured newspaper went, "Allies want to expand the use of illegal land mines." The story line went to the effect that for them to respond to our mines by endangering more children by emplacing more of them was analogous to fighting for peace or fucking for chastity. The writer didn't actually use the term "fuck," of course, though she implied it.

I was just as happy that the enemy weren't using mines. The homemade booby traps and trip-wired grenades were bad enough.

The enemy also began using daytime sweeps to try to find us or our caches of weapons. They usually weren't too successful. For one thing, we generally didn't have to fight them if we didn't want to. For another, we'd hidden our goodies very well. For a third, we only had to keep existing, keep inflicting *some* casualties on them, make the roads insecure, attack their "face," and eventually they'd probably get sick of it and go away.

Even so, we did fight back from time to time, if everything seemed favorable. It usually cost something though.

"Look over there, *Centuriona,* by the big tree."

From the thick bushes in which I crouched I looked and did see...not quite see; I could *sense*...something. A shadow, maybe. I looked again and the shadow moved, only a little.

The tree was a huge silverwood, easily ten or even twelve feet thick through the trunk. Cut down it would have been worth a small fortune. Its branches spread out, dominating the jungle and plunging everything beneath it into twilight.

But, in that twilight, the shadow *had* moved.

I had one of my squads out on a routine combat patrol. Routine, that is, if you can say so about something where you have absolutely no idea about what you'll run into but are reasonably sure you won't like it when you find it. Routine, when every step is a new and unique exercise in fear,

Not that the patrol was random. We were checking out known gaps in our mines and traps, and routes parallel to them; places the enemy might be found.

Like I said before; if we just rolled over and let the enemy have his way, we'd lose. We had to go out and fight his ambushes and sweeps on terms that favored us as much as possible. And we had to do so often enough that he wouldn't start thinking he could go anywhere safely. We had to make them afraid of us. That's all *friction* in war is about: Fear. No fear, no friction. No friction, and war really does become an industrial operation, with victory going to the side with the biggest, most efficient machines. Obviously, that wasn't us.

The shadow moved again. I concentrated. *There it was, the outline of a soldier.*

Getting down myself, I pointed at the squad leader, squatting a few meters behind me, to get her attention and direct it to the enemy. Then I gestured left, right, down and pointed a fist towards the enemy patrol to show her what I wanted. She did much the same thing to her two team leaders and her machine gun crew. The squad began to fan out quietly, one team to each side, the machine gun team and squad leader to me. The girls were quiet as librarians as they crept up on line.

Under and around the big tree I never got more than a glimpse, the merest sensing, of any movement. The enemy weren't expecting us, necessarily. But they weren't taking any chances either. They were learning.

I put my hand to the machine gunner's shoulder and squeezed it to steady her. She gave the tiniest little nod of understanding or maybe thanks.

In the woods before us I began to catch many more glimpses of the enemy patrol. Unfortunately, I still had no sense of how many there were. Nor were any substantial number of them exposed for any length of time. I'd see one, then he'd disappear. Then I might catch sight of two more before they disappeared.

When I started adding up the glimpses I'd had in my head I came up with a few too many for comfort. There was no way this was a squad. There were at least fifteen of the villains out there, and that meant—since it was more than a squad—that my girls were most likely facing a platoon. Thirty to forty enemy troops was more than I cared to tangle with, especially since they'd have artillery dropping on our butts within minutes—yes, that's how good they were with it—of our opening fire.

Reluctantly I looked behind me for an easy way out. Then I thought about how close they were and decided that we probably wouldn't make it. I turned back to the enemy platoon and tried to make out a radio. Then I thought, *Nah, what's the use. A platoon will have more than just one.*

I didn't have a radio. And even if I'd had one, it probably wouldn't have been able to reach one of my mortar crews. (I'd taken a half dozen "refugees" and added them to the mortars to make two fairly full strength crews. You can train a monkey to drop a shell down in a tube . . . but he's not likely to stay there when the enemy shoots back. That takes what we laughingly call, "intelligence.") But even if I had one, and even if I'd been willing to risk one of my mortar crews, it would be far, far too long before they'd be able to help me. They'd have to hear my request, then run like hell to the nearest mortar. That was buried probably a kilometer or more away from them. The squad would probably get stopped by an enemy check-point on the way to the gun. Even if they weren't stopped and got to the mortar in double quick time they'd have to unbury it. Then, when they fired, the enemy artillery would be on them like flies on crap. They used some very sophisticated radar to backtrack a flying shell to its point of origin. *No mortar,* I decided.

I looked at the scout sniper I had brought with me. It wasn't Zuli but another girl, Marielena. She was olive, like me, and kind of scrawny. I was glad she wasn't Zuli, actually, because while I didn't want to lose Marielena, I couldn't *afford* to lose Lucinda. Mari had ended up carrying a sniper rifle because she was a somewhat better shot than most and I had the rifle to spare. She was, maybe, seventeen and a little awkward still.

"Mari," I whispered, soft as baby's breath, "I need you to duck back about a hundred and twenty or so meters—quietly, you hear me?—then quarter circle around to our right. When the enemy gets with twenty-five meters of us I want you to start shooting at them. Concentrate on the ones nearest us, here. It would be nice if you hit one or two but I don't insist on it. Got it?"

She went without a murmur.

To the rest, through the squad leader, I passed along the command, "No matter what, wait for the machine gun to start off." The machine gunner, herself, I continued to squeeze into quiescence.

For the next several minutes I mentally bit my fingernails to the quick. The whole time the enemy platoon—oh, yes, it was definitely a platoon—kept creeping closer, slowly and with exquisite care. They never exposed enough of themselves for me to risk having the machine gunner initiate our little ambush. Damn, but they were getting better in a hurry!

The nearest was about fifteen meters, fifty feet, in front of our line when shots began ringing out from my right. Mari.

She didn't hit any of them that I could see. But she definitely got their attention. A fusillade of shots, everything from rifles to light machine guns to medium machine guns to forty millimeter grenades went in poor Mari's direction. The enemy very quickly shook himself into a rough line and began assaulting Mari's general location, making short rushes by individuals and small teams.

Mari's marksmanship, never of the absolute best, got noticeably worse. I'd almost swear one of her shots hit the tree I was hiding behind.

Then three things happened at once: the rightmost soldier of the enemy assault line jumped—unwittingly—right on top of one of my girls; the remainder of that squad was in nearly perfect line with my machine gun; and Mari screamed. It had to have been her, they had no women in their infantry.

I didn't have to tell the machine gunner to open fire. So many targets, after the strain of waiting, were more than she could resist. She started to blast away to her front, all of the rest following her lead. I can't say they were aiming all that well; few do.

But, God, the *chicas* put out some fire. Everybody had loaded a drum magazine, seventyty-five rounds, rather than the usual thirty. For just half a minute, or perhaps a little less, we put out more bullets than a maniple, even though we were firing burst rather than full automatic. The barrels were *smoking* when the magazines went dry.

And that's what saved us... most of us. The enemy couldn't tell the exact number of bullets flying his way. But, let me tell you, a thousand rounds, give or take, going off in thirty seconds makes a terrifying racket. Even more, every bullet added its own "crack" in flight, two if it actually hit something solid, which in the jungle it typically did. That was about two or three thousand distinct sounds of menace, in half a minute. Hell, it scared me; I'm not surprised that the bad guys decided, each on his own, to retreat, and reconsider. They pulled back completely out of sight, though they were competent enough to throw some fire in our general direction to wreck our marksmanship.

The machine gun maybe got one or two more of them as they backed off. I can't say so for sure, though. The one *Amazona* upon whom the enemy soldier had jumped was still trying to fight it out, hand to hand. Neither of them could get at a knife or bayonet and they were punching and scratching at each other, firearms useless and quite forgotten. I think the poor bastard had just realized he had a hand full of tit when I stuck him through the kidney with my bayonet.

I told the squad leader to get her people out in a hurry. Some of them had been hit, though none too badly. It wouldn't be long before their artillery began chopping us to hamburger. I accompanied the rest for a few minutes then went for Mari. I figured I had to.

She was a mess. Worse, she was conscious. She didn't even yet have the grace of shock to take the pain away. When I reached her she was writhing on the ground, trying so hard not to cry out she'd bit part way through her own tongue. I really don't want to talk about what she looked like; what they'd done to her. I had to fight down the urge to panic ... and to throw up. I guess training helped there, because I didn't do either.

But she managed to ask me, words smearing around her bloody tongue, "Please stop the pain, Centurion? Please, anything. Maria, please? Anything? Something? Please, Maria."

There was *so* little time. Already the artillery was dropping on where the patrol had been. I knew what I had to do. I just didn't want to do it. But the look of agony of her face was more than I could stand, either.

I flicked the selector to "R" for "rounds," single shot. Mari stopped thrashing and tried to force a smile when she felt the warm muzzle against her head. She began to pray, her lips forming the words with little sound. I prayed with her: "Our Father, who art in heaven, hallowed be thy name, thy kingdom come ..."

When she seemed more immersed in the prayer than in her pain, I closed my eyes and shot her, once. Then I cried as I slung her body across my back and carried it away through the jungle shadows. You see, I had to hide her so the enemy wouldn't feel he'd done well.

Marta had to go into hiding not long after that. We got word that they'd found that old recruiting ad and identified her from it. Not long after that, they identified me.

Which just goes to show that Carrera had his limits, intelligence-wise.

Interlude

In geosynchronous orbit, unheard and unseen by the primitives below, the Old Earth Ship, *Spirit of Peace,* coursed through space. *Peace*'s eyes and sensors focused on the jungle far below. She and her sisters of the United Earth Peace Fleet—between them the most sophisticated intelligence gathering tools in Terra Nova's history—saw everything that moved on the surface of the planet. Some of the newer ones—including the Spirit class—actually used radar to look into the ground. Still other sensors keyed on magnetic fields to identify large pieces of metal, a tell-tale sign of soldiers. From a number of ships, suborbital drones filled in gaps, both in area and in intelligence gathering technique. A steady stream of information beamed from *Peace* to the surface.

Below the ships and the drones, but still high enough that a man could not breathe the air unassisted, soared reconnaissance aircraft, some Zhong but mostly Tauran, based out of Cienfuegos, a Tsarist Marxist-ruled island in the Shimmering Sea. These, too, used their sensors—infrared, magnetic, visual and radar—to find targets on the ground.

Still closer to the planet, lesser aircraft—fighters, bombers, helicopters—used their eyes and their cameras to find an elusive foe.

Yet each of these methods failed in one or more particulars. Cloud cover frequently blocked normal photography. The layers of thick jungle always blocked it where jungle existed. Rain could dilute, interfere with, and distort the heat of a human body. Strips of aluminum hung from trees, radar scattering and absorbing nets, the carbon-based and hence radar-absorbing trees themselves; all these rendered even ground penetrating radar problematic.

Still, these methods produced literally millions of images and bits of information. These were collected at a headquarters far from the action. Thousands of overworked, bleary-eyed men and women labored around the clock to make sense of what the images showed...and of what they did not.

Occasionally, they found something. This something was then subjected to the most minute scrutiny. Parallels were drawn, analogies made, judgments rendered. By the time the something was sent in the form of useable information, more often than not it was too old to be of use. Almost as often, the something found was found in a populated area where it could not be engaged by any heavy or indiscriminate firepower; so bad an image would that make on the evening news.

Yet it was not all in vain. From time to time an image would show something interesting, other images would confirm, orders would ring out and a small patch of Terra Nova's surface would be scoured of life. Sometimes.

Below the satellites, below the aircraft, far below the headquarters that collected so many images, small groups of men crept through jungle, walked nervously through savanna. Sometimes they did so in response to information given them from on high, even though they knew that, often enough, this would have long gone stale. More often the small groups of men hunted for information—targets—for themselves.

Usually, the hunting was in vain. Metal they could find... often. Heat signatures were all too plentiful and all too often in the wrong place. Photo images might well show the face of an enemy, or of an ally, or of a neutral. Few heat signatures could definitively tell the difference between a group of men and a herd of large animals. No method, none, could look inside the human mind and heart.

CHAPTER FIFTEEN

Despite the hopes expressed by observers like Betty Friedan—
who assured readers of her *The Second Stage* that women
warriors would, as women, have more sensitive concern
for life than do male warriors, hence would be a force
for caution and against brutality in any future war—such
sentimentalism strains credulity.
　　　　　　　　—Jean Bethke Elshtain, *Women and War*

You cannot qualify war in terms harsher than I will. War is
cruelty, and you cannot refine it; and those who brought war
into our country deserve all the curses and maledictions a
people can pour out.
　　　　　　　　—William Tecumseh Sherman, to the Mayor of Atlanta

The light of three moons filtered through the firing port over Marta's
head. She looked old beyond her years, weary beyond the ability of
any amount of sleep to cure, and thinner than Maria had seen her
since she'd resigned from Cazador School. With her eyes closed,
one hand lightly holding her rifle to her thigh, her rear end on a
firing step and her back against the rough-hewn logs of the bunker,
she said, "Thank God the Taurans won't let the Zhong use any real
mines. We'd never have gotten away if they did."

"Rough night?" Maria asked, just as if most of the nights weren't
rough.

"No words," Marta answered. "Just no fucking words."

"Find some," Maria ordered, more harshly than she felt.

Eyes still closed, Marta nodded. She knew Maria needed every
scrap of operational information that could be found.

"They've started putting up wire," Marta said. "Long barriers. I think they intend to cut our area into sections then sanitize those sections in sequence. We ran into one we didn't expect—it wasn't there yesterday—and cut our way through rather than go to the ends that they might be watching.

"About two kilometers past where we cut through, we ended up in a running firefight with one of their patrols. Chance thing; they weren't expecting us and we weren't really expecting them. They didn't hit any of us and I kind of doubt we hit any of them. But I figured we'd better run for it.

"'Course, I didn't try to escape through the same section we cut through; I found a different place. But if it hadn't been wire, if it had been a minefield, we'd have stumbled into it before we even knew it was there."

"Lose anybody?" Maria asked.

Marta opened her eyes, though they stayed unfocused and her head still rested on the logs behind her. "No," she said, "but the wire's a new kind, more like razor-sharp metal tape. Arias cut the crap out of her hand on it. Goes right through leather gloves. Nasty shit."

"Ya done good, Marta," Maria said. "Go get some sleep."

Marta didn't answer except to nod. She closed her eyes again, let her chin fall, and in a moment was softly snoring.

How do I use this? Maria wondered. *How do I keep them from using the wire to separate and pen us up? Mines watch themselves to a degree. Wire they're going to have to put people to watching. I foresee a lot of work for Zuli in the coming weeks and months. And—I think—the wire's going to let us know where they'll have small teams out on their own, but stationary, where we can destroy them.*

Then, too, wire can be cut. So it has to be checked. That means men walking the line of the stuff. That makes it almost as much of a burden as an asset. And maybe we can make it more so.

From the crest of a hill, from the progressivine-fringed edge of a copse atop that hill, and not so far from where some of the enemy's wire made a dog leg, Sergeant Ponce, the engineer, watched through binoculars as the enemy helicopter touched down. It was the fourth time she'd seen it do so in her field of view. The intervening trees and hill made it impossible to tell whether any troops had been dropped off at any given one of the touchdowns.

It was the same basic model the legion used, a Volgan IM-71. The legion had bought its helicopters; the Zhong pirated the design and built their own.

Zhong are little folks, Ponce thought, *even smaller than us. They could have had forty men packed into that thing and have dropped off ten at each touch down. And if they have, I've no way to tell.*

She consulted her map. *I think they're not really looking for us. I think it's a wire inspection detail. That matches the touch downs...pretty well, anyway. So where are they going to check...?*

Ponce slithered back through the vines into the copse, to where she'd left the three women with her. Each of them, and Ponce herself, had a directional antipersonnel mine in her pack. These things resembled nothing so much as very shallow buckets—or saucepans with inverted covers—with straplike handles that, with the attached spike, could be used to aim them or to affix them to trees.

"Get the mines out, girls," Ponce ordered. "We're going to do a little wire integrity team discouragement."

Two hours later, when one of the Zhong squads dropped off by the helicopter had an unfortunate incident with four directional mines, Ponce and her girls were sharing an unpleasantly warm beer in a bunker, three kilometers away.

"Who's out there?" Marta asked. "There" was a patch of mixed rain forest and savannah over which three Zhong helicopter gunships—maybe working in conjunction with some of their infantry—were trying to flush some of the guerillas out of hiding to the open where they could be killed.

The gunships were working like an oversized team of raptors, two circling overhead while one searched out the floor with noise and fire.

"Lola Saavedra and her fire team," Sergeant Ponce answered. "Assuming they're still alive."

Marta reached out and pushed some tall grass out of the way. *Too far for naked eyes,* she thought, rolling to her side to take out a compact pair of binoculars. *Or even the integral scope on the F-26.* Holding her hands cupped over the lenses to reduce the chance of glare or flash giving her position away, she scanned left to right, looking for the team under attack. Finding nothing that way, she thought, *But if the Zhong are firing, they, at least, think they know where the girls are. Or might be.*

She adjusted her aim, concentrating on the areas where rocket and cannon fire occasionally lashed down. *Nothing.*

"Eleven o'clock," Ponce announced in a dead voice. The sound coming from the hunting gunships changed slightly in pitch. Marta shifted her view again.

"Shit," Marta said. In her view one of the girls—she was certain it was Saavedra herself—had broken from cover and was running, weaponless and with rucksack abandoned, across an open area for a thicker section of trees on the far side. The woman's mouth was open and her eyes wide with sheer terror.

Marta looked up and saw that one of the circling helicopters had come down and was swinging to line up with Saavedra's break for safety. She thought she could see the Zhong pilot's toothy grin, even through the glare of the windscreen.

"Run, Lola, run," she whispered, shifted her binos down to where her Amazon footraced for her life. For a moment, Saavedra had her face turned away, toward the pursuing helicopter. She didn't seem to slow even though she needed to see where she was going, which was something in her power, a lot more than she needed to see what was coming to kill her, which was outside of her ability to influence.

"Watch where you're going," Marta said, softly. "Watch where... shit."

Twin puffs of smoke bloomed from pods slung under the gunship's pylons. Mere moments later, the ground behind Saavedra erupted with two blasts from high explosives. Predictably, between not watching where she was going, and the shock of the explosions close behind, the Amazon tripped and fell. She rolled and was up in a moment, this time with her head and eyes firmly fixed to her path. Two more explosions went off close behind her, this time close enough to knock her down on their own. Saavedra managed to get back up to her knees and one hand.

Marta could have sworn the woman was looking right at her at the moment half a dozen rockets impacted all around her, swallowing both her image and her life in a storm of fire, smoke, and hot pieces of flying steel. Past her, at the far treeline, Marta made out faint images of Zhong infantry beginning to emerge.

"Shit!"

"I'd rather dance ballet on and around their booby traps," Marta said, later on, back at camp.

"Your tits are too big to dance ballet," Maria answered, not unreasonably.

Marta ignored the jibe, continuing her rant, "I'd rather crawl through a field of their homemade mines, with snipers and artillery zeroing in, than have one of those things on my ass.

"Saavedra was *looking* at me, Maria. She was looking *right at me* when they engulfed her."

Which is probably what's really bothering her, Maria thought. *That's a pretty intense and personal experience.*

Truthfully, it's getting to where my women's almost sole relief from fear is when they're in one of the refugee camps. Then the gunships can't tell the difference between the civilians and the soldiers. And, while they've demonstrated a certain ruthlessness with regard to civilian casualties, at least when the Taurans aren't looking, ordnance is expensive and they don't seem to like wasting it too often.

True, sometimes if we're in one of the deeper shelters the enemy almost never seems to have a clue. But moving from place to place, where no civilian ought to be, at night? That's just become an invitation to be collanderized.

And sure, we fight back with our light antiaircraft missiles; small arms, too, if the gunships come low enough. The gunships, though, seem to be able to take a fair amount of damage. The best we can hope for is to drive them away, temporarily. We've never actually shot one down.

Still, the damage builds up, when we manage to inflict some. Also, there are only so many of the aircraft for a fairly large area. We've got a partisan war raging over more than fifteen thousand square miles. A few dozen airplanes and about three times as many helicopters aren't too many for such an area. From the Zhong's point of view, I'm sure, they're never even enough. This is especially true given that each one spends a fair amount of time—many hours—in a maintenance hangar for every hour spent hunting us. And my women drive up the amount of time in maintenance dramatically every time we get a couple of hits on one, too.

Thank God, I've got properly trained—which is to say irrational— troops who will accept the considerable personal danger involved in taking on an aircraft with rifles for something that's really very unlikely to bring any immediate personal benefit.

Maria knew how to get her friend out of her funk. "Since you don't seem too worried about the mines and snipers, Marta..."

"I would rather have *none,* thank you, Maria," Marta answered, sensing what would have been coming. "The only good thing I can see is that the gunships can be dangerous to both sides. Zuli told me that she found some bodies while leading a patrol. She said there were about four enemy troops that had been shot up something awful by the old mill down by the *Rio Tetona.*"

"About?"

"Yeah. Her exact fucking word. 'About.' That's how bad they'd been hit. She just couldn't tell. No way we could have done it, not that kind of butchering. She thought she should leave the weapons and equipment alone so that the enemy would have no doubt but that we hadn't done it. I sent her to drop a message to the enemy as to where they could find the bodies." Marta paused. "Maria?"

"Yes."

Her voice held terror. "No shit; those things really scare me; the gunships, I mean."

Maria patted Marta's cheek and answered, "I know. Me, too." *And still, it's an ill whore that blows nobody any good. I wonder if...*

"Why this encampment?" Zuli asked Colonel Nguyen, who had volunteered to lead the mission. A small loudspeaker hung by the old Cochinese's side. The moons shone down big and bright, though the light of one of them was diffused by an intervening cloud. There was expectation of rain later on in the evening.

"Every revolution..." Nguyen said, "is people...on other side. Inform. Report. Help enemy. We gots...you women gots...nobody this place...your side. Don't know why. Seen over, maybe. No, that not right." Nguyen thought for a moment and then said, "Oversight. Is oversight."

"So?" Zuli asked.

"Is way to fix enemies of revolution...enemies of people."

"You're the boss," Zulucinda agreed, white teeth shining in a serious black face. "What now?"

"Now we wait. Keep girls out...spread. Umm...spread out. Rain start. I lead. You follow. Bring everybody. Bring big gun."

The rain was pouring down as Nguyen led off, his sprightly steps belying his age. Behind him came five of the eleven infantry

Amazons with Zuli, then the twin 23mm antiaircraft gun with its four-girl crew, a light mortar with three women and a mule, and then the other half of the infantry. The antiaircraft gun, drawn by a mule on its vestigial wheels, clattered and clinked slightly, but not enough to be heard over the rain. They entered the encampment by a side trail, avoiding the Zhong checkpoint at the main one.

Zuli slung her .34 caliber rifle, drew her dirk, and whispered to another woman, "Follow me." Nguyen nodded approval as he saw the shapes, one tall and black, the other short and brown, disappear into the wet darkness.

Nguyen pointed at a barely visible elevation and said to the corporal in charge of the gun, "You, set up there. Point south. Hide with tree cuts." He looked at the tiny mortar crew but said nothing as they were already setting up in the center of the encampment. "Rest girls, surround camp."

Zuli came back, wiping her dirk on her trouser leg. She towered over the diminutive Cochinese. "The guards are dead," she said, matter-of-factly. "So are their replacements. The whole undisciplined rabble of a crew was asleep."

"Is good. Now wait."

As the sun arose, the rain began to lessen and then to cease altogether. There was a thick fog rising in the valley between the encampment and the nearest group of Zhong, a large platoon or small company under ponchos on the other side, perhaps two and a half kilometers away.

Nguyen handed over his loudspeaker to Zuli and said, "Now. Do what planned."

Zuli nodded and turned the volume on the loudspeaker down to a fairly low setting. Then she lifted the microphone to her mouth, and shouted, "All right you bastard enemies of the people; out of your tents and huts. NOW!"

I like this girl, Nguyen thought. *She's got the right words for the occasion.*

As the civilians came stumbling out, many rubbing at their eyes with sleepiness, the women surrounding the camp arose from the ground and, rifles across chests, directed any who might have tried to run back to the center of the camp. Then the Amazons on the perimeter began to push inward, herding the people into a mass.

"Separate out the children," Zuli ordered. Once this was done she had four of her women lead the children off, through the fog to the sanctuary of the jungle. Some of the mothers tried to follow but Zuli was having none of that; the older children had to carry the babies.

To the adults, Zuli said, "Into the holes we had you dig."

The Amazons kept the parents in the camp, in their holes, at gunpoint while Nguyen waited.

When the sun was fully up, but not very high in the sky, Nguyen pointed at the corporal leading the mortar crew. She immediately bellowed, "Hang it!"

One of the others lifted a mortar round and placed the finned tail over the muzzle, holding it there with her hands.

"Fire! Continuous fire."

They managed to *kachunk* out a dozen rounds before the first one hit. It exploded up in the tree, above the poncho-sheltered Zhong. Even at this distance, and even over the sounds of the outgoing shells and their terminal explosions, the women could hear voices raised in consternation intermixed with screams of fright and pain coming from their enemies.

"Slow; fire slow," Nguyen ordered. "We's gots them's attention. No want lose." Zuli passed the order to the mortar crew who dropped down to a sustainable rate of five rounds a minute. Even so, the remainder of the thirty-six shells they'd already sent flying continued to drop about every other second for the next minute.

"There," Zuli pointed. In the distance, sun glinting on glass, were two aerial flashes that told of approaching helicopters.

"Fire all left round," Nguyen said. "Quick-quick. Use up and mortar girls run." The rate of fire went up again to something approaching the maximum.

After another fifty or so blasts, the mortar went silent. The women on the crew began to disassemble it until Zuli's shout reminded them, "Skip the fucking mortar. We've got plenty. Just go."

Nguyen waited another minute after the mortar fell silent. Then, judging range carefully, he said, "Big gun girls, fire now."

That order, too, Zuli passed on. Four of the Amazons sprang to the concealed 23mm and began tossing the cut branches lying over it off to the sides. One of them jumped into the metal seat, grabbed the handles and applied the pedals to make sure the thing would still traverse. The lead Zhong helicopter was about

eight hundred meters distant when a stream of fist-sized tracers began their intercepting arc. Not expecting this, the Zhong
pilot flew right into the stream of shells. His underside began
to disintegrate under the pounding even before he lost control
and arced off to crash into the trees. The other Zhong helicopter,
apparently shocked, pulled up and veered off out of range. The
Amazons were too well disciplined to cheer, but a quick glance
at their faces said they were pleased as punch to get some of
their own back.

"Now he call help," Nguyen said, with an anticipatory smile.
"Need help take care of ever-so-bad girls." The ever-so-bad girls,
not having a target in range, quickly reloaded their piece.

"Set thing on auto!" Nguyen called. "Wicked-naughty girls run!"
The Amazon infantry still at the camp scampered off, followed
by the four-woman gun crew who followed, their 23mm cannon
spewing out random crap behind them. Also behind them, the
Zhong helicopters proceeded to devastate the camp from which
had come the fire that had struck down one of their own.

"Teach sharp lesson," Nguyen said, looking over his shoulder
at the smoke and flames rising above the camp, "about just who
you support better."

Nguyen, the old guerrilla fighter, had no moral issues with
punishing a camp full of informers and traitors. That said, when
two of the helicopters broke off their punishment of the camp,
heading toward the direction the children had been taken in, he
said, "Ooo ... bad shit. Still ... maybe useful."

Rank be damned, Maria fumed at Nguyen when she was told.
"If those people didn't hate us before they sure as hell do now.
Godammit that was just plain murder."

Nguyen smiled almost indulgently. In his heavily accented
Spanish, he answered, "No say ... refugees—those who live—blame
enemy for attack camp. They know we cause. But we not cause
attack chop up kids. That enemy do. And civvie-traitor-fuckers
learn three things important. One: Enemy no care, no matter what
say. Two: Enemy no protect. Also no matter what say. Three: We
punish. That camp? No trouble this after."

"No!" Maria raged. "No, it won't be. That's because it doesn't
have that many people left!"

Nguyen shrugged, "So? And have some, yes. And there other

people, other camps, other villages. They learn lesson too. The gunships do teaching for us."

Nguyen finished, "You feel bad kids? What difference make, what you feel? What I feel; what difference? It happen. Maybe wish hadn't, but this war. Bad things happen."

"Those," Marta muttered, bitterly, "are some bad news. I wonder what took them so long?"

Ponce, with Marta and Maria, plus a couple of girls for security, overlooked one of the intersections of the main coastal highway and a feeder road from one of the ports. She answered, "I guess it's taken that long to build up one of the ports enough to offload such heavy equipment. Then, too, initially they'd have been restricted to the near vicinity of the port. The bridges in their area didn't have a prayer of holding up under a tank's load. But the Zhong have been busy with reinforcing the bridges, building new ones, and finding useable fords."

Maria said nothing as she followed a column of four heavy tanks through her binoculars. Past the tanks, but still within her field of view, engineers were setting up a prefabricated bridge over a chasm.

Finally, Maria put down her field glasses and said, "Girls, this is a 'bad thing,' as we say in the business. Soon enough the Zhong engineers will have managed to put up decent bridges in enough places that the tanks will be able to run pretty much anywhere that isn't heavily wooded."

Marta shook her head, saying, "Fuck! More than half of our area is open farmland. Worse, not too many of the mines we planted will take out a tank. None of those we'd planted off the roads will."

"Damn it!" Maria fumed. "Somehow, I never really expected them, not deep down. Things have been so bad I couldn't imagine them getting much worse."

"So?" Sergeant Ponce said, "Who's never made a mistake? So forget the mistake, Centurion. Concentrate on the fact that we've got a problem."

It was good advice; Maria took it. "Our entire defense, because that's what we've been doing, despite the fact we've been attacking more often than not, has depended in large part on antipersonnel land mines. The tanks will clear out antipersonnel mines with irritating, invulnerable ease. They'll just run right over them, setting them off. As often as not the crews won't even know unless they're unbuttoned. Even the antivehicular mines we've put in the roads won't do any more than break a track. And that'll just piss the bastard tankers off."

"So what do we do?" Marta asked.

"Request some real tank killer mines and go after the bridges," Maria answered. "And try to get them when they're out of their tanks."

A couple of Zhong tank crewmen were hurt once, when they set off an antipersonnel mine while trying to get their track back on their tank. That was the only real success with AP mines.

The Amazons tried to take out the bridges, when they could. One of the two problems with that was that the enemy watched the bridges pretty carefully. The other was that the Zhong could put bridges up faster than the Amazons could knock them down.

They had antitank weapons that would take a tank out, if they could catch it from a vulnerable angle, the sides or rear. This proved easier said than done. For one thing, it required considerable luck to find oneself in position to make that shot. For another, the tanks always worked in pairs, at a minimum, and always had infantry close at hand. Even if an Amazon found herself in a position to take a likely shot, the odds were good that the wing tank or the accompanying grunts would spot her and fire her up before she could do it. And even if not, they would pursue like furies if she shot and missed. The women did try just that a couple of times. It was not something they would afterwards recommend with any enthusiasm.

The night sky was completely overcast, with a deluge of rain threatening to pour down at any moment. In short, it was perfect.

There were four tanks in Maria's area supporting the infantry battalion she'd been fighting. Of that number she was sure, having made a very careful count of them. She did have a weapon that could take one out. Rather, she had three of them—not four, unfortunately—and three only if they all worked.

One night, when the rain was pouring down so hard she didn't think the Zhong had a prayer of spotting her or her troops from the air or ground, they rolled one of the "Davids," under its own power, to within about two kilometers of the place where the tanks were based when they weren't actively escorting or hunting.

The Amazons had kept the main gate of the place under observation for some days. They knew it always took a few minutes for the pair of tanks on patrol for the day to pass through. Maria lay very low in the position from which she'd kept the gate under observation. The gate through which the tanks would pass lay about four hundred meters distant.

Maria kept in touch with the operator of the David through a field phone and wire she had run out behind her on the way to the observation post. The Amazons had been issued a few of the phones and a limited amount of wire, just enough to be useful. Maria had also had the refugees on the lookout for any commo wire the Zhong might lay. This was not so much because the wire was useful in itself but because it tended to lead you right to them in both directions. Unfortunately, they didn't use it much, preferring radio by far. And why not? *They* didn't have an entire space fleet trying to pinpoint *their* radio signals.

Lightning flashed, followed by thunder. Almost immediately, a sheet of rain came down that might as well have been solid water.

Four hundred meters from the gate, about two hundred meters from Maria, along the dirt road that led to the gate, Marta and a half squad of Amazons lay flat on their bellies in the rain- and track-churned muck, laying a half dozen of their hard to come by track-breaking mines. When they were done they crawled back out of sight, except for Marta herself who veered her course to pass by Maria and her sole guard, Arias.

"Job's done."

"Camouflaged?"

"Pretty well. It wasn't hard to scoop out some depressions in this crap and cover the mines. And they were already mud-colored."

Unseen, Maria nodded. "Okay, good. Now we find out if those wonderful thermal imagers they use can see that little difference in temperature in this weather."

Marta began to lie down next to her chief.

"What do you think you're doing?"

"I'm not leaving you."

Maria answered, "If I am killed, you're in charge. Don't even *think* about arguing. This is an order; get out of here."

Marta grumbled, but she left. Alone, Maria turned her attention back to the gate, captured Zhong night vision goggles strapped to her head. This close to the enemy, she didn't think the Earthpigs would notice the thing's electronic signature, even if they could pick it up. She tried to ignore the cries of the *antaniae*—*mnnbt, mnnbt, mnnbt*—and the howling of a pack of monkeys.

She heard a heavy diesel roar that was soon joined by another. In her grainy green image, one of the sentries at the gate lifted up a barbed wire "knife rest" and moved it out of the way. Looking past that, she saw first one, then another Zhong tank moving to the gate. Each of the pair seemed to be carrying infantry on its back deck, about a half a dozen per was Maria's estimate.

The tanks passed the gate, slowly and carefully. It was unlikely that the tank crew gave a fig for the gate, but they didn't want to have to clean barbed wire out of their tracks. The first one stopped, about one hundred meters past the gate, waiting for the other to join it. When it did, both moved out at a slow pace.

The night suddenly strobed bright as the first of the pair rolled right over one of the mines laid by Marta and the women with her. The sound reverberated through the jungle, setting *antaniae* to screeching and even non-nocturnal birds to flight. The howling monkeys kept up their howl as they retreated as fast as possible from the blast.

Risking a rise of her head, through the night vision goggles Maria saw that one tank was stopped dead. Nearby, on the ground, a few of the infantry that had been riding it were being given first aid by their comrades. Inside the camp, an ambulance's siren began to hoot.

It didn't look to Maria as if any of the Zhong were dead. The other tank of the pair and the infantry that had been riding atop it were taking up positions to guard the damaged one until they could get it moving again. They knew a stopped tank was a vulnerable tank.

Maria picked up her field phone and squeezed the large button on the side several times to catch the attention of the operator of the David. When she knew she had it, she whispered one word, "Roll."

"Roger," said the "driver."

More than a kilometer distant, she flicked the engage switch of her control box, then thumbed the short control stick forward.

Ground began to roll past in the grainy, fisheye image on her screen. It was a truly rotten picture; the worst of Volgan crudeness and legionary frugality.

"Maybe if it weren't pouring cats and dogs and darker than three feet up a well-digger's butt this might work," grumbled the operator. She began cursing into her own phone about not being "able to see a damned thing."

She need not have worried so much about that. Within minutes of the first tank being disabled, before the David could have reached the area, the night sky was lit by four huge flares hanging under parachutes. Yes, the rain reduced the effect, but still; there were *four* of them up there.

Maria cursed as her goggles blacked out with the sudden burst of light. *Shit,* she thought, tearing them from her eyes. *I hope they're not damaged. I wonder why they used illumination; they've got all those night vision devices. Maybe the mechanics working on the tank requested it.*

The metal shell casings around artillery- and mortar-delivered flares tend to go off in unpredictable directions once they break free. Maria heard a rattle something like a distant freight train just as one struck the ground with a frightful *thud* not more than fifty feet away from her. Knowing that the casings were heavy and knowing they could kill her if one hit, Maria started to tremble a little.

The operator of the David called over the phone, "Centurion, I can see both tanks, maybe two minutes away. Which one do you want me to go for?"

Maria thought about that for a few moments. *If we take out the undamaged one we—at best, maybe—get it and its crew, the accompanying infantry being dispersed . . . then they'll fix the damaged one and use it again. But, on the other hand, there are a number of people clustered around the damaged tank. If we go after that, we might get the crew, a number of wounded—to hell with their wounded—some medics—to hell with them too—and that mechanic team that's helping fix the track.*

Besides, the undamaged tank might spot the David and get away. It's much faster, anyway. And I can still hear the engine turning over. On the other hand, the damaged one's going nowhere fast.

She forced the tremors from her voice. "Go after the first one. Go after the cripple."

"Roger."

Risking another peek up, Maria saw when the Zhong started to fire their rifles and machine guns. The David's hull sparked wherever it was hit. The enemy fire increased as the miniature tank speeded up suddenly, sprinting for the crippled tank. One crewman tried desperately to crawl back inside the tank; maybe to use the heavy machine gun or the main gun.

Only it was too late for that.

Maria's eyes saw spots and her ears rang. *So that's what fifty tons in flight looks like,* she thought in wonder. *Some spectacle.*

The David had gone right underneath the tank before the operator set it off. The explosion had buffeted Maria half senseless, close as she was. Then there was a huge chunk of machinery flying up and out of an ugly cloud of black smoke. Every man aboard had his neck broken in an instant when the tank suddenly lurched upward.

Maria couldn't see what became of the men clustered around it. She suspected there wouldn't be a lot left.

"We're still losing," Marta said later back at camp.

"Maybe so," Maria admitted. "But tonight was a good piece of work. We killed fifteen or twenty of the enemy for no loss ourselves. If you don't count the David, that is, and I don't. The tank has got to be a total wreck: Suspension ripped off, belly plate buckled and torn, turret mechanism and engine most likely destroyed beyond hope of repair. Better still, they're not going to be so damned bold. And, with only three tanks left, they won't be able to send out a pair every day like they have been."

"We're *still* losing," Marta insisted.

"Don't *say* that," Maria ordered.

"Yes, Centurion Fuentes," Marta answered, bracing to attention. "Now if that will be all..."

"Marta..."

"If that will be *all, Centuriona*?"

Marta left the bunker and went out into the falling rain. It didn't matter, she was already wet and perhaps nature's shower might clean off some of the dirt. She walked to a *bohio,* a shed of wood and grass, and sat down on a stump, feeling lower than whale shit.

It was a dirtier trick for me to use her rank against her than it was for her to use it against me. She's my friend and I made her feel less than she is. Jesus, does everything I touch or care for have to turn to shit?

Still, orders or not, I'm essentially right. Yes, we've gotten what some might call a favorable kill ratio. That much is true even if that someone counts the men from Pastora's platoon—Marta felt a sudden constriction in her throat at the thought of Pastora's cooling corpse and what they might have become if he hadn't offered himself and his men up as a sacrifice on the altar of the nation. She forced that down, as she did every time he came unbidden to her mind. *Never mind that now; nothing to be done. But even counting the Cazadors who were killed or captured the first day, by any objective measure we're doing well.*

Counting civilian dead, of course, the forces against us are doing better than that. The enemy probably thinks he's doing still better, but that will be a result of reporting dead civilians, along with dogs, cats, and cows, as dead guerrillas. By that count the enemy commander is a hero.

Naturally, that Zhong commander has to report all those spurious kills. Otherwise, he would certainly have been relieved. "Face," as Colonel Nguyen said.

And we're not immune. What was Pastora's sacrifice but "face?"

But we're not losing on body counts. His troops are quick learners; all the girls think so. Even if their commander, himself, is both an idiot and a coward. He hasn't learned much because he rarely ventures out of the deep, safe bunker he made his troops dig for him.

They could be quick learners, and it wouldn't be so bad. But they're quick learners who can replace their losses more or less indefinitely. So long as their society's and government's political wills hold out and as long as the Taurans are willing to foot the bill and provide the shipping for support.

They'll even replace the tank and crew within ten days, maybe less. The most we can hope for out of that is that they won't quite replace the devil-may-care attitude the tankers had. Not that that wouldn't be a big help. It isn't about kill ratios, anyway, not to me it isn't and, if she'd admit it, not to Maria, either. The Zhong can replace losses. Ours, on the other hand, are severe, crippling, and almost permanent. In the short term, our losses are irreplaceable, and at more than a personnel management level. Weapons, ammunition, all other supplies? *Those we can get more of, if only at the rate of a trickle. But the women we've been losing are friends.*

Marta shorted with derision, directed at herself. *No, they're not just friends. They're family really, the only family I've ever known that cared for me and that I loved and that had some permanence. But how permanent can we be when we're being butchered like cattle?*

She reached into a pouch on her combat harness and pulled out a small can of *shoug,* a mix of peppers—mostly Joan of Arc and Holy Shit, with a very small admixture of Satan Triumphant—that had entered the legion's combat feeding system from its time in Sumer. The can was already opened and resealed with one of the plastic tops that came in the rations. She pulled the plastic top off and set it aside. From the same pouch she pulled out a foil-sealed packet of chorley bread and ripped it open. She tore off a piece of the bread and dipped it in the *shoug.*

One advantage of this shit, Marta thought, wincing as she popped the assemblage into her mouth, *is that it hurts so much to eat it takes away other pains.*

They say that somewhere out in the jungle, no one in the platoon knows where, though I think Zamora does, Gorgidas is training some women as replacements. Some of those we recruited ourselves, thanks in good part to the enemy's lavish and, often enough, indiscriminate use of firepower. We've have been able to send off a few score of women recruits to be trained. We call them, "women," but I know the girls we sent off were, some of them, only fourteen or fifteen years old.

Again, Marta tore off a piece of the yellow bread and dipped it. She waited a moment before consuming the stuff. With a shudder, she took a bite from the bread, leaving the remainder clutched in her fingers. She waited for the burn to subside before eating that.

Doesn't matter, anyway. They'll never in the short term match the quality of the carefully trained Amazonas *we've lost. And where new officers and centurions are going to come from no one has the slightest idea. I'm not up to the job. I learned that at Cazador School. Kill in anger? I could do that, here and back when I was in the* classis. *Kill in cold blood, or even plan to? Shit; I couldn't kill a rabbit. And we're going to need replacement officers and centurions. But Camp Spurius Ligustinus and Camp O'Higgins were bombed off of the map on general principle, early on.*

I hope they didn't erase all the traces of Maria's brother's grave. I know it hurt her when we got the word.

Carefully, Marta replaced the plastic top on the can of *shoug* and returned it to her pouch. Enough was enough. She kept the bread out, and continued munching on that.

Ah, Maria, she mentally sighed. *Pity you're straight as a tanker's bar. I wouldn't push myself on you, not that and then wreck everything. But if you weren't so very straight, I could see us being a lot more than friends. Oh, well.*

And maybe that's why I'm such a bitch. On the other hand, given my life story to date, if we were more than friends today, you would be dead the day after. I suppose I'll take what I can get and keep.

Perhaps the best measure of the Amazons' success was a backhanded compliment. Not so long after the women had taken out the tank with the David, Tauran helicopters began winging into the area carrying several companies of Gallic Gendarmerie to reinforce the Zhong. The Gendarmerie were mixed soldiers and police, possibly only half as good at either job as specialists were, but amazingly good at rooting out insurgents and partisans. With every incident, bullet, bomb, or protest, it wouldn't be more than a few hours before they'd have found where the shot or shell came from, or who was carrying the protest signs, and have people collecting up evidence and collecting up people.

And there was evidence to be gathered. No training program is perfect. The Amazons had never been trained to consider that the fingerprints on the brass cartridge case of a fired bullet could give them away. But the Gendarmerie began fingerprinting and photographing everyone in the area, with all the names, faces, and prints fed into a data base. They started issuing ID cards as well. The Amazons didn't have access to a computer that could duplicate the cards. Nor did they have any warning of what was going on. Pretty soon the enemy had pictures of many of the troops.

Fortunately, the Gendarmerie didn't often know which pictures were *Amazonas* and which were legitimate refugees . . . yet. Even so, they had their successes. A couple of Maria's girls were grabbed off the street and locked up. The Gendarmerie didn't announce the captures, as one might have expected. This made Maria worry for her *chicas* more than she would have otherwise.

Then the enemy started moving the refugees.

"It's only so we can feed you better," they said. "It's only to protect you from the wicked, bad, evil, naughty terrorists who've been plaguing you." That this would also leave great tracts of depopulated land where they could shoot up anything that moved without any bad press? That part they didn't talk about.

When they first started clearing out the civilians the Amazons didn't know it right away. Communications and intelligence are always big problems for guerrillas. Maria and Zamora did know that some of their girls in the outlying camps had dropped out of sight.

Maria found out what was going on when a couple of the girls carried Zuli into her bunker one night. Zuli was shot up middling bad, though conscious still. One of the others was hurt as well, but not badly.

"There was no place to hide, Maria," Zuli gasped out. "We'd planned to take a couple of potshots at them, then duck back to the refugee camp by the bridge. We took the shots—I got two of them . . . I *think* I got two of them—but when we went back to the camp even the tents were gone. They must have moved them while we were sneaking into position."

One of the other girls, the one who hadn't been hit, spat out, "It was a fucking nightmare. Just a fucking nightmare. Like she said, Zuli got off maybe two shots before the damned helicopters were on us like flies on crap. They fired us up, then came around and fired again. We ran. Didn't matter. We couldn't shake them off. We tried to hide under water. No go, they shot up the stream with rockets. I thought we'd lost them for a while, when we started getting near the encampment. Lost them? Hmmph. They were waiting for us. They shot the whole area to shit. That's where Zuli got it. Marisa took one while we were trying to carry Zuli off. They must have run out of ammunition after a while. Otherwise they'd have toasted all three of us."

Maria sent the unhurt girl to get some rest, then let the medics take off Zuli and Marisa. Then she sent for Marta to take over for a while. With Marta in position, she began the trek cross country to see Zamora and Nguyen. The three talked about it, hiding underground in one of Zamora's bunkers that was nearest to Maria's sector. They talked about the problem—argued about it, really—at great length. The only solution they came up with . . . nobody liked.

✧   ✧   ✧

The Gendarmerie had managed to move six more encampments before Maria returned. With her came Zamora, two more squads, and Colonel Nguyen.

In that time a thousand people that they could otherwise have hidden among weren't there anymore, or not anywhere useful, anyway. There was a strip two miles wide and six miles long which no Amazon could enter, not and expect to come back again. *Anything* that moved in that strip of land was shot to pieces.

The pattern? First would come a few artillery shells near, but not on, the encampment. The next day collaborators would be escorted in to talk to the people, to tell them how it was the fault of the guerrillas that the camp was nearly shelled. Then there would be more shells—or maybe an air strike; close enough to terrify, sometimes close enough to kill a few.

After that a Zhong patrol would walk through. If they took fire, reinforcements would fly in, then the encampment would be plastered and the survivors would be evacuated by helicopter. If there was no fire, the camp would be secured and the people put under close guard. Then the interviews would begin ... the *private* interviews. It didn't really matter what was said in those interviews. The Amazons could never trust anyone that had spoken to the Gendarmerie in private. Then troops would pass out food and candy to show what great guys they were!

Within a few days would come a half dozen or more trucks, escorted by Gendarmerie in armed vehicles. The people would be told that a big operation was going to move through the area and that they'd better get on the trucks with what they could carry or they might all be killed.

Then they'd find themselves in a camp behind wire and under guard.

Ponce's finger traced on the map. She said, "The scouts reported all the signs as having taken place here. They're going to move the civilians sometime soon."

"It's a trap," Marta said.

Zamora disagreed. "We don't know that," she said. "It makes perfectly logical sense that those people are just next on the list to be moved."

Maria peered closely at the map. "I agree. We've been giving the Zhong unholy hell near that place ever since they showed up here."

"Can we stop them from moving those people?" Ponce asked.

Zamora and Nguyen both shook their heads. "No," Zamora said. "If the Gendarmerie follow their usual pattern those people will be gone by tomorrow morning. Not a chance we can do anything about it."

Nguyen pointed to the map. "There," he said, "that next."

Zamora looked and pondered. Finally, she said, "I concur. That one." She breathed a reluctant sigh, then added, "We have to prevent it. We have to show the refugees that there is no safety but only blood, terror, and death in dealing with our enemies."

Nguyen nodded. Even *he* didn't like what was to come. "You must cruel be. Is...sometimes...only kindness."

Marta shook her head. "You can stand me against a wall and shoot me," she said, "but I'm not going to do this. This is cruelty beyond the pale."

"Cruelty?" Zamora snapped. "You want to know what cruelty is? It's when you have to hurt innocent people, people who have been given no choice in what they do, because if you don't hurt them, and hurt them far worse than the enemy can or will, you'll lose, and all your friends' sacrifices, all the innocent blood spilled so far, will be for nothing."

"Yes? Well I still won't do it."

"That's why I brought two squads from outside the area," Zamora said. Her chin and eyes dropped slightly as she said, "I wouldn't have you ambush people you know." *Instead I'll ambush people I don't know for you. As if that's a lot better. Shit.*

The first order of business was to distract the enemy. That became Maria's job. Accordingly, she ordered one of her squads to let themselves be seen near the cleared strip. She knew that meant she might lose some of them. But the enemy's attention had to be attracted away from what they'd really be doing.

Next Zamora dispatched half a squad to get an ambush site ready, one roughly between the camp in question and where the refugees were being collected.

What was left of the rest of the group with her, Zamora called in to one of the deeply hidden base camps that had been dug long before as a safe haven, a place to rest, train, plan and prepare. The mortar team was sent to get ready for another, related, mission.

When Zamora judged her fragment of a command to be ready she led them to the ambush site the advance party had picked. Nguyen accompanied.

They moved through another pouring rain that lasted all night. Zamora was not overly concerned about being spotted from the air. Even so, they kept off of the trails and away from view. Halfway to the ambush position the mortar team split off, sans mortar, heading towards the big refugee camp the enemy was building. They risked a radio call to Zamora some hours later to say they were on site and would have their gun up in an hour or so, as soon as they dug up it and its ammunition.

The occupation of the ambush position went without incident. The two squads occupied the holes that had been dug and reinforced with overhead cover. This was only half for protection from artillery. Mostly they didn't want the Zhong, the Taurans, or the Earthpigs to pick up their heat signature if the rainy weather cleared. It must have worked, since later on the rain and clouds did clear and there was no subsequent attack.

In the rain, the ambush party put out their own directional mines, Volgan jobs that were considerably larger and nastier than the more usual variety.

The sun arose after some hours of waiting, and the girls' level of tension went up with it. None of them were looking forward to what they had to do.

Least of all was Zamora. *God, I could use a cigarette, to say nothing of a drink. Both are out of the question, of course. And I can't even bitch about it because I* volunteered *for this crap. Damn. I so don't want to do this.*

Two hours after sunrise, a convoy of trucks and machine-gun-armed light vehicles passed the ambush. The Amazons didn't fire a shot. They hardly breathed.

Zamora watched the convoy with disgust. It seemed about half and half female and male Gendarmerie. They were joking, flirting with each other, too, some of them. They were doing everything, in fact but watching out for danger. *Don't they know there's a fucking war on? Or am I upset because it's obvious now that* they're *not going to stop me from what I'm going to do. What the hell is the good of even having an enemy if they can't stop you from sending your own soul to Hell.*

The column was led by a small truck with what looked to be an automatic grenade launcher on it. *No problem with that,* thought Zamora. She was right. The grenade launchers weren't very dangerous provided one were close enough to them to keep the grenades from arming before they hit.

Next were three empty cargo trucks, covered with tarps. Then came another gun vehicle, three more trucks, and a final gun vehicle bringing up the tail.

Zamora's hand reached for the "clackers," the firing devices for the directional mines. *If I open fire now, before those people get on the trucks...*

Squatting in the bunker next to her, Nguyen saw and understood the look on her face; understood too what the movement of her hands meant.

"Convoy not target," he whispered fiercely, grabbing her hands in his. "People is target. People and what think."

Zamora looked away. She and the others continued to wait, hoping the enemy would show some sense and take a different route back than they had used going in.

They didn't. The Gendarmerie had turned refugee evacuation into a drill, by then. They certainly didn't take long getting the civilians into the trucks. Zamora was almost surprised by how quickly the convoy came back up the road.

Back in Cazadora School and CCS many women had developed a sort of trick to enable them to face the daily miseries, dangers, and mutually administered beatings. They would step outside of themselves, so to speak, thinking, rather feeling: *It was not me beating my best friend's face to pulp. No, me—the me that was me—stood off to one side watching without interest or involvement while a body that looked like mine beat or was beaten. It was not my friend being beaten, but someone I had never seen before, didn't know or care about. It was always someone else, never me, that broke a friend's arm or smashed her nose to pulp.*

The convoy neared. Zamora stepped outside of herself. Her hands grasped the firing devices for the mines, almost of their own volition, as if it were a drill. No emotion showing in them, her eyes followed the convoy. Those eyes saw two young kids, perhaps they were brother and sister, sitting up in the back of one of the trucks themselves watching the scenery go by behind them. Zamora's mind could not, at the time, see children on a lark. She had orders. She saw targets. The children were still sitting, pointing fingers at the sights, when Zamora stepped even further outside of herself and—one in each hand—squeezed the firing devices.

The directional mines weren't convex like most of those used in the world. Instead, they were concave to focus their thousands of little steel cylinders onto a particular target before scattering them.

Zamora had fired just as the lead vehicle was precisely in the kill zone. It flipped over, a mass of metal and fiberglass scrap, along with some disassociated scraps of meat, immediately. The other one was pointed at a truck. The truck careened off the road, spilling refugees and fragments of refugees from its sides. It hit a tree and burst into flames.

Even before the truck hit, however, the rifles and machine guns of the two ambushing squads opened up. The two siblings Zamora had seen yet not really seen were bowled over in an instant, along with what were probably most of their adult relatives. One machine gun, in particular, played over the occupants of the trailing gun jeep. Zamora saw clearly—yet, again, didn't really see at all—as one targeted Gendarmerie was wrapped around the pintle on which her grenade launcher was affixed, her body jumping and fragmenting with each impact.

The ambush party fired like that for perhaps two minutes, then Zamora blew her whistle to signal "cease fire." Part of the platoon assaulted out into the kill zone, shooting all the enemy troops again to make sure, but only killing some of the adults among the refugees.

"Spare children," Nguyen called. "They carry word out!"

Meanwhile, Zamora called on the radio for the mortar team to begin to fire on the big refugee camp. They sent sixty rounds toward it in just over three minutes, twisting the traversing and elevating cranks to get a spread of fire on the targeted camp. Then, per orders, they bugged out. She'd told them not to waste time trying to salvage the mortar.

About the time the first distant "crump" of outgoing mortar shells could be heard, Nguyen was back.

Zamora looked at him, recognition of reality coming back to her face, a look of nausea growing.

"I won't do that again," she announced. "Never again. I don't care what you say. I don't care if you outrank me. I don't care. Never again, hear me?"

Nguyen told her she wouldn't have to, not with any luck. Then the women split up, to doff their uniforms and weapons, put on civvies, and make their way back to their respective camps. Zamora didn't begin to cry until she got home...and in private. A part of her thought it was cruelty to be left alive after having to do something like that.

Zamora could still function, if not so well, the next day and the next. A scout reported to her concerning what the mortar shells had done at the camp.

"Where did this information come from?"

The scout answered, "From some civilians who fled it. It seems that three of the camp's new inhabitants—all women, the civilians were positive on that—anyway, three of them rushed one of the guard positions with sticks in their hands and killed the occupants. Then they took over a machine gun and tried to engage the rest of the guards. They shouted out for the refugees to flee, that this was a rescue by the legion. The refugees fled en masse, not to be rescued, I suppose, but to avoid being killed. The camp's guards—some of them—panicked and opened fire, killing a fair number of the civilians. All the refugees swamped the wire then, running for their lives. Our sisters died well, I was told."

Zamora noticed a funny thing, thereafter, for certain very odd values of "funny." *Between the mortar crew and the enemy guards who'd panicked, so the scout said, one hundred and seventy-one refugees had been killed. That was about twenty civilians for each member of the mortar crew. Nor did the mortar crew actually kill any Zhong soldiers or Gallic Gendarmerie themselves. Curiously, they aren't overmuch bothered by what they had to do. The girls in the ambush, on the other hand, killed maybe a half a dozen Gendarmerie and no more than three civilians each, yet are emotionally devastated and look like they'll stay that way for a long time.*

Fascinating concept, morality as a function of what you see rather than of what you do. Perhaps that was how enemy pilots are able to sleep at night. I wish I could sleep at night. Why must we always become just like what we fight?

Of course, she had them *all* on her conscience. Nguyen noticed the next morning.

"Snap out of it, Tribune," he ordered with his quaint, almost French, accent, after he had stopped by Zamora's bunker and caught her crying.

"It's just so...so...damned sickening, sir."

He didn't, quite, sneer. "Terror make sick, yes?"

"Yes...sir."

Nguyen took a deep breath, then let it out slowly. "Tribune Zamora...you young. So listen older, maybe wiser, man. All armies terror use. Anyone use weapons that hurt, kill, any army still issue bayonet, terror use. It is, always been, always be, primary instrument war."

"But not on civilians," she cried.

"Ah." Nguyen shook his head. "That nonsense."

"If we do these things, we're no better than they are. We're no better than the Salafi *Ikhwan*."

"More nonsense," Nguyen said, heatedly. "Double nonsense. You fall in same trap as Salafis."

Zamora didn't understand and said so.

"How big Salafi, when at biggest? Tiny, yes? How often they really risk lives? Rare, yes? Why? They cause, it have no support. That why tiny; that why don't take real risks. Because have faint support, these peoples, they never win. So, all suffering they cause? It wasted. Pure waste. Wrong. Immoral.

"Now you peoples, you gots support. You fight, you risk, you lose friends. You do this can, because you support have. You use terror, with righteous, because you win, eventually. End justify harm, justify terror."

"The ends do not justify the means," Zamora protested.

"No? Then what they justify?"

Interlude

There are many ways of gathering and transmitting important information. Little Balboa had no spacecraft or satellites. It had no high altitude aircraft. It had few really sophisticated sensors.

It had a lot of eyes. Deep behind Tauran lines, in the south along the Transitway, between the bleeding edge of the battle and the port of Cristobal—still held, *barely,* by Fourth Marine Legion—small teams of Cazadors waited underground. They emerged but rarely, and then, more often than not, merely to confirm that no enemy were in their area. Sometimes, they emerged to find there were enemies in their area. Often those teams did not make it back into hiding. This, too, was information of a sort. This information, in itself useless, became priceless when matched against the reports, and failure to report, of dozens of other teams. In the constricted area between the Port of Cristobal and the line of defense built along the Gamboa River, the knowledge of where the enemy was not was the same as the knowledge of where he was.

Sometimes the reports came by remote radio. At least as often they came by courier pigeon.

On a huge map, the positions of the Tauran Union forces had been plotted with commendable accuracy. Carrera knew where they were because he knew where they were not.

Still, Carrera looked at the map as if willing it to yield more information than it could. So intent was he that he didn't notice when Parilla entered the huge war room.

"Patricio? Patricio! Are we ready?"

So intent was Carrera on the map that it took him a moment to realize someone was talking to him. He turned his face away from the wall and answered, "Hm? Oh, excuse me, Raul. Almost."

"Almost?"

"The guns are in position. Since the island has held, the legions have long since been shifted to the north. We are paying a high price to make the enemy deploy along the Gamboa the way we want him to. Still, they are conforming. Jimenez in Cristobal awaits the order. Our three Q-ships are ready to enter the Shimmering Sea. The Air Defense Brigade is straining at the bit to shoot back. Only one thing remains."

"The diversion?"

"Yes . . . that."

"You don't want to do it, do you?"

"Frankly . . . no."

"But you will do it."

"Yes. Of course. Damn me."

"When?"

"Very soon."

CHAPTER SIXTEEN

Scientific vivisection of one nerve 'til it is raw
And the victim writhes with anguish
like the Jesuit with the squaw.
—Kipling, "The Female of the Species"

Maria:

Right after that, they stopped trying to clear the civilians out of the way so they could get at us. It wasn't because of those Gendarmerie we killed, nor even because they were overly concerned with civilian life in general. Rather, I think it was that the civilians themselves refused to be moved.

I didn't see it, but I was told that the next time the Taurans and Zhong tried to relocate a camp, all of the people just sat down and refused to budge. Some TV news type was present. She'd probably been expecting some such thing, some kind of refusal, after the ambush of the truck convoy and the mortaring of the big camp.

Maybe if she hadn't been there the enemy would actually have used their weapons on the civilians to force them to move. I don't know, but I think they would have. They threatened to, for certain. I do know that when those people were forcibly picked up and put on the trucks, they got off again once they were set down. And, despite threats, the Zhong wouldn't shoot; at least not with that camera going they wouldn't.

It was about that time that the enemy stopped really trying to hunt us on the ground. Whether that was because their commanders were taking heat for the casualties they had suffered, because of a change in their strategic plans, or because they just didn't see the point anymore, I haven't a clue.

Even the small patrols they sent out didn't have the fighting heart they'd once shown. Oh, sure, sometimes they'd really try. But, as often as not, they would find some spot where it was extremely *unlikely* to run into us, then hunker down for the night. They were, in plain words, playing it safe. We went after those bolder enemy squads with a vengeance when we could. Call it reinforcement training.

And if they did a sweep, they did it in maniple strength, nothing less. Sometimes they swooped in on our area with what looked like a whole battalion. It was kind of flattering, in a way. It sure wasn't very dangerous for us. Did you ever try to move a maniple quietly, through the jungle, at night, less still a cohort? We just avoided them.

But if they'd given up on the ground, their flyboys hadn't given up from the air. No, they were no better at finding us now than they had been before. I don't think they were really trying for us, however. Any target that showed up in a thermal sight at night would do. The more targets, the smaller the area, the better.

The refugee camps took it hard. Some people began moving away from them. Some, if they could avoid us, started defecting to the enemy's camp. Most didn't, however. After all, Zuli had mostly recovered from her wounds.

We began seeing strange devices in unlikely spots.

"Sniffers," Colonel Nguyen announced, with some disdain. "Seismic detectors." The former, he explained, sampled the air for traces of human beings. Going to the bathroom had just become a dangerous enterprise. Urine and feces were the chemical traces they were most likely to pick up, he said, though we'd have to watch for smoke, insect repellent, anything both strong and volatile. *Antania* breath would do in a pinch. Though catching the nasty little bastards... blech.

The latter detected any kind of foot or vehicular traffic by the energy transmitted through the ground. Beating those involved us manufacturing... well, have you ever seen the little devices where the wing turns a windmill and the windmill makes a tiny wooden man pound a tiny wooden hammer onto a tiny wooden anvil? We made a simplified version of those we called "thumpers."

Then we placed them everywhere there was an acoustic sensor that we could find or that we used frequently as a route.

The danger lasted for maybe two days. That was how long it took us to place the thumpers and randomly place kerosene-, urine- and feces-soaked rags all over the area. For fun, once, we put a bunch of them in a deeply wooded place where there were no civilians or troops. We also made a dozen little firepits that we put on time delay fuses. We carried in some large chunks of metal as well. Then we went to a hill a couple of miles away to watch the festivities. We didn't have any popcorn for the show and so made do with canned *shoug* and foil-wrapped *chorley*.

It began with artillery fire. Then came the jets and gunships, more artillery, napalm...the works.

I later heard that the Zhong reported an estimated one hundred twenty "terrorists" killed.

I had actually had one of my troopers suffer a sprained ankle from stepping in a hole...as we were leaving.

Remember all those extra weapons and supplies we'd been given early on? I started to have a use for them. The more the Taurans bombed on or near the camps; the more the civilians were endangered, hurt or killed; the more of them decided that maybe they ought to support us in an active way. In a roundabout way, the enemy was forcing us into becoming more of the democracy they claimed we were not. The roll of potential voting citizens was going up rather faster than casualty figures were dropping it; at least in my area they were.

With all these new replacements—including the tiniest dribble sent to us now from our *Gorgidas* training maniple—I split up my platoon to provide cadres. Not that there was much left of it, even including the few Cazadors remaining. One squad and half the mortar crews I kept with me, out in the brush. The rest I split up, one Amazon or Cazador for every two or three camps.

"Teach them to defend themselves," I said, passing out extra rifles to the troops.

"Train them to fight," I said, passing out cases of ammunition. "But don't have them do it much. Run away if the enemy gets close.

"Make lots of booby traps. Plant many mines," I said, when I broke into the caches of explosives and detonators. "And don't forget the foot traps Madam Nguyen showed us about.

"And dig in!"

Of course, the more the camps began to look like military sites, or moved to get away from the bombing, the more they became targets. But, then again, the more they became targets, the more people went to my girls and boys and asked to be enrolled and armed. I think it more than evened out.

For the Zhong, though, and the Gallic Gendarmerie, it rapidly became a nightmare. When this had all started they could have been reasonably sure of someone taking a shot at any given group of them every few days. They could be sure, as well, that the shots would be aimed by someone who knew how to shoot. Usually no one would get hit, of course, unless it was Zuli pulling the trigger. Usually no one does. But they'd have to duck anyway.

The percentage of people who really could shoot had dropped. That didn't mean anything, though, because the number of people shooting had gone through the roof. I'd passed out over three hundred rifles, mostly older, more primitive ones and sundry captures, to willing hands. They were untrained hands, to be sure, but could the enemy know that? No. They had to treat every shot fired at them as if Zuli were behind the rifle stock. Which, sometimes, she was.

Bang. They dive for the ground. I couldn't speak the language, but I knew what they were saying: "Anybody hit?" "Hell no, but if blood were brown we'd all have medals." "Where the fuck did it come from, Sarge?" "C'mon. C'mon, soldier boys. Back on your feet. Get moving. We haven't got all day." "Fuck that! I signed up for college money and to pass out free food to Uhurans. I sure didn't sign up to get shot! Besides, I've got my stress card right here." Whisper, whisper, from the sergeant to the private. They're back on their feet, start to shuffle forward a few meters.

Bang.

You can have a lot of fun doing this sort of thing. And nobody gets hurt, usually.

Sometimes though, they do, and not always the ones you might want to see hurt.

I was shadowing a Zhong maniple once, for a couple of days, careful to keep myself and the girls with me at a safe distance. Don't look askance, they outnumbered us about twenty-five to one.

This maniple was having a tough time of it. They'd come in by helicopter to a landing zone about four kilometers from a medium-sized refugee camp, established a quick perimeter defense, then collapsed that and taken off into the woods. They were moving through an area where our control of the population was solid; most of the people had already signed on with us, at least for part-time work. A number, maybe a half a percent or so, had volunteered for active service. We hadn't had time to train them worth a damn, of course, but they had already gone a long way toward making the area a nightmare of booby traps and mines.

This poor enemy maniple had no idea what it was getting into. The first warning they had was when one of their troops set off a directional mine, one of the Volgan jobs we used. From the little brush-covered hill from which I was watching I saw one unfortunate boy's legs torn off. Another one behind him took what must have been about two hundred chunks of steel cylinders through the chest and belly. The last one lost his eyes and face. Only the second one was given the mercy of dying quickly. The other two just screamed and screamed while their overworked medic tried to do something, anything, to help. It made *me* wince to hear it, and I was responsible for it.

That maniple halted for the ten minutes of shrieking before a medical helicopter could be brought in to evacuate the two wounded, then another five for a second chopper—this one without Red Cross markings—to take out the body. When one of my girls asked me if she should shoot up the second helicopter I shook my head "no" even though we had a fair chance of damaging it from where we watched.

The Taurans hadn't been moving another ten minutes before someone shouted out a pained cry for help. I hadn't heard any explosion so I guessed he'd run into one of the staked foot traps we'd taught the refugees to make. Those things were sickening. We'd dig a small hole then put in a barbed stake pointing straight up from the bottom. From the sides we'd put in two more stakes, those ones also barbed. Then we poured in something nasty, usually bolshiberry or progressivine juice, but sometimes it was human shit, to cause infection, and camouflaged the hole.

When somebody stepped into the hole one of a few things could be expected to happen. Sometimes they'd break or twist an ankle. That wasn't so bad for them. Slightly more often the stake pointing straight up would go through the sole of the boot and right through the foot. Sometimes it slid off the sole and went into the calf. Even if the enemy soldier didn't do either of those things, unless he was very careful pulling his foot out the two stakes pointing down would impale his calf or ankle. If the poor bastard actually managed to impale his foot and then tried to pull it out of the hole quickly, he'd end up with three wounds, all of them agonizing—lots of nerve endings in the human extremities—and no good way to get out of the trap.

Sometimes we'd booby trap the pit with a grenade, directional mine or other explosive device so that even if the guy got his foot out he'd die anyway, usually taking a friend or several with him.

It took even longer this time for a helicopter to get the wounded man out.

When the Zhong maniple began to move again, this time almost all their eyes were on the ground and the trees. They really weren't looking for us anymore. I took the chance and began to follow just a bit closer. I could, because I had someone—a young boy—from the nearby refugee camp to guide us around the mines and traps.

The next thing they hit was a mortar shell that had been hung from a high tree. Somebody pulled a wire, probably with his foot, releasing the shell. He shouted a warning to the others while diving to the ground himself. They all hit the ground in time—nobody was even scratched that I could see—but they were pretty shaken up by the whole thing.

Normally a mortar shell won't explode unless it's been armed by that tremendous kick in the pants from being fired out of a mortar. We'd played around with the fuses for these shells, however.

The enemy might have made as much as a kilometer of progress by nightfall. I didn't risk trying to ruin their sleep. One never knew when a gunship might be loitering out of hearing.

Next day, it all started again. Then again the day after that. I personally counted twenty-three of their troops hurt or killed for no loss of our own. I was feeling pretty good about it, even congratulating myself, when the Taurans reached one of the refugee camps.

You know, war crimes aren't committed by abnormal people. They are committed by quite normal people in very abnormal circumstances. I can look back now and almost feel sorry for what we did to those boys. Not the ones we hurt, nor even the ones we killed, but I can almost feel sorry for the ones who had to live after they did what they did.

I didn't feel that way then, though. All I felt was helpless rage and hate.

They went through the camp like a storm. Anything or anyone that got in their way, dogs, kids—didn't matter—was shot down. A little boy—couldn't have been more than two—was trying to get his dead mother to rise up. One of them put his muzzle to the back of the little boy's head and just blew his face off.

There were two of them who stood above an open shelter firing down into it. They even stopped to reload and fire a second magazine each into the pit. I didn't know what they were shooting at until later. It had been a family, I think, because when I looked at the bodies the next day I found a pile. Children on bottom, mother above where she'd died trying to protect them, an old grandfather on top of all where he'd died trying to protect his daughter or daughter-in-law and grandchildren. At least that's what I assumed the relationships were. But maybe I was wrong, almost any decent man will give up his life for almost any woman. Almost any woman will die for just about any child.

I'd had one of my girls in the camp. I saw her cut down running for her rifle to try to fight back.

One whole family—I think it was a family of seven—made a run for it. I couldn't see who was shooting at them but I did see them drop, one at a time. Whoever did it shot the adults first, then the kids.

One of the enemy, it might have been the commander, an officer anyway, tried to stop the massacre. His troops just ignored him, though. When a group of maybe forty civilians was rounded up, this guy drew his pistol to try to protect them. I couldn't see who shot him. He just clutched his stomach and fell. Then a dozen of them turned their guns on the civilians until they'd all fallen. Two of the enemy walked among them, shooting again anyone who showed any sign of life.

I wish I'd known who that Zhong officer was. I'd like to have recommended him for an award from our side. Yes, that's permitted within our regulations.

I watched all this, unable to take my eyes away, until I heard a strangled sound coming from behind me. It was the guide we'd taken from the refugees. Two of my girls were lying on top of him. One held a hand over his mouth. The other pinned his arms. They whispered comforting noises—I suppose they were supposed to be comforting—in the boy's ear while he wept and struggled. It looked like he might succeed in getting loose, so the one pinioning his arms loosened her hold just enough to be able to hit him on the back of the head with a smallish rock. He lay quietly after that, unconscious.

By the time I looked back it was over. The camp was dead, burning. So I led my little patrol in one direction, sick at heart, while the enemy maniple left by the other. One of the girls, a big husky *Amazona* named Edilza, slung the unconscious boy across her shoulders to carry him off. He didn't weigh much. He was only twelve... and now an orphan.

So tell me. What else could I have done?

That's the precise question I asked the boy, once he came to. He just answered we could have fought, at least given him a rifle to fight, even if he or all of us would have been killed to no purpose.

I told him back, "We're here to win, boy, not to make futile gestures. They'll pay for what they did, but they'll pay when *I'm* ready." I sent the boy to join my growing group of male guerrillas, the one I was rebuilding around the Cazadors who had survived so far. I understand he became one of their more ruthless and efficient cutthroats very quickly.

The Tauran press must have gotten hold of the story. Certainly they grabbed the Zhong by the stacking swivels. That entire maniple was pulled out of country shortly after the massacre. I don't know what ever happened to them. On the plus side, that left only four infantry maniples, two of them from the main battalion, their weapons maniple, and their headquarters in my area. And, naturally, recruiting went up even more. Some people might have blamed me and my girls for some of the enemy bombing, especially the bombing we'd brought down deliberately on them. They didn't blame anyone but the Zhong and the Taurans for the massacre.

Which wasn't really fair. The fact was that the slaughter was almost entirely my fault. You can't expect soldiers, any soldiers from any country, to just take what we were doing to them indefinitely. The most you can do is delay the time it takes for their discipline to break. To do that, though, you've got to give them their revenge from time to time.

Revenge for what? Well, for seeing their friends and comrades butchered and killed by an enemy they can't usually get to grips with to fight. Revenge for booby traps and ambushes.

If you don't do that, they'll take things into their own hands. Always.

What could they have done? They were holding some dozens of prisoners who had plainly committed war crimes, by Zhong rules, if not Tauran. Some of them were my girls, captured out of uniform. Others were refugees *cum* part-time guerrillas who'd been caught carrying arms or explosives, or planting mines or traps. From the point of view of the enemy troops my people were getting away with murder . . . literal legal murder. A wise commander would have court-martialed and strung up those prisoners right in the open where the Zhong soldiers could see.

That just might have saved that refugee camp. Then again, maybe not. That maniple had taken an awful lot of punishment in a short period of time to an enemy they couldn't see.

Then, too, it wasn't as if every mine and trap they'd hit hadn't been planted by one of the people in the camp they destroyed or some other one. It wasn't as if the people they'd killed, the adults and adolescents, anyway, hadn't been the very ones who'd been killing their friends at a safe distance.

By the way, if you ever go to a real war, and you like yourself as much afterwards as you did before, there's something very, very wrong with you.

Zamora came to see me not long after the massacre. She'd brought just one other *Amazona* with her as an escort, a woman I didn't know very well.

A messenger had brought me advance word that she was coming, so I broke open one of my dwindling store of ration packs for the occasion. We hadn't seen each other in months, it seemed, so why not celebrate a little?

Zamora seemed so dog tired when she arrived. It couldn't have been the trip. That, she had said, had been easy, if slow. No, she was tired deep, deep inside, tired of living, it seemed to me.

I led her into the bunker I was using for my command post. Once there, Marta handed her a canteen cup full of juice (oh, not real juice, just that dried stuff that comes in pouches and tastes somewhat better than the dog piss it resembles). Then she began to pour grain alcohol into it. It comes canned, with the ration packs, enough for two ounces per troop per day. I expected her to stop Marta's pouring but she didn't until the damned cup was at about one hundred proof.

She asked for a cigarette, too, so I opened the can of those and handed her one. Hands trembling, she lit it, smoked it, then took another one which she lit from the stub of the first.

I may not have mentioned it, but the only alcohol I'd ever seen Zamora take was that one beer at Botchkareva. And she'd never smoked before where I had seen. She didn't say anything until she'd drunk about half the canteen cup, which took a remarkably short time. By then the tremors in her hands had subsided.

"Do you do that much?" I asked.

"No . . . yes. But just the last month or so. The cigarettes and booze help a bit. For a while anyway. But it always starts up again."

"Marta, why don't you go and check on that wire laying detail Arias has out?"

She looked at me curiously, shrugged and left.

Then Zamora told me about what had been happening to her, in her area. It wasn't a pretty story. She'd had it worse than me. The Zhong battalion in her area had a *real* commander. Zamora started to cry while she talked. She didn't sob, or anything like that, but the tears just rolled down her cheeks while she spoke.

"But I could deal with that," she said. "I could deal with it right up to where the civilians started turning on me. Oh, Maria, nothing worked. I'd have the collaborators killed but there'd always be more. That fucking bastard chopped off the food to feed those peoples' families unless they cooperated. Those people weren't given any choice but to help the enemy. It was that or watch their kids slowly starve. Finally I had to give the order to kill the family of one of them. Everybody . . . the wife . . . the kids. I didn't know what else to do. Nguyen said it would help the cause . . . and it has. But that's when my hands started to shake. Maria, I'm so *sick* to death of this." Tears flowed the entire time.

I let her cry herself out, then asked, "What brought you here?"

She took another sip from her cup, another drag from her cigarette, then told me. "There's an aircraft of some kind going to land at an open space a few miles from here tomorrow night, or maybe the next. It's carrying orders for the whole tercio, what's left of us. Our chunk of the stump of Fourteenth Cazador Tercio, as well. I'm supposed to meet it, pick up the orders and get them to headquarters. I'll need an escort from you."

"Sure. No problem. Now go to sleep. You'll be safe here. And the bugs won't eat much. I'll set up the escort. Six troopers and myself?"

She nodded, maybe too tired to speak, maybe too much alcohol. She forced herself to get out, "It's the field that's northwest of the Padilla farm. You know the place?"

"Sure. You just go to sleep. I'll set everything up."

The message didn't come the next night, nor even the next. Nonetheless, we staked out the field for a third evening. It was almost morning and we were just beginning to lose hope when it suddenly materialized right in front of us. There was never a sound, but one second the air above the field was clear; the next there was a sleek, graceful looking thing with wings, pulling its nose up to a stall a few feet from the ground.

We reached the craft just as the pilot was sliding his canopy back. Zamora stuck a weapon under the man's nose and said, "Morgan."

"Drake," the pilot answered, then asked, "You all from the *Tercio Amazona*?"

"The *Tercio Amazona*, yes," Zamora answered. "Who are you?"

"Warrant Officer-Pilot Montoya, Rafael. One Thirty-Eighth Aviation *Ala*. I've got orders for you . . . and a few goodies that might come in handy."

Montoya handed over the orders, a middling thick sheaf of papers, then—standing on one wing—he began to unload some equipment from the space behind his own seat. He placed the various boxes on the ground with some care. There were maybe two dozen, all told, in different sizes.

"How many of you are here?" Montoya asked.

"Eight, total," I answered.

"All women?"

"Yes."

He seemed to be doing some calculations in his head for a moment, then said, "There's no way you're going to be able to carry all this stuff any distance. I doubt that eight men could. Let's stash most of it. You can come back for it over the next few nights."

That seemed like good advice to Zamora and me. We and two

of the others, with Montoya helping, moved all the boxes into the nearby woods, then camouflaged them as best we could.

Sweating under the load, I grunted, "What is all this junk?"

"Jammers. Half are radio jammers. The other half are to mess with the enemy's global locating system. There are instructions on how to use them inside the boxes. I understand they're pretty good. And from what I gather, you're going to need them soon."

The pilot, Montoya, looked to the east where the sky was beginning to light up. "There's no way I'm getting out of here now," he said. "Can a couple of you give me a hand camouflaging this thing?"

I told him we could. Then he, myself, and two more women began stretching a net over the aircraft and making its outline as irregular as we could.

Montoya stepped back and looked critically at our handiwork. "Have to do," he announced.

Carrying eight of the boxes, Montoya with two, six women with one each, and the last two women pulling security, we all set out to return to our base camp.

Back at camp, a sleepless Zamora began poring over the orders Montoya had brought us. She wasn't drinking but her chain smoking made the inside of my bunker pure hell. Unable to stand such dense smoke, I left her alone.

Maybe Montoya had felt the same way. He followed me out.

I asked him, "What was that thing you came in?"

"The glider? A Condor Mark III . . . recon and courier version."

"Glider?"

"Well . . . an auxiliary propelled glider. Pretty hush-hush. We've got a bunch of 'em; over twelve hundred, I think. That's including the fighter and light bomber versions. But Carrera won't let us use them for anything but recon and courier work."

"That's what you do mostly, courier duty?"

"No." He shook his head. "Mostly I do recon."

News! He would have a better idea of how the war was going than we did. I asked him about it.

"I don't know any secrets. I can tell you what I've seen. Mostly it's a stalemate. Eighth Legion still holds the island . . . three quarters of it, anyway. I've flown over it a few times but I couldn't see anything except for fire and smoke. An occasional patch of skeletonized trees. Some ships bringing in supplies for the enemy or evacuating his dead and wounded.

"The defenses at Cristobal are still holding, but our Fourth Marine Legion is pushed back almost to the causeway that leads to it. That and a few outlying fortresses. The town's just a mound of rubble anyway; rubble and charcoal with a bunch of bodies buried in there somewhere.

"The big news is along the river. Second Legion stopped the enemy's airborne corps dead cold. The bad guys are building up their supplies for a set piece battle to force their way through Second Legion and over the river. Our boys are still digging in. They've done damned well, actually, considering that almost all their artillery was overrun when the Taurans surprised us by landing from the Shimmering Sea side. Fortunately, they got most of the troops in what had been the rear area out to safety."

I asked him, "How's the City holding up under the bombing?"

"Not bad," he told me, "not bad. Casualties among the civilians are high, of course. But we're digging more new shelters for them every day. We're hanging on."

"Just hanging on? We're going to lose, aren't we?" Oh, God, all the pain and misery, the useless death and destruction, and we were going to *lose*.

But he surprised me. Shaking his head, he said, "I don't think so. Really I don't. You women have done great out here. You've made all of us proud. Because of you the enemy's not going to be able to turn our flank from this direction, not any time soon. We're safe to the south because they are *not* going to take the island. Fortress Cristobal? If human flesh and sheer will can hang on to the dump, Legate Jimenez's Marines will do it."

The pilot's face sort of screwed up, as if there were something he wanted to tell me but wasn't sure that he should. Finally, he decided to. "There's something else, too. Something that's been bothering me for months now. The troops that are awaiting the enemy on the beaches in front of and to the east and west of the city? Carrera should have moved them north to aid Second Legion once it became obvious that the island wouldn't fall. He didn't do that, near as I can tell. And why did Second Legion's artillery get overrun when the Taurans came from the Shimmering Sea side? Surely Carrera knew there was an invasion fleet out there. Hell, I know he did because *I* reported it. Me, among others.

"And the four legions pinned down on the beaches near the City? I've seen them, or something that looked like them, and from the ground and close up, too. But I don't think they're really those legions. The troops' uniforms are too new, most of them. And they're doing things that don't really make sense; showing themselves too much, for one thing. And the artillery doesn't seem manned up to strength, either. I'm just a dumb shit pilot who didn't graduate high enough in Cazador School to go to OCS or CCS. But it sure looks fishy to me."

"So what do you think it is?"

"I think those divisions aren't on the beaches, maybe never were. I think they're just behind Second Division waiting to meet the attack from the north. Maybe even to counterattack. Maybe they're underground. I know we did an awful lot of digging in that area."

I thought about that for a moment or two, trying to remember some detail from before. Then I remembered what I'd been searching for. "The enemy isn't bombing that area much, is he?"

"No," Montoya answered. "From what I can see there's been damned little done there. And they've never carpet bombed the area like they have the island and the beaches. Too afraid of hitting their own POWs, I'd guess."

Montoya thought for a while, then said, "Clever bastard. Carrera *does* have those four legions there. Hmmm, with the mech legions and Second Legion that would be seven. Plus the Tenth Artillery. Oh, are the Taurans in for a surprise when they attack." He laughed. He had a pretty nice laugh, too. But since he was only a warrant and I was a centurion...well, "of all the sad words."

Still we could talk and we did for hours; until the sleepless night caught up with us. Then he went to sleep in one bunker. I went to another. Rats!

I'd kept a couple of my girls guarding the field where Montoya's Condor was waiting. When we got there, they reported to me that it hadn't been found or disturbed in any way that they had seen. We quickly stripped it of its camouflage net, which Montoya carefully stowed aboard. Then he began attaching straps to various points on the glider. He pulled a large package out from his rear compartment and hooked the straps up to some shackles on it. A medium size metal tank was connected to the package by a hose. Montoya turned a small handcrank. There was a sound of rushing gas and the package began to expand. It was a balloon.

"Good-bye and good luck, Centurion Fuentes."

"Godspeed, Warrant-Pilot Montoya."

He began to climb into the cockpit.

"Wait," I said. Then I ran over and gave him a quick hug and a chaste little peck on the cheek. "Take care of yourself. Who knows, maybe we'll see each other again when the war's over, maybe after we're out of the legion." I whispered, "I hope we do."

"I hope we *can*," he whispered back, a wistful smile on his face, before finally seating and strapping himself in. "But, yes, Centurion, I'd like that."

In a few minutes his glider began to rise almost straight up, pulled by the balloon. *Ah, clever,* I thought, as I waved good-bye.

To the smirking girls with me I said, "Not one bloody word. Understand?"

Interlude

Movement attracts the eye. Where there is none, the eye often closes, goes to sleep. Movement in one area will attract the eye and the mind away from lesser movement in another. This is human nature.

Though the ships of the United Earth Peace Fleet, the satellites, the spy planes, and their sensors continued to watch over the whole of Balboa, movement was attracting the eyes and minds of the human beings who analyzed the data the sensors sent back.

Thus, the area where the Amazons conducted their partisan campaign had begun to attract a great deal of notice. Radio messages were intercepted at an unusual rate. Small squads and platoons were sometimes glimpsed moving by the uncaring satellites' unwavering eyes.

Aircraft were ordered in, fighters, bombers, gunships. As they left destruction behind them, still more attention was directed onto the area to measure the effects of the destruction. This greater attention found even more signs of activity. More aircraft were sent.

Back at their bases, back on their carriers, the aircraft began to show signs of failure. A transistor would burn out in testing, sometimes. A rubber wheel would show signs of excess wear, sometimes. Parts would be used, more parts ordered. Bombs would be used, too, and these were more time-consuming to replace.

When the maintenance and logistic loads had grown to alarming proportions, it was proposed that the scale of the effort be reduced...to save the aircraft for the main assault over the Gamboa River. A phone call from Zhong general to his commander, and from that commander to his old Academy buddy, the president, led the president to call the president of Gaul. Gaul, being a key part, perhaps the key part, of the Tauran Union, some wheels, political wheels, were set to spinning. The aircraft continued to fly. Still, their numbers grew fewer with time and those that flew began to show signs of serious maintenance issues. Accidents increased noticeably.

With so much effort, so much analysis, being directed at the Amazons, much less was left for the rest of the country. Thus it was that no one took notice of minor changes in vegetation north and south of the *Rio* Gamboa. No one observed the occasional column of troops that could have been glimpsed breaking cover as they moved forward. Tanks long hidden underground were not noticed as they were dug back into the open. The few human beings still at the task often missed what the sensors often found.

Much concerned with numbers, with the measurable, the Zhong and Taurans began releasing estimated body counts from the aerial effort.

Occasionally, these bore some relation to reality.

Wiser heads eventually interfered. They pointed out that, if there were to be an attack, and if all the aircraft were down for maintenance as they were likely to soon be, there would then be no air support for the troops on the ground.

Neither a president, nor any government whatsoever, could change that.

CHAPTER SEVENTEEN

By oppression's woes and pains!
By your sons in servile chains!
We will drain our dearest veins,
But they shall be free!
Lay the proud usurpers low!
Tyrants fall in every foe!
Liberty's in every blow!
Let us do or dee!
    —Robert Burns, "Scots wha hae"

By the Rising of the Moons.
    —Irish Traditional Song, Terra Novan version

"What are you so fucking cheerful about?" Marta asked Zamora, appending, "Ma'am."

Zamora did seem positively cheerful about the orders, once she'd had time to digest them. She'd even managed to chop her drinking to a reasonable amount, with dinner. She still chain smoked whenever she could, though.

"Oh, just ready for a change, I guess."

"A change? From living, if you call this living, to dead, you mean?"

"Shut up, Bugatti," Zamora said without rancor. She didn't bother to deny the charge. "Now as I was saying, the main effort is going to be for Fifth Mountain Tercio to attack the two ports in the east. Two battalions each, with their support, are going to go after *Puerto Armados* on the *Mar Furioso* side and Capitano, on the Shimmering Sea. One battalion will stay behind to partially secure their base area. The Lempiran Mountain cohort with one of ours is going for Capitano. The Valdivian Mountain cohort, also with one of ours, attacks *Puerto Armados*. I understand a couple of batteries each of light artillery have been degaussed and buried within range of each port. There are also supposed to be some light tanks well hidden within range of each port, though I have no idea where. So, at least, the *Montañeros* have some chance of getting to their assault positions undetected. They surely would be detected if they had to try to move their heavy equipment forward. Still they are going to be vulnerable to air attack.

"Carrera doesn't want that. In fact, he wants them to have the best possible chance. He also wants them to have skies overhead as nearly free of enemy aircraft as possible. That's where we come in, us and Fourteenth Cazador Tercio."

Marta gave a snort at the mention of the Fourteenth. That snort was not without reason. The Cazadors had grown—maybe better said, regrown—considerably since the first dark days when they stood alone against the Zhong Marines. Most of their higher leadership, however, was gone. Also, most of their new soldiers were pretty poorly trained in comparison to what their earlier soldiers had been.

Not everybody who graduated Cazador School ended up in a leadership position. Many of them, in fact, proved themselves to be great soldiers, tough as nails, determined to a fault...and completely incapable of leading others, lacking that little spark that no training program can give but that makes all the differ- ence in the world in combat.

Some of those ended up in the Aviation Legion Jan Sobieski. Montoya was one of those. Others went to man the small ships and submarines of the *classis*. Still others ended up as "*tropitos*" in the Fourteenth or one of the other special tercios or cohorts.

"We can't count on the Cazadors," Marta insisted. "They have a lot of men who are just fine soldiers but who can't, can't, CAN'T lead."

Zamora sighed. Her happy expression vanished. "Yes, I know," she agreed. "And those men have been forced to become squad leaders, platoon centurions, and platoon leaders for a bunch of troops many of whom are little more than rabble."

"It isn't as bad as all that," said Maria. "Some of those men are learning things about themselves they never suspected. Some of them are turning out just fine."

"Most are fucking not, Maria," Marta said. "And you know it. Not the ones in our area."

These were being led by a former corporal named León whom Maria had brevetted to optio, the same rank as Marta.

"Look, Maria," Marta continued, "León may be a great guy, a really nice guy. He's . . . *okay-at-best,* for the merely routine things. He can teach his boys all the skills and tricks of the trade. But he just can't keep his head together in action."

"So what do you propose, dear?" Zamora asked.

"León has this sixteen-year-old boy working for him," Marta said. "Maria brevetted him to sergeant. Now *that* boy, Robles, has all the earmarks. He's a little fucking tyrant, too, arrogant and ruthless. Even so, the rest of the Cazadors, new and old, worship the little shit. That's no surprise because when León freezes up, as he usually does, young Sergeant Robles carries him through. And, no, I do *not* like Robles, not a bit. If he were my child, I would put him up for adoption. But the little bastard is *good.* He's a natural, in fact."

"What? You want me to fire León?"

"Frankly, yes. He'll fuck it all up."

Though looking directly at Zamora, Maria answered, "I won't do that to the man, Marta. I just won't. Besides, with Robles' help, I think we have a chance to carry out the mission."

Marta threw up her hands in disgust.

Zamora continued, "Now that I have your attention . . . *again* . . . Our mission is simplicity itself: *take the town and the camp . . . destroy same.* No one is saying this. But it is true anyway. You— all of us—are to *get the enemy to use their aircraft on ourselves so they're not available to use on anyone else.* Anyone like Fifth Mountain."

"All you have to do, Maria, is assemble your—what is it; forty-seven women and thirty-one men?—link up with myself and the maniple's third platoon, plus Weapons, then we will assault two or three hundred well armed and well dug in, most likely desperate, Zhong troops. And all of this under artillery and mortar fire, while half an air force scours the ground from the air. Oh. Joy."

Zamora laughed a little. In a way, that was comforting to the others. "Fortunately they're mostly support troops. If they were infantry, we wouldn't have a prayer. As it is, we do."

Again, Marta burst out, "A prayer? A fucking prayer? Sure,

we do: Our Father, who art in Heaven ... The only simple thing is going to be the burial afterwards ... because the enemy won't likely bother to bury us and there aren't going to be enough of us left over to do it for ourselves."

"Shut up, Bugatti, and listen for a change. I have a plan."

Zamora pointed with a stick to a sand model dug out of the ground. The end stick circled several marked areas, then traced routes that were also marked with yarn on the dirt.

"The first trick," she said, "assembly, isn't going to be that hard. We travel in small groups, using the refugee camps as way points, hiding among the civilians until nearly the last minute. Where there are no camps we have dugouts we prepared months ago. Sure, we can expect to lose some, and the civilians are going to take it hard when the enemy starts dropping random artillery fire and air strikes around, maybe even on, the camps ... most likely on the camps.

"Rehearsals in our assembly areas are going to be a problem. We can't really do a full dress rehearsal. If the enemy sees us—and they would see us; their aircraft are prowling constantly—they'll cream us, with air and artillery, both.

"So, the maniple XO is going to have to go for the nearest fire base and at least keep their heads down for some hours. Ex, you get one of our platoons for that, plus a couple of sections of the Fourteenth. You also get a package of the jammers that attack the enemy's satellite navigational systems, their GLS. I don't want their artillery to know that their asses are lower to the ground than their heads are."

The XO looked dubious. "Ma'am, It's damned unlikely that the enemy is going to let us just waltz over their artillery. I'd expect anything from an infantry platoon to a *battalion* to come to the rescue. I can handle a platoon. I can't handle three maniples, plus."

Zamora shook her head. "Not indefinitely, no. But you don't have to. If they come ... okay, when they come, they aren't likely to come by truck, so you're going to have to use some of the Cazadors to pin any reinforcements down right on their landing zones."

"Now, when you tell me that the artillery is neutralized, we— Maria and I—go in after the town."

"Cristina ... what if the XO never tells you?"

"Then we go in anyway, Maria."

✧   ✧   ✧

The Amazons had a chance of surprising the Zhong as to what they were going to do. There was no practical chance of surprising their enemy about the fact that they were going to do something. Some weenie in one of the Zhong or Tauran intelligence sections was sure to notice an increase in the number of civilians moving out of the area on their own. Even though the Amazons would tell the civilians nothing, word tended to get around anyway.

Then there was the high tech problem. Not too hard to beat in small numbers and while stationary, it could be expected that their remote sensors would pick up an increase in urine traces in the air where there hadn't been much before. No doubt, too, the spy satellites and aircraft would start showing more heat signatures moving through the jungle at night.

The potentially biggest give away, though, would have been any detectable increase in Amazon reconnaissance activity. There wasn't any increase, though. Maria and the others had been sacrificing men and women all along on recon missions—just as they'd been trained to do—so that when patrols really were sent out to find out important things, it wasn't out of the ordinary.

Still, whatever they saw, and however they saw it, the enemy was soon blasting at random throughout the entire area—air, artillery, mortars...

"I think they may even be using naval gun fire on us," said Marta as she watched a distant hill erupt in a volcano of flame and smoke. "My God..."

"Cheer up, dear. Mostly they're missing."

Marta shivered. "They don't always miss." She shivered again, remember a squad of Cazadors as they'd approached a link up point the previous day. Two enemy fighter-bombers had dropped out of nowhere and laid eight napalm canisters right on top of those men. Where there had once been nine human beings became an instant inferno highlighted by nine human torches. Marta couldn't hear even them scream, not over the roar of the flames. She saw them burn to ashes, though. Even their bones were consumed.

Thank You, God. Thank You that it wasn't me or mine.

Marta and Maria listened as the radio reported an unusual calm over the City and the Gamboa Line. Few Zhong or Tauran aircraft were to be seen. Some of that was, no doubt, the pounding the Amazons were taking. That couldn't be all of it, however. They were being hit, but not *that* hard.

"Maybe the enemy is saving their aircraft to support a major push."

Maria thought about that but countered as being just as likely, "Maybe they've all come down with maintenance problems. Montoya told me that, even with his simple Condor, an airplane spends many hours in the shop for every hour in the air."

"I hope. I hoped to fucking hell they aren't saving *all* their aircraft for us."

Someone once said that there's nothing like a death sentence to clear the mind.

The women's minds were pretty clear. When everybody expected that the night was to be their last full one alive their minds were clear enough to know that they might never have a chance to show any kindness to their friends again. They would touch, gently, on the slightest pretext, maybe just a hand on a shoulder, maybe a pat on the head. Sometimes they didn't even bother with an excuse at all. They were trying to say "good-bye" and "I love you, sister."

With Zamora's permission Maria broke open a number of cans of the legionary rum, just enough for everyone to have a decent drink. Since it was a sort of farewell dinner, they used the canned rations lavishly.

It was so sad to see old friends together, probably for the last time. It was sadder still to watch one of the new girls with one of the older ones who had taken her under her wing.

Maria, Marta, and Zamora sat together. They were the last three left in the unit from the old maniple, that first maniple at Botchkareva. It was some comfort to sit with old friends while choking down canned shoe leather and "undifferentiated meat with differentiated sauce" as three of the canned main meals were not-too-affectionately known.

As dinner neared completion, Zamora cautioned Maria, "You be careful, hon. Make it back to your little girl."

"I've been trying not to think too much about Alma ... Cristina, why don't you have any kids of your own?"

Zamora looked as if she were weighing an imponderable decision for a moment. Then she looked at Maria very seriously and said, "Because I'm a lesbian."

Maria's eyes widened. Marta's became saucers.

"I had no idea," both women said simultaneously.

Zamora nodded, sucking in and biting both lips together. "I'm pretty discreet. 'Nobody's wife, nobody's girlfriend, none of the help.' And I wanted to be important, to matter. That would have been a lot harder in the lesbians' unit. I'm also not the 'marrying kind.'"

Maria knew. *Zamora has no intention of surviving the operation. She would never have admitted to it if she had.*

Marta looked at Zamora carefully. Zamora looked back, questioningly. Then Marta stood up, took Zamora's hand, and began to lead her out of the bunker. "I'd invite you to join us," she said to Maria, over her shoulder, "in a heartbeat. But you're straight as an arrow and you wouldn't like yourself much in the morning."

"Incoming!" All the women hugged the ground closer than any lover as a dozen mortar shells walked across their assault position. When the shell-fire lifted, someone was screaming nearby, crying out for her father. "Daddy! Daaaaady!" The cry broke off in deep sobs.

"Who is that?"

"I don't know who... MEDIC!"

A body flopped to the ground next to Maria. It was Zamora.

"Maria, the XO tells me that the artillery is about as neutralized as it's going to get. She said that reinforcements are pouring in by air and the Cazadors are *not* holding them. She'll be lucky to get away at all if she waits much longer. You've got to go in now!"

"Incoming!" Again they pressed themselves to earth to avoid the deadly flying splinters.

Maria lifted her head very slightly and shouted to Zamora over the mortar blasts, "Are you out of your fucking mind? I can't order my girls into *that!*"

"It's now or never, Maria. You've got to go!" She thought what her position didn't allow her to say. *I'm so sorry, Maria, my friend.*

Maria, not dissimilarly, thought, *Shit. Shit. Shit!*

"All right. All *right!*" Maria picked up a Yamatan radio, feeling herself step outside of herself as she did so.

"Michele Six; Michele Six; this is Mother Superior, over."

The radio crackled back, "Michele Six, over."

"Fire your prep, over."

The words, "Shot, out," barely preceded the faint distant *crump* of the Amazons' own mortars, flinging their loads heavenward to fall onto the enemy camp by the town. Almost immediately, the Zhong mortar fire lifted.

They're back-plotting the flight of the shells to return fire on my mortars. Good luck and good-bye, Michele.

It took maybe half a minute for Michele's fires to start falling on the camp. Two mortars were playing over the enemy tents in the center, two more were flailing the bunkers nearest to Maria and Cristina. The last pair walked white phosphorus from left to right to lay a blanket of smoke between the assault line and the enemy riflemen and machine gunners. The mortars had been ordered to try to keep their fire away from the town.

Maria rolled over onto her back and shouted to two otherwise useless boys from the Fourteenth to start the illumination. These began popping off hand-held flares as fast as they could. Some were green, some white. Together with the explosions and the smoke the flares lent the landscape a very surreal quality, all bizarre shapes and flickering shadows.

The flares were the signal to begin the assault. Maria hadn't worried overmuch about the Zhong or the Gendarmerie screwing things up by using flares themselves. They had so many very nice and expensive starlight scopes to see by, it was unlikely they would use flares that would only hurt them and help their attackers.

To Maria's right a brace of machine guns under Marta began to hammer through the smoke screen at the bunkers beyond. They couldn't see anything, of course, but they hoped to make the enemy nervous enough to aim high or wide. That was the theory, anyway. Maria heard Marta's voice over the racket. "Come on, murder the bastards! *Mátalos!*"

Into the radio, Maria said simply, "Breach team in."

A dozen men from the Fourteenth began loping forward, sections of what appeared to be very heavy poles clutched in their hands.

Maria watched the men, half expectantly, half fretfully. She'd had to use men for this job as the bangalore torpedoes they were going to use to blow a hole through the Zhong wire were too heavy for all but the very biggest and strongest of her *Amazonas,* her combat engineers. She needed those women for something else.

Marta had objected earlier that the men weren't reliable enough for the job, that the Amazon engineers should do it; breach the wire.

"It takes more—pardon the expression—*sheer balls* to do what I need those women for than the bulk of the Cazadors can muster anymore," Maria had answered.

Most of the Cazadors made it to the first concertina fence unscathed, though an unlucky burst cut down two of them. One of those screamed for help but had to be ignored for the moment.

Splitting into two groups, the Cazadors lay on their bellies at the wire and began joining the explosive sections and feeding the assembly forward under it. The whole time they lay there Zhong machine gun fire chattered only a foot or less over their heads.

Maria had figured on four sections of torpedo being enough to cut one lane through one concertina fence. There were three fences to get though, two lanes each. The dozen men carried four torpedo sections each, each section of about ten kilograms. She'd wanted a little extra, just in case. And if the bangalores weren't needed to make it though the wire? They made pretty good general purpose demolition charges.

Little Robles—the sixteen-year-old sergeant—shouted, "Fire in the hole!" three times.

Everyone in the attack force, men and women, both, scrunched down against the blast. Shortly after it came, dirt, rocks and bits of wire pattered down on them.

Maria looked up even as the stuff was falling to see Robles shoving men forward through the breaches they'd made.

The first set of breaches was the signal for the rest of the assault party to begin moving forward. They moved up by short rushes and hops, not firing themselves much for fear of hitting the breach team. Some of the girls were hit even despite the short hops; random fire from the enemy. The rest continued on.

Maria couldn't make short, safe little rushes. For one thing, she had to be able to see what was going on. For another, the woman carrying the radio she was depending on to control the attack was too overburdened to keep getting up and down continuously.

Again they heard "Fire in the hole!" three times from Robles. Even the radio operator had to duck for that. The twin blasts shook their bodies and rattled their brains.

From behind, Zamora was calling out encouragement, "Forward, *chicas.* Forward."

Kneeling on one knee, Maria was trying to call the mortars to get them to shift fire when she heard, "Falcon! Falcon!" The shout became general. She looked up to see where the enemy aircraft were coming from and going to. Marta's tracers pointed her view in the right general direction.

One of the attacking aircraft, the highest above the ground, dropped a big flare, probably so the others could see what they were aiming at and to hell with their own side's starlight scopes. The other aircraft went straight for Robles at the wire.

Maria guessed, *I suppose that they won't want to cut the wire themselves. Damn. Napalm.*

The whole scene in front of her eyes suddenly lit up as bright as day, a long sheet of pure flame. One . . . person—she couldn't tell if it was a man or a woman anymore—ran directly towards her, screaming and dripping liquid fire, fingers clawing at face and eyes. He, or she, or it, dropped about fifty meters in front of Maria, still screaming, still burning. The attack abruptly stopped.

Maria couldn't take her eyes from the horrid sight until her RTO pulled her back to the ground, handing her the microphone and yelling, "It's the mortars."

Michele Six—her name really was Michele—was half sobbing into her radio. In the background Maria heard what had to be mortar or artillery fire coming in a steady drumming.

So much for Michele, at least for a while. The shelling of the camp abruptly stopped.

Can't think. CAN'T think. Zamora saw the attack failing, knew it would fail unless someone made a breach in the wire . . . and soon.

She looked about her for someone to order into the attack, someone who looked big and strong enough to move nearly one hundred pounds of explosive by hand. No one. Zamora's gaze went to her own fairly beefy hand.

Someone. She got up and ran forward.

Marta immediately noticed Zamora's sprint. *Oh, no. Cristina, if you die I will never forgive you.*

She began to tongue-lash her now silent and shocked machine gunners. "Can't you see what the CO is doing, you dumb twats? Get some fire on those people."

She saw Zamora disappear into the smoke.

Zamora felt her gorge rise as she stumbled through the tangle of ripped wire, smoldering vegetation and charcoaled bodies.

Through first one breach, then another, until finally she came upon a neat line of burned lumps in the rough shape of men. One of those lumps was small; Robles, age sixteen.

For courage in face the face of the enemy above and beyond that normally expected of a soldier of the Republic, Zamora recited, as she pulled tubes of explosive from what must have once been hands. One such lump stuck to the bangalore, charred finger wrapped around the long, dark tube. When she had gathered four, as much as she could hope to carry, she stumbled and fell all the short—though seemingly endless—distance to where the breach was supposed to be but wasn't. A series of hammer blows knocked her legs out from under her. Zamora fell.

Over the roar of battle Maria heard a voice crying out. It was Zamora, screaming, "Fire in the hole...fire in the hole...fire in the hole." The last was very weak.

The explosion that followed was not.

Maria knew. She stood nearly straight up and began running forward. "*Adelante las Amazonas!*" Her girls must have heard her; they followed right enough. They'd fixed bayonets long before. These glinted in the flare- and flame-lit night as they surged ahead.

Maria and her RTO ran straight forward. They couldn't see a thing, what with the smoke from the white phosphorus, the demolitions, the napalm, and the burnt grass. They stopped abruptly, throwing themselves to the ground, when they saw three tracers streak across their path a few feet to their front.

Which way is the breach? Which way is the breach? Maria had gotten so confused she couldn't tell if it was to her left or right. The RTO didn't know, either. Finally she flipped a mental coin and came up with "We'll go right from here." It was the right decision.

When she found the breach she also found Vielka Arias and another girl crouching over a half-shredded Zamora. Zamora's hands weren't shaking and she looked perfectly calm, even detached. Maria knelt beside her.

"Hello, Cristina," she said.

Zamora's eyes shifted, lost focus, then gained it again. She looked up at Maria. "Not gonna make it, am I?"

"I've seen you look better."

"It's okay. I don't want to make it. I don't want any more nightmares. I don't want any more sickness in my stomach. It's okay." She coughed up some blood, spat it away, and said, "Now go take this place."

Good-bye and God bless, Cristina. Maria bent over and smoothed Zamora's hair away from her face, then lightly brushed the dying woman's lips with her own. Then, reluctantly, she turned her attention back to the fight.

I've got to find a way to signal my troops that the breach is here.

The way stumbled upon her a couple of minutes later.

The Amazons hadn't had much use for pipers of late. For this occasion, though, Maria had foregone one rifle to put one of them back on her pipes. She told the piper, "Blow anything you please, but do it loud and do it *now!*" The piper did, the noise of her war pipes rising even above the firing and blasting. It was perhaps not the best rendition ever played of "Scots Wha Hae," but it was heartfelt. More importantly, it worked.

The first group to reach Maria at the breach were the remnants of the Cazadors, under the command of León.

She looked at León and his men intently for a moment. *Do they have any fight left in them? Yes!*

"All right, you crew," Maria shouted, over the rattle of the battle and the din of the pipes. "Sergeant León, straight through the breach then strike right into the heart of the camp. I want you to get the tanks before their crews can man them. Destroy them if they've already been crewed. Then find and smash the enemy's command post."

León nodded, dumbly, and led his men forward.

As groups of old and new Amazons found the breach, Maria sent them left or right to clear the line of bunkers around the perimeter of the Zhong camp. She stayed near the breach itself trying to see what was going on and bring some order out of the mess. Some more enemy aircraft flew by but, since the Amazons were now in and among their compatriots, the planes didn't attack.

The air defense team fired a couple of missiles at them anyway. One, Maria thought, might have been a near enough miss to send one plane limping home. At least that plane turned off while the others moved up to a higher altitude.

Marta led the machine guns to Maria. Her still substantial chest was heaving with the strain of sucking in enough oxygen to keep her body going. "Where now?"

"Wait here," Maria answered. "Catch your breath. Then head

that way." She pointed towards the general location of the enemy command post. "Support León and his apes."

Marta just nodded while trying to catch her breath. She hadn't quite caught it yet when she ordered, "Follow me" and disappeared into the night, machine gun crews in tow.

From the breach Maria could hear firing—*and a lot of small explosions, probably grenades*—to both her left and right, as well as to her front. *I haven't heard the big cannon from a tank yet, so maybe we've gotten lucky there. We'll see.*

See? She couldn't see much, beyond a bunch of burning tents and shacks...and bodies, of course; far too many of them hers. The two boys she'd had on the parachute flares must have run out because the sky overhead was clear of any lights. But for the flames and occasional explosions it had grown very dark. She pulled out those night vision goggles she'd captured seemingly so long ago, put them over her face and scanned.

Maria saw them by the light they made themselves, four huge steel behemoths spitting flame on her right flank, rolling it up. The goggles flared out and went dark, then came on again.

Over on the right the girls were trying...and dying, shot or smeared under half-meter-wide treads. They would have all been chopped but for one Amazon with an RGL who waited for the last tank to pass over or near her, then hopped up on the back deck. She fired her warhead right down onto the top of the turret. She was blown off, broken and dying. The tank stopped in its tracks.

You made a good bargain for us, girl, one grunt for one tank.

It just wasn't the kind of bargain logical mathematics will teach one to make. "A rational army..."

The other tankers must have been confused and frightened already. When the rearward tank died without the others knowing how, the remaining three simply pulled into a perimeter of their own, defying all comers, but not advancing any farther.

Those Amazons remaining on the right, willing to live and let live for the moment, perhaps, found what cover they could and hunkered down. On the left the Amazons were clearing out the enemy bunkers one by one.

Then the Cazadors got into it. One of their few survivors later admitted that when they'd seen the women under attack by the tanks they couldn't help themselves; they just had to charge to the rescue.

They didn't rescue anyone. They were shot to pieces for no

gain. Worse, they had been almost on top of the enemy command bunker when they'd turned around to "save" the women.

Though in her own mind Maria was never sure if it was quite fair to say there was nothing gained from the men's self immolation. The three tanks backed off a couple of hundred meters. That was worth something; if not enough. It certainly didn't make up for the men's not having taken out the command bunker or caught the tanks earlier.

"Incoming!" *Mierda*. Maria threw herself to the ground for the hundredth time. The RTO was a little too slow, the inertia of the radio on her back keeping her upright a fraction of a second too long. A shell splinter took the top of her head off. Her body fell across Maria's, pinning her to the ground briefly. Maria felt a sticky, lumpy wash of wet, nasty stuff all over her face and uniform. She started to shake and pray, feeling very tired.

It was normal. Mind-numbing terror tires one out quickly.

That was just an adjusting round, an unlucky chance shot. Maria visualized the satellite jammers and what sort of job they were doing on the enemy's automated fire control system. She was pretty sure they were having to do things the old fashioned way. It was also a very slow way.

A half dozen girls reported to her. Two of them carried monstrously heavy flamethrowers strapped to their backs. It was the engineer section.

Maria asked the senior—and largest—of them, "Sergeant Ponce," an Amazon in fact as well as title, "do you believe in God, *chica*?"

When Ponce answered, "Yes," Maria added, "Then let's hope he believes in us. Come on, *ingenieras*. Follow me!"

The seven of them sprinted as fast as they could to the left. When they reached the point of the group clearing that side of the perimeter they halted.

"There's a set of four bunkers there, Centurion," the squad leader gasped out. "We tried to take them but . . . I've lost four of my girls."

"Grenades?" Maria asked.

"Can't get close enough. We tried." Her finger indicated several bodies that had not quite made it close enough to the bunkers to use grenades.

The little subcomplex of bunkers was about twenty or twenty-five meters to the front. Maria ordered Ponce to, "Toast 'em."

Stabbing tongues of jellied flame licked out to saturate the firing ports of, and entrances to, the bunkers. The occupants began to scream. They were fear screams though, not pain screams. They lasted only until the fire had burned up all the oxygen in the bunkers. Then they died away.

A few of the enemy tried to escape, maybe even to surrender. The women didn't have time for that. They shot them down. Nobody who resists an assault, inflicting casualties right up to the last minute, can expect to be given a chance to surrender. It just doesn't work that way.

Maria told the left section leader to keep clearing ahead. With the engineers, she, herself, started to move into the center of the camp, toward the command bunker. They had to fight almost the whole way forward. There were Zhong troops running all over the camp. Some were panic stricken and harmless. Some were still trying. It didn't matter. The women shot all they came across. Those who were already on the ground, dead or wounded, they slashed or stabbed with bayonets...to make sure.

When they reached their command bunker Maria found a couple of Cazadors who apparently had resisted their primal urge to rescue damsels in distress. The senior of them told her, "We've got them pinned inside. They can't get out. But we haven't been able to get in either. Grenades don't seem to do much. The entrance seems to be baffled somehow...or maybe the interior is."

"Have you seen my platoon optio?"

"She was here, Centurion. But she cut off to the right. I don't know why."

Dammit, Marta, where the fuck are you?

"How much jellied gas do you have left in the tanks?"

Ponce answered, "Maybe about half full, enough for a few bursts of a couple of seconds each."

"Okay. Ponce, take three girls and one flamethrower with you. The other one and two troops go with me. You men cover the bunker's sole exit. Nobody gets out."

Ponce struck first. The two women with her opened up with their rifles at the firing ports that dotted the outside of the bunker. Then Ponce stood up and began to try to jet her fuel right through another port.

Someone must have seen her stand and fired on her; made a lucky shot. It didn't hit her, but it did hit the tank of jellied fuel.

As if in slow motion, the first spurt of flame burst from the ruptured tank. The spurt became a fireball. Ponce's face turned from determination to surprise to horror. The fireball expanded. The hair on her head flashed into smoke. Her eyes melted a moment before the flame covered her features. Ponce screamed. She, and the two *Amazonas* with her, were caught in the fireball from her burst tank.

Maria wanted to vomit, not for the first time. Instead she prayed. *Our Father, who art in heaven . . .*

Maria's side of the bunker was an easier approach than Ponce's had been. There was a sharp drop of about three feet that covered her as she crawled closer to it. She felt her knee come to rest upon a rounded object that felt a lot like a pole. It was a pole, a pole made of sections, one of the ones used to hold a camouflage net above the ground. There were more of them about.

Maria thought . . .

"I've got an idea. You two with the flamethrower, gather up four of these pole sections each. Join them. Then cut something to tie a grenade to the end. On my command we'll pull the pins and shove the grenades right through those firing ports. Flamethrower, after you hear the three bangs put the nozzle right into the middle port and let 'em have it."

She had to tell them twice, so rattled were they.

After several minutes, one of the woman said, "Ready, Centurion."

"On three," Maria commanded. "One . . . two . . . *three!*"

Even over the sounds of battle raging around, they could hear the people inside that bunker as they scurried like rats to try to find some cover from the three little bombs that suddenly appeared at the ends of poles at the bunker's ports. There was a *boom, boom, boom,* the last two coming close together.

Even before Maria shouted, "Go, go, go!" the woman toting the flamethrower was already scampering up to the firing port. She pushed the nozzle into the center port and squeezed the trigger.

Flames burst out of all three, more or less simultaneously. The people inside must have been still alive, most of them, despite the grenades. They shrieked.

The *ingeniera* shrieked too as the back draft of flame began to roast her hands. Still, even with her hands roasting, she kept the fire up until her nozzle sputtered out. Then she dropped the nozzle and slid to the ground, sobbing as quietly as she could.

Maria ran to her, stripped the tank from her back, then dragged her back by her feet.

"Don't you go into shock on me, girl. No time for that." To the larger of the two *ingenieras* left with her, Maria said, "Put her across your shoulders and get her out of here,"

Maria risked taking a stand and looked around at the ruins of the camp. *I don't know the full price we've paid but it looks like a good night's work to me.* Tracers—red and green—crisscrossed back and forth over the entire area. Looking toward what she knew was the enemy motor pool, she saw the sky was red with flame. Their tents were burning, too. No fire was coming from their mortar position. *A good night's work,* she thought. *Mission accomplished.*

Marta again huffed up, still leading the surviving machine gunners. "I saw a group of them trying to rally. We shot the cocksuckers up pretty good. I doubt they'll stop running anytime soon, the ones we left."

In the distance the women thought they heard helicopters, a lot of them.

"I'm surprised it took them this fucking long," Marta commented.

"Me, too...a little. If the enemy *are* sending reinforcements there is no way we can hold the camp and town."

"No," Marta replied, "not with the survivors being as exhausted as they are. Besides...there aren't that many of us left."

Maria agreed. "We don't have to stay. Our orders were to trash the place, not to hold it after trashing it." Again she looked at the flames and smoke on every horizon. "I think we've trashed it. Gather the girls and start pulling out."

From the cargo pocket of her uniform Marta pulled out one of the two star clusters she'd put there earlier. They were both red, the signal to break off, get out of the camp, and split off to the various hides.

Marta fired one, then the other. When the second one burst into bright red light she and Maria went into a low crouch and started moving back to the breach.

Ordering Marta on ahead, Maria waited at the breach while her remaining girls and boys passed through. The reports they gave as they passed told a heartbreaking story. The platoon was ruined.

I hope that the rest of the maniple is in better shape. She didn't dwell on that, being too mind-numbed, even to mourn. That would come later, and in private. When Maria had seen what she assumed had to be the last of her troops out past the breach she started to follow.

Maria had made it maybe halfway through the wire when something, a delay-fused shell more than likely, went off close behind her. That was the last thing she felt for some time.

Interlude

The first man off of the helicopter said, "Damn, what a mess!"

The second man said nothing; he was too busy throwing up.

The third man, a sergeant, said, "Quit jawin', quit gaggin'. Get your butts out to the perimeter. That way!"

Even the sergeant felt his stomach lurch, though, as he viewed the scene around him.

Death had held a feast for some of its friends. None of them had decent table manners. Bodies and parts of bodies lay every which way.

Most noticeable was a burned out tank. The driver was wedged partway out of his hatch. The tank's own gun had blocked his further escape. He had burned slowly, the sergeant surmised.

Not far from the wreck of the tank, a smear on the dirt linked an upper torso and head at one end, feet at the other. The expression on the face was ghastly to behold, especially on a woman.

Other soldiers, friendly and enemy, lay sprawled in every conceivable position. Some hung on barbed wire. Some could be seen, were one to look, crouched down in the bunkers in which they had died. It was not wise to look too closely, however, as some bunkers had been treated with flame. The bodies in these stank abominably.

The sergeant paused to cover a woman whose skirt had blown up to her waist. He shook his head, regretfully. "I always did like the pipes," he said, to no one in particular.

Around the camp its former defenders sat, apathetic, staring into space. That...or they continued shrieking as an overworked medical team attempted to give what help was available.

400

The sergeant paid these last no mind. As he led his men to reseal the breach in the wire, helicopters—many more of them—whooped to a landing.

Ahead of the sergeant a soldier shouted, "Hey, Sarge. I found a live one."

CHAPTER EIGHTEEN

So far from God and so close to the Tauran Union
—Diana Porphyry, Helvetian politician

Maria:

I awoke screaming. Something between my legs and on my right nipple was hurting me... badly. My body shuddered and spasmed out of my control. My arms and legs twisted and twitched against the bindings that held me to a metal chair. I was naked, my legs held open by whatever held me to the chair. My eyes were covered by something, tape and gauze it must have been. Distantly I heard a whirring sound. Other than that, I was alone with my agony.

I didn't know how I had gotten there. The last thing I remembered was waving some of my girls through some barbed wire. Had I been killed? Was I in Hell? *My Lord, my God, why hast thou forsaken me?*

Eventually I came to realize that the whirring and the pain were related somehow. When it increased so did my agony, my uncontrolled screams, and the spastic twitching of my body. When it slowed down or decreased in volume sometimes the pain just dropped to the level of intense discomfort.

It never quite went away. Even when the whirring stopped altogether I still burned between my legs and on my breast. But at those times I could cry because I didn't have to scream. I could also sense things that my mind couldn't quite latch on to when the pain was more intense. I smelled charred wood and flesh. *I am in Hell,* I thought.

I began to pray out loud. But I could barely hear my own

voice saying "O, my God, I am heartily sorry for having offended thee..." I wished for a priest. *Are there priests in Hell?*

I don't know how long this went on. An hour? An eternity? Suddenly the pain dropped to a mere burning and the wrappings around my eyes were torn away. Half-deafened already, I was blinded by the light.

Two women, Gendarmerie women, stood by a field telephone. I was unfamiliar with the patch on their left shoulders. I still don't know what three tranzitree blossoms means. Wires ran from the phone to me. A man, a Gendarmerie officer, towered over the women, gesturing and shouting. He pointed at me, then at the telephone, and shouted some more.

Not Hell after all. Not exactly.

Another man began to detach the wires. He had to probe in some intimate places to do so. He could have raped me for all I cared just then. He could have done anything if it would only stop the pain. When the wires were detached he considerately draped a coarse cloth over me, then began to cut away my bindings. I felt more pain as blood rushed back into hands and feet long deprived.

The officer gave me a cigarette, offered me some water. He spoke Spanish with a funny, but understandable, accent. At least I could understand him if he looked directly at me and spoke very loud. He asked me my name.

"Maria," I answered. "Maria Fuentes." It was hard to talk after all that screaming.

"Look, Maria, I'm terribly sorry for what those two did to you. One of them lost her husband here at this place. Another lost her boyfriend. They blame you for that."

"War," I answered through my scream-strained throat.

"Yes," he agreed. "A terrible thing, isn't it? But tell me, why did you attack this place? You must have known it would cost you dearly."

"War," I said again.

"Yes, well, you had better come with me." He led me outside. Once my eyes adjusted to the fierce sunlight I recognized the command bunker we'd destroyed. He took me to their eating place. On the way I saw a line, a long line, of bodies. Ours.

Zuli was there. She looked so natural in death. Almost as if I could nudge her and bring her back awake, back to life. Zamora was a few places down from Zuli. She wore a smile I hadn't seen on her since long before. Ponce and the other two after her I could not recognize by individual features. The three pitiful little balls, all curled into a fetal position, were side by side. The Cazadors who'd been burned to death were a larger group of carbonized lumps, farther down the line. One body, badly mutilated but unburned, still clutched a set of pipes in her arms while the breeze tugged at her kilt.

I stopped hobbling and started to cry. The Gendarmerie officer was very considerate. He let me alone for however long it took.

At the mess tent he coaxed me and encouraged me to eat something. All the while he kept saying what a terrible waste it all was. I said nothing.

Suddenly, he stood to attention. An officer senior to him began to berate him viciously. Two women, the same two that I'd seen before, stepped up to stand on either side of me. They gripped my arms.

"Fuentes, Maria. Centurion, Junior Grade. Service number 112-47795."

"Why the attacks?" one of them demanded. "Why now?"

"Fuentes, Maria. Centurion, Junior Grade. Service number 112-47795."

The electricity from the telephone cranked up a bit more. I guess they were in a hurry. There are less painful ways but they tend to be slow. If you're in a hurry, the old fashioned way is best. I screamed and spasmed. "Fuentes, Maria..." I passed out again.

"Maria, please Maria. You've got to tell them what you know. Why did you women attack? What was the purpose? I can't stand to see them doing this to you. Please tell them."

It might have worked. It almost did. But then I remembered some counterinterrogation training we'd had at Cazador School.

Good cop; bad cop. My "rescuer," Fournier his name, was the good cop. The others were bad. I spit in his face.

Once I realized this, it was easier to hold out. I got more information from Fournier than he did from me, although I didn't have any real use for it. I discovered, for example, that of the twenty-nine attacks we had launched, only seven—mine included—had actually succeeded in breaking in and trashing an enemy base. I learned that our casualties were over a thousand men and women, against maybe half that for the enemy. We would be hard put to replace those losses. The question was whether the enemy would be willing to replace theirs.

I hadn't been able to find out anything about how Fifth Mountain had done. But, since they wouldn't tell me, I had to guess that we'd managed to pull enough air onto ourselves that the *Montañeros* had most likely succeeded. I felt a little better from the thought.

"Fuentes, Maria ... Centurion ... Junior ... Grade. Service ... number ..."

I'd have broken, eventually. Anyone will. And that's okay. Information is only good for a while. After a period of time it just isn't useful anymore. Then you can spill your guts. Besides, I didn't really have any information. I'd told them we'd attacked because we'd been ordered to. Which was true.

But I had my suspicions. Montoya had told me more than maybe he knew. We had been ordered to attack all across the occupied area for no more reason than to suck up enemy air power, to wear it out so that it would be down for a few days. Why? I couldn't be sure. Maybe Carrera needed a few days breather to adjust our forces without interference from the air. Maybe he just needed to give the boys a break from constant air attack. Maybe ...? Who knew.

Around midnight they threw me into a little dark room with only a tiny, barred window and only one, locked, door. I rested on the bare concrete, my arms and legs too cramped to move to the cot that stood against one wall. Besides the pain, I was suffering from profound humiliation. The electricity had made me lose control of my bowels and bladder. The swine hadn't even let me clean myself up.

I forced myself to stop sobbing, biting my tongue, clenching my teeth and what I could of my fists, and forcing slow deep breaths into my lungs. They might be able to force sound out of me with their damned electricity. I'd be damned if I'd give them the satisfaction of hearing me cry if I didn't *have* to.

It was cold, there on the concrete. A half inch or so of water had gathered, not enough to drown myself; unfortunately, so I thought. Drowning would have been a mercy.

I thought about ways to kill myself. They'd left me nothing, not even any clothes or a blanket I might have been able to unravel into a cord to hang myself with. All that was available was maybe to try to beat my own brains out against a wall. And for that I lacked the strength to even try.

I thought about holding my breath 'til I turned blue, thought of Alma and laughed a little. Then—still thinking of Alma—I did cry after all, but not loudly.

Alma? Would I ever see her again? Probably not, I supposed. I knew I would never see most of my friends in this life. They were lying in a shallow grave the enemy had dug outside the wire. Earlier Fournier had taken me up to see them shoveled into the clay. I guess he thought it might help to break me. It hadn't. I was proud of those girls. I was even proud of the idiot boys.

Had it been worth it, all the suffering and death? Had it been worth it, everything I'd gone through to become a soldier? I didn't know then. It would be a while before I found out if it had been worth it or not.

I fell asleep thinking of happier times.

A long, continuous, low rumble awakened me. It took me a while to figure out what the sound was. Have you ever heard several hundred machine guns firing sustained fire from a couple of kilometers away? Neither had I, but that sound was what I imagined it would be like.

I wasn't all that curious at first. Little by little, though, curiosity arose. I made a tentative stretch of an arm, then another. Cramps shot through them. It wasn't all that unbearable, considering what I been through already.

The legs were worse. Maybe more muscle means more pain from cramping. Still, I was able to get to all fours and crawl to the wall underneath the window.

The wall was a problem. It wasn't smooth, but it offered no holds to my fingers either. I managed to use it, however, to support me partially while I forced myself to stand. The window was still too high to see out of.

I got my fingers hooked onto the inside sill and pulled, willing my feet and legs to stretch upward. That was hard. They'd taken a small hammer to several toes in each foot. Likewise to two of the fingers of my left hand. Both my thumbs were dislocated.

The sound grew louder as my head neared the window. Finally I could see. But I couldn't have told you what I was seeing. I didn't know for sure which direction the window faced towards. I guessed it was west.

There to the—west?—I could see what was creating the sound. It looked like a million strobe lights flashing continuously. The light was reflected from and through the clouds. More than ever it seemed like those several hundred machine guns. I tried to count the number by adding up however many flashes I saw in what I guessed was half a minute. I couldn't count the flashes that quickly. I gave that up after several tries.

Much closer, I saw and heard helicopters landing and flying off. More reinforcements to replace the units we'd destroyed here at the enemy base? So I assumed.

No longer able to support myself at the window I let go my grip, relaxed my legs, and slid back to the concrete floor. As I did so, I painted the wall and my back with something very unpleasant that must have been stuck to my backside.

I still didn't know what it was, that sound, those flashes. I knew it could have been the enemy's artillery blasting their way south to the City. If so, it was more likely both the enemy's airplanes and artillery doing the blasting. I had no real sense of time, hadn't had since I'd been awakened by the electricity. Maybe they'd been able to get their air fleet back up and flying while I'd been unconscious. Maybe.

A bit more likely, so I thought, was that our artillery and the enemy's were dueling for the Gamboa Line and the bridges and fords over the river. I considered, and almost completely rejected, the idea that it was mostly ours, the legion pounding our way south to relieve Cristobal.

It didn't matter in any case. Not to me. I was going to die there, I was sure, either in that stinking pit or from cardiac arrest in the metal chair they strapped me to in order to work on me. Or maybe they'd just put a merciful bullet in my head when they realized that I wasn't going to break, that I would never break in time for it to do them any good.

About Alma I wasn't worried too much. Carrera had told us

he'd banked a really large amount of money in Helvetia to take care of the widows, widowers, and orphans of the war, no matter who won it. And Porras would live long enough to see Alma into college, a job, or marriage. Maybe all three. Porras wasn't really all that old. I hoped Alma wouldn't miss me too much.

I heard a lot of helicopters landing and taking off. I didn't know why. I'm not sure I even cared. I fell back to sleep, my shitty back resting against the shitty wall.

I blinked. Light streaming into the room through the window had woken me up. Daybreak. Time to get reacquainted with the torturer. I began to shake. Yes, it was from fear.

I heard footsteps on the floor outside my cell, two sets of them. The shaking grew worse. I couldn't control it. I'm not afraid of being hurt. Only a fool isn't afraid of pain that you can't control, that robs you of any human dignity, and that might last forever.

I began to pray, mostly for strength, though I mentioned to God that a quick death would be an acceptable alternative.

The lock to the cell clanked open. I heard a knock.

"Why should they knock?" I asked myself aloud. "They own the place."

The door opened slowly. "Centurion Fuentes? Maria? Maria! Are you in there?" a voice asked, uncertainly, in La Plata-accented Spanish.

EPILOGUE

Rise Again! Rise Again!
Though your heart it be broken or life about to end.
No matter what you've lost, be it a home or love or friend,
Be like the *Mary Ellen Carter*, Rise Again!
                    —Stan Rogers, "The *Mary Ellen Carter*"

Marielena Mistral, Recruit Private, Service number 127-10976:

It was right after I heard about the massacre that I decided to join up. All the recruiting offices near my town were closed. Still, all I had to do was find one of the undercover people. He hooked me up with the sergeant. The sergeant filled out my papers, took my oath of enlistment, gave me a little traveling money, some directions, and sent me on my way.

I went through seven different way stations—rarely having the slightest idea where I was—before I arrived at the training base deep, deep in the jungle.

It wasn't much of a base; just some tents and dugouts, those, and a large number of people carrying weapons. The people were mostly in uniforms. A number, like myself, were still in civilian clothes. Most of those, also like me, had just recently decided to join and only just arrived for training.

The men who ran the base were very nice to me and the other girls. I'd expected a lot of shouting and screaming, a lot of the meaningless harassment one saw in the movies. It wasn't like that at all; not at first, anyway.

Those men gave us uniforms to replace the tattered civilian clothes we'd arrived in, fed us decently, then assigned us in groups of ten or twelve to some of the tents. Before leaving us alone, they pointed out where the nearest bomb shelters were and explained to us what to do if we heard the siren that meant an aerial attack was imminent. The camp had been hit before, they said.

As we went to sleep, all we could talk about was the counterattack. A great victory, the rumors said. A great victory, but perhaps not a final one. The Taurans and the Zhong had a vote too.

The next morning, we were unceremoniously hustled out of our tents and put into four ranks, one rank about a meter and a half behind the other. One of the sergeants explained to us what to do when we heard the command "Attention." We practiced that a few times until he was satisfied. Then he told us to stand "at ease" while we waited for the platoon centurion to show up. The sergeant had a slightly feminine quality to his voice, but he seemed to know his business well enough.

The first I saw of the centurion was a glint of gold at the base of her throat. It stood out even in the faint light that penetrated the jungle canopy overhead. My head turned in the direction of the glint and I saw her, held up by two other soldiers—they looked like women to me; one looked very *much* like a woman to me. The centurion shook off their help and began walking stiffly, and with a pronounced limp, toward us. The sergeant, still facing us, hadn't seen her yet.

She was a short little woman, very pretty, olive skinned, rather older than the rest of us. She was very pretty, that is, if you overlooked her eyes. Those were cold and hard, with maybe a touch of madness to them.

Her left hand was covered completely in a cast. There was a smaller cast on her right hand, mostly holding her thumb in position. The fingers of the right hand were free, grasping a stick about two feet long, with bronze at the tips.

"*Madre* Maria," I heard someone say. "Whoever she is, she's wearing the Gold Cross!" I didn't yet know quite what that meant.

The sergeant heard that, glanced over his shoulder, and saw the woman. He came to attention himself, then called us to the same position. Smiling, he whispered, "God help you all." Then he turned around and saluted the woman with the stick.

In return, she touched the stick to the brim of her hat, then said, "Post." The sergeant walked off smartly to one side. I didn't see where he went to.

The woman, the centurion, stood silently appraising us for a few moments, disgust shining clear in her features. She looked over each of us; you could feel her eyes on you, measuring you. You could feel, too, that you just didn't quite measure up... not to her.

Still silent, the centurion walked stiffly over to the girl at the right front of our formation. That girl was a little bit plump.

The centurion stopped in front of the girl, looking her up and down. She said, finally, "You, little sister, are fat. You shall lose that weight... or I shall skin you. Clear?"

Speechless, the plump girl just nodded, quickly and shallowly. The centurion stuck the pointy end of her stick under the girl's chin and said, "When I ask you a question, *Ballenita,* you will answer it in a loud and clear voice. You shall also append 'Centurion' to the beginning and the end of your every answer. So let us try this again. Is what I have told you clear?"

Shaking, her voice wavering still, the plump girl answered "Centurion. Yes, Centurion!"

The centurion removed the point of the stick from the girl's chin and walked to the next in line. "You don't look smart enough for this," was all she said before going on.

By the time she came to stand in front of me, I thought I had already heard every insult known to womankind... and even learned a few new ones. To me she said, "Too much little girl in you. That will change." It hadn't been a question, so I didn't answer. I was certainly too afraid to answer her back. She slapped my face with her stick, even so, but just hard enough to sting a little. I forced myself not to cry out. Satisfied, she nodded and moved on.

When she was finished, the centurion moved—still limping—back to in front of the platoon. She said, "I am Fuentes; Senior Centurion Maria Fuentes. I am responsible for turning you little maggots into soldiers... Amazon soldiers. When that is done to my satisfaction, I will be responsible for leading you into the area where the enemy is polluting our soil... and for leading you against him.

"Now the Taurans may kill you, here or later. I may kill you myself, or send you somewhere to do something that will get you killed. That is what war is about; that is what being a soldier is about. I am going to train you to kill... and I'm going to train you to die, if die you must. If you do not like that, get out now, while you still can. I don't need or want you unless you want to be here...on *my* terms. Remember, the enemy cares even less for your opinion than I do...and I don't care at all.

"But if you stay, and if I decide to keep you, and if you live, there will be something true for which you may thank God. When women all over the world are second class citizens of their own societies, you will not be. You will be the equal of anyone, anywhere, anytime.

"The price for that equality will be fair..."

Glossary

AdC Aide de Camp, an assistant to a senior officer.

Ala Plural: Alae. Latin: Wing, as in wing of cavalry. Air Wing in the legion. Similar to Tercio, qv.

Amid Arabic: Brigadier General.

Antania Plural: Antaniae, Septic mouthed winged reptilians, possibly genengineered by the Noahs, aka moonbats.

BdL Barco de la Legion, Ship of the Legion.

Bellona Moon of Terra Nova.

Bolshiberry A fruit-bearing vine, believed to have been genengineered by the Noahs. The fruit is intensely poisonous to intelligent life.

Cazador Spanish: Hunter. Similar to Chasseur, Jaeger and Ranger. Light Infantry, especially selected and trained. Also a combat leader selection course within the *Legion del Cid*.

Chorley A grain of Terra Nova, apparently not native.

Classis Latin: Fleet or Naval Squadron.

Cohort Battalion, though in the legion these are large battalions.

Conex Metal shipping container, generally 8' × 8' × 20' or 40'.

Consensus   When capitalized, the governing council of Old Earth, formerly the United Nations Security Council.

Corona Civilis   Latin. Civic Crown. One of approximately thirty-seven awards available in the legion for specific and noteworthy events. The Civic Crown is given for saving the life of a soldier on the battlefield at risk of one's own.

Cueco   Regional Spanish slang: Derogatory term for homosexual; queer.

Dustoff   Medical evacuation, typically by air.

Eris   Moon of Terra Nova.

Escopeta   Spanish: Shotgun.

Estado Mayor   Spanish: General Staff and, by extension, the building which houses it.

FSD   Federated States Drachma. Unit of money equivalent in value to 4.2 grams of silver.

Hecate   Moon of Terra Nova.

Huánuco   A plant of Terra Nova from which an alkaloid substance is refined.

I   Roman number one. Chief Operations Officer, his office, and his staff section.

Ia   Operations officer dealing mostly with fire and maneuver, his office and his section, S- or G-3.

Ib   Logistics Officer, his office and his section, S- or G-4.

Ic   Intelligence Officer, his office and his section, S- or G-2.

II   Adjutant, Personnel Officer, his office and his section, S- or G-1.

Ikhwan   Arabic: Brotherhood.

Jaguar   Volgan built tank in legionary service.

Jaguar II   Improved Jaguar.

Klick   Kilometer. Note: Democracy ends where the metric system begins.

Kosmo   Cosmopolitan Progressive. Similar to Tranzi on Old Earth.

Lorica   Lightweight silk and liquid metal torso armor used by the legion.

LZ   Landing Zone, a place where helicopters drop off troops and equipment.

Maniple   Company-sized military formation.

MRL   Multiple Rocket Launcher.

MTP   Member of the Tauran Parliament.

NGO   Nongovernmental Organization.

Noahs   Aliens that seeded Terra Nova with life, some from Old Earth, some possibly from other planets, some possibly genetically engineered, in the dim mists of prehistory. No definitive trace has ever been found of them.

Ocelot   Volgan- or Balboan-built light armored vehicle mounting a 100mm gun and capable of carrying a squad of infantry in the back.

Meg   Coastal Defense Submarine under development by the legion.

Paracaidista   Spanish: Parachutist.

PMC   Precious Metal Certificate. High denomination legionary investment vehicle.

Progressivine   A fruit-bearing vine found on Terra Nova. Believed to have been genengineered by the Noahs. The fruit is intensely poisonous to intelligent life.

Push   As in "tactical push." Radio frequency or frequency hopping sequence, so called from the action of pushing the button that activates the transmitter.

PZ   Pickup Zone. A place where helicopters pick up troops, equipment and supplies to move them somewhere else.

Red Fang	An individual short range communication system, linked through the F-26 rifles and M-26 light machineguns.
RGL	Rocket Grenade Launcher.
RTO	Radio-Telephone Operator.
Satan Triumphant	A hot pepper of Terra Nova, generally unfit for human consumption, though sometimes used in food preservation and refinable into a blister agent for chemical warfare.
SPATHA	Self Propelled Anti-Tank Heavy Armor. A legionary tank destroyer.
SPLAD	Self Propelled Laser Air Defense. A developed legionary antiaircraft system.
Tercio	Spanish: Regiment.
Tranzitree	A fruit-bearing tree, believed to have been genengineered by the Noahs. The fruit is intensely poisonous to intelligent life.
Trixie	A species of archaeopteryx brought to Terra Nova by the Noahs.
Yakamov	A type of helicopter produced in Volga. It has no tail rotor.

Legionary Rank Equivalents

Dux, Duque: indefinite rank, depending on position it can indicate anything from a Major General to a Field Marshall, Duque usually indicates the senior commander on the field.

Legate III: Brigadier General or Major General. per the contract between the *Legion del Cid* and the Federated States of Columbia, a Legate III, when his unit is in service to the Federated States, is entitled to the standing and courtesies of a Lieutenant General. Typically commands a deployed legion, when a separate legion is deployed, the air *ala* or the naval *classis,* or serves as an executive for a deployed corps.

Legate II: Colonel, typically commands a tercio in the rear or serves on staff if deployed.

Legate I: Lieutenant Colonel, typically commands a cohort or serves on staff.

Tribune III: Major, serves on staff or sometimes, if permitted to continue in command, commands a maniple.

Tribune II: Captain, typically commands a maniple.

Tribune I: First Lieutenant, typically serves as second in command of a maniple, commands a specialty platoon within the cohort's combat support maniple, or serves on staff.

Signifer: Second Lieutenant or Ensign, leads a platoon. Signifer is a temporary rank and signifers are not considered part of the officer corps of the legions except as a matter of courtesy.

Sergeant Major: Sergeant Major with no necessary indication of level.

First Centurion: Senior noncommissioned officer of a maniple.

Senior Centurion: Equivalent to Master Sergeant but almost always the senior man within a platoon.

Centurion, J.G.: Sergeant First Class, Typically commands a platoon but is sometimes the second in command.

Optio: Staff Sergeant, typically the second in command of a platoon.

Sergeant: Sergeant, typically leads a squad.

Corporal: Corporal, typically leads a team or crew or serves as second in command of a squad.

Legionario, or Legionary, or Legionnaire: private through specialist

Note that, in addition, under legion regulations adopted in the Anno Condita 471, a soldier may elect to take what is called "Triarius Status." This locks the soldier into whatever rank he may be, but allows pay raises for longevity to continue. It is one way the legion has used to flatten the rank pyramid in the interests of reducing careerism. Thus, one may sometimes hear or read of a "Triarius Tribune III," typically a major-equivalent who has decided, with legion accord, that his highest and best use is in a particular staff slot or commanding a particular maniple. Given that the legion—with fewer than three percent officers, including signifers—has the smallest officer corps of any significant military formation on Terra Nova, and a very flat promotion pyramid, the Triarius system seems, perhaps, overkill. Since adoption, regulations permit but do not require Triarius status legionaries to be promoted one rank upon retirement.

Afterword

Nah. Sometimes a book just has to speak for itself. If you have a question, ask (www.tomkratman.com, hit "contact," or in the KratsKeller at bar.baen.com); I'll try to answer it.

Well...maybe one thing. Yes, I think it could be done, both *Gorgidas* and *Amazona*. But pretty much only in the way I've described.

ACKNOWLEDGMENTS

in no particular order of merit:

Major (now Colonel) Kat Miller, Sam Swindell, Mo Kirby, Bill Crenshaw, Sue Kerr, Matt Pethybridge, the 'flies, Toni Weisskopf, the late Jim Baen (who rejected this way back, thereby giving me the opportunity to rework it extensively), Dan Kemp. If I've forgotten anyone, chalk it up to premature senility.